Other People's Skin

Also by TaRessa Stovall

The Hot Spot
Proverbs for the People (with Tracy Price-Thompson)
A Love Supreme: Real-Life Stories of Black Love
Catching Good Health: An Introduction to Homeopathic Medicine
The Buffalo Soldiers

Also by Tracy Price-Thompson

Gather Together in My Name
Knockin' Boots
A Woman's Worth
Proverbs for the People (with TaRessa Stovall)
Chocolate Sangria
Black Coffee

Also by Elizabeth Atkins

White Chocolate
Dark Secret
Twilight

Other People's Skin

Four Novellas

Edited by
TRACY PRICE-THOMPSON
and TaRESSA STOVALL

ATRIA BOOKS

NEW YORK LONDON TORONTO SYDNEY

ATRIA BOOKS

A Division of Simon & Schuster, Inc.
1230 Avenue of the Americas
New York, NY 10020

First Atria Books trade paperback edition October 2007

ATRIA BOOKS and colophon are trademarks of Simon & Schuster, Inc.

For information about special discounts for bulk purchases, please contact Simon & Schuster Special Sales at 1-800-456-6798 or business@simonandschuster.com.

Designed by Davina Mock-Maniscalco

Manufactured in the United States of America

10 9 8 7 6 5 4 3 2 1

Library of Congress Cataloging-in-Publication Data

Other people's skin : four novellas / edited by Tracy Price-Thompson and
TaRessa Stovall. — 1st Atria Books trade pbk. ed.
p. cm.
1. African American women—Fiction. 2 Identity (Psychology)—Fiction. 3. Human skin color—Fiction. 4. Hair—Fiction. I. Price-Thompson, Tracy, 1963– II. Stovall, TaRessa.

PS647.A35O84 2007
813'.010892870896073—dc22
2007018846

(trade pbk.) ISBN-13: 978-1-4165-4207-0
ISBN-10:   1-4165-4207-8

Contents

Editors' Note   vii

My People, My People   TaRessa Stovall   1

Other People's Skin   Tracy Price-Thompson   67

New Birth   Desiree Cooper   169

Take It Off!   Elizabeth Atkins   273

Acknowledgments   367

About the Authors   369

AS BLACK WOMEN in America, negotiating the minefields of daily life can be a daunting task. With an erosion of our core value system and a mass media that bombards us with repeated images of inferior, stereotypical black womanhood, we are often given the message that it is somehow wrong to love our sisters and our natural black selves. Thus, cultural and ethnic pride, self-edification, and a sense of a shared responsibility for our own are often elusive ideals that we must work hard to reclaim.

We all know it takes a village to raise a people, and as women of the village we must strive to cultivate an environment where our daughters thrive on a steady diet of sisterly love and mutual support. Too often black women pass judgments on one another based primarily on physical characteristics of skin tone and hair texture, when in reality we are all linked in a sisterhood of one blood, one heart, one soul.

Other People's Skin seeks to heal this rift among black women and to cleanse our sisterly souls of this polluted by-product of America's legacy of race-based slavery. The crab-in-the-barrel mentality that at one time may have been necessary for our individual survival has now become a purveyor of our collective demise.

There is safety in numbers, our sisters! It is time to gather our community resources and use our talents and efforts to correct the ills that breed dysfunction and prevent us from rising as a unified body of black womanhood and realizing our full potential.

It is our hope that each story in this first volume of our Sister-to-Sister Empowerment Series will bless you with a healthy dose of self-love and provide a healing balm for our generational scars.

We hope that through our literary efforts you are able to find a gem of solidarity in this work of fiction that is useful in your every-day life. May you wish for your sisters the same love, serenity, and prosperity you crave for yourself. May you be blessed with the utmost peace and balance, and as you travel along the roads of self-discovery with Carmella, Euleatha, Catherine, and Dahlia, may you always remember . . . if the hat fits you must wear it!

Tracy Price-Thompson and TaRessa Stovall

Other People's Skin

TARESSA

My People, My People

STOVALL

Chapter ONE

Niggaz and flies,
I do despise . . .
The more I see niggaz,
The more I like flies . . .

TRIED TO SHOO those words from my mind as I listened to our
biggest client explain what was wrong with the model we'd chosen for a major ad campaign.

"I like the concept, basically." Helena Booker smiled through
clenched teeth that were, like every aspect of her appearance, so
dazzling they appeared unreal. "But," she said with a sigh, "this
model just doesn't fully express the spirit of my product. You do understand what I'm saying, don't you?"

Helena was as gorgeous as she was condescending. Her rich
brown skin, regal bone structure, and jazzy couture strut had
made her one of the first black supermodels chosen to usher in
the "Black is Beautiful" sentiments of the 1960s. She'd parlayed
that into a successful stint as a network news anchor, then
chucked it all to start a line of cosmetics for women of color. Age
hadn't diminished her beauty, and in her early sixties she was as

awesome as ever to behold. She always made me feel frumpy, with her short, stylish coiffure, artfully applied makeup, and high fashion attire. I looked her up and down, my mental calculator clicking. Her mouthwatering winter white silk designer suit cost more than the mortgage payment on my condo. Her matching Manolo Blahnik stiletto heels equaled the note on the new BMW I still couldn't afford. And her diamond and platinum Van Cleef and Arpels jewels were probably worth more than my entire life savings.

Her royal highness Helena stood before me and the creative team I led, grinding her fabulous designer heels into the center of my last nerve.

"Now Helena." I forced a smile. "For five years you've trusted our judgment, and for five years we've delivered, have we not?"

She raised a single eyebrow, diva-style.

"You are the undisputed queen of cosmetics for women of color, and we are the advertising experts." She didn't so much as nod her agreement with this obvious truth. "We all agreed that this new product line, Hot Chocolate, calls for a campaign that emphasizes the new, the bold, the future of global beauty. Inspired by your vision, we looked everywhere for the perfect face to represent this new line of cosmetics. We looked at every black supermodel, actress, and singer. We pored over photos of up-and-comers. We even stopped a few sisters in the street.

"But *she*"—I turned to point at the gigantic color poster behind me— "says it best. This woman is the face, the body, and the spirit of Hot Chocolate."

"I disagree, Carmella," Helena sniffed. "She simply doesn't convey the image I had in mind."

I bit the inside of my cheek and took a long breath. "You of all people must be aware that this model, Amira, is the hottest thing since the hair weave. She rules the Paris runways! She's been on the covers of several *white* magazines, not to mention all the major black ones. She's got fashion writers all over the world scrambling to come up with new superlatives to describe her."

Helena flicked a hard glance at Amira's towering image, then bored her eyes into mine. "Carmella, normally I respect your opinion and yes, you-all"—she pointed her chin at my team, who sat stoically through this madness—"usually do a very good job for me. This model may be popular now, but maybe she's a tad overexposed. We wouldn't want someone whose identity overshadowed the product line, now would we?"

Right. So the folks like Jada Pinkett Smith and the other superstars you told us to go after wouldn't have overshadowed the product. I swallowed my annoyance and said, "Helena, Amira has it all—the look, the charm, the star power. Like your product she is distinct, a cut above. Just look at her one good time and tell me I'm wrong."

I turned to feast my eyes on Amira's magnificence. Her rich blackberry skin, voluptuous features and awesome bone structure were a praisesong to the beauty of the motherland. Her closely cropped, natural hair was an upraised fist and a high five on the black-hand side. Her bold curves and long, shapely legs convinced you of what scientists had recently confirmed—that the first woman on Earth, the original Eve, was an African. Her glowing smile blended the harmonies of Stevie Wonder's "Isn't She Lovely" with the words of Maya Angelou's *Phenomenal Woman.* Mississippi-born Amira, whose mama had crowned her with a name that means "Queen," was every African female ruler, every runaway slave, and every homegirl throughout the diaspora rolled into one. There was—there could be—no one more perfect for the Hot Chocolate ad campaign than she. Reenergized by the power of her beauty, I turned to Helena with a buoyant smile. "Do you see what I mean?"

I was startled to see that Helena didn't seem to be able to look at Amira's picture for more than a few seconds. And she was more agitated than I'd ever seen her.

"This woman simply will not *do!*" Her voice dropped an octave and went up a notch in volume. Helena and I had disagreed in the past. But something about this was different. It felt personal and dangerous. I tried to think of what to say next.

Rodney, my ultrasuede-smooth boss, magically appeared at the conference room door to save the day. "Helena, our team has worked long and hard on this campaign. Just tell us what you need and we'll fix it, sugar," he drawled in his irresistible Southern baritone, shooting me a look of warning.

"You-all are not listening to me," she snapped. "I want a new model. She's all wrong. I just don't like the way she looks."

I studied Helena for a long, tense moment, then heard the words float from my lips before my good sense or professional instincts could stop them. "But Helena, Amira looks *just like you.*"

The whole room held its breath. Rodney moved toward Helena, his hands outstretched in apology. She stopped him with a raised palm and spoke in a growl. "This campaign will launch in one month. We *will* stay on schedule. And you will find another, more suitable model by the end of this week. Or I will be forced to take my business elsewhere. She leaned forward to glare at me. "Do I make myself clear?"

My mind and vision flared crimson, and I fought the urge to slap the pretty right off her smug face. Before I could fix my lips to speak, Rodney intervened. "Not to worry, Helena," he drawled, quickly blocking her view of me. "This isn't a problem. In fact, we have several other ideas—and models—we think you'll be quite pleased with." He graciously held her sleek, floor-length fur coat (which was probably worth more than my entire college education) while she slid her arms into the sleeves, then wrapped her manicured fingers around his elbow as he walk-talked her toward the elevator.

I scanned the stunned faces of my creative team. They were young, gifted, black, and looking mighty stressed. Nakenge was a crackerjack copywriter whose conservative, dress-for-success image made everyone take her seriously despite the fact that she was fresh out of college with wide eyes and a baby face. Her round, tortoise-shell glasses, neat ponytail, and classic pearls at her ears and throat said "young woman on the way up" in no uncertain terms. Morgan, my Black American Princess from a wealthy family, was a multital-ented creative force whose flowing dreads and bright African attire counteracted her fancy pedigree and invited the world to meet her on her own terms. Rounding it out was Mitch, a lean, mean retired military officer with a love of and serious talent for graphic design. A perfectionist whose quiet reserve masked a wicked sense of humor, Mitch hadn't taken long to adjust to working for a woman who was younger than him. And his calm energy provided a much-needed balance to our female mood swings.

I loved my team, and normally I had no problem pumping them up and steering them toward success. But at the moment I felt more like gobbling a pint of chocolate ice cream and ranting at the gods who put Helena Booker in charge.

"Whatever happened to 'Black is Beautiful?'" I grumbled, gaz-ing back at the poster of Amira as if she could provide the answer.

Rodney strode back into the conference room. "Team," he said, "I know you've done a lot of hard work, but it's still not over." They listened attentively, pens ready to record his every word. "Bring in every head shot you can find. We'll reconvene at nine o'clock tomorrow morning for a fresh start." I turned to gather the materials from our failed presentation. "Carmella, can I see you in my office, please?"

"I'll be right there," I replied, taking down the poster of Amira and rolling it tightly. That damn Helena. She *knew* this campaign was right. She was always picky, demanding the best, but this wasn't about quality. She knew our ads were the reason that Black Beauty had become a household name and a multimillion-dollar company. I didn't know what her problem was, but I wasn't backing down without a fight.

"Go right in," Rodney's assistant said. "But I warn you—he's pacing!"

Bad sign. I opened the door, took one look at his tight jaw, and prepared for battle. Then I strode into what I called the Maroon Palace. Rodney, a proud Morehouse Man, paid homage to his alma mater by decorating his office in the school colors of maroon and white. His stately mahogany desk and the high-backed chairs placed neatly around his office emanated power and confidence. Colorfully classic artworks by masters such as Romare Bearden, Jacob Lawrence, and Faith Ringgold showed Rodney's aesthetic taste and investment savvy. Few papers ever littered his gleaming desk, and the scarlet Oriental rug created an atmosphere of plush quiet that was missing from the rest of the agency.

As always when I was in the palace, I felt the urge to stand up straight and mind my manners. I watched him pace across the office, noting his dapper Italian suit, smoothly trimmed hairline, and aura of leadership-in-motion. Many a woman had lost her head over Rodney's handsome good looks, Southern charm, and impressive business achievements. I knew him too well to be swayed by his external assets. I knew the rhythm of his stride—he was trying to figure out how to "manage" me. But I planned to beat him to it.

"Carmella, what happened back there?" His voice was neutral and his step never faltered.

I clutched my Amira poster like a lucky charm and helped myself to a seat. "Helena's obviously lost her mind. I guess she's forgotten that we're the ones who put her products on the map. Can you please talk some sense into her, Rodney? She always listens to you."

"She's made up her mind. She doesn't like that model so we have to find another one."

"Do you have any idea how many strings I had to pull, and how much we had to pay, to get Amira to work with us? If we wait any longer, we won't be able to afford her!"

He stopped pacing and moved to the seat behind his desk. The window he gazed out of was twice the size of the one in my office. And his view was of the city skyline, while mine was of the building next door. He swung his eyes back to my face. "Carmella, if she doesn't like Amira, then Amira's out. As our oldest client—not to mention the one who pays us the largest retainer—Helena is always right."

"Not this time, and you know it."

"Here's what I know," he said, ticking off the list on his fingers. "One. You and your team are the best in the agency. Two. You came up with a kick-ass campaign. Three. The client likes the campaign. She just doesn't like the model. Four. You've been through this a million times. And five, I know you'll come through like the creative genius you are. In the next couple days. Because we simply have no choice."

"Rodney, Amira *is* Hot Chocolate, and it would be a mistake to give in to Helena's hang-ups, whatever they are."

"This isn't like you, Carmella. What's the problem?" Rodney frowned at me. "You've been playing this game long enough to know that we have to please the client. So you and Helena disagree about the model. You'll find one who's more to her liking."

I unrolled the poster and waved it in his face. "This is who the campaign was created for. Without her, it falls flat. Look at her, Rodney. She symbolizes everything we're trying to sell. Black Beauty cosmetics aren't just about looking good. They're about feeling good, being proud, and accepting your own beauty. The very sight of Amira says, 'You can be an African queen like me, honey, and still keep it real.'"

"I don't disagree with you, Carmella. Do I need to remind you that our job is to give Helena what she wants? We're doing fine. The agency is growing. But we still need her business."

"She needs us just as much as we need her," I said. "Where would she be without us? Remember the Mocha line? She didn't like the concept, but when it blew up and put her in the Black

Enterprise top 100, she acted like the whole campaign was her idea in the first place. We have never failed this woman, never made an error in judgment, and she's got the bottom line to back me up."

"That check she pays us every month makes her the boss."

"But it doesn't make her the expert on advertising. That's what she's paying us for. Don't we have a responsibility to tell her when she's wrong?"

Rodney rose and resumed his pacing. "Carmella, this isn't about your judgment as a pro. You're a star. We've got the awards to prove it. But I need you to—"

"Kiss up to Miz Thang so we can afford new carpeting or a new piece of equipment?"

"Or yearly bonuses for my top producers?" he asked pointedly.

"When did it get to be like this, Rodney?" I stood in front of him, forcing him to pause. "I left the biggest, most successful white agency in town to help you build the dream—our dream—of a powerful black agency. When did it get to be all about the money? What happened to using our black genius, our talents and skills to bust out of the box and make a difference?"

Rodney frowned, then spoke slowly with no trace of his honeyed drawl. "It's about reality, Carmella. Ideals are fine, we all have them. But look around you. I've got overhead, a staff—and you certainly don't come cheap."

"You're right. I don't come cheap." My hand found its way to my hip. "And neither do my instincts. I haven't been wrong yet, have I?"

"Carmella, we're not debating your track record—it's impeccable. That's how I know you'll come through with everything we need to make Helena happy."

"If you ask me, Helena's got some serious issues, and it's going to take more than a new model to solve them."

Rodney rubbed the back of his head, a sign that he was out of patience. "I'll look forward to seeing you first thing in the morning for a fresh start. Okay?"

I rolled up my poster and shook my head. "Whitefolks can get on your last nerve. They can even drive you stone out of your mind when they do wrong. But I swear, it takes your own people to truly break your heart."

Chapter TWO

MY OFFICE was only a few yards from Rodney's, but the walk back felt like a mile. I picked up a batch of phone messages from my assistant, Deborah, and sat down to face the lineup of unread emails beckoning from my computer screen. I responded with half a brain, scheming for ways to keep Amira in the campaign and Helena happy at the same time.

Compared to Rodney's Maroon Palace, my workspace was a closet. But I was grateful because it was a lot better than the tiny cubicle I'd had at the white ad agency. I'd convinced Rodney to let me paint the walls a soft teal (though he's so cheap, he insisted that I do the painting rather than hiring a pro). My wall décor was eclectic: my high school diploma, college degree along with the honors and awards I'd racked up, were to the right of my desk. A collection of framed ads from favorite campaigns—including Helena's Mocha line—were on the left. The petite window with the non-view was behind me, slightly to the right, surrounded by hanging plants. Across from my desk was my idea wall, covered in corkboard. It held a rotating gallery of works-in-progress, ideas for future campaigns and anything else that might inspire me. I winked at the collage of Amira photos I'd posted there. "Sorry, Queen," I whispered. "We lost this round. But I'm not giving up on you yet."

As I straightened the seemingly permanent piles of paper on my desk, I felt a presence at my office door and looked up to see Shane Kelly, a freelance photographer whose studio was in our building. He waved a large manila envelope at me. "Hey, Carmella," he grinned, "Got a minute? These are from yesterday's shoot." He stood close enough to unnerve me.

I took the envelope. It was always a pleasure to look at Shane's work. Almost as much fun as looking at him. With his honeyed skin, hazel eyes, wavy hair, and athletic physique, most folks expected him to be in front of the camera rather than behind it. It's a shame, I thought, but I'm just not into the light-skinned pretty boys. I prefer my men dark chocolate, thank you, and not so movie-star smooth. Shane was nice, but I'd spent months ignoring the vibes of interest he sent my way.

I invited him to have a seat and checked out his shots for a series of motorcycle ads. He'd set up the motorcycle against a vivid sunset. His composition of the shot emphasized the sensual thrust of the machine against the glory of Mother Nature's streaked backdrop. "Shane, these are outstanding. I'm sure the client will love them."

He looked pleased. "I found the perfect sunset and bam! It all came together."

"You the man with a camera, no doubt about that," I admitted. "I guess that's why we keep hiring you, right?" I circled the best shots and returned the envelope. "I need this by end of day tomorrow," I said, glancing at the calendar full of deadlines on my desk.

"No problem."

"Great. Thanks." I went back to my emails.

I looked up a moment later to see him still sitting there. I jumped up and grabbed the Amira poster. "Shane, would you mind giving me your opinion of something?" I asked.

"Not at all," he said, looking way too comfortable in that chair.

I tacked the poster to the back wall so he could get a full view.

"Nice composition," he murmured.

"Thanks. But I'm really more interested in your opinion of the model. Does she say Hot Chocolate to you? Does she represent black womanhood at its finest?"

"I'd love to shoot her," he said wistfully. "I'd light her differently, though. You see that angle there?"

"Shane, just focus on the model, please."

"Oh, yeah. Amira, right?"

"Yes. Don't you think she's perfect for the product?"

He studied the poster for a long minute. "Works for me. Why?"

"Oh, the client doesn't like her. Wants somebody . . . lighter-skinned, longer-haired, you know."

"Helena Booker? I'm not surprised," he said.

"Really?"

"No. I've always found her to be kind of color-struck."

"And how's that?"

"Well, leaning toward lighter-skinned models, as you mentioned. Used to be married to a white guy, too."

"I had no idea."

"He was Italian, not American, you know. Word is she gave up everything for him—her family, her country, her career, *and* the brother back here she was engaged to. Even stopped modeling to play housewife in a French villa. And she took it real hard when he left her."

"Why'd he do that?" I hated to admit how much I was enjoying hearing about Helena's bad times.

"For a white woman, an Italian woman, a plain, chubby home-girl who could throw down on the pasta and cannoli, " Shane said. "Word is that's what put the 'itch' in Helena's personality. Of course, I can't swear it's true. You know how folks in the fashion world gossip."

"Well, it might explain some things, I guess," I muttered. "But it still doesn't solve my problem."

"Which is?"

"Forgetting about Amira—and the fortune we paid to get these shots— and finding a new, 'more acceptable' model in the next couple days. Unless I can come up with a way . . ."

He nodded. "I have faith in you, Carmella. You'll figure something out."

"Thanks for the vote of confidence, but this really bothers me. Not just professionally, but . . ."

"Personally?" he asked.

I nodded.

"I know what you mean," he said.

"How's that?" I asked, more sharply than I'd intended.

"Folks trippin' off of color, especially *your* people," he teased.

"Honey, today, they're *your* people. Any more of this mess and I'm turning in my 'colored card.'"

We shared a small laugh. "Great work, Shane. I'll look for the finals about this time tomorrow?"

"You've got it," he said, letting himself out. "Ciao."

I tried not to sneak a look at his jean-clad rear bumper as he walked away. Nice brothah, great-looking for that type. I'll bet he's real high-maintenance, though. He probably spends more time in the mirror than I do. And besides, girl, he is not your flava at all!

Chapter THREE

DEBORAH BUZZED MY LINE to say that Ebonee, my "little sister" from the church mentoring program, had arrived for our weekly appointment. "Send her in." I smiled, hoping her youthful energy would rub off on me.

"Hey, Carmella." Ebonee smiled, and I rose to hug her. Petite and curvy, she wore the tight flared jeans and stomach-baring shirts that young girls sported to flaunt their pierced bellybuttons. Her hair, a mass of braided extensions, was pulled back and then up in the back, dancing around her head even when she stood still.

"Tell me again why I'm buying you a new outfit for your birthday, please."

"It's not just any outfit, Carmella. It's my dress for the Winter Dance," she reminded me. "Mom said it's okay if we get a strapless one." She grinned mischievously. "For real."

"All right," I said, grabbing my coat and purse. "There are some serious sales goin' on at the mall and I'm praying that we hit a good one."

While I wheeled my aging but trusty Honda through late afternoon traffic, Ebonee explained that her boyfriend, DaJuan, had gotten on her nerves. So she and her girlfriends were going to the Winter Dance as a group. "Will DaJuan be there?" I asked.

"Of course he will," she trilled in her little-girl voice. "And I'll be looking so good he'll have to get his act together."

That girl dragged me through every clothing store in the mall. Two hours and dozens of dresses later, she fell in love with a black silk sheath, strapless and classically chic.

"What do you think?" she asked, preening in the mirror.

"It's a gorgeous dress, Ebonee, and it fits you like a glove."

"Good! That way DaJuan can see what he's missing."

"Does it come in any other colors?"

"I dunno." She shrugged. "Why?"

"Well, black looks good on you, but I think a bright color might look even better." I ran off to find some other choices in her size. When I returned with a deep red version of the dress, she looked surprised, then mumbled something under her breath.

"I'm sorry, what did you say? I couldn't hear you."

"That's nice, but I think I'll stick with the black." Her normally open face had closed up the way it was when we'd first met.

"You won't even try the red? That'll really get DaJuan's attention."

She shook her head quickly. "It's not my color."

I paused awkwardly. "Ebonee, you look fantastic and I'll be happy to buy the black dress for you and the shoes and accessories as I promised. But why don't you try on the red version, just for fun?"

It shocked me to see her eyes fill and hear her voice crack. "Carmella, I don't wear red. It doesn't go with my complexion."

I felt my blood pressure rise. This beautiful young girl with glowing dark skin was afraid to wear a vibrant shade because somebody, no doubt a well-meaning mother, aunt, or grandmother, had filled her head with that old foolishness about staying away from bright colors.

"Okay, Ebonee." I sighed. "I know you'd look just as gorgeous in this one, but it's your choice. Why don't you go ahead and get dressed so we can find some jewelry and shoes?"

She nodded and we shopped until dinnertime, finding everything we needed to complete Ebonee's glamorous ensemble. We collapsed in a restaurant booth, so hungry we ate without talking until we'd finished dessert.

"You know, Ebonee, your application for that fashion design program is due soon. Do you need any help getting it together?"

"I'm almost finished." She smiled. "Thanks to you I know what I'm going to do when I get out of school. And my grades are coming up, so I'll be able to get into a good college."

I patted her hand. "Girl, you're so brilliant and beautiful you can do anything you want to do. Why don't we go over the application when we get together next week?"

"A'ight." She smiled, and we lugged her bags to my car for the drive to her house. Like most of the young people in the mentoring program, Ebonee lived in the 'hood, where danger and temptation greeted her every time she stepped outside of the apartment she shared with her mother, three younger siblings, and two cousins. As we shared a warm hug, I reminded her of how proud I was of her for doing so well and sticking to her goals. Lord knows it isn't easy for young folks under any circumstances, but Ebonee was determined and strong.

"You have fun at the dance—and be sure to get a picture for me, hear?" I called as she walked up the stairs. "And I don't care what anybody says," I whispered, driving off. "You can wear any color you want."

Back in my condo, I settled onto the couch, looking for something on TV to make me forget my troubles with Helena. But I couldn't get away from her. The commercials we'd created for her aired on nearly every channel during prime-time. "Black Beauty," the tantalizing male voice crooned in the jingle, "the only one I see, you are a vision of possibility . . ."

I wondered what Helena's loyal customers would think of her little color hang-up. I turned off the TV and flipped through the latest fashion magazines, scanning each sister's face. Are you the one? I asked silently. While any of the models, singers, and actresses I saw could have sold a line of cosmetics, none of them came close to Amira's power or sizzle.

I prayed for the inspiration to work some serious magic on the Hot Chocolate campaign. "Hmph!" I said aloud. "What I really need is a spell I can put on Helena to give her some sense."

Pouring myself into a strawberry-scented bubble bath, I meditated on the contrast between the snowy suds and my coppery skin. Nobody had ever told me to stay away from certain colors or shades because of my complexion. Come to think of it, my complexion had rarely been mentioned when I was growing up. It was simply a fact of life. As a child, I'd loved my color, always believed that it warmed and protected me. In fact, I'd secretly pitied whitefolks since their skin didn't seem nearly as sturdy or comforting as mine.

I snuggled into bed and fell asleep, dreaming of double-dutch, of lotioned-legs in all shades scissoring the air with intricate steps and rhythms. I recalled the rhymes we carried from one generation to the next, our voices harmonizing with our soles as our hearts thumped to the rhythm of the whirling ropes. We were jumping into womanhood, full of possibility. Clapping hands, slapping fives, feet tapping faster than breath, we danced those magic steps into our bones.

I held onto the edges of the dream as I rolled into wakefulness, trying to remember a time when blackfolks accepted each other without judgment or prejudice. I showered and ate, straining to re-call life without the color games we played among ourselves. While dressing and combing my hair, I envisioned Ebonee sporting a deep red dress that brought out the undertones of her velvety skin. I bal-anced the somber navy of my favorite wool gabardine suit with a bright red shell in Ebonee's honor, topped with a vibrant red, navy, and gold Hermès scarf. Then I cursed the foolishness that kept her from adorning herself in the brightest shades of the rainbow.

During the walk to the train station and the swift ride to the of-fice, I tried to assess the faces of black people around me without la-bels or prejudice. Tried to imagine loving instead of dividing ourselves. Yearned for a way to heal the festering wounds and smooth the whipping scars that had branded our souls as surely as they had risen upon the backs of our enslaved ancestors.

But neither memory nor imagination could bring the relief I craved. And by the time I entered the brownstone building where I spent the better part of my days, I felt sadder than I had in a very long time.

Chapter FOUR

LORD, I SILENTLY PRAYED, pressing the button for the eleva-tor, please hit me with a dose of creative inspiration between here and the fifth floor. My job is riding on this, Lord, and I can't afford to be unemployed. Help me just this one time and I promise I won't ask for another thing . . . at least not today.

The elevator doors were closing when a large, male hand wrestled them open. Shane darted in with a grin. "Hey, good morning!"

I nodded, trying to ignore the tempting scent of his aftershave. It was a shame for a man to smell that good. Especially a man I wasn't attracted to. We exchanged comments about the weather and he reminded me of our appointment that afternoon. I nodded briskly, squared my shoulders, and strode into the conference room to greet Rodney and my creative team, hoping they couldn't read the despair lurking beneath my faux smile.

Rodney welcomed everyone, reminded us that we had to move quickly, and hustled out to an appointment before we could ask any questions. I stood and smoothed my skirt with sweaty palms.

"All right, team. The bad news is we're back to the drawing board. The good news is that we have plenty of great models to choose from, and most of them are in the range that Helena's looking for. Color range *and* price range, I hope."

Their faces were open, expectant. "Let's go through these pictures, categorize them by types, and pick our favorites, okay?"

It took us most of the day to narrow down the pile of photos to four finalists—all of them with complexions in the safety zone. I was tired already but had a ton of other work to do.

"All right, team. Great job. Helena will be in day after tomorrow to check these out. Can you have comps made up with each of these new faces so we can see how they work with the campaign concept and slogan, please? We'll need them by midday tomorrow." They scurried off to pull everything together while I trudged toward my office.

"Boss, you look whupped!" Deborah said sympathetically. "Don't forget, Shane's bringing those pictures by." Her eyes twinkled. "If you're too tired or busy, I'll be happy to help him out."

"Oh it's like that, huh?" I teased.

"You don't mind, do you?" she asked coyly.

"Not at all," I replied. "Y'all would look cute together."

"Honey, Shane would look cute with anybody. Or rather, anybody would look good with him." She sighed.

I marveled at Deborah's transformation from crisply efficient professional to girl with a crush. "He is fine," I agreed.

"So why aren't you gettin' with him?" she asked pointedly.

"Not my type, honey."

"Who's not your type?" Shane asked from behind me. Why hadn't Deborah warned me?

"Hey! I was just wondering where you were," I lied, pivoting to face him.

"Right here, right on time as always. But you haven't answered my question," he said, his eyes lingering on the hollow of my throat, then climbing back up to my eyes.

I turned away so he wouldn't see how flustered I was becoming. He followed me into my office, where I took the sheath of photos from his hand. After a quick inspection, I signed my approval on his invoice.

"Great as usual, Shane. Thanks. Just give this to Deborah on your way out, okay?"

"Sure." He smiled, hesitating. I gave him a questioning look.

"I was wondering whether you'd seen this article," he said, sliding a folded newspaper page onto my desk.

"I haven't even had time to . . ." I began, then stopped when I saw the headline, "Shades of an Identity Crisis."

"Yeah, well, it kind of pertains to what we were discussing yesterday and I thought you might be interested," he said almost shyly.

"Thanks." I nodded, eager to read the story in private. "I appreciate it."

"Sure. You're welcome." He stood and paused. "I know we have this . . . professional relationship, but um . . . well, maybe we could grab a quick lunch together sometime?"

"You've kind of caught me off guard, Shane," I stuttered, wondering why it was always the men I didn't want who seemed most interested in me. "I need to get through this thing with Helena. Then I'll let you know."

He nodded and left quietly. It's never a good idea to mix business with pleasure, I reminded myself. Shane must fight women off day and night. Maybe he just sees me as a challenging conquest, another name to add to his list. Or maybe he's simply a nice brothah who really is interested. No matter, because his type simply doesn't turn me on. Too smooth, too pretty, too light, bright, and bourgie. He is our best photographer, though, so I'll have to let him down easy. Maybe this is the time to hook him up with Deborah, I mused, picking up the newspaper he'd given me.

I was drawn into the tale of young black women in Africa and the Caribbean using bleaching creams to lighten their skin. "Being lighter means you're prettier," one teenage girl explained. "You get more attention and you're just treated better all around."

"I do it because it makes me more important," another young woman said, even though she was one of many suffering from permanent skin disorders caused by the bleaching creams.

The story went on to describe how the bleaching caused severe acne and skin cancer and, in some cases, darkened the skin. I pinched myself, hoping this was another of my crazy dreams, but couldn't stop reading. "I want people to see me as more than a poor ghetto girl, and being whiter would make me happy," one woman said as she made her first purchase of the cream.

I started to curse the sheer madness of it all when Rodney peeked into my office. "Got a second?" He sat before I could respond. "How's it going?"

"We've narrowed it down to four finalists, all of whom Miz Thang should find acceptable. The new comps will be ready tomorrow. We'll review them, pick the best, and go from there."

"Good." He grinned. "I knew you'd come through, Carmella."

My eyes fell on the newspaper story, and I swallowed my anger. "Well," I said with a sigh, "it ain't over till the diva sings."

"What's wrong?" he asked, concern shading his face. "You don't seem like yourself."

"I'm just really tired, Rodney . . ."

"Well, maybe you should take some time off. Once Hot Chocolate is up and running, of course."

"Yeah right." I couldn't remember the last time I'd taken a day off. "I'm about to head out. I'll see you first thing in the morning, okay?"

"Great job as always, partner," he enthused. "You know you're the best, right?"

While my mouth said "thank you," my mind wondered how I could be "the best" when I felt so damn low and out of fuel.

I organized my desk for the next morning, called it a day and slipped out, hoping no one would join me on the elevator. I needed time and space to sort out the impact of Helena, Ebonee, and the bleaching cream story. If I were a drinking woman, I'd be dancing with a bottle. But since I wasn't, I hoped a walk home in the dark winter air would give me a new perspective. I stepped over cracks, chanting a hated childhood rhyme under my breath:

> "If you're white, you're all right
> If you're yellow, you're mellow;
> If you're brown, stick around;
> but if you're black, *get back!*"

"My people, my people," I muttered, searching out our faces in the crowd that whizzed around me. Why are we still trippin' off of our different shades? Why do we keep weighing ourselves down with this mess? Light skin, dark skin, "good" hair, "bad" hair. Every black person I knew had been touched by the madness, either directly or indirectly. My stick-around brown complexion put me squarely in the middle of the color bar, neither light nor dark enough to attract much attention or force me to defend myself against charges of being "stuck-up" or "ugly." But I'd watched the sad drama played out in school classrooms as teachers favored lighter-skinned students, heard it in playground taunts and threats, and felt it pulling families apart as one child one was called too much of one thing or not enough of the other. My family wasn't hung up on the color thing, but it came into our house through television and magazines.

The hunger to see more black folks in the media led me into advertising. I wanted to create healthier images of black people. Maybe help us to quit fighting among ourselves and accept each other. That fire still burned inside me. But the Helena Bookers of the world seemed determined to stand in my way.

For every Amira, there were countless light-skinned, longer-haired black beauties trotted out to represent the safer, more familiar brand of black allure. So when this tall drink of deep chocolate strode onto the scene defying the notion that she wasn't qualified to represent, the world took notice. I rejoiced. I thanked God. I took it as a personal victory in the war against African-American self-hatred. I remember the first time I saw a photo of her dominating the Paris runways. I claimed her audacious beauty as a personal victory in the war against my people's self-hatred. Her warm elegance gave little dark girls permission to love themselves. Her confidence made believers and skeptics alike take a second look. And the sheer power of her beauty caused everyone to look inward and reassess his or her definition of womanly glory.

Well, okay, maybe not everyone. I recalled the night a group of sistahs standing behind me in the supermarket fussed over Amira's appearance on the cover of a leading black magazine. She'd already been on the covers of *Vogue* and *Elle*. But, for some reason, her sculpted face smiling from the front of *the* black women's magazine was too much for their eyes or their nerves. "Why'd they have to put *her* on there?" one woman whined. "She's not even pretty!"

"She looks all right," another woman said in a nasty tone, "but she needs a weave!"

"Or maybe some of Michael Jackson's skin cream!" a third one tittered.

I grabbed a copy of the magazine and steeled myself to face the three young women, knowing before I scanned their faces that they'd be melanin-drenched and blind to their own beauty. Leaving my cart full of groceries in the aisle, I hurried past them and out of the store, my appetite ruined. Right then and there, I vowed to make Amira the focus of a major ad campaign. And when Hot Chocolate came up, I knew the fit was perfect. If only it weren't for the self-haters of the world.

I stepped around the steam rising from a sidewalk grate, the sights around me blurring as the two childhood rhymes merged in my mind. I figured the screaming traffic would drown out my voice as I spat the words in anger:

"Niggaz and flies . . .
If you're white, you're all right . . .
I do despise . . .
If you're yellow, you're mellow . . .
The more I see niggaz,
If you're brown, stick around . . .
The more I like flies . . .
But honey, if you're black, you'd best just *get back,*
get back, get back . . . "

"What's that you say, young lady?" A deep, smooth voice cut through my thoughts. The first thing my eyes fell on was the hat. It was a rich milk chocolate with a wide black band. The inside was a threadbare silk of the same rich shade. Like its owner, the fedora was a bit worn but still quite elegant. It sat on the sidewalk, filled with bills and coins. A few inches away, pointing at the hat, was a

pair of deep brown Stacy Adams shoes with pointed toes just like
the ones my grandpa wore. My eyes traveled upward to the man's
dark brown slacks and white shirt, which shone with the sheen of
too many pressings, cuffs a bit frayed but neat and clean. A beige
and white tweed overcoat a few shades lighter than his lightly
creased skin topped a brown sweater vest. He perched on a tall
stool, long legs anchoring him to the concrete, an old-timey guitar
across his lap. His salt-and-pepper hair was neatly trimmed, as was
a narrow mustache above generous lips. He's always sharp, I
thought with a grin. And always strumming, singing, or signifying.
The low rumble of his words snapped me out of my reverie.

"Seems to me I heard something about liking flies and getting
back. Is it something you want to talk about?"

Though I'd seen him every day for years, it wasn't often that
we had a conversation. Most days, we traded glances and nods of
greetings. Occasionally, he'd throw a song lyric my way as though
he was singing specifically to me. And more often than not, I'd
keep my spare change in my coat pocket so I could toss it into the
hat as I passed, downplaying the clink of coins by looking the
other way.

This day, the comforting look on his face invited my confidence.

"It's us . . . blackfolks. I just get so frustrated with the way we
put ourselves and each other through changes because this one is
light and that one is dark. Why can't we get past this mess and on to
more important things?"

He nodded patiently. I realized I must sound like a lunatic.
"Look, I'm sorry. I didn't mean to . . ."

"Reminds me of when Billie sang that song of hers, 'Strange
Fruit,'" he murmured, strumming a few chords.

Southern trees bear a strange fruit
blood on the leaves and blood at the root.

"I remember that song!" I exclaimed. "But it's about lynching, isn't it? And I was talking about. . . ."

"Same thing. Young lady, have you ever wondered how we got started hating ourselves the way we do?"

All the time, I wanted to say, but he didn't wait for my response. A woman rushing by bumped into me, and I stepped closer to the building he leaned against. "You don't think we just woke up one day and decided to drive ourselves crazy, do you?"

I shrugged. "I really don't know. I've wondered, off and on, why we do it. But what's that got to do with a bunch of racist white folks tying a rope around some brother's neck and hanging him from a tree?"

"Do you know why they call it lynching?"

I shook my head, mesmerized by the pain and beauty in his eyes.

"Back in the 1700s, the American slave owners were having problems keeping us in line. Seems the transplanted Africans were prone to uprisings, rebellions, and frequent escapes. Business was suffering for the slave owners. Then they heard of a man named Willie Lynch, a slave owner in the West Indies who'd come up with a way to keep slaves in line."

The stop-and-go tire squeals and beeping horns provided a staccato backdrop to his flowing voice. I leaned in more closely to make sure I didn't miss a word.

"The American slave owners invited Willie to come and help them. 'We're desperate,' they cried, 'can't keep these Negroes down.'

"Well, ole Willie Lynch, he came to the U.S. Told them not to worry, he had just the plan to solve their problems for generations to come. The secret, he told them, was to get the slaves to hate themselves more than they hated their owners.

"'Well, how do we do that, Willie?' they asked.

"'Listen here,' he said. 'It's not enough to whip and chain their bodies. You've got to whip and chain their hearts and minds. Then their bodies will stay right where they are, content to serve you. All you have to do is get them to fighting among themselves. Take one group and treat it better than the others. Turn them against each other. Young against old. Male against female. Light against dark. Tell them the ones with straighter hair are better than the ones with curlier hair, and so on. Break up their families. Sell children away from their mothers, husbands away from their wives, sisters away from their brothers. Break the men down. Make them watch you rape their women, fill them with your seed, have your babies. When the men get riled up, kill one or two as an example. I guarantee you, the others will back right down.'"

I was hit with a sudden shiver, but whether it was from the terror of his story or a new chill in the winter air, I didn't know. I pulled my red wool coat more closely around me.

"The American slave owners did just what he said. Soon, the slaves stopped rebelling and started fighting among themselves. So that, young lady, is the story of Willie Lynch."

I realized I'd been holding my breath. As I exhaled, the wind lifted my hair from my shoulders and whipped it into my face. We studied each other for a long moment. This was by far the longest and most involved conversation we'd ever had. We usually stuck to topics like the weather, upcoming holidays, or new sights in the neighborhood.

"That's a great story," I said. "I wonder how come I've never heard it before . . ."

"Let me tell you something else you may not know." He smiled, showing strong, white teeth. I wondered if they were dentures. "I haven't always been on this corner. And I'm not a musician by trade. Believe it or not, I am actually a somewhat learned fellow." He grinned. In that instant I realized that, despite our glances, greetings, and occasional encouragement to "Have a good day!" we didn't even know each other's names.

"I'm Carmella." I smiled, feeling strangely timid. "Carmella Daley."

He made a motion as if to tip the hat that sat near his well-shod feet. "And I am Dr. Stanley Phelps, retired professor of African-American history." He read my raised eyebrows as a question mark.

"So what am I doing on this corner with a guitar and a hatful of money?" he asked, chuckling. "Well, music has always been my passion. But halfway through graduate school, I met and fell in love with the most beautiful woman in the world, my dear, departed wife Mae Sue, may the good Lord bless her soul." His face brightened, he straightened his back, and the years fell away. "We married, had six children—four girls, two boys—all shades of the human rainbow. I gave up music and devoted myself to supporting my family. Life was good, and when I retired, I realized that I wanted nothing more than to add a little music to the world.

"As for that." He gestured toward the hatful of money. "I'm blessed to have a decent retirement income. Every dime of that money goes straight to charity, for those less fortunate than myself."

He picked up his guitar and resumed his song, the full weight of sorrow and rage humming beneath the carefully enunciated words:

"Southern trees bear a strange fruit
blood on the leaves and blood at the root."

I thought about the story he'd just told me, and wondered whether that's where the term "lynching" had really come from. Maybe my street corner music man was just a fanciful griot, a teller of myths and fables to those of us who needed something to help us make sense of our inner turmoil and maddening contradictions.

I half believed he was an angel sent to bring me back from the brink of madness. As we smiled gently into each other's eyes, I thought how much he'd always reminded me of a favorite uncle who always brought you the gift your parents said was too expensive or impractical, the one who sneaked you sugary treats behind Mama's back and told you stories even better than those in the books you devoured by flashlight long after bedtime.

As he finished singing, we were assaulted with sudden sheets of rain that seemed to come from nowhere. I clutched my coat even more closely, waiting for him to grab his belongings and leave the corner. He reached for the hat, stuffed the money into his coat pocket, and invited me to take the chocolate fedora from his hand. "Here, put this on your head."

"Oh, thanks, Professor, but I can't possibly do that! I appreciate it but really, I'm fine. I was going to wash my hair anyway . . ."

"Never argue with a gentleman who's rescuing a damsel in distress, young lady," he chided, tilting the hat toward me.

"No, really, I . . ."

"Take it, I insist. You can return it tomorrow."

Nearly drenched, I hesitated, then accepted the hat and set it gingerly on my head. "I'm not really a hat person . . ."

"It suits you." He smiled.

"I don't know about all that . . ." I protested weakly, giving in to the seduction of his chivalry.

He waved me away as he slung his guitar strap over his shoulder, folded and lifted his stool, and strode toward a nearby café. "Just remember what I said. And remember, no matter how angry you get, we are all *your* people. Never forget that."

I nodded and clasped the hat to my head, helplessly in love with his elegant charm. Why aren't there any men like him my age? I grumbled to myself, jogging slowly toward my building as the rain grew more vicious. If I had been born a few decades earlier, I'd have given dear, departed Mae Sue a run for her money. May the good Lord rest her soul.

STUMBLED GRATEFULLY into my apartment, peeling wet clothing from my body as quickly as I could. Ah, sanctuary. I couldn't live without the bustling sensory riot of big-city energy. Rushing cars and people made my pulse dance and kept my brain clicking. I'd lived in the hustle all my life and couldn't imagine calling any other environment home. But my soul also needed the soft colors and comforting sensations of my small twelfth-story home. The pastel walls soothed my senses and wiped city stress and soot from my skin. My pillowy furniture felt like sinking into Mama's warm arms. First-time visitors to my place were often surprised by the contrast between my sleek, tailored attire and business style and the plush, lacy, near-Victorian mood of my private space.

Brewing some tea, I grabbed a towel to pat my hair dry and glanced into the bathroom mirror, noting that the mane my mother called my "crowning glory" had been a source of pride, shame, and guilty vanity throughout my life.

As long as I can remember, folks referred to it as "that hair," as though it were something separate from the rest of me. The thick waves I inherited from Nana Daley, my father's half–Native American mother, set me apart from my kinkier-haired sisters, Deirdre and Santina. Strangers would measure my unremarkable Negro features against my hair and ask, "What are you, child? I mean, you're mixed with *something*, right?"

When I shook my head, assuring them that both my parents were black, they'd eye or even touch my hair and say, "Well, you sure have some good hair." Then they'd glance at my sisters, lower their voices and say, "That's something special, child. I hope you appreciate what you've got."

I wasn't sure whether special thanks to God were warranted, since others seemed much more excited about my hair than I was, but I tried to appear grateful. My only complaint was the mayonnaise that Mama rubbed into my thick waves and encased in plastic wrap "for deep conditioning." But it didn't seem as punishing as the grease and hot comb ritual my sisters endured, squinting their eyes against the sizzle of frying hair and yelping when the comb singed their foreheads or ears. Deirdre shot me looks of naked envy, wondering aloud why *she* had to undergo such torture when I was spared. Santina just sucked her teeth and stared straight ahead like a prisoner counting the days until her escape. Sure enough, when she went off to college, Santina discovered braids, and as a grown-up schoolteacher, she now alternates between braids and twists, swearing that she's "allergic" to perms and pressing combs.

Deirdre faithfully smoothes her kinks into bone-straight tresses always cut in the latest fly style. Me, I've stuck with my shoulder-grazing pageboy, parted on the left, since college. I've fantasized about new hairdos but haven't had the nerve to experiment. I grew up with Mama's endless warning to "leave that hair alone. Don't put anything in it, daughter. It might turn and never come back." So I have a light perm every few months and keep the classic blunt cut that spells security to me.

"This," Mama would say as she wove my hair into tight, thick plaits, "makes you more than just everyday pretty; it makes you special. Now all my daughters are pretty, but the way your hair grows just gives you advantages. Don't mess it up now, hear?"

I swallowed her words whole and grew up fearing any change in the climate of my hair texture. I combed and brushed it softly, oiled it gently, kept perms to a minimum, avoided swimming pools in case the chlorine made it permanently kinky, and sidestepped trendy styles in favor of the tried and true. When a man was attracted to me, I secretly feared it was because of my hair alone, though I didn't dare ask. Any lover who lavished too much attention on my head made me anxious, and I'd awaken, heart pounding, after a nightmare of my hair falling out in clumps and leaving me bald and abandoned.

I picked up the fedora to dab the raindrops from it with a dry towel. I hope I don't ruin it, I thought, smiling again at the professor, his music, and his story about the conspiracy to make slaves hate themselves so they'd stay on the plantation. On one hand, it sounded kind of far-fetched. But, if it was true, it explained some of the things that were bothering me.

Don't be so sensitive, I remembered my mother's voice chiding me as I got my feelings hurt or my temper in an uproar about one thing or another. Life is unpredictable and people are crazy, she'd counsel me. Just learn to take it in stride.

Sorry, Mama, I thought. I still haven't learned to do that. I was excited about Amira because I want to make a difference. It's rare that one gets a chance to help black folks feel better about themselves through advertising, but those fleeting moments are why I chose this business and why, after honing my skills at *the* powerhouse white agency, I pursued my dream of working at a sharp, dynamic black firm that shared my commitment to images that were empowering and real.

I picked my way through dinner while channel surfing through dozens of boring shows. I must have dozed off because next thing I knew, I saw myself in our conference room arguing with Helena about what defined a black woman's beauty. Suddenly, a white man sporting colonial dress walked in. "That's right, hate yourself!" he shouted. "Reject yourself! Reject your own! Gaze upon your dirty self in the mirror and wish you were something—anything—else. You can't see who you are. You can't see any kind of truth. And do you know why? Because I've blinded you and I'll keep you that way!"

There was something familiar and scary about him. "Mr. Lynch?" I asked, as Helena smiled nervously.

"You will address me as 'sir,' wench!" he sputtered. "And take that wig off your head. Who do you think you're fooling?"

I grabbed a handful of my hair and pulled it hard, looking him defiantly in the eye. "This is all mine I'll have you know."

"A gift from a European ancestor, no doubt." He smirked. "And far too lovely for your face."

I stared at him in disbelief, then looked at Helena, who cowered in a corner, rubbing the skin on her forearm like she expected a winning lottery number to appear. "Try this," he suggested, handing her a jar of bleaching cream.

"Just go away!" I shouted at Willie Lynch. "We're not listening to you. Nobody believes your stupid lies anyway!"

"I beg to differ," he intoned, strolling across the front of the room. "My work has been so effective that you no longer need slave owners to beat you down and turn you against each other. You're doing it on your own!" His loud, mocking laugh shocked me awake.

I sat up on the sofa to hear the same laugh coming from a character on the newest black sitcom, a young man one step from being a new millennium stereotype. How can a show with blacks writing, directing, producing, and starring in it be just as insulting as the stuff that whites used to crank out about us? I am losing my mind, I realized, turning off the TV to get ready for bed. Please, Lord, stop the crazy dreams. And please keep my hair on my head.

The next morning I overslept, which got the day off to a bad start. I grumbled through my shower and pulled on my tapered black pants, topped with a bright coral sweater and long gold necklace. Ignoring the morning paper, I raced through a bowl of cold cereal and inhaled a cup of black coffee, and was halfway out of the building when I remembered. *The hat.* I ran back to grab it, then hurried to the corner to return it to the professor before hailing a taxi to work. But he wasn't there. No stool, no guitar, no Stacy Adams shoes, nothing. What if something had happened to him? How could I find him? And what was I going to do with this wonderful hat that didn't belong to me?

I spotted a taxi and threw my arm up to hail it. Inside the cab, I closed my eyes to the driver's maniacal driving and promised him an extra tip if he got me to the office on time. I practiced deep breathing and tried not to get seasick from his sudden stops and squealing swerves. He got me there with three minutes to spare. I threw him his fare plus a hefty tip and was about to close the door when he said, "Hey, lady! You forgot this!" I turned to see his outstretched hand holding the fedora.

"Oh, yeah, thanks." I grabbed it and rushed into the building. After a morning of calls with other clients, I met my team in the conference room to review the sample Hot Chocolate posters with the new models.

They watched my face as I inspected the previous day's choices, blown up to poster size under the Hot Chocolate logo. I never would have picked any of these models, lovely as they were, I thought. Too bland. But it was Helena's party, not mine. And I had a feeling she'd like any or all of these midrange faces just fine.

"They look great," I said. "Y'all done good. Just run them by Rodney, make any changes he suggests, and have them back here by the end of the day, okay?" They nodded happily.

Not long ago I was like them, on fire about my work. Lately everything felt like an endless chore that sucked my spirit dry. Where had my passion gone? Oh yeah, back in my office, in a poster tacked to the wall, embodied in a girl named Amira who was good enough to sell the world's finest designer fashions but not Helena's cosmetics for women of color.

Let it go, I told myself, rubbing the tight spot at the back of my neck. Don't let that crazy woman get to you.

Without warning, I was struck by a craving for junk food from the corner vendor. I grabbed some money and plopped the hat on my head, enjoying the way it made me feel frisky and a little mysterious. Not bad, I thought, catching a glimpse of myself in a storefront window. I looked like a woman with a purpose, on my way to someplace important, instead of a frustrated advertising executive suffering from burnout and a bad attitude.

Savoring every bit of my greasy hot dog, salty pretzel, and tart lemonade, I turned down a side street I'd been wanting to explore. Shadows chased autumn sunbeams in and out of corners while pedestrians scurried by like cockroaches at the first blast of light. I window-shopped at an antiques store, avoided the urge to splurge at a funky shoe-and-accessory boutique, and swung through a vintage thrift shop with clothing so delightful I wanted to skip work and play dress-up.

Back on the sidewalk, I felt, then heard, a faint but persistent throbbing. It was the beat of a drum, an African drum, beckoning me home. My hips began to sway under my heavy coat, while my back longed to arch and contract in a sensual, wordless call-and-response. Smiling, I followed the sound into a tiny sliver of a store called Diaspora. A blast of yummy incense greeted my nostrils. Walls draped with brilliant fabrics delighted my eyes. I felt sedated, hypnotized by the mellow atmosphere. "Greetings, my beautiful sister, African queen," a voice tinged with a Caribbean lilt snaked into my ear.

I turned to see a smiling brothah with bushy locks and eyes that seemed to be laughing at life. We nodded a mutual greeting, then I allowed myself to be seduced by the amazing fabrics and colors around me. Running my hand over some mudcloth or draping an Ethiopian shawl over my head, I longed to reconnect with ancient pieces of myself that had been scattered across time and place.

I was flipping through some African magazines (with midnight-colored, full-featured women gracing the covers) when a small, homemade pamphlet caught my eye. On the front was a crudely drawn picture of a strong black man roped around the neck and hanging from a tree, and below that the words, *Let's Make a Slave— The Willie Lynch Speech of 1712.*

The pamphlet was in my hand before I knew it. I added a package of coconut incense and a tall, fragrant orange candle and placed them in front of Mr. Dreadlocks with a twenty-dollar bill.

"Ah, I see you've come for knowledge, my sister," he intoned in that gorgeous voice. "This," he said, pointing at the pamphlet, "may very well change the way you see many things. Not saying it will. But it definitely could." His fingertips brushed my palm as he gave me my change. I shivered from the delicious tease of his touch. Now this is a man I could get excited about, I thought. But before I could get my flirt on, my eyes landed on the clock above his head. Time to get back to work, I noted, hating to break the spell. Maybe I could come back on payday and buy a large piece of fabric to hang on the wall near my sofa, I thought longingly.

I took one last sniff of the incense on my way out. "Oh, by the way," dreadlocks called out as I opened the door, "nice hat."

See, that's the thing about brothahs that always gets me—never fails. How they can be lover, stranger, friend, or kin, and no matter what mood you're in, no matter how stank the funk of your blues, they can say the one thing guaranteed to coax a smile. I thanked him with a laugh and strode back toward the office with a lighter heart.

My joy was short-lived though, because who did I see coming out of Rodney's office but Helena Booker, sheathed in a burgundy leather pantsuit and shod in coordinated Prada boots. What was she doing here? I nodded a quick greeting and tried to hurry away. "Oh, Carmella," she purred, "I can't wait to see your suggestions for Hot Chocolate tomorrow."

You saw my suggestion, I thought bitterly, and it was too much for you to handle. I'm sure you'll love the watered-down versions just fine. I flicked a quick grin in her general direction and sauntered into my office, shutting the door firmly behind me. I had just hung up my coat when I heard a brisk knock.

"What *is* it?" I nearly growled.

"You dropped this in the lobby," Shane said, peeking through to show me the *Let's Make a Slave* pamphlet. "I called after you but you didn't seem to hear. Are you all right?"

"Yes. No. To be honest I don't know," I said, sinking heavily into my chair and indicating that he have a seat. "This color madness is making me crazy."

"I remember this story," he mused, flipping through the pamphlet. "A history prof in college made sure every student of his knew about Willie Lynch."

History prof? "What was the professor's name?" I asked excitedly.

"Let's see . . . Dr. Phillips, no, that wasn't it . . ."

"Phelps? Stanley Phelps?" I asked.

"Yeah, that's it! Tall, fly brothah with salt-and-pepper hair and Stacy Adams shoes. Reminded me of my grandpa. Hey, I didn't know you went to . . ."

"I didn't. But I met Professor Phelps the other day. He lent me this"—I held up the hat—"and when I went to return it to him this morning, he wasn't there."

"I could swear I heard that Phelps was dead. Are you sure it was him?"

"Yeah. He's very handsome, nicely dressed, plays the guitar on a stool at the corner near my place. I met him last night. And he told me the story of Willie Lynch. I know it's him. Come on, let's see if we can find him!" I jumped up.

"Uh, Carmella, it's the middle of the afternoon."

"Right. So?"

"I just thought you had . . . work to do?" he looked at the pile of papers on my desk.

"Yes, but this is more important. I have to give this hat back to Professor Phelps. Wouldn't you like to see him again?"

"Okay." Shane shrugged, hoisting his camera bag onto his shoulder. I set the hat on my head and he appraised me slowly. "Damn shame."

"Do I look that bad?" I asked.

"No. That good. Damn shame you have to return the hat. It looks great on you. I'd love to shoot you in it."

"Thanks," I said self-consciously, annoyed that his comment made me feel pleased. "Let's go."

We took the train and walked briskly toward the corner. I slowed as we got close enough to see that the professor wasn't there.

"Shane, I'm worried. He's been here every night that I can remember. Do you think he's hurt or sick or something? I have his hat and no idea how to reach him."

"It's all right, Carmella," Shane said, putting his arm around my shoulder. "I'm sure he has other hats."

"This is the only one I've ever seen!" I snapped, pulling away from his embrace. Business and pleasure—two separate things, I reminded myself. "And I have to get it to him!"

"Carmella, I don't want to upset you any more than you already are, but I could swear I heard that Phelps died years ago. Maybe this was someone else, you know, a well-dressed bum . . ."

"He wasn't a bum!" I shouted. "And he told me his name, and about Willie Lynch. I just want to return his hat, don't you understand?"

Shane stared at me like I'd gone insane.

"I'm sorry," I whispered. "It's just that . . . what if something's wrong and he needs our help? How are we supposed to find him?"

Next thing I knew, we were inside the corner coffee shop and Shane was ordering us hot drinks and sandwiches. He amused me with tales of his college escapades and impressed me with the story of how he'd defied his family's dream of him becoming a doctor like his father, grandfather, and great-grandfather to pursue photography.

"Believe me, they thought I was crazy," he said. "Boy, how you gon' make a livin takin' pictures? What kind of security will you have with that? Do you think we sent you to one of the country's finest colleges to learn how to press a shutter button?"

"And you became a photographer because . . . ?"

"I went to college to study engineering. Got a scholarship and everything. In my junior year, I took a photography class to satisfy an elective, and bam! I was hooked. I liked seeing better than being seen. There's nothing like trying to make a vision come to life."

His eyes sparkled with the satisfaction of doing what he loved. I wondered when mine would have that look again. "My parents tolerate my profession," he continued. "They've stopped hoping that I'll come to my senses. But they're real proud of my brother the lawyer. Graduated top of his class, about to make partner in a big bucks firm. But you know what? He says he envies me."

"Why?"

My exciting lifestyle. You know, the travel, the variety, the chance to work with beautiful women . . ." His gaze deepened.

"It's getting late," I noted, feeling suddenly nervous.

"Do you have to go already? It's great just talking with you. About something other than business."

I nodded. "You've been very patient and gracious. I'm sorry I lost it out there."

"No problem. Maybe you're supposed to keep the hat. It looks like it was made for you," he said.

"You're wrong, but thanks for the compliment." I rose, and he did the same.

"Can I walk you home?" he asked eagerly.

"No thanks. I'm . . ."

"Carmella, I won't bite. Unless you want me to, of course."

"Shane, I'm really not comfortable . . ."

"Okay." He raised his hands in surrender. "No more bad jokes. No pressure, I promise. But please consider letting me shoot you in that hat, okay?"

I nodded, and we said our good-byes outside the restaurant. Aw, Shane, I thought, if only you looked more like the dreadlocked brother in the African shop. Then maybe we could check each other out. But as fine as you are, I just don't lean in that direction.

I stood staring at the corner as though I could will the professor into being there. His disappearance worried me. Nerves on edge, I noticed a crowd of well-dressed blackfolks crowding into the bookstore across the street. Hmmm, I thought, crossing the street for a closer look, I wonder what's going on. Inside, a chic, full-figured sister with oversized black glasses and expressive hands was there to read from and sign copies of her book, *The Beauty of Soul.* I grabbed a copy to check it out. It's probably the same ole same ole, I thought dejectedly. Then I noticed Amira's face smiling up at me from the book's cover and decided to see what Ms. Sister-Author had to say.

After being introduced as a fashion writer, Lori Underwood stood behind the podium to address the growing crowd. She said that *The Beauty of Soul* was written to celebrate black women of all shades, shapes, ages, and sizes. I took a seat. "I wrote this to satisfy the hunger we have to see our true beauty, not just what's fed to us by the media," she explained.

"You see, there are people who make millions—no, billions— of dollars from our desire to change ourselves, to cover our natural glory and conform to some other standard. But we don't have to sell ourselves short or deny who we are in order to succeed." The woman next to me nodded vigorously. "We set our own standards, and we set the trends, not only here in America but all over the world. We are leaders, not followers, in fashion and beauty. That's what this book is about!" The crowd murmured excitedly.

Lori Underwood read a few passages, quotes from women of different ages and sizes about how they've struggled to see and accept their own beauty and feel good about what God gave them. Then she came out from behind the podium to walk among the audience and said, "You can see here in this book, or in this room tonight, that we are the most colorful, diverse, and unique women in the world. Few other races can look like we do, yet we come in so many colors and combinations that we look like every other race. We break all the rules, and we make new ones as we go along."

Folks were raising their hands overhead and throwing out "amen" like it was Sunday morning at the corner church.

"I wrote this book to celebrate the incomparable beauty of black women across the spectrum," she continued, her voice taking on the cadence of a minister helping her flock to see the light. "You are beautiful, I am beautiful, we are all beautiful right here and now. True freedom is realizing how wonderful you really are and accepting that some folks just can't handle our beauty. But that's okay," she said reassuringly. "Because we're going to teach them how."

The crowd jumped to a standing ovation. There was a rush to purchase copies and then to get in line for Lori Underwood's autograph and a dose of her positive energy. "We've been needing a book like this," the woman in front of me confided to her friend. "Uh-huh," her friend replied. "I can't wait to show it to my husband. He's always talking about how Asian women are so this and so that. This book proves there's nobody like a sistah!"

I liked Lori Underwood's book and admired her confident style. After she graciously inscribed the book to me, I took her hand and said, "I just want to thank you, not only for including all of us in your definition of beauty but also for putting my girl Amira on the cover. That makes a strong statement, one that we all needed to see."

She leaned in to speak in a near whisper. "You don't know how I had to fight to get her on the front of this book. It was hell, do you hear me? Folks said I was crazy, that it would hurt book sales, that her type of beauty was just a fad. It was a long, hard battle, I swear."

"Well, I'm going through something similar myself—with Amira, as a matter of fact."

"Really?" she asked, and we quickly exchanged cards. "Let's talk soon. Stay beautiful. And thanks for supporting the book!"

I hesitated for a moment. Maybe I should buy Helena a copy. Nah. She'd probably take one look at the cover and take off running. If she wants one, let her buy it herself.

I felt the beginning of a new idea pulse at the back of my brain. But a few feet from the bookstore, my mind was suddenly wiped clean by a handmade poster. On the left side of the poster was a picture of Michael Jackson as a child. On the right was a more recent picture of him. Across the top were the words, "Where's the Michael We Used to Love?" My eyes darted between the two images. As a child, Michael's skin was the same warm brown as mine, his dark eyes twinkled, his full lips were raised in a delighted smile, and his three-inch Afro crowned his head with pride. As an adult, he looked like a corpse—whiter than white, his altered features tragically grotesque. Lank, greasy hair hung framing a skeletal face. His skin looked lifeless, his eyes were cold and empty, and his lips seemed ready to scream or cry. Not only was it impossible to identify him as the beaming little boy on the left, but he barely resembled a member of the human race.

I tried to look away but couldn't. What had made him want to mutilate himself beyond race, beyond gender, perhaps beyond the human species altogether?

My head whirled with the beginning of a new idea. I couldn't name or picture it, but it was definitely forming. After walking aimlessly, I found myself inside a beauty salon.

"Can I help you?" asked a young gum-popping sister with a burgundy-striped weave.

I stared at her, realizing I had no idea why I was there. It wasn't time for a perm or trim. "Yes, I'd like a haircut," I heard myself say.

"Do you mean a trim or a cut?" she asked, looking around for a hairdresser.

"A cut. Short." Whose voice was that coming from my mouth? Who was telling it what to say? I stared at myself in the mirror, snatched off the hat, and repeated the request.

Gum-popper squinted at me as if to say, *That hair is real and you want to get rid of it?* I recognized the look and nodded in response. She shrugged and called out, "Benita! Benita! Got a lady here needs a cut!"

A pleasant-faced middle-aged sister ambled out from the back and invited me into her chair with a smile. "How you want it cut, baby?" she asked.

"Short. Tapered. Close to the skull but not a buzz or crew cut."

"This all yours?" she inquired.

I nodded wearily, closed my eyes, and leaned back into her strong hands. When I opened my eyes half an hour later, the first thing I saw was the long chunks of hair laying on the floor, looking like piles of discarded yarn. The second thing I saw was the strange brown girl in the mirror. I blinked a few times, then stared again. My features seemed to say, *Didn't know we were here, did you? Well, take another look, 'cause we're front and center now.*

Was I ordinary without my crowning glory?

Would any man ever again look my way? Had I lost my identity or gained a new sense of myself?

"That's real nice," gum-popper said with a smile. "You'll need to come back in a couple weeks for a trim, okay?" I tried to read her eyes while I paid her. The compliment seemed sincere.

I walked back to my building feeling naked and vulnerable, even with the hat on. For the first time in memory I was without my security blanket, my shield, my coat of armor. I was nearly bald. And I had no idea why.

THE MISSING PROFESSOR HAUNTED ME. I called the police, area hospitals, and the nearest homeless shelter to ask if they'd seen a Dr. Stanley Phelps. No one had. Checked information—no one by that name was listed anywhere in the county, or the zip code, for that matter. The hat sat on my kitchen table. It seemed to be watching, trying to tell me something.

"Well, where is he, then?" I asked it. "Was he ever there at all? You're proof that I didn't imagine him, right?"

You've lost it now, I told myself, talking to a hat about some man whose existence you can't seem to prove. Tomorrow I'll call the university. Maybe they can help track him down.

I flipped through *The Beauty of Soul,* enjoying the rainbow of faces Lori had chosen to celebrate. I marked a page where a chocolate-skinned model sported a vivid red dress, looking simply divine. The book was a revelation and a relief. There were other people out there who got it. Maybe there was hope after all. But before we could get to the solution, we had to understand the problem.

I picked up the Willie Lynch pamphlet and skimmed the text inside.

Gentlemen, I greet you here on the bank of the James River in the year of our Lord one thousand seven hundred and twelve. First, I shall thank you, the gentlemen of the Colony of Virginia, for bringing me here. I am here to help you solve some of your problems with slaves. Your invitation reached me on my modest plantation in the West Indies, where I have tried and proven some new methods of control, along with the old technique of imposing fear. I have come up with a sound method of controlling your slaves.

Only a few miles up the river, I inhaled the scent of a

dead slave, probably hanging from a tree. Gentlemen, you are not only destroying valuable assets by these hangings, you are responsible for the increase of uprisings among slaves. Every time slaves run away, you lose profits, you suffer occasional fires, your animals are sometimes killed, and your crops are left in the fields too long for maximum profit.

In my bag here, I have a foolproof method for controlling your black slaves. I guarantee every one of you that, if installed correctly, it will control the slaves for at least three hundred years. My method is simple. Any member of your family or your overseer can use it.

I use fear, distrust, and envy for control purposes. These methods have worked on my modest plantation and it will work throughout the South. Distrust is stronger than adulation or respect. My list of differences is as follows:

Age. Take your old slaves and pit them against the young slaves, and vice versa.
Color. Take your lighter-skinned slaves and pit them against the darker-skinned slaves, and vice versa.
Intelligence. Take your smart slaves and pit them against the dumb slaves, and vice versa.
Sex. Take your female slaves and pit them against the male slaves, and vice versa.
Hair. Take your fine-hair slaves and pit them against the coarse-hair slaves, and vice versa.

Gentlemen, I guarantee that after indoctrinating your slaves with this formula, it will become self-refueling for hundreds of maybe even thousands of years. However, for this plan to be successful, your white servants and black overseers must distrust all blacks. But your black slaves must love and trust your overseers. The overseers can win the love and trust of the slaves by doing small favors for selected slaves. This will give you informants among slaves, and it will create divisions among the slaves, which are the components for control.

Never miss an opportunity to apply this formula. Have your wives and children apply it. It is a fool-proof plan, and if intensely and properly applied for one year, the slaves will remain distrustful of one another, for their enslavement will be psychological.

I read the pamphlet again, slowly, then fell asleep with images of Helena, Ebonee, and a new line of Michael Jackson bleaching cream dancing through my mind. Exhaustion won out, and my slumber was heavy and dreamless. Until I sat straight up in the bed at three a.m., my brain on fire.

I leaped out of bed, ran to the kitchen table, grabbed a tablet and pencil, and began writing and doodling furiously. It was as if my conscious mind was still asleep and the ideas were pouring straight from someplace beyond waking awareness.

My hands ached from scribbling and sketching, but I couldn't stop. Sweat beaded on my forehead; I wiped it with the back of my hand and kept going. A few times I reached back to twirl a piece of hair around my finger, not realizing how much of a habit that gesture had become. Startled by the lack of warmth on my neck, I shook my head to clear it, and kept writing.

All of the turmoil and revelations of the last few days came together in an idea that had the power to change my entire career. Dawn rose as I filled the last sheet of paper with pencil marks. I rushed through my shower, jumped into my clothes, shoved the papers into my briefcase, and grabbed the hat on my way out the door. The cool silk of the hat's lining teased the skin above my ears in a delightful way. Surely the professor would be back at his corner, and I'd return his hat and tell him about all the things that had happened in the last couple days. I strode toward the corner, listening for his guitar.

The corner was bare. It was too early for the morning crush of pedestrians. I stood awkwardly, fighting the panic that rose in my chest. Where *was* he? Didn't he know I needed him now?

I finally walked to the train station, feeling the weight of too little sleep tempting my eyes to close. I was so tired I was dizzy, but I couldn't rest until I brought my brainstorm to life. I charged into the office before anyone else, flicking on lights and machines as I went.

Splashing cold water on my face in the ladies' room, I caught a glimpse of myself in the mirror. There's just so much *face*, I thought, wondering whether I'd made a mistake. Without my trademark hair am I Carmella Daley or an imposter, a clone? Whatever had possessed me to march into that shop and tell them to hack off my hair? I couldn't even imagine what my mother would say. Was it true what she'd always told me—that my hair was what made me pretty, special, worth looking at? Would any man ever want me now?

Well, it's too late now, I reasoned. What's done is done. And I kind of liked the feeling of lightness around my head.

My office seemed eerie with no one around, but I welcomed the solitude. Diving back into my new project, I jotted, outlined, sketched, and planned an advertising campaign far bigger and better than anything I, or our agency, had ever attempted. It was bold, it was challenging, perhaps it was crazy. But I didn't have a choice.

I was kneeling on the floor, taping together pieces of poster board, when Deborah came in. "Boss? May I ask what you're doing on the floor this time of day? You weren't working all night, were you?"

"Deborah, come in. Close the door. This is the biggest, most important campaign I've ever done. I can't give up the details, but I need you to clear my schedule and yours for the next two days.

We have got to get this ready for a presentation tomorrow after-noon. Get us on Rodney's calendar—I don't care what he's doing. Tell him it's urgent and I want everyone at the agency to attend the unveiling of this campaign. Then get the the team up here, ASAP, please."

"Fine. Great. Consider it done." She waved her hand impa-tiently. "What I want to know is, *what happened to your hair?*"

"Oh, that," I said, still working on the poster board. "It's gone. I mean, I had it cut."

"Any special reason?"

"Since when does a sistah need a reason to get her hair cut?"

"Heeeeey, no offense meant. I wasn't trying to imply that you need a reason. It's just that, well, Carmella, your hair . . . I mean, it was you."

"No, Deborah. It was hair. Just hair. I'm still me. In fact, I may be more me than I've ever been."

We stared at each other awkwardly. "Look," I said, jumping up to give her a hug. "I didn't mean to snap at you. You're the first one who's seen it and I was so wrapped up in this new campaign that I never even thought about how to explain . . . anyway, it's not some-thing I planned to do. It just kind of happened. Spontaneously, you know?"

She nodded. "Okay. Well, I like it." She smiled hesitantly. "It's a shock at first, but it's workin' for you, boss. Now I think it's time for me to get busy on this top secret mission."

I sure hope I don't have to explain my shorn head to everyone, I thought, slapping the hat on my head to deflect further inquiries.

I closed the door and immersed myself in my new baby, the campaign that would scratch the growing itch inside me. Fingers flying over the computer keys, I burned up the phone lines, calling in favors, scouting out the right celebrities to make this thing fly. Later for Helena and Hot Chocolate, I thought. This was bigger and badder than anything I'd done for any client or campaign. *This* was the climax of my entire career. And I wasn't going to let anyone ruin it.

Omigod, Helena! I glanced at the clock—the meeting with her was in fifteen minutes. I wrapped up my call, saved my file, and had Deborah buzz my team into the conference room. We ran through a quick preview of the comps, and I smiled my approval. "Y'all have done a marvelous job," I said.

I read the quizzical looks on all their faces and touched the hat self-consciously. "I've become attached to this hat . . . it's a long story, no time to tell it now. Oh, and I got my hair cut, too. But it's no big deal, no cause for panic. Just a woman's prerogative to change things up, okay?"

They exchanged looks that said they couldn't wait to get away from me so they could discuss just how and why I'd lost my mind. Before I could set them straight, Hurricane Helena sashayed into the conference room, a vision in a violet St. John knit pantsuit, her slender, highly-arched feet in matching Ferragamo pumps, and her ears adorned with huge amethyst earrings.

"Rodney tells me we have cause for celebration," she said. "I'm looking forward to seeing your new, improved ideas for the Hot Chocolate campaign."

Lord, hold me back, I prayed, thrusting the corners of my lips into a reasonable facsimile of a smile. "Good afternoon, Helena." I sighed, the high from my creative rush fading fast. "My team has worked long and hard to come up with some new ideas. We think you'll be pleased." The new posters were unrolled and hung with a flourish.

Helena's eyes danced approvingly over the two models we'd selected—each generically beautiful enough not to offend a single soul. They both had camera-friendly bone structure, satiny complexions, symmetrical features, and dazzling smiles, all topped with clouds of spiraling curls. Their looks were more reassuring than inspiring, more comforting than hot and definitely more mocha latte than chocolate. But I was beyond caring. "I think I prefer . . . this one," Helena announced, indicating the sultry, doe-eyed waif on the left. "Her look really says Hot Chocolate. Don't you agree?"

I ignored her invitation to spar. "Your decision is law, Helena. The girl on the left it is." I turned to one of my creative assistants and whispered, "What's her name again?"

"Kaylee," he answered.

"Why don't you tell Helena about her?" I suggested.

"Me?" He was so shocked his voice squeaked out. I bit back a laugh.

"Yes, you. She was your choice, wasn't she?"

"Yes, but . . ."

"Go for it."

Helena cocked a brow in the direction of our whispering. I stood. "Helena, Mitch is the one who suggested this model, and I think he should be the one to tell you all about her. Mitch."

He stood and cleared his throat, then proceeded to delight Helena with the chosen model's pedigree and status in the marketplace. Helena nodded approvingly, following his every word. I should've let Mitch deal with her a long time ago, I thought, happy to have made a successful match and taken the pressure off myself.

Rodney walked in, startled to see Mitch making a presentation while I sat doodling on my notepad. "What's up?" he asked softly, sliding into the chair beside me.

I shrugged. "Mitch's choice was Helena's favorite, so I thought I'd let him run with it. Matter of fact, Rodney, I'd like off of Helena's account altogether."

"And why is that?"

"My team is more than capable of handling her. Plus, I have something new, something *really* hot that I'm working on. But I won't be able to tell you about it till tomorrow."

I laughed at his puzzled expression. "Chill, boss. You know I wouldn't let you down."

He lifted the hat from my head and peered at me closely, tracing his finger around my new hairline. I laughed self-consciously, then realized that everyone in the room was staring at me.

"Well, well," Helena said, "what have we here?"

"Just a new hairstyle," I murmured. "It was an impulse, actually. Can't even explain why I . . ."

"It's nice." Rodney grinned. "It's really you."

The others chattered their approval, and I caught a pensive look on Helena's face. Before I had a chance to wonder what she was thinking, Rodney moved to her side to seal the deal on her approval of the new model.

I slipped unnoticed out of the room, my relief at Helena's agreement threatening to give way to exhaustion.

"Boss, your phone has been blowin' *up*!" Deborah gushed, handing me a thick stack of messages. "Lauryn Hill, Quincy Jones, Spike Lee . . . what are you cookin' up in there?"

I shook my head, laughing. "Top secret, I told you. When will my team be here?"

"They're scheduled for one o'clock. Should I order you a sandwich or something?"

I didn't feel hungry, but knew I was running on fumes. "Sure. Turkey, please. Thanks."

Reading the messages gave me another surge of energy. Seems that folks were as excited about this as I was. Or at least intrigued enough to call back.

When my team arrived, I gave them a quick explanation of my poster boards and sketches, enjoying the growing excitement on their faces.

"This is deep," Mitch said. "Looks like this could be the revolution," Morgan agreed. I nodded as we settled into a brainstorming session. Once they had their assignments, they hurried out, chatting happily about the bold new campaign.

The rest of the day passed in a blur of more urgent phone tag, cryptic emails, and frantic note taking. By the time I paused to take a breath, it was seven-thirty and everyone else had gone home. I'd been in the office, working nonstop, for nearly twelve hours. Though my brain was still churning, my body demanded food and sleep.

On my way out of the building, I passed Shane in the lobby. I tried to get by with a quick nod of the head, but before I got to the door he said, "Whoa—hold up!"

"Yes?" I said without turning to face him.

"There's something about the way you look tonight . . ." Before I could respond, he was circling me, camera in hand, clicking away. "I told you that hat was made for you." He took a few more shots, then paused and lowered the camera.

"What's goin' on under there, Carmella? Don't tell me you cut your hair," he teased, lifting the hat from my head. "Aw yeah, that's it!" He raised the camera and started clicking even faster this time. "Great haircut. Love it. Shows your face, your bone structure, your eyes . . . and those lips! How did I miss those before?"

I smiled in spite of myself, but still I was in no mood for foolishness, no matter how flattering it might be. "Shane, I really have to be . . ."

"See, the hair is like a curtain that lets you glimpse the face but never truly see it. Now that the curtain is gone, I can see just how beautiful you really are." He straightened up and lowered the camera, along with his voice. "I am serious, you know. I find you very, very beautiful, Carmella."

I tried not to let my anxiety show. "Shane, you're handsome, you're fun, you're smart . . ."

"But I'm just too light skinned, is that it?" he asked. I couldn't tell whether he was being sarcastic or serious.

"What did you say?" I bristled. "That's the most ridiculous thing I've ever heard."

"Is it, Carmella? I know I can't be the only one feelin' the chemistry between us. I think you're attracted to me. Why won't you give it a chance?"

We held eyes for a wide, silent moment. "Well?" he asked, all the teasing gone from his face and voice.

"It's just that my life is so complicated right now. And I don't believe in mixing business with pleasure," I added weakly.

"Yeah. I get it," he said curtly, snapping the camera into its carrying case.

"I don't think you do, Shane."

"Well, are you attracted to me or aren't you? If you're not, then hey, it's strictly business from now on. But tell me, is what I'm feeling a one-way street?"

"How am I supposed to answer that, Shane?"

"Well, Carmella, I think you just did. You take care of yourself." He started to walk away. I pushed open the lobby door, feeling even more weary than before. The last thing I needed was some spoiled-ass man who thought every woman should want him.

"You know," I heard him say to my departing back, "there's more than one way to be color-struck."

I froze halfway through the door. How dare he accuse me of being color-struck! Who the hell did he think he was anyway? That's exactly why I've always avoided his type—they were arrogant and full of themselves. Calling me color-struck! Me of *all* people. He must be out of his natural mind.

I stood outside the building taking deep gulps of cold air, ready to whip my anger on the next person who passed by. Raising my hand to clamp the hat on my head during a strong gust of wind, I felt something come off in my hand. The black band that encircled the crown of the hat had come loose. Just what I needed. Now the hat looked as forlorn as I felt. Home, bath, bed, my body begged. But it was overruled by an urge to do something for the hat.

Next thing I knew, I was slipping into Diaspora, inhaling

mango-scented incense and moving toward the wall of fabrics. I crossed my fingers, hoping I'd hear dreadlocks' dreamy voice. Maybe that would wipe the sting of Shane's accusation from my mind.

"May I help you?" The young woman was brisk, professional, almost cool. "We just got a new shipment of Kente cloth. Would you like to see some of it?"

"Sure," I murmured, "I'd love to."

Together we looked at several kinds of the woven cloth whose bold colors had come to symbolize an affinity with African people and pride. I took off my hat and showed her the newly bald space at the base of the brim. "I'm kind of looking for something for the hat," I said. She flipped through bolt after bolt of fabric, each brighter and more gorgeous than the next, but none of them seemed right for my borrowed headpiece. I had no idea what the professor's taste might be. But it didn't seem right to let the hat lay bare.

"A strip of this would look beautiful on your hat," said a familiar voice. "See how well the gold in the Kente sets off the brown-tones?"

"It's not really mine, though," I started to explain, turning slowly to savor the sight of dreadlocks' round face and laughing eyes.

"Watch this," he said, moving behind the counter and returning with a large pair of scissors. Moving with a tropical languor, he snipped a narrow length of the Kente and deftly wrapped it around the base of the hat. "Here. Try it on."

I put it on my head, searching for a mirror. The young woman held one up with a smile. I nodded at my reflection. The Kente picked up the undertones of my skin and brought the hat to life. "Good work, honey," she crooned to dreadlocks. "Thanks, love." He beamed at her. I glanced down to see matching gold bands on their left ring fingers.

Damn! The one man I've seen in months who gets my attention and he has to be married! This is definitely not my day. I paid for the cloth, hoping they couldn't read the disappointment on my face. It was too late to take the train, so I hailed a taxi, half dozing as I rode home. I kept hearing Shane's voice and seeing dreadlocks' face. Yeah, I liked darker-skinned men. So what? Hey, the blacker the berry, the sweeter the juice, right?

As the taxi rounded the corner, I opened one eye to check for the professor, but there was no sign of him anywhere. Was it possible that I'd never see him again? Shane swore he'd heard the professor had died. Then again, Shane thought he knew everything.

"Lord, deliver us from the madness of Mr. Willie Lynch and all the mess we put ourselves through in his honor," I prayed before collapsing into dreamland. If my new campaign did even a little to make that kind of difference, I'd be more than satisfied.

Chapter SEVEN

THE MORNING WAS A WHIRL of preparation. With Hot Chocolate back on schedule, I could focus on the unveiling of my latest inspiration. Deborah and my creative team helped me set up the conference room. Chairs were rearranged so everyone in the agency could attend. I even considered inviting Shane but decided against it. He'd have to find out how wrong he was about me on his own time.

At one o'clock, the room was filled with people and expectation. I took a deep breath and said a quick prayer. This would either soar or fall flat on its face. But it simply had to be done.

Deborah killed the lights and we began in total darkness.

"Black is Beautiful, right?" Patti LaBelle's voice said.

"At least that's what some of us claim," Spike Lee's voice accused.

"But we don't all believe it, do we?" Erykah Badu's voice asked. A chorus of children's voices mockingly sang:

> If you're white, you're all right.
> If you're yellow, you're mellow.
> If you're brown, stick around.
> If you're black, get back, b-b-b-back.

The lights came up on a video with a parade of stars, from Vanessa L. Williams and Morris Chestnut to Philip Michael Thomas and Maya Angelou, each sharing a few words about learning to love your black self, whatever shade you may be. Queen Latifah, Busta Rhymes, and Take 6 put the story of Willie Lynch to music. Lauryn Hill and Brian McKnight joined Kirk Franklin and Sounds of Blackness in a song entitled "Unity." Tavis Smiley explained how we were putting nooses around our own necks and hanging ourselves from the trees of ignorance and self-hatred. We unveiled billboards, magazine ads, bus and subway posters, TV spots, movie trailers, radio quips, and internet digicards with a rainbow of well-known black faces—including Amira's—and our slogan: "Stop the Lynching. Start the Love." I showed off our website, www.stoplynchingstartlove.com. I reeled off the growing list of celebrities who were happy to lend their support. I named prominent writers and journalists who had agreed to write up the campaign—including Lori Underwood for the *New York Times*. I described the public unveiling of the campaign, to take place on May 19, Malcolm X's birthday, at the site of the African burial ground in downtown Manhattan.

"This is more than a campaign," I explained. "It's a new movement to stop the self-hatred, stop the madness that's holding us back as a people, and help get us strong again. No more talk about who's too light or too dark, or whose hair is 'good' or 'bad.' We've got to dump that toxic waste and start loving ourselves and each other. Stop our children from killing themselves and each other. Start proving that black *is* beautiful—in *all* of its variations and shades."

The lights went up. The room was hushed, then it filled with shouts and applause. Rodney rose to embrace me. "This is *it*, Carmella. Outstanding. I have just one question—who's the client?"

"We are." I smiled.

"I don't understand."

"We're doing this pro bono, Rodney."

He opened his mouth to protest, but I cut him off. "We've never done much pro bono work, and this will tell the world more about us than anything else we've done. This will put us on the map for real. The phones will be ringing with folks begging us to work with them. Just trust me and my instincts on this, boss, okay?"

"Carmella, this is going to cost a fortune."

"I'll underwrite the campaign," a familiar voice said. I whirled around to see Helena.

"Who let *her* in here?" I whispered to Rodney. But he didn't answer.

"Helena, did I hear you correctly?" he asked.

"Yes," she said, stepping forward. "This campaign is simply wonderful, utterly brilliant, and I would be proud to be associated with it. In fact, I would consider it a very worthy—and appropriate—investment for Black Beauty cosmetics."

"Well." Rodney chuckled, obviously relieved. "What do you say, Carmella?"

In an instant, my dream had become a nightmare. I had calls in to several multimillionaire business leaders, including Magic Johnson and Oprah Winfrey, and was hoping they'd come through. Helena Booker sponsoring "Stop the Lynching. Start the Love"? My head started to pound.

Still, as Rodney would say, a bird in the hand is worth two in the bush and Helena was in his hand, at least. "I'm waiting to hear from a few other potential sponsors," I said, trying to smile graciously at Helena. "I'll have to let you know in a day or two, all right?"

Her slow nod made it obvious that Helena wasn't accustomed to being told no or put on hold. But she managed a halfway credible smile.

Deborah came to drag me back to my office, flinging more messages at me. "I've never talked to so many famous people in my life! And they're calling personally—I'm not hearing from agents or managers, you understand? Blair Underwood, Jasmine Guy, Mariah Carey . . . I can't believe it!"

"Have we heard from Magic Johnson or Oprah Winfrey?" I asked.

"Not yet. But look at those phone lines! They won't stop."

The word was spreading, and folks wanted on board. I was shocked at how many of them said they'd been hoping something like this would come along. So I wasn't the only one who felt hurt and frustrated when black people did each other wrong.

I was ready to call it a day when Rodney stepped into my office. "I'm impressed, but not at all surprised," he said proudly. "And I hope you take Helena's offer seriously. She's quite sincere."

"What was Helena doing at my presentation, Rodney? Did you go behind my back?"

"It wasn't planned, I swear. She stopped by a few minutes before it started, saying she had something important to discuss with me. I told her I had to attend your presentation first. I couldn't very well let her sit in the lobby or in my office." He shrugged. "I didn't think it would be any big deal."

"Maybe not a big deal," I said. "But ironic as hell, considering her little hang-ups."

"Why are you so cynical? A sponsor is a sponsor. And she seems sincere about wanting to help with this new campaign."

"Yeah, sure. What's her motive? Slapping the Black Beauty

logo all over our materials? Taking credit for the whole concept? You know I don't trust that woman, Rodney, especially when it comes to—"

"Has it ever occurred to you, Carmella, that I just want to make a difference?"

My head snapped up to see Helena at my door. "May I come in?" she asked.

"I appreciate your offer, Helena, but I need a few days."

"Fine," she said. "I'll wait to hear from you then?"

I nodded, hoping I never had to take her up on her offer.

"First she hates Amira, now she wants to sponsor my new campaign," I said. "Can't help but be suspicious, boss."

Rodney rose with a smile. "Enjoy the success of this new, uh, venture." I knew the very thought of a pro bono campaign hurt him to his capitalistic little heart. "Get some rest—you've earned it—and we'll talk tomorrow. I've got to go meet with a *paying* client, if you don't mind."

More calls, but not the ones I'd been waiting for. "God," I prayed, "you'd have to have a sick sense of humor to have Helena sponsor this campaign. I'd rather not have to take a dime of her money, so please let Oprah or Magic call. Thank you. Amen."

I wanted to keep working, but my body was about to go on strike. I took the early train home, my Kente-adorned hat snugly on my head. I was shocked to see the professor, back at his spot on the corner, strumming his guitar. This time, his clothing was black, as was the ebony fedora hat filled with bills and coins on the sidewalk in front of him. I approached tentatively, pinching myself hard to make sure I was awake, blinking rapidly in case I was seeing a mirage.

"Professor Phelps?" I asked.

He nodded and gave me a big smile. "Well, how have you been, young lady? You're looking quite well."

"Thank you." I removed the brown hat and held it out to him.

"The black band came off and it didn't look right, so I was hoping you'd like the . . ."

"I do. I like it a great deal. But I won't take it. You see, it's your hat now."

"Well, if you don't like the Kente, I can find another black band."

"That's not it." He chuckled. "I gave that hat to you. As a gift. I don't want it back. You see, young lady, you've grown into the hat. That's what makes it truly yours."

I smiled, wanting to tell him everything but unsure where to start. I tried to focus my mind long enough to speak coherently, but before I could begin he nodded at the hat lying near his feet and said, "Beauty and fedoras come in all shades, just as love does."

"I'm sure you're right," I agreed, "but I'm not involved with anyone at the moment."

"Have you asked yourself why?" he inquired.

I shook my head and at that moment I saw the face of Richie Dawson, a light-skinned playmate from elementary school. Richie and I went from being best friends in kindergarten to boyfriend and girlfriend in the fifth grade. We still played and studied together, but the energy between us turned from carefree to sweeter and more complex. We were just beginning to look at each other differently when some boys teased Richie on the playground. "Richie likes Carmella! Says he wants to be her man! Is that your girlfriend, man? When you gonna kiss her, huh? Why don't you do it now?"

Richie's golden face blushed red and he turned into a stranger before my eyes. "Man, that girl ain't none a my *girlfriend*," he sneered. "I don't like nobody." I felt the sick sensation of shame and rage knot my stomach. I wanted to drop off the earth.

In that moment, my heart broke. Not from romantic love, but because he'd wiped our friendship from his heart without a second thought, all behind some teasing from a bunch of silly boys. I think it was then that I decided I didn't like light-skinned boys. Funny, I'd never thought about the reasons I felt that way. Maybe Richie's youthful betrayal had set the stage for my rejection of Shane.

A blast of frigid air brought me back to the present. The professor strummed a blues riff, his eyes half-closed. I enjoyed the smiles of passersby as his music wafted above the traffic to float into their ears. What's that he had said—that I'd grown into the hat? As he finished playing, I said, "Professor, I have so much to tell you, but . . . well, mostly it's just really good to see you back. Here. Where you belong. It didn't feel right with you gone. And I was worried."

"I appreciate your concern, young lady, but there's no need to fret. Ole Professor Phelps isn't going anywhere yet."

I wanted to hold him tightly to me so he wouldn't disappear again. Instead, I clutched the brown hat tightly to my chest, admiring the way the Kente brought out the browntones. In the fedora, and in my own skin.

Chapter EIGHT

AFTER A RESTFUL WEEKEND, I was back at the office full steam. My campaign grew by the minute. Rodney kept leaning on me to accept Helena's offer, but I tried to hold out for other support. I was fully energized, better than ever, on fire with more ideas every day. Convinced that the hat was my good-luck charm, I wore it even in the office, reluctant to let it out of my sight.

Helena showed up midweek, knocking tentatively at my office door. I waved her in and invited her to sit down.

"I guess you're wondering why I volunteered to underwrite your new campaign. Especially after I rejected your model for Hot Chocolate."

I waited without responding.

"Well, Carmella, your remark that day hit home. You know, when you said that Amira looked like me. I didn't want to admit it, but you were right. I thought about it and realized I had some unfinished business to take care of. But I didn't know where to start. How do you look inside yourself when you know you're going to hate what you see?"

"Helena, there's really no need for you to—"

She closed her eyes and gave a shuddering sigh. "When I saw Amira, I saw myself. I heard all the voices saying, 'She's so pretty. If only she wasn't so dark,' when I was a child. I saw the eyes that saw me as pretty, and the 'but' that kept them from really seeing it for themselves. Like so many of us, especially in my generation, I accepted all the light/dark, straight/nappy stuff. I didn't question it. But I was determined to overcome it."

I scanned the collage of Amira photos on my bulletin board. Let my eyes drift to the window, over my wall of awards, and back to Helena's face. For the first time since I'd known her, she looked vulnerable, almost on the brink of tears.

"I grew up thinking that if I could just be a model, a famous model, it would change things. Maybe then I could get people to see the pretty and not just the darkness of my skin. I don't know what made me think I had a chance. Back then, Lena Horne was all the rage. But I made it, probably due to the newfound black pride of the 1960s. In Europe, I was treated like a queen. My skin was more precious than a rare jewel. But no matter how successful I was or how famous I became, I felt sad and ugly inside."

Her eyes opened, and they shimmered with tears. "Even now, with all that I've accomplished and all that I have, the hurt doesn't go away. It haunts me at night. It keeps me feeling like a helpless child. Amira *is* me. She's the me I showed the world. She's the beauty I never really believed I had.

"I know it's too late to get her for Hot Chocolate. But I want to be part of your new campaign. Like many of us, I've been scarred by the skin-hair thing. Like most of us, I hated the whole thing but felt powerless to stop it. But now, I'm ready to stop being part of the problem, as they say, and start being part of the solution. If you'll agree to work with me, that is."

I was at war with myself. As much as I wanted to tell her to go to hell, I wanted the campaign to fly. And the words she'd just spoken hit me straight in the heart.

"I just don't know, Helena."

"I know I can be unreasonable. But when our buttons get pushed, we all are. I take the 'Stop the Lynching. Start the Love' campaign very personally. Besides, if you can reach an old diva like me, you know you've got the power to help others change."

"Look, Helena, some things are still up in the air. I can't give you a final answer until I know what's going on. It may take a few days, it could take a week. But I will consider your offer."

"I appreciate it. Thank you." She stood and prepared to leave. "By the way, Carmella, I love your new look. The hat and the haircut. You have a lot more style than you realize."

I was so shocked at the brief glimpse into Helena's soft side that it was several minutes before I could move. Pinch. I was awake. And getting tired of squeezing my flesh to prove it.

It was the next day before I saw Shane. He darted into the elevator, looked like he was about to speak, then thought better of it and nodded silently. We both watched the floor numbers flashing by. He still smelled delicious. And he still got on my nerves. We finished the ride without speaking.

Magic Johnson wasn't available for a response. Oprah was still reviewing the request. Costs were mounting and Rodney was leaning on me to accept Helena's offer. Fine, I told him. Set up the meeting.

The next morning, I found a large manila envelope on my office chair. Inside were the photos Shane had taken of me in the lobby. No invoice, no note. The photos were stunning. Maybe he and Helena were right. Maybe I did look all right—no, maybe I was beautiful—hair or no hair. It was an idea that would take a while to digest, but I could get used to it. I smiled.

Well, since he wasn't coming to me, I guess I had to go to him. I tucked the envelope of photos under my arm, told Deborah I'd be out for a few minutes, and climbed the two flights of stairs to his top-floor studio. I couldn't remember the last time I'd been up there. His name was stenciled on the door in square black letters, and someone had drawn a picture of a camera below it.

After knocking twice, I was about to give up. Shane opened the door expectantly, his face clouding up when he saw it was me.

"How much do I owe you?"

"For what?"

"The photos. They're really great."

"Consider them a gift."

"I want to pay you, Shane."

"I won't accept it. Just consider the pictures food for thought."

"How about some real food?"

"Is that an invitation?" He looked like he was afraid to smile.

"I'd like to take you to dinner."

"What for?"

I sighed. "To express my appreciation. What do you think?"

"A business dinner?"

"Does it matter?"

"It does to me," he said.

"Shane, I'm sorry," I said.

"You don't have to apologize to me, Carmella. Different strokes for different folks. I'm used to women not wanting to date me because of my looks. Seems there're more of those nowadays than the women who want to marry or have children with me 'cause they think I'm movie-star material. But you know what? I'm just a regular guy, just a man. No game, no shame. And no hard feelings."

"Look, I'll admit I've had a bias."

"Don't worry about it. I guess we all do."

"But we can all grow, right?"

"I don't know, Carmella. Can we?"

"I have a confession," I said softly.

"What's that?"

"I am."

"You are what?"

"I am attracted to you. I've tried to avoid it, but I have to admit it's there."

"So?"

"How's tomorrow night? For dinner."

"Let me check my calendar and get back to you." He smiled.

"Don't wait too long, Mr. Camera Man." I winked. "You don't want me to change my mind."

He winked back and closed the door.

Time to meet with Helena. I gave my phone one last hopeful glance before joining her and Rodney in the conference room. It was silent. But I could swear I heard God laughing.

I'd had Rodney draw up a contract outlining all my terms. As we turned to the document, I strode over to Helena. "We can do this," I began, "but we're playing by my rules. I welcome your support, Helena, but that's what it is, support. Not direction. I retain all decision-making powers in every aspect of the campaign." I waited for her to withdraw her offer, half wishing that she would. Instead, she simply nodded and smiled.

Each of us signed all copies of the contract. I extended my hand for a seal-the-deal handshake.

Helena hesitated. Lord, what was it now?

"Carmella, I know I can be impossible. But I really think this campaign calls for something a little more . . . personal. If you don't mind." She took a step toward me and awkwardly opened her arms.

Before I knew what I was doing, I'd stepped into them and we were hugging like long-lost girlfriends. Rodney beamed. God's laughter had turned to applause. "Take that, Willie Lynch," I said. "I know that's right," Helena said, slapping my palm.

We set up a series of future appointments and I returned to my office. Looking out the window at the bustling city below, I twirled the hat on my finger. The sun seemed to wink at me from behind a winter cloud. I set the brown fedora on a hook above my coat. I guess we can all grow. After all, I'd made a date with Shane and a bold new deal with Helena.

Maybe there's hope for my people after all.

TRACY

Other People's Skin

PRICE-THOMPSON

Chapter ONE

I ENTERED THIS WORLD on the wave of a violent midsummer heat, north of Venice, south of the French Quarter, on the wide mouth of an oxbow lake. My first drops of sweet milk were suckled in a spacious wood house crawling with Spanish moss and shaded by loblolly pines. According to Ma'Dear, mine was the year of the great drought, and instead of the river belching forth schools of laughing gull and black skimmer fish, folks in our tiny back-swamp on the Mississippi Delta were up to their chins in scorched caking mud, which, whispered by some, was the exact same shade of my newborn hide.

Shortly after my birth, Peaches fainted. The sight of me was far too much for her to bear. She came from good stock, she cried, panting through the pains of my afterbirth and holding her milky arms out as evidence of her purity. A LeMoyne, she insisted. A direct descendant of the distinguished Jean Baptiste. And until I came along to highlight the stain on her pedigree, her silken brown tresses and fine chalky skin had been more than enough to prove it.

Papa wrung his hands as Ma'Dear revived Peaches with strong herbs and coaxed her into a sitting position, gently urging her to nurse the howling infant rooting for her full breasts. As her elder daughter hovered at her elbow, Peaches accepted the swaddled bundle that was me, and with trembling arms lay my wriggling body atop her still-bulging belly. Pinching the thin cloth into a tent between her thumb and forefinger, she peeled back the soft blanket and peeked inside, her eyes wild and cautious. She permitted herself only the briefest confirming glance before swooning and letting the blanket fall to protect her from my stare. With her face drained of color and her hair floating in a mad halo above her skull, she pressed the back of her hand to her forehead and wailed in horror, "But this can't be none of my child! I ain't got nothing but French, Spanish, and Indian in my blood!"

Her pale brow furrowed in mild curiosity, eight-year-old Paline leaned close to our mother and lifted the blanket to judge the anomaly for herself. She gave me, her squalling baby sister, a short but critical examination before declaring with a cynicism that truly befitted a LeMoyne, "Then Papa must have some bull, muskrat, and *nigger* in his."

〜

Peaches refused to nurse me.

Papa could not meet the glare in Ma'Dear's one good eye as he placed a gentle kiss upon my forehead and implored her to tend to me, as she had tended him, his mother, and her mother before her. Washed and oiled, I was soothed by her chants as cradled in her ancient arms I sucked from clean rags dipped in goat's milk and sweetened with bits of steeped peppermint bark. Ma'Dear used both hands to knead and shape my skull, beginning at the forehead and working her way back from my crown. Loosening my blankets, she used her finger to sketch several markings upon my chest, belly, and around my eyes. That done, she turned me onto my stomach and examined my plump baby bottom, then peered closely, searchingly at the brown skin of my back. Humming a foreign chant, she used the tips of her fingers to gently roll the soft flesh high on my shoulders and smooth it down nicely along my lower back and spine. Satisfied, she flipped me back over and covered me once more, but not before whispering, "Your life ain't gonna be without hardship, daughter. But neither will it be without love."

⁓

The shame of it all was too much for Peaches to bear, and if Papa had been a sounder, more assured man, perhaps the accusations in her eyes would not have cut him so. Seething her disdain, Peaches towered above him as he lowered his forehead to her ample breasts. Papa was a handsome fellow: smooth complexion, straight hair; it was the evenness of his temperament that kept him on trial in his own home. But his was a crime of passivity. He had never pretended to be that which he was not. It was only to appease her that he went along with her charade, but he could have told her this was a possibility. After all, he *was* a Negro. One could look at him and realize this. But she insisted on putting on airs, on reconfiguring her family tree and his as well.

Yet not a soul in the bottoms was fooled; in fact, our neighbors frequently joked that the LeMoynes (Top Jar had long since shrugged off his own surname) were just another one of those shamming-ass, backwoods nigger families who went from dipping snuff and gut-laughing like bottom folks, to sipping tea with their pinkie fingers sticking straight out like twigs and talking like they had goat shit in their mouths.

Just imagine!

The fools had been fixing to hightail it to N'awlins and adopt a pedigree and a shit-free asshole, then strut around trying to pass for white! Hmm, well let's just take a looky-see here . . . with their fair skin and fine hair, Peaches and the two older children just might make it. And, the locals admitted, if you glanced at Top Jar from the low end of a hooch jug and didn't stare too hard perhaps he might just fool you too. Shucks, they reasoned. Mulatto, quadroon, octoroon—just a bunch of fancy words for a nigger who done been cut four or five times.

But that *baby*?

Messed up them grand notions but quick! Only thing that little one was gonna pass for was exactly what she was! Talk about an arrow that zipped when it shoulda goddamn zapped? Chile came out looking like a whole pot of wet coal! Look just like a pretty black china doll, but her mama couldn't stand her. Like to give herself a high-falutin heart attack when Peaches looked down 'tween her thighs and seen all a that black rolling out of her like a pool of Texas tea. Thought Ma'Dear had fixed her with the evil eye, mixed her up a special down-home brew, and put some North Cacka-Lacky mojo on her high-yella ass that would last a lifetime.

⁓

And speaking of passing and Ma'Dear, how was they planning to explain the old woman, some folks wanted to know. The younger ones laughed and shook their heads. They'll hide her in the kitchen, the women surmised. Set her behind a pile of rotting potatoes and call her the serving maid. Better yet, the hooch-drinking farm boys ventured, they'll bed her down in a shed with the horses and mules. Have her chewing coarse hay and smelling of horse balm. At that, the elders would smile and wipe the sweat from their brows with a sigh. These timeworn relics of the Delta had something that their younger brethren surely didn't: memories. They knew the bayou would dry up and spit out alligator dust before Peaches cast out Ma'Dear. When it came down to the old woman even Top Jar, as titty-whipped as he was, wasn't fool enough to let his wife go but so far. Some swore Ma'Dear was a saint; others claimed her as a conjure woman. But whatever you chose to call her, certain things were clear. No one, but no one crossed Ma'Dear, and as I could certainly testify, there wasn't a soul who could keep her where she did not desire to be.

~

Peaches was casual about giving me a name. Since I did not meet her expectations, the time and energy required to carefully select it seemed trivial and inconsequential.

"Look woman," Papa implored her, and for the first time since my birth there was a hint of authority in his tone. "The gal belongs to us and she gots to have a name."

"I know who she belongs to, Top Jar. It was me who carried and birthed her."

"Then for God's sake, woman. Give her a name."

Months passed.

Papa had been promoted and given a transfer. The family would move twelve miles west to Sweetwater. There, Peaches would finally get her dream house. Chez LeMoyne. Fully equipped with a small eat-in restaurant with checkered tablecloths and red vinyl stools.

The day of our departure dawned with a bitter chill in the air. The river meandered in a southerly flow and called out invitingly to the whippoorwills soaring overhead. Everything had been loaded up the night before and all that remained was the transporting of the human cargo.

"Why her ears so dark around the edges?" Peaches questioned Ma'Dear. "Lawd have mercy. Please don't tell me she ain't as black as she gonna get."

"It takes a while for some lit'luns to find they true color." Ma'Dear bounced me on her hip and slid her gnarled fingers through my tangles before placing me in a small chair that Uncle Bubba had built for the ride in Papa's car. "And black ain't the worst thing this chile can get. Some believe getting ignored is worse than most anything else."

"I'm trying, Ma'Dear. Lawd knows I'm trying."

Ma'Dear gave Peaches a long, hard look, the glare from her single eye a vivid cone that completely encompassed the pale face before her. "Well then, Miss Peaches LeMoyne. Don't nothin beat a try 'ceptin a failure. Jarrett says the chile needs a name. What you want us should call her?"

"Call her what you wish," Peaches said quietly as she reached down into my car cradle and stroked my dark cheek with one pale finger. She shuddered despite herself. "Call her what you wish."

Ma'Dear waited until Peaches had shut the door on the empty room, then she lifted my dimpled six-month-old body high into the air once more. With her lips stretched over her toothless gums she uttered into each of my ears the gift of two very strong names: the first of which honored my ancestors, the second of which indicated the change in my life that was sure to come.

Euleatha Oyi-Yansi LeMoyne was born.

Chapter TWO

I ROSE BEFORE DAWN TO WASH HER. With only the glow of a small bed lamp to guide me, I entered Ma'Dear's room and methodically went about my morning's work; drawing the heavy drapes apart with a hook-ended pole and pulling back the white lace curtains just in time to catch the twinkling vestiges of a faded July moon. I watched quietly as the darkness inched into light, trailing lazily across the sky before breaking apart in a kaleidoscope of patterns created by the predawn birth of the Louisiana sun.

Purposely, I went about my labor, ignoring the sheet-covered form on the bed as I poured water from a chipped jar into the clay-

potted ferns, pausing to break one or two of the most badly with-
ered leaves off at their stems and crush their wasted petals between
my cold fingers. Papa had wanted to assist me this morning and
even Peaches had shown a bit of rare kindness and volunteered to
help dress her, but I'd refused all offers. This here business was between me and Ma'Dear, and the duty that had been prescribed at
my birth was now written in stone and sprinkled like dust into the
crevices of my soul.

Her night table was cluttered though not in disarray. I busied
myself replacing the lids on several clay jars filled with cherry bark,
mint leaves, and spider root. They were of no use to her now. The
large bottle of swine tea, which I'd never been able to stomach, went
directly into the plastic-lined trash can at my feet. There were some
things that Ma'Dear and I had never been able to agree on, and
swine tea and broiled owl were two of them. After all, there were
three generations of life in between us and almost ninety years
stretched the span of our births. Rightly so we didn't always see eye
to eye.

After discarding the perishable herbs and storing the others in
one of the two large hatboxes I'd taken from the larger of her velvet-
lined cedar trunks, I retrieved a face bowl from the chest of drawers
and filled it with lukewarm water and powdered bouquets from her
small bath. I pushed the door shut for privacy, then turned to face
her, grateful for the starched cloth draping her body and momentarily shielding my view.

She had known the exact time and day of her departure. Had
prepared for it with the ease of a long trip, even looked forward to
its coming. "There's much worse things than dying, Eulie."
Ma'Dear had sighed. "With all the hatred in this world sometimes
death can be a blessing." She'd refused to tell me when she would
leave. Just kept begging me to love everyone as hard as I could, regardless of what I thought of them. "You don't know what all is in
they hearts, Euleatha," Ma'Dear admonished me whenever I com-

plained about Peaches and Paline, " 'cause you ain't learned yourself to wear they skin."

"Don't need to wear it to know it makes them think they're better than me," I told her. "And look like they wouldn't be so proud of wearing it either, seeing where it came from."

She made a clucking sound. "Believe it or not, you got some of that same blood running through your hot veins! The black race ain't been pure since we was stolen from Africa."

"But that wasn't none of our fault," I countered and shook my head in disgust. "How folk can glorify the part of them that comes from somebody's raping and brutalizing I will never understand. And to top it off, not only do them white folks got us loving them, they got us hating almost everything about ourselves." I'd frowned a youthful expression of rage and vigor as I tried to make her understand what burned so deeply within me. "Ma'Dear, you know yourself that Peaches is as black as you and me, but she'd kill herself before she'd admit it. That's why she so hateful to dark folks. Makes her come face-to-face with the part of herself she would rather hide 'cause she thinks that part of her is ugly. The white man got us thinking like that, and if I got any of him in my veins I sure ain't bragging on it! He got himself one heck of a reputation for stealing and raping and pilfering and causing black folks pain, and I for one will never be proud of that!"

Ma'Dear chuckled at my cultural indignation. "You ain't got no patent on pain, daughter. Believe it or not, everybody got it hard sometimes no matter what they look like. I usta know me a woman who looked just like Peaches. She was a brave lil thang but died young, she did. High yalla, hair like chocolate silk. Had a cute lil mole right above her lip. Black gals hated her on sight. Said she thought she was somebody. Thought she was better'n the rest of them 'cause she looked near white. Well, I knew better'n that. She actually preferred dark skin, so it was her who secretly envied them. She didn't show it, but she was full of their same sorrow. In fact, I knew 'bout her sorrow firsthand. Watched it roll down her back, dripping black like midnight tears as it soaked into the ground. Yeah, this-here gal I once knew bore her share of pain and somebody else's. Some folks just suffer on the inside where it can't be seen. Others suffer and don't even know they sufferin'. Ask 'em and they'll tell you they doing just fine."

I wasn't so sure about that. I figured Ma'Dear must have been feverish and talking out of her head, because I'd been living around Peaches and Paline for all my days and I had yet to see either of them suffer a lick. Bright skin and green eyes was like money in the bank around these parts. Because of their hair and coloring, everything came easy for them. Hardly ever lifted a finger outside of the kitchen and the town folk fawned over them so bad it was almost embarrassing. Especially the elder menfolk. No fool like an old fool. Oh Miss Peaches! You sure are looking fine this mo'ning! Cheeks plump an' yellow . . . sweet an' ripe, jes like your name! Can I help you tote that bag? You got anything need lifting round the house? Any windows need washing? Pots need scrubbing? Send that boy of yours down for a haircut. We'll have him looking right handsome now, the little rascal! And Miss Paline, *same thang* go for you. Anything you got need fixin', and I mean, *anything,* you jes give a holler, ya hear? Hmph. Ma'Dear didn't know everything, 'cause if there was ever such a thing in this world that women like Peaches or Paline would have to work for, it had yet to be created.

Standing at the head of the bed, I braced myself. I knew what had to be done; tradition demanded it and Ma'Dear had schooled me well. She was to be laid out and buried in the same day. No way around that. And no stranger would ever handle her. No blood would be drained from her body and replaced by foreign, repugnant fluids. It had always been this way, from the days of the slave ships and beyond, and she had made me promise to carry out her instructions and sear them upon my progeny for all eternity.

My fear was thick and palpable and could have easily immobilized me had not my pain been so raw and my sense of obligation so keen. With a deep breath I pushed the fear down where the hurt and longing lived, and reminded myself that I belonged to Ma'Dear. The same Ma'Dear who'd been born a slave and lived to see her freedom, who had birthed a daughter and buried a husband all in the same day, who had held her baby sisters in her arms and stared down the man who killed their mother, the same Ma'Dear who had survived several lifetimes of yanking back sheets and getting right down to the business of living.

I wasn't frightened enough or foolish enough to disobey her.

As I slid the ends of the sheets from beneath her form and pulled back the top corners to expose her face, I was only mildly surprised by what I saw. Ma'Dear's skin tone had always changed with her mood. How she looked depended on how she felt on a particular day. There were days while standing near Paline or Junior when she appeared to have less than a drop of black blood in her veins, her skin insipid and pale and as soft as an unbaked Carolina biscuit. On other days she was seared golden with the buttery glow of deep-dish hot-water cornbread. Some mornings I was greeted by a face I can only describe as Indianish: lush and fertile and red as the blood-soaked battlefields of the deep South. And there were other days still, when rocking me in her arms and soothing away some hurt or slight, Ma'Dear's eyes floated like moonbeams and peered at me from skin the exact shade of a Mississippi sky at half past midnight.

In death, however, Ma'Dear gravitated to middle ground. Today her skin resembled the scooped-out earth of a freshly dug grave: rich and fertile. I could almost imagine dipping my finger into the well of her cheeks and reveling in the sweetness of her brown sugar, because on this day, my seventeenth birthday,

Ma'Dear looked like a freshly baked ginger cake with an entire bottle of chocolate syrup drizzled over her head.

I dipped the heels of a soft rag into the scented water and carefully soaped her face and ears, then washed and rinsed her thin tufts of white hair. As I gazed upon the atlas of Ma'Dear's face I could only imagine the wonders of her hundred-plus-year journey. Jagged paths of wisdom curved away from her tranquil smile and scaled the crests of her cheeks. Highways, furrowed and paved with tenderness, formed an outer loop beyond her eyes, bisecting and linking smaller, less traveled roads. A thoroughfare of joy, its borders sprinkled with life's hills and valleys, ran along the perimeter of her lips, their surfaces a placid oasis brimming with laughter and love. In the conduit cast by her aquiline nose grew a shady forest, a perfect place of rest for the road-weary traveler. In the beauty of Ma'Dear's face I saw a genogram of her ancestors. Of their challenges and tribulations. Of their victories and triumphs. And of me. The zenith, the apex, of their existence.

The facecloth hanging from the bedpost was used to pat her skin dry. Next, I pulled the sheet down to her waist and used a pair of scissors to cut away her nightclothes. Rigor mortis had come and gone and her body was cool to the touch, pliant and cooperative. As the cloth fell away from her and the first traces of her skin came into view, I marveled at its suppleness, its clarity and tone.

I was five the summer I first gazed upon Ma'Dear's nakedness. She was bathing in a yawning claw-foot tub, its twin spigots trickling clear water over her shoulders and back and breasts. My feet dangled above the hardwood floor as I sat perched upon the closed lid of the commode, watching her, feasting on the wonders of her ancient flesh as she immersed herself in the heady mixture of water and crushed petals and herbs. In my innocence I'd been fascinated by her oddities. My intellect was not yet keen enough to question the strangeness of what my eyes saw.

"Oh, Ma'Dear," I yelped when she swiveled around to give her toes a turn under the thin streams, "why come your feets look like mashed-up rutabagas?"

She grinned. "Chile, feets like this come from walkin in other folks' shoes."

Then a sly look stole over her and Ma'Dear dipped her right shoulder just an inch, granting me the briefest glimpse of her naked back. I recoiled in surprise, slamming my head on the thick porcelain toilet tank and nearly knocking myself unconscious. "Oh! Ma'Dear!" I hollered. Unsure of exactly what I'd seen, my five-year-old eyes brimmed with tears as much from the knot on my head as from the strange disfigurement of her back. "Why come your back got like that?" I shrieked. "What somebody done to make it look that'a way?"

Ma'Dear's smile faded and a strange look crossed her face, "Euleatha Oyi-Yansi," she whispered, the words tumbling from her mouth like a bag full of sorrow. She aimed her thumb over her shoulder. "This back right'chere? This come from living in other people's skin."

I swallowed hard against the memory and began soaping Ma'Dear at her neck, making small sudsy circles on her gaunt chest, then cleansing the pair of flaccid breasts that had nursed my great-grandmother and brought comfort to my grandmother and father and then finally, to me. When I finished washing Ma'Dear's breasts, I covered them with half of the sheet before allowing my hands to travel south toward her sunken stomach. Out of respect I averted my eyes from the hairless triangle of her sex, preferring instead to do my business by touch and complete the area as quickly as possible. I washed her sticklike thighs and pulled the sheet down over her groin and folded it just above her knees, the oldest-looking part of Ma'Dear's body. Scrubbing knees, she'd called them. Wizened and arthritic, the skin hung from them like animal hide: tough and calloused. Her calves were limp; her ankles were devoid of flesh, nearly all bone. Her toes were as I remembered them: knotted and gnarled, the same dark appendages that had haunted me as a child.

I was just about done. I folded Ma'Dear's hands upon her chest and carefully rolled her frail body over until she lay flat on her stomach. With great trepidation I pulled away the last shreds of her nightgown, sweeping the thin garment free in one smooth motion. I could scarcely believe my eyes as I stared at her exposed flesh in unreserved amazement.

Ma'Dear's back bore the colors of humanity. Her skin was a kaleidoscope of colors: patches of black, bits of brown, snatches of the palest white, tiny sections containing the creamiest shades of yellow and the deepest tints of red the human eye could stand. Every color was equally epitomized; not a single skin tone went underrepresented. I saw all the shades of Asia, of Africa, of Russia, of England, of Palestine, Israel, Ireland, North and South America, you name it, all of humankind was there, etched in indelible ink upon Ma'Dear's back from shoulder to shoulder, neck bone to coccyx; the graphic portrayal of God's wondrous globe, the end result of several lifetimes of loving and giving and living . . . in other people's skin.

Chapter THREE

THE FRONT ROOM was not in its usual state. Papa and Uncle Bubba had spent the morning setting up rows of folding chairs and polishing the cherrywood breakfront to a high glossy shine. Candles flickered in large glass vats atop the claw-foot highboy, and the heavy green drapes had been parted to reveal the hand-crocheted panels that hung beneath them and filtered out the mid-summer morning's rays.

Ma'Dear was a vision of loveliness. A delicate package wrapped in linen and lace, her shrouded frame was but a tiny wrinkle in the yards of sequined fabric and lay deeply inside the satin-lined pillows of her burial bed. Her coffin was a simple rectangular box carved from a young oak that was felled during a spring twister and carefully sanded and shellacked under Uncle Bubba's watchful eye. The top half of the lid was upright, braced open on a shiny hinge made of brass. The bottom half of the lid had been nailed shut, a wreath of yellow roses resting upon it in sweet repose.

Twin ceiling fans stirred up an uncommon draft and the faint aroma of orange peels and brewed mint leaves hovered in the air. The slight breeze caressed my skin and I turned away from Ma'Dear and shivered, drawing my shawl high upon my shoulders. The double doors swung inward and a small groan escaped me. He paused in the vestibule, his features so unlike mine. Me the spitting image of our father, him a broken man with our mother's face: slug colored and drained of all compassion. I watched him half swagger and half limp his way over to where Ma'Dear lay and instinctively moved to place myself in the space between them, wanting for all the world to bar him from her righteous presence, to shield her dignity from his toxic view.

"You did good, Eulie." He nudged me aside as his eyes swept over her body. "She don't hardly look dead at all, but why'd you hafta go'n wrap her up like a goddamn mummy?" He leaned in closely and frowned as best he could. "You sure she gone? Look like the old gal is playin' possum to me—'cept she ain't snoring or cutting loose none of them antique farts."

"Junior!" His name felt sour on my tongue. "Boy, you best watch your trifling mouth! Even without a breath in her body she's worth ten of you."

Junior threw back his head and laughed, his mouth open so wide I could read his thoughts.

As pure and saintly as Ma'Dear had been, she had never been able to pass those traits on to me. I was a child despised; years of painful taunts and mistreatment had toughened my spirit and I walked around with hell in me. In a constant state of rage and resentment. And right now I was on fire. Burning with the urge to take my fist and give Junior a little color—right around his eye—but instead I glanced at Ma'Dear and lowered my voice. "For God's sake, stupid. Have a little bit of respect for the dead."

"Oh, I gots respect. Got more than enough respect. I respect the fact that I ain't gotta empty that nasty pee bucket no more, or go blind from seeing her wrinkled ass sticking out the washtub." He pinched my arm painfully and grinned from one side of his mouth, then picked up a wooden chair with one hand and turned it around backward before straddling it between his legs and cautiously lowering his weight. The bulge of his right thigh was prominent through the fabric of his pants. His left leg hung useless, malformed, and incomplete.

He leaned his forearms on the coffin and peered closely into Ma'Dear's still face. "Damn, Eulie. You'n granny look just alike, did'ja know that? The two of you together are blacker'n an empty skillet! No wonder she was always sweet on you. Y'all could 'bout pass for twins!"

"You spoiled yellow freak," I hissed. "Ain't worth the snot in her nose! You got half a brain to go with that half a body. Say another word about my mama and I'll—"

"You'll what?" His good hand snaked out and clamped down hard on my wrist, his knuckles white, his voice like steel. "That old coon wasn't none of your mama. Your mama is in the kitchen calling for you, needin' you, while you out here foolin' round with that dried-out sack of hog feed!"

"Turn her loose, Jarrett Junior."

Neither of us had heard Papa push through the door. Bull-chested, with arms as thick around as my thighs, he filled the door-way and cast a shadow over the room. His overalls were stained and splotched over his faded brown shirt. Sweat darkened the brim of his old army cap and his work boots were covered in dried paint and curled upward at the toes.

"Boy, when you gonna learn," Papa's words rang deadly although he never spoke above a whisper, "'bout mishandling wimmens?"

Junior took his time releasing my arm, but stood respectfully and lowered his gaze. He was nearly as tall as Papa when he stood on his good foot, although he would never measure up to Papa's thick, strapping build. He was too willowy, light in the ass like Mama, and no matter how much booze he drank he stayed trim. Papa spent his days pushing timber; Junior spent his days popping 'tang.

"Ain't hurting her none, sir," Junior mumbled. "Just come to check on Ma'Dear and tell Eulie Mama's calling for her to help out in the kitchen."

My big brother was a lying sack of shit and there wasn't a soul between Jefferson and Broward counties who didn't know it. Papa's eyes crawled off Junior and questioned me. "That right, Beanie? You supposed to be in the kitchen helpin' your mama?"

I sighed. My anger dissipated and sorrow reclaimed my soul. "Yessir. But I needed to talk with Ma'Dear. Wanted to tell her—"

"Beanie baby, don't you think she know what's in your heart?" He nodded toward Ma'Dear's body. "All these years she been learnin' you and you been tending her? You ain't got no need in standin' over that shell and talkin' into the air. All Ma'Dear ever needed to hear from you she heard it while it counted."

I nodded and began to weep. Instinctively Papa glanced around the room, then looked furtively over his shoulder before drawing me briefly into his embrace. I used to think my Papa loved me. The first five summers of my life were spent underfoot at the lumber plant where he was the chief foreman, boss man to a crew of thirty. Jarrett Senior. Most honorable man in all of Broward County they called him. A King Solomon in overalls. And me, Top Jar's string bean. His beanie baby. His mirror image stained dark with pigment. Namesake of his grandmama, safeguarded by his great-grandmother, tortured by his children, and hated by his wife.

By the time I was six Papa's outward expressions of love for me had all but disappeared. He didn't dare display any affection where someone might catch him. Especially Peaches. To make up for it he'd tiptoe into Ma'Dear's room late at night bearing sweet treats and corn-haired doll babies with china-blue eyes and red-checkered dresses. During those rare moments Ma'Dear and I would giggle like schoolgirls while Papa hugged and tickled me and planted sloppy kisses on my forehead, but unfortunately those moments were few and far between.

By and by it grew painfully obvious to me that light skin and straight hair were prerequisites for family love and a carefree life, and when I was younger I'd pretend that Papa and I were really married and that Peaches and Paline were evil witches who'd cast a spell over us and turned me black and ugly and made Papa their unwilling servant. There were one or two occasions when I allowed my daydream to float me into the actual world and got slapped with a cold dose of reality when looking to Papa to defend me from Peaches's disdain or Paline's wrath. "I scrubbed them pots! I did too scrub them pots! Papa seen me scrubbing them, didn't you, Papa?" In that split second between the sad apology in his eyes and the noncommittal shrug of his shoulders indicating his refusal to stand up for me, let alone take my side, I hated him.

But now I rested my head in a comfortable spot high on the rock of his chest and let my tears fall. Papa was right. That was just a corpse lying in the pine box before me. My great-great-grandmother lived in my heart. I sighed and opened my eyes and studied his face, a face so like mine but with skin that was much, much lighter. Papa glanced toward the door with guilt in his eyes. Like he expected it to open up on a constable with his gun drawn and a warrant for his arrest. The charge? Comforting me.

"Gone." He squeezed me tightly before releasing me and pushing me gently toward the door. "Git on in there and help out, Beanie. Theys gonna be plenty of folks callin' on Ma'Dear today and you don't wanna keep Peaches waitin too long." Dutifully I moseyed down the narrow hall that led to the kitchen. As big as I was, I'd wanted to stay in the safety of Papa's arms. Wanted to tell him just how much I was gonna miss Ma'Dear and how I didn't know if I could keep on living in this house without her. I'd wanted to tell my papa how hard it was to live in my skin, subjected to Peaches's rage, Paline's wrath, and Junior's torture, with no Ma'Dear to fend for me. I'd wanted to tell Papa a lot of things, but instead I kept my mouth shut and headed toward the kitchen. Because I'd already learned the hard way that when it came to high-yellow women with big breasts and green eyes who called themselves Peaches or Paline, my Papa had done lost all his senses.

~

Senseless or not, Papa made good money for a colored man and had showed his natural tail when it came to constructing our house. An intricately designed three-story stucco perched back from the road on a long winding drive, ours was the largest and grandest property in the middle-class parish of Sweetwater and sat a half a spit from the rolling colonial homes of the white elite. There were three smaller houses and a large colonial on our left and a large red ranch-style house to our right. The west wing of our house was where the family lived and slept, and the east wing branched off to a conduit that had been specially designed for Peaches's restaurant. Ma'Dear and I had been chased up to a set of small rooms in the attic above the garage, complete with a private bath and a small skylight. Paline had a cathedral room next to the master bedroom, and Junior slept in a bedroom right off the front room, which wasn't really a front room at all. It was actually centered on the west wing of the house and overlooked a small creek that ambled lazily in the spring and swirled with ice chips during the winter.

Keith G'Orge was my age and lived with his lawyer parents in the big, white-columned colonial directly next door, and the owner of the red ranch was the lip-licking widower Peets, the town alderman whose cunning eyes had claimed Peaches even before our moving van was done unloading.

The passage hall leading from the front room to the kitchen was a twenty-foot green-carpeted walkway. Its wide path was lined on either side with an assortment of tall, wicker-potted plants and opened onto a wide ceiling-to-floor glass window called the lookhole that gave full view to the goings-on inside the industrial-sized kitchen. The stainless steel ovens, Frigidaires, and matching cutting tables faced away from this glass wall, which Peaches used as her personal observation point. From the head cook to the chief bottle washer, Peaches ruled with an iron fist and distrusted everyone except Paline to follow her orders. Having Papa put glass where sheetrock should have gone was just one of her many ways of snooping and checking and making folks miserable.

One of my chores before heading to the kitchen each morning was to polish that thin glass with old newspapers soaked in lemon rinds and vinegar until it almost disappeared, and each night I prayed for God to roll enough soot off those stoves to cover that look-hole and keep Peaches's eyes from scorching our necks, but each morning it was transparent and sparkling. So clear it looked like it wasn't even there. In fact, more than one newcomer to our home had attempted to gain entry to the kitchen by walking straight through that clear sheet of glistening glass.

While Peaches and Paline manned Chez LeMoyne and served

up some of the best crab cakes, corn fritters, monkey bread, and pecan pies this side of the Chattahoochee, I was relegated to the kitchen as a scullery maid, where I swept and scoured and polished the cabinets and countertops until it was easy for me to see my own frown. "Hey, Eulie, peel that pile of taters! Come, Eulie! Scrape out these here pans, You! Eulie! Pour some lye down this here drain." The only chore deemed too menial for me to perform was the floors. As bad as Peaches was, she drew the line there and had years ago hired Mr. Thomas, Sweetwater's sin on sobriety, for the job. "Ain't no child of mine"—her green eyes would flash and she'd make a show of tossing her thin curls— "gonna blacken her knees scrubbing *nothin'*." Then she'd pose with her hand on her hip and call out her favorite threat, "Humph, Top Jar ever let times get that hard 'round here we'll just have to mosey on down the road to Mister Peets's."

The kitchen staff hated my mother. If lightning hadn't struck the shithouse in Washington and left times so hard for black folks, even those west of the bottoms, there'd be nobody left in the parish—hell, in the whole damn county—willing to work for Peaches. Not for food or for money. As it was, she just did manage to keep an assortment of folks on call and a full-time motley crew: a middle-aged drunk to do the floors, and Julius Greentree, a one-eyed dishwasher, busboy, and overall handyman, and a young obese Spanish woman by the name of Fannie who marinated meats and prepared side dishes and who referred to humans as though they were her favorite foods.

When I wasn't scrubbing something or the other, I took care of the vegetables. According to Peaches it was sin to sit in a chair while chopping, and if she had her way J.C. himself would strike you down for licking a spoon. Lord have mercy on the trifling wench who neglected to wrap her hair, or the loose-lipped soul who yakked too much while dicing potatoes or peeling onions. Like a pale apparition Peaches would appear out of nowhere, her high-yellow flaming red, arms crossed, lips pressed into a tight, disapproving line, piercing her target with a heat-filled evil eye that burned straight through the glass window to scorch with a fire more deadly than that in any of the industrial stoves.

I was nearly seven when I staged my first hunger strike. There was peace in the shadows of the hall on Sunday mornings, and safe beneath the leaves of a rubber tree plant I'd watch them through the look-hole while waiting for the after-church crowd to arrive: Paline, bloated in a tent dress and sandals while mashing sweet potatoes, Peaches with her hair pulled back in a wavy bun, makeup perfectly applied, draped in something red—silk or cashmere—and stirring a steaming pot of gumbo or frying up a batch of crab cakes.

On this particular Sunday morning a man walked through the front door of Chez LeMoyne and surprised us all. Peaches peered through the serving window and got so flustered she dropped her ladle and splattered her clothing with hot lard. Paline's hand immediately went to her hip, and even from where I sat I could feel the evil rolling off of her. Staring at the man as he lowered himself onto a red vinyl stool, I was suddenly struck with a horrific realization: We were a black family who owned a black restaurant on the black side of town, yet we suffered no black people at our tables. Peaches's clientele were either well-to-do white folks who rolled into Sweetwater slumming in droves for a taste of her jambalaya, dirty rice, and steamed crawdaddies, or they were an assortment of Creole, Cajun, Indian, or Spanish who had looks and coloring very similar to hers.

Dear God, I prayed silently as I pressed my body into the puke-green carpet and tried to disappear, *please help this hungry man standing before Peaches who, like me, couldn't pass the paper bag test to save his life.* I almost died outright when she stared down her nose at him like he was a mangy dog and then cussed him slam out, telling him just how cold it would get down in you-know-where before a black, ratty-ass nigger like him would darken her doorstep and eat a forkful of her food.

Later that evening after refusing my supper I repeated every word she'd said to Papa and Ma'Dear. I could tell right off that Papa didn't believe me but Ma'Dear knew I never lied, so she did her best to comfort me by pointing out that Peaches did not discriminate. My mother was fair in a warped kind of way, she said, because even the soul who was obviously Negro but slid in at least a shade lighter than that infamous sandy-colored sack was shit out of luck if he wanted a seat at Chez LeMoyne. Peaches would take his money and thank him kindly, but the most he could hope for was a plate piled high and wrapped tightly—and passed out to him from a window hole in the back door.

It was three whole days before I could be convinced to accept even a sip of her water.

Chapter FOUR

M Y SISTER was at the sink when I entered the kitchen, whining and complaining about having to work on her day off. She was high-strung and took nerve pills, which according to Ma'Dear were no more than pastel-colored sugar tablets. After shooting me a hateful look she went back to her chores muttering, "I s-s-see somebody finally decided to bring they tail in here and help out like they got some s-s-sense."

Paline was a witch. Even though she was bright skinned and had them funny LeMoyne eyes, she stuttered, was shaped funny, and suffered from what Ma'Dear called "female trouble." Paline was thick around the shoulders and had a full, soft tummy, and once when I'd peeked through the bathroom keyhole and seen her getting out of the tub, I saw thick black hairs slicked between her pale breasts and almost broke my neck as I stormed upstairs to report the news to Ma'Dear.

Hairy titties or not, Paline was pampered something terrible, and while Peaches and Papa catered to her every whim, it looked like the whole world virtually bowed to her will. From the time I was small Paline made it clear how much she despised me, and I couldn't remember us ever having one real conversation where she failed to either curse me or ridicule me in some shape or fashion.

Fannie was at the cutting table deboning salmon, and Peaches stood over a large, steaming vat stirring roux for gumbo. She wore a sleeveless red shirt with a pair of crisp red pedal pushers, and with her hair pulled back in a bun and a white gardenia stuck on the side, she looked young and innocent. She glanced at the fussing Paline but did not say a word.

". . . Getting my d-d-damn Indian up . . . Don't know what kinda plans I mighta had f-f-for my Sunday. Can't even get no real help to come in here on the Sabbath and this little w-w-wench got the nerve to insist Ma'Dear be laid out today when she ain't the one in here d-d-doing none of the work."

These days Paline hardly ever spoke directly to me. Instead she fussed at me, around me, and tossed her loaded staccato statements up in the air to explode and rain down on my head like shards of hot shrapnel.

"Why come Paline is so much prettier than me?" I'd asked Ma'Dear once when I was small. Ma'Dear had pursed her lips before speaking. "Actually, you the pretty one. Even Paline knows that. But pretty is what pretty does," was her final response, and over the years Paline had grown uglier than an empty glass of buttermilk in my eyes. Not only was she top-heavy with hairy legs and pendulous breasts, but when she got mad, which was nearly all the time, she flared her nose like a horse and stuttered madly until two rosy spots rode high on her cheeks.

"Up in here," she continued, "m-m-messing 'round with dead folks when there's shrimp to be peeled and c-c-corn to be shucked."

She reached into the pantry and took out a tin of Bon Ami. Sprinkling it over the countertop, she continued her monologue. "Couldn't wait till Monday to stretch her out. Nooo, got me 'round here p-p-putting on the hog and cleaning up on my day off for all that riff-raff what's sure to come tracking through here looking for a free meal . . . Shoulda carried Ma'Dear to the undertaker w-w-where the rest of the stiff folks go! Shit, this *is* the seventies, and as poor as these black f-f-folks is 'round here, most still got sense enough not to show their d-d-dead from the front room."

"And it look like some folks," I said, "would have sense enough not to show their asses from the kitchen."

"Mud hole!"

"Old maid!"

"Mama should have d-d-dunked your nappy head beneath the bayou waters when you was born . . . come here with a head full of steel wool and looking like a r-r-raggedy-assed panther."

"Shut up, w-w-witch."

"See there!" She threw the rag in the sink and pointed a dripping finger at me. "Don't m-m-make me snatch your high ass outta joint! That's why don't nobody want you around here. Always got to r-r-ruin everything!"

"That's why you *still* 'round here," I snapped. "You might be yellow, but you shaped funny and you got long titties! Plus you meaner than a swamp snake! Ain't fit to be no man's wife and that's why you almost thirty and ain't none ever asked you!"

Her chest rose and fell with the heat of her anger. Peaches ignored us as she continued to stir the pot of roux, and Fannie's hands were a blur as she patted and formed the salmon into thick orange hunks and pretended not to notice us.

"You'd best tame her, Mama." Paline dried her hands on the sides of her dress and advanced toward me. "Make her go scrub down the front steps or something, just get her outta my s-s-sight. She's stinking up the whole d-d-damn kitchen." I stood my ground.

Tense and coiled. Paline was heavier, but I was a good foot taller and like Papa, I was all muscle.

Just let her try me today.

Peaches's eyes were cold as she looked over her shoulder first at me then at Paline. She placed the large spoon in its holder and covered the pot of bubbling roux with a shiny lid. After wiping a trickle of sweat from her brow, she turned to face us with her hands on her hips. "Go on upstairs, Paline. Take your medicine and lie down for a spell." Peaches waited until Paline was gone, then rubbed her hands on her apron, untied it, and hung it from a row of hooks behind the kitchen door.

Finally she turned to me and said, "Today is your day Euleatha. All that grieving you doing for Ma'Dear got you acting crazy and sounding like a fool. But remember this: Where you tear your drawers is where I cut your ass, so if you wanna start catching hell up in here, keep on raising sand like you just did. Tomorrow gonna bring something different and you'd best believe it, 'cause that long-titty old maid that just left out from here? That is my child, and when you mess with her you is messing with me." She gave me a long, dangerous look, then sashayed out the kitchen leaving me and Fannie with our mouths wide open.

"She didn't mean that." Fannie rushed over to me and put her arms around my shoulders. "She's just upset over Ma'Dear, that's all."

"What I ever do to them?" I whispered as the tears overcame my resolve and slipped from my eyes. "What I ever do to make them hate me so?"

"Nothing, *chica*. You've done nothing. It's their own self-hatred that makes them so unbearable. That is something I will never understand about you coloreds. You hate each other based on the very things that should bind you. Look, Eulie." She forced me to look at my reflection in the shine of the refrigerator door. "Your skin is the color of a sizzling porterhouse steak. Yummy. Your sister looks like a skinless chicken breast marinated in sesame oil and herbs. Yummy. Both fill your stomach with good meat. So what's the problem? You people hate your blackness because you can't escape it. That's what's wrong with Miss Peaches and Miss Paline. What they hate in you is everything they really hate about themselves."

Racking sobs bent me over at the waist and I shook my head wildly. "But I'm her daughter too!" I wailed. "How can Peaches be so cruel?"

Fannie tore off a paper towel and made me blow my nose as she used her meaty thumbs to wipe the water from my eyes. "What do you expect, *chica,* huh? Just what do you expect from a woman who looks like a whole damn pan of mashed potatoes with butter?"

"I wish . . ." I sniffed like a small child. "I wish I'd never been born."

⌇

I paused in the doorway and let my eyes scan the crowded front room in search of Cissy. You could tell the bottoms folks from the residents of Sweetwater just by the color of their skin. Sweetwater boasted a largely Creole and Cajun heritage, although there were quite a few whites milling about today out of respect for Ma'Dear. Bottoms folks tended to look just like the sweet soil they toiled in: rich and dark, as if Mother Nature herself had designed them to harvest provisions and cultivate humanity.

Someone had draped an elegant lace netting over Ma'Dear's coffin to keep back the flies, and every window on the ground floor was pushed up high in an attempt to combat the intense heat. There was a steady buzz of voices filling up the room, and a slow thumping throb began to dance behind my temples as I appraised my family members. Peaches stood near the fireplace dressed to the nines in a hip-hugging scarlet dress with matching fish net panty hose, her manicured nails painted whorehouse-red. Laughter tinkled from her bright mouth as she leaned in close to console the widower Peets, who stood licking his lips like a fox in a chicken coop.

With an alcohol stench rolling off of him so strongly he could have revived Ma'Dear, Mr. Thomas staggered around with a drag-toe gait, annoying folks by passing out the funeral programs and then snatching them right back again, while Junior backed Tressy Granfield into a dim corner, no doubt doing his best to talk her into dropping her one decent pair of Sunday drawers.

Seemed like all of Sweetwater had turned out for the event, and even some from far beyond. Minnie Funkhouse sat next to her husband Hill, and Julius Greenbriar cuddled his infant son, whose mother Nell had ran off to try her luck in Hollywood two months after his birth. Even Mother Watts, who Ma'Dear swore ran a gambling house on her sandy parcel of land by the railroad tracks, was there helping herself to handfuls of pigs in a blanket that were being passed around on shiny silver trays.

With her hips perched on the edge of the curio, Paline looked like two screams and a holler—her light gray dress bunched up too tightly around her whale of a waistline, while the crooked seams ran amok down the back of her sheer gray stockings and crawled toward her thick ankles. I'd passed Papa in the corridor on his way to the shed to get another block of ice, and in the instant when our eyes met I'd seen myself illuminated in his face and felt a small touch of Ma'Dear's love.

As Fannie lumbered past with a fresh tray of iced tea, I spotted Cissy and her parents on the far side of the room sitting in a back row. Tears of relief welled in my eyes as I made my way toward them, toward the comfort and safety they'd come to represent over the last seven years of my life. Cissy and I had been friends since the fourth grade, although if she hadn't been smart enough to cover my salt with her sugar we could have ended up as enemies.

In those days Sweetwater's school district had consisted of an administrative office and an adjoining two-room brick building. The front lawn was landscaped every other day by the same man who emptied the trash cans, scrubbed the blackboards, and retrieved hats and mittens, fallen from pockets or carelessly tossed aside, from the large fenced-in playground in the rear. The smaller room in the schoolhouse belonged to Mr. Baptiste, the K through sixth-grade teacher, and Miss Fontaine was responsible for grades seven through twelve, which she taught in the larger room.

Being born a LeMoyne had landed me next to Tara Lenape for my first three years of school and had caused me more trouble than the piss-colored slew-footed heifer was worth. Mr. Baptiste called Peaches in during the second week of fourth grade and told her I was smart. Too smart to keep getting in so much trouble every day. Said if I tried hard maybe one day I could go to college and become a doctor or some kind of engineer.

College? Euleatha? Peaches laughed and sucked her gold teeth. Euleatha don't know her ass from a hole in the ground. She told him she would no more think about sending me to college and throwing her good money after bad than she would think of casting pearls before swine. Instead, she slapped me across the lips in front of the whole class and said if I couldn't keep my mouth shut in school she could make it so I didn't come back. After all, she could use the help around the house, and since our good governor had been so slow in integrating the public schools in Louisiana she didn't think he'd kick up too much of a fuss if one little nigger girl decided not to attend.

Mr. Baptiste cleared his throat and hemmed and hawed and assured her that things between Tara and me were not quite that bad. Said if me and Tara couldn't get along then maybe he could try rearranging his seating methods and keep us at opposite ends of the room. In fact, he just remembered. That wouldn't be necessary at all. The problem had just fixed itself because in a few days we were getting two new girls, the daughters of Sweetwater's new postmaster, Cissy and Martha Lemmon. Martha, a big-boned freckle-faced girl of twelve, was assigned to Miss Fontaine's room, and Cissy, a slight, shy-looking girl of nine, would be assigned to sit right next to me.

From the moment I laid eyes on Cissy Lemmon, I despised her. She was dark, even darker than me, and funny looking to boot. She arrived at Mr. Baptiste's class during the third week of fourth grade clutching her mother's hand like a big baby, nervously twisting her dress from side to side, making it sail like a blanket in the wind with her eyes cast downward toward her cuffed, ankle-length white socks. Her face shined brightly under a thin coat of Vaseline, and her knees were dark and knobby as they peeked from beneath her dress. Although Cissy was as black as tar and my sister paler than death, something about her clothing put me in the mind of a younger Paline, and from that point on everything about her, from the starch in her yellow crinoline dress and matching bolero jacket, to the shine on her leather satchel, enraged me. It also tickled me to no end to find that as black as Cissy was, she had the nerve to have a head full of thick, wavy, dirty-red hair, and the minute she slid behind the double desk and sat beside me I'd wanted to yank fistfuls of her red straw out by the roots and slap that second-class underdog look right off her silly face.

In Sweetwater the younger children got to eat lunch first, and as I chewed through my cheese sandwich and sipped warm milk I was mesmerized by the sight of the new girl. My mouth watered as she opened a brown paper sack and neatly pulled the foil off of a hunk of crispy golden fried chicken so big it had to be a breast, then nipped daintily around the edges until all the pretty deep-fried skin and crust was gone and only the pale lean flesh underneath remained on the bone.

At recess I shrugged off my normal crowd of hooligans and followed her out to the playground, marveling all the while at her attire. Her shoes were real Mary Janes and looked fancy enough to wear on Sundays: black patent leather with a shiny silver buckle on the sides. The bows on her ankle socks were the same color as her dress, and she even had matching yellow ribbons hanging from the ends of her twisted red pigtails. I was dressed as usual: two thick plaits Ma'Dear had braided that hung straight down my back, faded cutoff shorts left over from a pair of dungarees worn so long there'd been holes in the knees, and one of Paline's cast-off shirts that was long in the sleeves and short two buttons.

My eyes almost popped out of my head when Cissy sat primly on the wide seat of a swing and I glimpsed a slice of her yellow underpants, which were the exact same shade as the beautiful fabric of her dress. I got real mad then. Peaches always bought those sort of frilly things for Paline, velvetine hoopskirts, A-line taffeta slips and satin bows. Seeing something like that on Missy Cissy was enough to make green smoke shoot out from my nose.

I continued to scrutinize her every move as she swayed gently back and forth on the metal seat. She swung low like a punk. If she was really something she would have stood up and pumped her knees a few times, then stuck out her leg and dragged it once or twice for leverage before spreading wider and taking herself up over the fence. It had rained steadily for two days in a row, and now mud puddles were as big as craters in the recessed, rain-soaked earth. There were several vacant swings available, but instead of choosing one I jumped over a wet brown puddle and marched right over to where she swung and demanded, "You want me to take you up?" Before she could fix her head to nod no, I put my dirty tennis shoes on either side of the seat beside her and forced her to stand up and grab onto the chain-linked handholds. Facing her, I pulled myself up as well, and placed one of my knees between her knobby legs, then pushed off quickly before placing my other leg against the cool metal of the handholds.

We stood nose to nose as we traveled like a pendulum. Back and forth, back and forth, with her breath on my face and our pelvises colliding, I pumped my knees like crazy, taking us up and up and up, until we were sailing high over the low, crisscrossed metal fence of the playground.

"That's enough," I heard her mutter through clenched teeth, but I ignored her pleas and continued alternately pumping and dragging, propelling us higher and higher until we crested above the top spikes of the tall schoolyard fence. The treetops spun past crazily. The schoolhouse became a miniature replica of itself. The swing jerked and arced up to a flat plane, then dangerously surpassed the straight-line angle and buckled precariously on its descent.

The knuckles clenching the chain links had gone damn near white. Her eyes bulged dangerously and her dark skin glowed a funny shade of green. Suddenly her whole body began to tremble violently, almost causing us both to lose footing. "Hold still! Don't look down," I warned, but of course that's exactly what she did. A moment later a warm spray of liquid splattered my bare legs and ran into my socks, completely soaking my raggedy kicks.

"Girl, don't tell me you pissin'?"

With her breath coming in short gasps and her eyes squinched shut, Cissy nodded miserably and two fat tears squeezed from between her lashes and slipped down her face. "I-I-I'm scared a heights."

"Hot dog!" I reversed the trajectory of my body, pushing against the winds until I slowed the motion and brought the swing down gradually. "Pissy Cissy!" I taunted her on the way down, enjoying my newfound power. "Just wait till I get offa here and tell everybody how you got so scared you peed all over me."

She opened her eyes and lifted her head to bless me with such an agonized look I was physically stricken by her pain. The expression on her face was eerily familiar. I'd felt pain like that hundreds of times—in the disgusted shake of Peaches's head whenever I walked into a room, at the end of clenched fists as Junior pinched my arms or twisted my plaits, on my unprotected skin as Paline opened her mouth and scratched me bloody with her barbed, thorny words. That I could bring such despair to the face of another stunned me, and as my foot slid in the urine and skittered over the edge of the swing, I fell backward and down, tumbling, tumbling until I plummeted to the ground and splashed butt-first in a convoluted heap in a pool of cold muddy water.

Waves of laughter filled the air as the other kids gathered 'round me pointing and stomping in glee. Humiliated, I attempted to pick myself up out of the sucking hole only to lose my footing and land back on my behind. Blotches of mud stained the stretched elastic of my socks and soaked through the fabric of my shoes to further dampen my toes. I sat there miserably as the kids formed a cruel circle around me, taunting and jeering. There was no way I could stand up, my shorts were mud soaked and plastered to my body. I was so embarrassed I'd forgotten all about my intentions to rat on Cissy for having an accident, so when she pushed through the crowd with a look of pure goodness on her face and shrugged off her bolero jacket, telling me to take it and tie it around my waist, I wasn't sure if the tears falling from my eyes were from shame or from thanks. I took the jacket, and then I took her hand.

Cissy pulled me out of the sucking mud and helped me wrap the jacket around my lower body. "I can't go back to class looking like this," I said miserably. "They gonna laugh at me till three o'clock."

"Who said anything about going back in there?" she said with a small smile on her face. She led me around the side of the administrative office, her crinoline skirts swish-swishing as we stooped under a small wooden railing. With my hand still in hers and mud caking the back of my legs, we ducked down low and waddled past the ground-floor windows where the principal and his secretary sat working at their desks.

"Where we going?" I whispered.

"Sshhh!" Her shiny shoes sinking into the wet grass, Cissy ran across the manicured front lawn and down a small footpath that led to the main road. The smell of wet pinewood was still in the air. "We going to my house. My mama got some clean clothes you can fit. That way you ain't got to go back home and explain nothing to your folks."

"But what about Mr. Baptiste? We gonna be in trouble for sneaking 'way from school!"

Cissy grinned. "Don't worry 'bout that. By tomorrow he won't be so mad. Besides, Mama will write him a note."

"Ain't your mama gonna be mad? Will she whip us?"

"Whip us?" Cissy gave me a strange look. "What she gonna whip us for? She's gonna help us is what she'll do. She my mama, ain't she?"

Cissy lived in a neat two-story house with white siding and black shutters. Three diaper pails sat near the edge of the driveway and the aroma of freshly baked fudge chocolate cookies met us as we skipped up the path. She led me through a screen door and then into a brightly lit vestibule where children's toys of every shape and variety imaginable were scattered everywhere. There was a big over-stuffed sofa in the front room, and two recliners and a wooden rocker. A large wooden plaque on the wall read:

COME IN, SIT DOWN, RELAX, CONVERSE.
OUR HOUSE DOESN'T ALWAYS LOOK LIKE THIS,
SOMETIMES IT'S EVEN WORSE.

Several small children dressed in old but clean clothing played merry and carefree. Two small boys fought happily over a red fire truck, tumbling over and over and squealing in delight.

"Who these kids?" I asked. I'd heard her mama had a house full of babies, but none of these kids looked remotely like Cissy. They ranged in skin color from vanilla ice cream to butternut to burnt kindling, and none had hair anywhere near the red on Cissy's head.

She pointed. "This one here is Babette, she's five. Over there by the sofa is Joshua, he just turned four. The baby in the rocker there is Rose, she's still pretty new, and the two boys fighting for that truck are Jeremiah and Obediah. They're almost three."

I asked incredulously, "They all belong to your mama? Ain't none of them the same color."

"Yep. They ours. Just that our skins are mixed up real good, that's all. My daddy is real light with red hair, and he likes to say 'the blacker the berry' 'cause—well, you done seen my mama. The rest of us are just somewhere in between."

"And they still love y'all?"

Cissy stared. "Course they do! We theirs, ain't we?"

Just then, the tall woman I'd seen earlier in the day stepped into the room carrying a tray full of cookies. "C'mon now!" she called out happily to the playing children. "Get over here and catch yourselves a cookie!"

I shrank back against the wall and inched toward the door in an attempt to hide myself. The thought of my muddy clothes superseded the pinching quake in my stomach as my nose opened wider and my mouth watered for a taste of those pretty brown cookies.

"Mama," Cissy began as she approached her mother. "Me and Euleatha came home from school 'cause we both had accidents." I cringed further into the wall but Cissy smiled and motioned me forward. "I made a mistake and let go of my water, and Euleatha slipped and landed in it."

"My Lordy," Mrs. Lemmon cried and looked at both of us. Her dark face was beautifully framed by short, natural hair. "Poor babies! You gals run on upstairs and get a bath while I put another batch of cookies on to bake. By the time you done they'll be just about ready to come out the oven. Good and hot." She smiled at me then said to Cissy, "Remember your manners. Be sure an' let Euleatha bathe first. And go through that trunk in your sister's closet and find something nice for her to put on while I wash out her clothes and hang them on the back line." Mrs. Lemmon took me by the shoulders and peered at me closely. "Well, nice to meet you, Euleatha. You tall for a girl, but well shaped. Pretty as a button too, with your smooth skin and all that thick hair. You gonna be a real looker, just like my Cissy. Your mama must be right proud of you."

My mouth was unhinged in amazement. I couldn't even imagine what would have happened had I cut school and tramped through Peaches's house, pissy and dragging another child with me full of mud, but I knew for sure it wouldn't have had nothing to do with fudge cookies and lemonade.

As I sat in that big ole tub full of warm water and Joy dishwashing liquid in that safe house full of different-colored babies and a whole lot of love, I pretended that it was my own mama who was downstairs baking cookies for me, washing my clothes out by hand, and calling me poor baby. For the first time in my life I felt almost normal as I splashed lemon-scented bubbles at Cissy and she laughed and squirted me with a water gun, and from that day forward I knew I had two whole people in the world who loved and cared about me. I made the number two with my fingers and laughed and laughed and laughed. Two whole people, I tell you, I had two whole people.

Until yesterday on the day before my seventeenth birthday when Ma'Dear decided to make that ultimate journey, and then suddenly my numbers were back down to one.

~

"Beanie," a calloused hand touched my arm as I made a beeline toward an empty seat near Cissy's father, Mr. Lemmon. Pausing, I raised my teary eyes to the childlike face of my Uncle Bubba. Buford LeMoyne was Peaches's older brother, and throughout my whole life I'd heard her telling folks, "Don't mind Bubba. You know he ain't wrapped too tight," but if you asked me, it was Peaches herself who wasn't playing with a full deck. Uncle Bubba was huge and burly but simple and sweet and good with his hands. He could build almost anything from a piece of bark or the stump of a tree, and some of the prettiest items in our home had been shaped by his own hand.

"Hey, Uncle." I grinned at him and he grinned back. He'd lost another tooth, I saw. One more piece of furniture missing from his parlor. "You okay?"

"I'm good, Beanie. You okay?"

"I'm okay, Uncle Bubba." This was part of our usual exchange, and I took his big paw and rubbed it between my own.

"I kin take care a you, Beanie," he said. "Now that Ma'Dear gone, Bubba be keeping P-Paline offa you an' takin care a you for Ma'Dear."

I gave him a small, miserable smile. It was gonna be hard to live in this house without Ma'Dear, that much was for sure, but I knew it would take more than sweet ole Uncle Bubba to get Paline's claws out of my back once she decided to dig in. I moved through the crowd heading for Cissy, stopping to accept condolences and make the appropriate responses as necessary. Entire families had shown up, from as far away as the bottoms, where I was born on the Delta, to major cities further north of New Orleans.

I slid into a chair next to Mr. Lemmon and he looked at me with sad eyes and frowned. Jean-Pierre Lemmon looked more white than black, although his nose was decidedly broad and Negroid and the pitch of his voice came straight out of Africa. His pale skin was blotchy from shaving as well as from the heat, and his tidy red hair had been freshly washed and cut. "Sorry 'bout your loss, Miss Euleatha. Ma'Dear was a fine woman. A fine woman, and she'll be missed indeed."

I thanked him as he switched seats, allowing me to sit next to Cissy.

"You okay?" she asked in a low tone. "Did you get everything done the right way?"

I nodded. "It was hard, but I had to do as she asked."

Cissy nodded knowingly.

"It took everything I had in me, but I got it done. Now its up to Papa. Him and Uncle Bubba got to get her in the ground before sundown to make the cycle complete."

Cissy gave me a wide-eyed look and then shivered. "It all seems so scary, Eulie. Messing with dead bodies and trying so hard to figure out what all Ma'Dear meant. You know she talked right crazy sometimes, but most of what she said made a lot of sense. Especially the parts about how things go around in cycles like nature intended, and how what kinda energy you give out eventually comes back to visit you." She touched my arm lightly and her hand was like midnight against the white fabric. "All that stuff makes a lot of sense, 'cause when you get down to it God knows Ma'Dear had it right. All that matters in this world is love."

Chapter FIVE

PAPA HAD WRITTEN THE OBITUARY, and Mr. Ross Dampier from the *Sweetwater News* had volunteered to print up two hundred copies of the one-page program. The cover was pale gray embossed with fancy black lettering that read, "Genessa 'Ma'Dear' Sanders," and underneath that, "Sunrise July 4, 1861 . . . Sunset July 29, 1971." To anyone else those dates mighta seemed strange, but they made perfect sense to me.

Although she'd been old by medical standards and had never seen a city doctor in her life, it looked like Ma'Dear coulda stayed around here at least twenty more years if she'da had a mind to do so. Tell the truth, I'd fully expected Ma'Dear to deliver my firstborn child just as she'd done for my mother and my grandmother before her, because with God as my witness, up until five minutes before her death Ma'Dear had been as healthy as a horse. Ever seen somebody just announce it was their time to die and then simply close their eyes and go? Me neither till I witnessed it with Ma'Dear. Yeah, for some folks one hundred and ten years mighta seemed like a way long time, but it looked to me like Ma'Dear had been just getting started.

"You just watch, Eulie," Ma'Dear had told me long ago. "The Sanders wimmens live to see a whole lot. Some of us see it as a blessing, others see it as a curse, but any way you slice it, length of years is part of your birthright. So live well, daughter. Live well. Now our menfolk? Humph. You can barely wipe the titty milk off a they chins before they sliding toward the grave. Jarrett don't watch all a that salt pork and fatback Peaches like to cook wit . . . she and Mr. Peets gonna be vacationing in the south of France using his insurance money. Mark my words!"

Ma'Dear had two half sisters. Younger than she, they shared a common father, but he was not Boxing Ben, the man Ma'Dear called her daddy. "Them are *my* baby sisters," Ma'Dear would say with a smile. "Half nothing! We was too poor to be splitting anything up thata way, including our blood." It seems Ma'Dear had been born ahead of her sisters, and whatever was happening back in those dark days of slavery had resulted in her mother having two younger children by her slave master.

"That weren't nothing particular," Ma'Dear said when talking about the white man's love of black flesh. "Whites took advantage of Negro wimmens in that manner all the time. They loved that part of us, the part that makes us so sweet. No, particular wasn't the fact that he climbed into her bed at night. Particular was what Mama put herself through just to pay him back."

Ma'Dear's mother had died in the same year that freedom came, and like Ma'Dear, both of her younger sisters were taken in by a woman they called Aunt Mattie, the slave owner's cook, and had left North Carolina shortly thereafter. Aunt Mattie and her husband, Uncledaddy, took the three girls, and along with their own children, moved to Louisiana. Ma'Dear chose to stay close and settle down in Louisiana, while her sister Genevieve moved to New York City and Genera married a visiting farmhand and followed him back to Arkansas. Just minutes after Ma'Dear's death Papa had sent each of her sisters an emergency telegram, and they'd promised to get here in time for the wake and funeral.

I stood on the porch twisting my braids back and forth and waiting for the two women I'd come to know as simply "the aunts," and although I'd never before laid eyes on either of them except for a grainy faded photo someone had taken of the three of them when they were very young women, it wasn't too hard to spot them when they arrived. Ma'Dear's sisters stood apart from the other folks that were either walking up the wide lane or pulling up packed so many to a car they looked like smashed Gumbies when they got out. These two just moved different. Like they'd seen more. Came from more. They climbed out of the hired black station wagon slowly. Road dust swirled about the tires as the hot sun stoked up embers in the dry dirt. The first one out was a bit taller than Ma'Dear but much thinner in the waistline. With skin the color of hominy, she had the eyes of an exotic dancer and a thick mane of soft silvery curls that fell past her shoulders. When she smiled, a row of dazzling white teeth flashed in her face and that's when I knew.

This one was the dish.

Auntie Genevieve or, as Ma'Dear used to call her, Mary Mack. She was the baby of the family and also, according to Ma'Dear, the prettiest. A midwife who lived up in New York City with her husband Buck Black, Aunt Mary Mack was notorious for her love of boiled peanuts and red-and-white peppermints.

I watched as Aunt Mary straightened her black skirt and smoothed it down over her hips. Even at her advanced age her figure was better than most I'd ever seen, and if Ma'Dear was right and this is where I got my small waist and saucy legs, then one day soon I was gonna have a little something to serve up on a platter too. I stood in the recess of the porch and watched as she reached back inside the car to help her sister get out.

This one was Aunt Genera, better known as Charming, the middle girl. With her was a cute little chocolate-skinned boy of about eight or nine. I knew he had to be Malcolm, her great-grandson. Aunt Charming had one child, a daughter they called Sugar Baby, and a few years back I'd overheard Ma'Dear telling Papa and Peaches that Sugar Baby's only son Zeke and his wife had just got burned up in a fire. Seems like the daddy got the boy out then went back inside for his wife, and both of them ended up burned and dead.

Peaches had made a smart-alecky comment about the pair getting their just due for being involved with Negro gangs like the Tomahawks and those troublemaking revolutionaries who kicked up unnecessary fuss like the Black Panthers. She'd asked Ma'Dear what kind of damn fool gets out of a burning house and then goes rushing back inside to save a woman, and Ma'Dear told her the kind of fool you got when you mix Sanders blood with Armstrong blood and not to worry herself 'cause she would never live long enough or get lucky enough to know a fool of that caliber.

Aunt Charming held Malcolm by the hand and took her sister's arm. They made their way up the porch steps to where I stood.

"Beanie?"

"Yessum." I was enveloped into two pairs of sweet smelling arms and crushed against bosoms that were made for comforting.

"Well ain't you just a tall drink of water! Chile, you every bit of what Genessa said you was. A for-sure string bean. I'm your Aunt Charming, and this here is your Aunt Mary Mack." I sniffed loudly. "What?" Aunt Charming gave me a questioning look, then wiped a tear from my cheek and reached up to smooth a few tufts of hair that had curled around my hairline. "Baby, you grieving?" She took my arm and sat me down on the top step, and Aunt Mary moved around to comfort me from the other side.

"I know durn well Genessa done schooled you and taught you the old ways. Her blood still in her? You got her laid out in time and did it all with your own hands, right?"

I nodded.

"Well." She looked relieved. "Then there ain't no need in crying. You done your part. She left here when and how she was supposed to. Just like we all will. Nobody gets to stay forever, even Jesus had to close his eyes 'cause he too was a man! You named for two powerful peoples, you know. There was two Euleathas before you. Euleatha the Brave and Euleatha the Wise. And both of 'em was special, just like you. Built strong and pretty too, just like you."

"That's right," Aunt Mary took up. "In fact, there's always been a Euleatha in our bloodline. Lord knows we've always needed 'em. How else we gonna keep things alive in our hearts if'n somebody don't make the trip back and see with they own eyes what's been done to us and learn to understand how kindness and selfless love can fix it?" She brushed a pale young spider from the steps and swung her legs around slowly. "Yeah, Ma'Dear picked the right one, I can tell. She named you right and proper, so dry them tears and keep living, chile. You'll see Ma'Dear again. And big Euleatha too."

I was puzzled. See who again? Couldn't be Ma'Dear 'cause she was laid out in the front room. They were talking nonsense but I had better home training than to tell them so. The heat swirling off of the two old ladies was giving me a headache and I longed to go back inside and find comfort next to the body of Ma'Dear.

The front door opened and Paline stuck her head out. "Whatchoo out here yakkin' for? There's fools running l-l-loose all over this house! Get your black ass on in h-h-here and help tame these roguish niggers before they try to m-m-make off with Mama's silver and every damn thing else that ain't n-n-nailed down!"

Two sets of mouths fell open as the aunts stared at the spot where Paline had just been.

"Lawd, Jesus!" Aunt Charming whistled low between her teeth. "The heat gits so bad down in Weeziana it makes folks cuss they own kin? That little red hellion must be Paline. Ma'Dear told us about her. The grown one who's still livin' at home. Look to me like she ain't so grown your mama can't cut herself a nice thin switch offa that tree over yonder and put something on Miss Paline to help set her tongue straight."

Aunt Mary nodded and pulled Malcolm close, smothering his little peanut head between her breasts. "Speaking of mamas, where is yourn? Seem like her and Jarrett woulda been waiting to greet a pair of old folks who crossed two and three states to get here in twenty-four hours."

"I'm sorry," I apologized automatically before standing up shakily and moving toward the front door. "Y'all must be tired and thirsty. Peaches said there are rooms ready for both of you, and if you like I can take Malcolm in the kitchen and get him something to eat and drink right now."

Pushing Malcolm in my direction, Aunt Mary froze. "Gal, what you call your mama?"

"Peaches."

She stared at me. "You mean you calls her by her first name?"

"Yessum."

"And why for is that?"

"'Cause she tells me to. Don't want folks to know she my mama."

"Why come?"

I hunched my shoulders and scratched my leg. "Said I was too black to be a child of hers."

They gave each other an ancient, knowing look.

"But that's okay," I quickly added, "'Cause she too light to be a mama of mine."

Aunt Charming spoke first. "Listen here, Euleatha. You cain't let what other people think or say about you be the thing what tells you who you are. I can see the hell raging in you and I'm sure Ma'Dear done seen it too, and her spirit can't leave here proper until your lesson done been learnt. You gotta learn to understand folks so that you can love 'em better. I done heard about how you been treated here and I reckon you got some hatred in your heart . . . maybe some for yourself and some for your mama as well, but you gots to learn folks before you can judge 'em. Gots to walk in their shoes, sleep in their beds, wear their clothes, and live in their skin."

I'd heard all of that before.

Aunt Mary asked, "When they plan on reading Ma'Dear's will?"

"Nightfall. After the burial. That's when she said it had to be done."

She nodded, apparently satisfied. "Good. Things be clearer to you by then."

"Look." Aunt Mary put her hand on my shoulder. "Genessa wasn't rich, at least not in the way some might find important, but I believe she's got something for you that will help you walk any path you choose in this life. A gift that will last you a lifetime, one that you can pass on to one of your chirren or even your grand-chirren, if your own kids turn out to be anywhere near as dumb as your daddy is."

I ignored the comment about Papa. It was no secret how big a fool he was for Peaches, and it would take more than me to stand against these two oak trees and defend him. But a gift? From Ma'Dear? My heart jumped. Could it be? Years earlier she'd sent me to fetch something from her smaller trunk. The one she kept under lock and key. I'd rambled and rambled until I came upon a beautiful gold brooch with tiny etched carvings running along the sides. I'd never in my life seen anything so beautiful and exquisite, and immediately I knew it had to be mine. For weeks on end I'd begged Ma'Dear for that shiny gold oval. When begging didn't work, I pleaded, and when that got old, I released my secret weapon and showed her a few tears. She had not been impressed. Instead she'd insisted that the gift she had for me was so great and so magnificent it would make that good brooch look like a dented penny and put it right to shame. At the time I couldn't imagine what Ma'Dear owned that could live up to such a claim, and I sure couldn't imagine it now. If only Ma'Dear had left me that brooch. It made perfect sense that the brooch be her parting and most special gift to me. Casting pearls to swine? I knew just how valuable that gold brooch must be. I saw it as the answer to my prayers. The bridge to my future plans, and for the first time in over two days I actually smiled.

⁓

Folks spilled out of the front room and milled along the corridors, in the parlor, and in every other room on this wing of the house. Cardboard funeral fans glued onto ice cream sticks waved to and fro, a symphony of blurred color that did little to cool the thick humid air. About twenty-five souls were seated upon stools brought out from Chez LeMoyne. Papa had asked Peaches if she'd allow a few bodies to sit inside the diner where there was an air cooler and they could eat proper at a table, but she'd stood there in her red sequined dress and matching three-inch stiletto-heeled pumps and rolled her eyes and said if they couldn't eat at her place last Sunday, and if they couldn't eat at her place next Sunday, what in the hell made him think they was gonna eat at her place *this* Sunday?

After knocking some of the road dust off their clothes, the aunts came downstairs smelling of gentian violet and rosewater, and sat with me on a long green chaise longue. Peaches sashayed over in her tight dress, and after air kissing them near each cheek and making sorrowful little noises, she strutted right back over to Mr. Peets.

A minute later Papa emerged from the kitchen, and after a curious look at giggling Peaches and a lip-licking Mr. Peets, he came over to hug and kiss Ma'Dear's sisters. The aunts might have been old, but Lord were they sharp. After talking briefly with Papa, they sent him to the kitchen for herb tea then eyed Peaches with great disdain as they shook their heads at Papa's retreating back.

"Ain't it a shame," Aunt Charming said, dotting her nose with a lace hankie, "when a man what comes from blood like ours just crumple over and collapse? And as big and strong as he is! All that man wrapped around her one little pinky finger."

Aunt Mary Mack fanned herself and agreed. "He must get it from his daddy 'cause he ain't none of Joy. That boy's mama was something else! Had enough spunk for two men . . . funny how she an' the brave Euleatha were the only Sanders wimmens to leave so soon. It like to kill Euleatha the Wise when that gal of hers died."

"True sister. So true. It's a sad thing when the momma has to bury the chile, and don't I know it? My only son gone these three years past . . . and Ma'Dear's brand-new baby resting in the same box with her husband . . . chile too young to even get herself a name . . ." Aunt Charming's voice trailed off and a faraway look crept into her eyes. "The day we put my Zeke in the ground it rained so hard and so long looked like the very heavens was protesting. It rained that same way when Genessa buried that girl baby and when the wise Euleatha buried her Joy."

I stood up as the organ player from Sweetwater Baptist Church began easing low melodies from her electric organ. "Let's go up front," I coaxed my aunts. The music was a prearranged cue for the family to take their seats. I led Malcolm and the aunts through the crowd of milling mourners and up to the family seats that had been reserved in the front row. I gave a pat to little Malcolm's head and then took a seat between Paline and Peaches.

"Whatchoo s-s-setting up under me for?" Paline hissed under her breath almost as soon as my legs hit the chair. "Drawing all that d-d-damn heat!" I ignored her and instead turned my attention on the still, slight figure of Ma'Dear.

"Genessa looks real good," one of the aunts exclaimed, "but she fixin' to sweat in all this wicked humidity."

And then Papa was before the room speaking in a deep, clear voice.

"Good afternoon, folks. I'd like to thank you all fer coming out on such short notice to say good-bye to our Ma'Dear. Sorry 'bout the heat, weren't much we could do about that, but I'll make this short so as not to keep y'all no longer than necessary."

Funeral fans fluttered in every direction and the smell of gumbo eased in from the kitchen. Papa cleared his throat and fussed with his striped tie before continuing. "Most of you been knowing Ma'Dear for quite a long spell so I consider you all my family. Some of you knowed her even before I was born, and you knowed my own mama, Joy Sanders, as well.

"And," Papa went on, and out of respect he made it a point for his eyes to sit an extra second or two on the elders in the room, the ones who had traveled from Venice and beyond, some who looked old enough and ready enough to scoot Ma'Dear over and take their own rest, "there is even some of you in here who knew my grand-momma, Euleatha the Wise. Ma'Dear's only daughter. I'm talking 'bout family, I tell you!

"But for the few of you who may not know, I'd like to tell you a little bit about this lady laying before us here today. This little lady who raised me, my daughters, my son, my momma, and my grand-momma. And taught us all how to love! Family, I say! They don't even make 'em like this no more!" A chorus of *No!* went up in the air.

"Naw," Papa's voice floated up to the ceiling, "you see, when they made ole Ma'Dear they broke the mold!"

Shouts of *Well!* and *Amen!* rose from the women in the church choir.

"But that's okay." Water dripped from Papa's chin and he low-

ered his voice and spread his arms wide to settle down the mourners. "What Ma'Dear brought to this world could never be matched.
The love she spread over all these people, over this great big family
setting right here in this room, can never be forgotten! Her voice
can never be quieted, and her *hands,* ha' mercy sweet Jesus, can
never be stilled."

Preach it, Top Jar, Preach it!

The rest of Papa's sermon was lost on me. He was a terrible
preacher anyhow. Lived right, but couldn't hardly drag him into a
church. As I sat there and stared at the body that had dried so many
of my tears and soothed so many of my pains, a bitter taste welled
in the back of my throat. All that stuff Papa preached about family
love was nothing but hogwash. What did these people care about
my pain? About my suffering? Other than the bottom folks, almost
every visitor in the house had formed an exclusive clan, an impen-
etrable circle of privilege where the price of admission was light
bright skin. There were only about ten dark faces in the room, including my own, and nobody here other than Cissy had ever bothered to really love me. Some days I found it hard to love myself.

But then, what did I expect? After all, when I looked around
this middle-class community of creamy skin and soft, wavy hair, the
reality of my existence was painfully clear. Dark skin held no merit
in these parts. It was a bitter reminder of all those bone-in-the-nose
African booty-scratchers who were dangling from nooses, high in
our family trees. Africans who'd been dumb enough or meek
enough to get themselves snatched off their own land and brought
to this country in chains. Who wanted to be reminded of that heritage? Peaches said the best thing that could have happened to the
Africans was to get some white blood running through their veins
to thin out those thick nigger lips and smooth out that rough,
kinky hair. Made them look less animalish and more human, she
thought. More European.

No, I shook my head and briefly closed my eyes. A child who came into this world looking like me was a stinging reminder, like a constant knife in an open wound, and if it hadn't been for Ma'Dear I would have perished in this house long ago.

And without her now I didn't have much chance of surviving.

I was on my own.

Papa finally finished preaching and took a seat near the window. Peaches made a big fuss of standing up and sashaying over to the coffin in her high-heeled shoes. She smoothed her dress over her flat tummy and curved hips and made sure all her assets were showing as she leaned over and peeled the lace netting away from the pine box.

The choir let loose with the first stanza of "Precious Lord" just as Peaches shrugged the netting completely away. As Ma'Dear's face came clearly into view and the choir poured waves of emotion into the funeral song, a dull pain struck me high in the chest; it dissolved my self-control and sent me slumping over onto Paline. Drenched in a cold sweat, I was powerless to fight back as my sister jabbed me in the ribs and shoved me away. I hardly felt her prods. My body jerked like a marionette as huge waves of grief engulfed me, crashing hard against the back of my throat, the pain pressing deeply into my chest as hot tears fell from my eyes and dripped onto my black skirt.

"Sit up straight!" Peaches snapped as she reclaimed her seat beside me. The room spun in crazy, obscene circles. Her voice came at me from over a great divide, miles and miles of endless earth separated us as I retched up air and clawed at my own face, my neck, the back of my hands, my short nails leaving purplish welts upon every exposed inch of my damp skin. My legs spread wide, I hung my head between my knees, searching for air, praying for deliverance from the torturous ache boiling inside of me. Merciless, my pain rolled onward, faster and faster, swirling its way up from my feet and splintering like scorching needles through my lungs, fragmenting my soul and pulverizing my heart as it broke free from lips stretched wide in a guttural animal cry.

"Quit m-m-making all that noise!" Paline jabbed me again.

Peaches hissed, "And close your goddamn legs and act dignified in front of all these folks!" She bared her teeth in embarrassment and delivered a stinging pop to my bare arm. "Dignified, dammit! This is Sweetwater not the goddamn bottoms!"

But my grief knew no boundaries. There was no containing it as I pulled away from snatching hands, ignoring the white-gloved ushers as they took one hand from behind their backs long enough to open small vials of ether as they gestured frantically with those cardboard fans.

"She catching the spirit!" someone yelled.

"She'll be catching hell when I get my hands on her!"

That was Peaches again, but I paid her no mind. She was now as insignificant to me as I had always been to her. Hands clutched at my legs and ankles as I found myself on my knees, a long braying sound bellowing from me as I crawled toward the spot where Ma'Dear lay. I kicked and flailed my feet until the hands fell away and I was free. Through the haze of my tears I concentrated on the still figure that seemed so close yet was so far away. The gulf between us looked eternal. I knew it would take a lifetime to reach her, but a lifetime was all I had and I was prepared to die on the journey. Crawling. Step by step.

The choir keened along with me, feeding the grief swelling in the room, fueling the mournful cries, swaying hands, and stomping feet as bodies first stood, then jerked and trembled as though electrified, before slumping over limply until white-clothed ushers raced to the rescue with smelling salts and cool cloths.

Somehow I did it. I crossed the river Jordan. I caravaned through the desert and climbed the mighty mountain. Finally, I kneeled on the cushioned satin stool before Ma'Dear. My arms were like lead as I grasped the sides of her pine bed and pulled myself up. Up, as I searched for a foothold for my knee. Up, as I stretched out my body and threw my leg over the edge of the smooth scented wood. Up, as I hoisted myself over until my thighs lay comfortably upon hers.

"Nooooo," I heard my uncle Bubba cry out. My shoulders were grasped firmly and I was hauled out of the pine box. Gasping, I slumped backward against his chest, my knees like jelly until I found myself bathed once more in the scent of gentian violet and Aunt Charming's soothing voice as she gathered me in her generous arms. I submitted to her embrace as she lowered me to the carpeted floor and rocked back and forth, humming an ancient tune and keeping the exact same rhythm that had once belonged to Ma'Dear.

One by one those who loved Ma'Dear came forward. Some hobbled on walkers or canes, others were supported under the arm by a nephew or a grandson. In bare feet and in classy leather shoes, wearing homespun cotton shirts and store-bought designer suits, the simple, the extravagant, the young and the old, in a solemn procession they thanked and praised and paid homage to the soul whose hands had eased out their babies and massaged their wombs, whose mystical herbs and magical fingers had soothed and cured all that had ailed them, whose wrists had flicked fire from countless tree switches whipping at remorseful legs and repentant feet, and whose sturdy arms had provided strength and courage while comforting their hearts and calming their fears.

The children skipped gaily and reached inside and touched an arm, or lightly smoothed a piece of lace on her shroud. Men and women alike wiped away tears as they kissed a cool cheek, a forehead, patted a hand. And some merely stood for a moment and smiled as sweet memories of the legend laying before them ran fleetingly through their minds and brought comfort and joy to their souls.

I stayed in Aunt Charming's arms for what seemed like hours, until every last body had traveled past and left a mark or a word or a touch with Ma'Dear. Finally, with my throat scraped raw from screaming, I sat mute as Papa stepped forward again and with tears in his eyes began closing the lid on the box Uncle Bubba had made with his own two hands.

As the pine cover was lowered, I took my last look at Ma'Dear and seared every bit of her image onto my memory. The lid descended lower and lower and my eyes greedily devoured the best thing that had ever happened to me and locked it away in the recesses of my soul. Fresh tears poured from me and leaked down my face, and Aunt Charming gathered me tight as a new storm vibrated within me and threatened to dislodge me from my being and hurl me out into a stratosphere of sorrow.

"Hold on, Beanie," she whispered in my ear. "This ain't the end, baby. Brace yourself. 'Cause this ain't the end. You got a long road to travel, daughter. So save some of them tears for later, 'cause before it's all over you are sure to cry again."

Good-bye, Ma'Dear, I wept as the top snapped shut and the last vestiges of my great-great-grandmother disappeared forever from my view. *You were so good,* I whimpered. So good. So damned good to me.

Chapter SIX

WE WERE WAITING ON THE LAWYER, Papa said. According to Ma'Dear's instructions the will had to be read before sundown, and seeing how it was a Sunday and all we'd be lucky if he didn't charge us extra to come out. The house was unusually quiet, the heat of the day dissipating with the night breeze. The guests had been gone for almost an hour now, fed and watered and sent on their way. Junior was slumped over the table, a belly full of gumbo, crab cakes, and cheap hooch sending low sleep sounds escaping from his parted lips.

I sat stiffly on the edge of the low-backed mohair chair, trying hard not to breathe in too much of the emotionally charged air swirling around the room. Behind me, Paline's glare was an inferno, scorching the fine hairs on the nape of my neck with her unbridled fury. I'd embarrassed them, Peaches had scolded me. Made them look like commoners. Like they were still rolling around in the bottoms instead of sitting in the finest house in Sweetwater. Weren't no need in carrying on like that anyhow, she said. Ma'Dear had done got her share of living and somebody else's too. Didn't make no kind of sense. Everybody knew black folks was prone to acting the fool at the drop of a hat. All that damn hollering when Ma'Dear couldn't hear it no way.

I felt relieved when the door finally opened and Uncle Bubba escorted a thin white man inside. He paused in the doorway and adjusted his wire-framed glasses, looking out of place in his wrinkled black suit and careless tie, unsure of whom to address.

"Umm." He walked over to the dining table and sat his tattered briefcase on top of a yellow place mat. The leather was badly worn in some spots and completely missing in others. He cleared his throat and wiped his palms up and down on the legs of his pants. "Good evening, folks. My name is Joseph Hansome and I was hired some years ago to draw up the will of your deceased family member . . ." He popped open his briefcase and sifted through a stack of papers on top. ". . . Mrs. Genessa Sanders."

He paused and smiled around the room, happy with himself, then continued. "Mrs. Sanders has asked that your immediate family be present during the reading of her last will and testament." He nodded toward Papa. "Are all of your family members here in this room right now?"

"Yessir." Papa nudged Junior and nodded. "Yes sir, we's all here."

"Good. Then if you could send someone to retrieve what she called her large black trunk, we can get right down to business."

Papa looked at Uncle Bubba who nodded, then left the room silently.

Peaches said, "Tell us Mistah Hansome, suh. Exactly what did Ma'Dear own that was worth leaving behind?" She stood and walked over to the window. "I mean, she's been with us for over twenty-five years and as far as I know she never worked a real job—"

"Well." The white man smiled. "Some things can't be measured by today's standards of—"

"Did she have any g-g-goddamn money!?" Paline jumped in. "Why we in here tap dancing in circles if Ma'Dear ain't h-h-had nothing? Why you wastin' everybody's time?"

A low growl came from Papa's direction that nearly caused me to fall off the edge of my chair. "Hesh up, Paline! For the love of God, hesh your damn mouth for once!" All five of us swiveled around in our seats to stare at Papa, and even Mr. Hansome shrank back, but Papa was not yet through. He leaned in toward Paline, rage quivering his shoulders and chin. "You ain't got no idea what Ma'Dear mighta had. She came from *nothing* and learned to make something out of it! She lived in this crazy world three times longer than what God has given you, so you betta watch your smart mouth and have some respect for the woman who raised me!"

Well I'll be damned, I thought. Papa was a man after all! Cussing Paline in front of Peaches? I had a feeling he would live to regret that slip of the lip several times over.

To my surprise, it was Junior who spoke up. "Settle down, folks. Don't nobody know what all Ma'Dear had up in them rooms. But whatever it is, it should probably go to Eulie seeing how she stuck by the old woman all these years."

"Eulie, *hell*!" Peaches stormed over to the table and Mr. Hansome scooted in his seat and jumped back a country mile. She jabbed her finger at Junior's nose. "It was me and Top Jar who been feeding Ma'Dear all these years. Feeding Eulie's ass too! Whatever Ma'Dear left here ought to be enough to cover a down payment on what she owes us!"

I was stunned. Junior? Sticking up for me? Surely there was a blizzard blowing ice cubes around down in H-E-double L.

"And what about Paline?" Peaches continued. "Ain't she got a claim to a birthright too?"

"Shut up, Peaches." Papa's voice was quiet and even. "Anything you or Paline mighta had a claim to you forfeited a long time ago by being so damn selfish and evil."

Okay, that was it. Hell had frozen completely over. *Watch it, Papa,* I thought. *You best watch what food you put in your mouth and sleep with one eye open.*

Paline jumped from her chair and I saw Peaches's eyes narrow down until she looked like a rattlesnake. "Fool," she spat. "You must be out of your cotton-picking mind! You best go somewhere and get outta all this heat, Jarrett Senior, until you can talk to me like you got some damned sense." She shook her head like she knew she'd heard him wrong. "I'll show you selfish and evil, mother-fucker. One more word out of your goddamn mouth, nigger. Just *one more word,* and me and these children will just pack our shit and mosey on down the road to Mr. Peets!"

Papa's broad shoulders slumped under the weight of Peaches's glare and he tucked his chin back in. He'd taken his stand and now accepted his defeat. Blinking rapidly, he pursed his lips and shook his head from side to side, but not another word passed from his mouth. Not one more word.

Paline snickered and I rolled my eyes at her in disgust. Junior threw up his hands and put his head back down on the table, and Mr. Hansome busied himself shuffling and reshuffling through the few papers in his briefcase.

I was glad when Uncle Bubba came back dragging Ma'Dear's heavy black trunk. I knew there was a key taped underneath the bottom on the left-hand side, but I kept quiet while Mr. Hansome made a show of tearing open a large white envelope and pulling out a few sheets of paper, then letting a small silver key tumble out onto the table.

"Okay." He pushed his glasses up and cleared his throat again. The room was so quiet you could have heard an ant sigh. "Without further ado, I'll go ahead and read the last will and testament of Mrs. Genessa A. Sanders: 'On the fourteenth day of August in the year of our Lord, 1954, I, Genessa A. Sanders, being of sound mind and body, do hereby appoint Mr. Joseph A. Hansome," he grinned, "that's me, as my lawful attorney in fact to bear witness to the drawing of my last will and testament—'"

"Dammit, skip all that legal mumbo-jumbo and get down to the nitty-gritty!"

Peaches had gone all red in the face, and after one look at her Mr. Hansome moved on quickly. "Okayyy, how about we just open the trunk and pass things out according to her instructions. First on the list is Jarrett Sanders Senior." He unlocked the trunk and took out a white square box. "The note here says that the contents of this box belonged to your great-grandfather, Mr. Boxing Ben Sanders."

Papa took the box with trembling hands and stared at it in great wonder.

"Don't stand there gawking, dummy! Gone and open it up!"

Papa cut his eyes at Peaches, but not a word passed his lips.

He fumbled with the fold of the box and managed to pull it free. Then he plunged his hands inside and slowly pulled out a pair of battered, timeworn leather boxing gloves. The rawhide strings were twisted and stiff, and the leather was all but scraped off the fists and knuckles, but traces of the original color still remained inside the black palms. The gloves spun around slowly as they dangled from the laces held in Papa's hands, and I made out the letters *Spau* embossed in gold on the inner wrists of both mitts.

Uncle Bubba sucked in his breath sharply, but nobody spoke.

Mr. Hansome covered the silence and said, "Er . . . I'll go ahead and read the rest of the note."

> *"Jarrett,*
>
> *Choose your battles wisely son but fight each one like you mean to win. What was born a man ain't meant to die a chile, so look beyond her pretty smile. Remember, rain don't always* pitter, *it's been known to go* pat, *and there's more than one way of skinning a cat.*
>
>

Love, Ma'Dear."

Papa stared at the gloves, then turned and looked sharply at Peaches. Suddenly his features became clear and even, and as he looked from the gloves to Peaches and back again, I saw something foreign creep into his eyes and a willful jut take over his chin. "Look beyond her pretty smile"? *Better watch out, Peaches,* I thought as Mr. Hansome began reading again.

"The next item listed here is for Jarrett Junior." His hands went back inside the trunk and came out with a small circular box wrapped in cellophane. Junior accepted the box and turned around, heading toward the door.

"Like hell," Peaches drawled, and Junior turned back with an impish grin.

He limped back over to Mr. Hansome and laughed. "Go ahead and read me some of Ma'Dear's poetry. Give me one of them old-timey riddles. I bet I can figure it out."

Junior opened the box and extracted a shiny sterling silver pocket watch. The chain was long and sparkly, and the timepiece looked heavy and antique.

Mr. Hansome read from the paper again.

> *"Jarrett Junior,*
>
> *Time, like youth, ain't nothing but a passing illusion.*

*A wise man squanders neither. A minute idle is a minute
wasted. Your clock is ticking.*

Love, Ma'Dear."

"Shucks." Junior laughed nervously. "Ma'Dear musta been
older than she looked. That ain't even had no kinda rhyme to it. It
don't mean a thing to me!"

All eyes returned to Mr. Hansome, who nodded briefly then
delved back into the trunk. I held my breath, sure my brooch was
coming out next. I'd already decided I'd sell it and use the money to
leave Sweetwater for good. Aunt Charming had invited me to
Arkansas and Aunt Mary Mack had even urged me to come to New
York City. I was thinking on Chicago, though. Maybe I could find
one of Huey Newton's groups and get involved with some real black
people. Do some organizing. Some changing.

"Okay. It says here the next item is for Deline LeMoyne."

I frowned. I'd almost forgotten Peaches had a given name. She'd
been Peaches for so long till I just naturally thought of her that way.

Again Mr. Hansome rummaged through the trunk. This time
he came out with a flat, rectangular box that was tied with a pretty
pastel bow.

Peaches gave a short laugh. "What all Ma'Dear got to say to
me? She ain't never liked me nohow. Always acted like Top Jar
coulda done better when everybody knows that's a straight up lie."
She took the box and snatched off the bow and flung it to the floor.
The inside of the box was lined with yellowing sheets of tissue
paper, which she scattered on the floor along with the bow.

Peaches looked suspicious as she took the item from the box.
She held it up so we could see it, and suddenly a sunny smile
creased her face. "Hot diggity! Ma'Dear knows how much I love me
some *me*! Now if this ain't the prettiest mirror I've ever seen!"

I had to agree. The mirror was shaped in a rectangle with elab-
orate carvings and designs along its polished oak border. From the

look of the piece I knew it had to be handcrafted and painstakingly stained, and for a moment I thought it might have been one of Uncle Bubba's pieces. I turned to ask him and saw a look of respectful admiration in his clear eyes. Whoever had carved the mirror had truly earned Uncle Bubba's reverence. Peaches twirled the mirror this way and that. She styled and profiled and examined her reflection from every possible angle.

Mr. Hansome cleared his throat and coughed a few times, then began:

> *"Peaches,*
>> *Pretty is what pretty does. Even the most treasured piece of fruit will eventually spoil. The true meaning of lovely can only be found when you look in the mirror and like what you see from the inside out. Remember, God don't like ugly, and beauty, while short-lived, runs only skin-deep.*
>
>> *Love, Ma'Dear"*

Peaches blushed ten more shades of red. "What the hell she mean by that, Top Jar? Y'all been up in here talking about me or somethin'? That old lady got her damn nerve. She better be glad she already in the ground, and pray I don't take a mind to dig her old ass up and tell her about herself!" She smoothed back a few wild strands of hair and stared at Papa. "You gonna explain to me why that old woman talked that trash about me! God don't like ugly? Then that must be why He loves me so!"

Paline stood up. "Well, after seeing w-w-what you all got ain't no need in me sticking around. Evidently Ma'Dear didn't have a pot to piss in, so if all you got for me is some old mess she done been saving since the year of the flood, you can just k-k-keep it."

"Just a minute." Mr. Hansome stopped her. "By law I've got to stay here until the will is read and everything is distributed according to Mrs. Sanders's wishes. I understand it's been a long day for you people, but there are only two things left, so please bear with me so we can all get some rest."

Paline stopped but did not sit down. I almost yelled out loud when Mr. Hansome took an oval egg-speckled case from the trunk and sat it on the table.

I swallowed hard as my heart hammered against my throat and fresh beads of sweat formed on the bridge of my nose. "That's mine," I said quickly and reached out to take it.

"No." Mr. Hansome held it high in his palm. "It says right here that this one is willed to Paline LeMoyne. Is that you or your sister?"

"I'm Paline." She gave me a sly look. "What you snatching so f-f-fast for? This must be the good stuff. Maybe Ma'Dear loved me b-b-best after all."

I was in agony as Paline lifted the egg-shaped lid from the hand-painted case. Nestled inside was my gold brooch, the deep-set jewels glittering at me mockingly.

"That can't be hers!" I insisted. "Ma'Dear knew I wanted that. I thought she was saving that for me!"

Paline laughed as she pinned the brooch to her wrinkled gray dress. "I guess you thought wrong, huh? Maybe you got another think coming to you!"

Tears welled in my eyes as Mr. Hansome read from his paper:

"Paline,
    If no man is an island and no woman an oasis,
    Then black gals gots to help each other keep a
grounded basis.
    When life gets tough and stomps you till you gots no
strength to stand,
    It ain't your skin that saves you, it's the grace in your
sister's hand.
                    With all my love, Ma'Dear."

I couldn't care less what message Ma'Dear had left Paline. She'd left her my brooch, and to me that was the ultimate betrayal. The events of the day overwhelmed me and I sobbed loudly into my hands.

"Stop being such a goddamn water bag!" Peaches snapped. "Ever since the day you was born you been crying about something or the other!" Peaches grabbed my shoulder and jerked me around harshly, "Listen up, Eulie." She wagged her finger in my face. "Ain't no Ma'Dear here to be wiping up your snot no more! And what you got to cry about anyway? Hesh up all that fussing over nothing. Paline deserves to have something nice and that's why Ma'Dear gave it to her."

Papa strode over and removed Peaches's hand from my shoulder. Without saying a word, he stared into her eyes as he stood beside me and gently rubbed the spot where she'd grabbed me.

"The last item in the box is addressed to 'Euleatha the Strong.'" Mr. Hansome delved in for the last time and came out with a large round hatbox, similar to the one I'd used to pack away Ma'Dear's herbs. I frowned but accepted the box from his outstretched hands and followed suit and opened it.

I gasped in surprise when I examined its contents. The last thing in the world I wanted or needed was what was in that box. Paline laughed as I pulled it out, and even Uncle Bubba had to snicker. Out of all the things Ma'Dear could have left me, she'd chosen to will me a hat.

An old brown Stetson-type fedora with a shiny black ribbon banded around its brim.

I turned it over and examined it from all angles, sure that there was something special about it that would explain why I, her closest friend, had been forsaken. The fedora had a brown silk sheathing on its interior, and a few thin sheets of tissue paper were plastered around the inner rim. It was a man's hat, and the brim looked flexible and pliant, as though it could be worn up or down, or slanted to the side in whatever fashion the wearer found suitable.

Paline intruded on my thoughts. "Well at least Ma'Dear had one thing right. Eulie can always use a hat to go over that head of n-n-nappy-ass hair. She shoulda l-l-left you a straightening comb to go along w-with it."

Peaches howled.

Junior snickered.

Papa frowned.

I was struck totally dumb. My visions of leaving Sweetwater were fading fast and my hopes for a peaceful future suddenly looked dim.

"Okay," Mr. Hansome said with a long sigh, "here goes . . ."

> *"Euleatha the Strong,*
>> *Shrug off your outer skin my child, and try on something new.*
>> *When the time is right to make your move, you'll know just what to do.*
>> *The past always reveals the truth, so there's no need to fear it.*
>> *Be patient, loving, brave, and strong . . . and if the hat fits you must wear it.*
>> *My love will keep you until we meet again, Ma'Dear"*

Chapter SEVEN

THE AUNTS WERE LEAVING on the 7:09 train. A car would arrive shortly after dawn to take them to the station where they'd be seated in a dining car to enjoy a leisurely breakfast while heading north to New Orleans. There, Aunt Charming would fly northwest to Arkansas, and Aunt Mary's flight would take her northeast to New York City.

I had to be on that 7:09. I didn't have much money, but I was sure one of the aunts would lend me some until I could get to Chicago and get on my feet. As I threw my essentials into two small cardboard suitcases that had belonged to my grandmother Joy during the fifties, I vowed the sun would never set on me in Louisiana again.

It hadn't been hard for me to arrive at my decision to leave, although the aunts had warned me not to run from my destiny. They said I had to play out the hand that had been dealt me so that Ma'Dear's spirit could pass on in peace. They said I'd been chosen to learn the old ways, but I had to earn this knowledge first. Knowledge they claimed, I could only get by laying down my hatred and staying put right here in Sweetwater.

But the aunts were getting on in age. Plus, they were light skinned. Neither of them had ever had any trouble passing the paper bag test, so what could they know about my pain? No, they were wrong. There was no place for me here and I was gonna find me some black folks who loved their dark skin if it killed me. I was sick and tired of these high-yellow folks in Sweetwater who hid behind their light skin and used it as a shield to hold up against me. As a trophy to dangle out in front of me. The fact that their lives were so easy caused hatred to well up in me, and I slammed my dresser drawer and yanked open my closet and pulled a few dresses off their hooks.

I took a thin, no-wrinkle brown dress off of a hook and paused. Dangling from the hook beneath the dress was a beaded necklace I'd all but forgotten about. It had been a gift from Cissy. A choker with alternating red, black, yellow, and green beads held together with a shiny gold clasp.

I lay the dress on the bed and held the necklace up to the light. "It stands for black power," Cissy had told me. "Black power in the colors of an African flag." I went to the mirror and modeled the tiny beads against my neck. On impulse, I opened Ma'Dear's hatbox and sat the hat on the dresser. It took me three tries, but I finally managed to clamp the gold clasp on the necklace to the black ribbon banded around the hat. I held the fedora in my hands and looked at it critically. There. The beads hung from the right side of the hat in a straight line and the vibrant colors somehow brought me comfort.

I slept fitfully that night, tossing and turning and staring around the small room I'd slept in for most of my life. I rose from the bed at 3 a.m. and gazed out the window at a face in the crescent moon, while lightly fingering the curtains Ma'Dear had taught me to sew. As I turned back to the bed my heart filled with sorrow, my eyes rested on the hat. Ma'Dear's final and most puzzling gift.

In addition to Euleatha, Ma'Dear had also named me Oyi-Yansi, which signified a change that was sure to come. Somehow I sensed that the necessary change was gonna have to come from within me, but other than stealing out of Sweetwater I had no idea what to do.

"Show me, Ma'Dear," I whispered softly. "I'm here. I'm waiting."

I wouldn't have to wait much longer.

⁓

I opened my eyes to the predawn sun and panic snatched at my heart. Trifling! How could I lay in this bed while my opportunities were downstairs about to climb into a taxi and leave me behind? I jumped from the bed and tore off my nightshirt, throwing it carelessly in the corner. Let Paline come in here and pick it up because if the good Lord was willing and the creek didn't rise, after today I'd never have to step foot in this room—this house—again.

I pulled the brown dress over my head and loosened the two long plaits that hung from either side of my head. With a few strokes of a wire brush my thick coarse hair settled nicely around my shoulders and I took a few deep, calming breaths.

Out of habit, I pulled the sheets and covers up neatly over my bed and fluffed my pillow, then I slipped into my Sunday-go-to-meeting shoes and hurried into Ma'Dear's bathroom to brush my teeth and splash cool water on my face.

I'd hidden the two small suitcases behind the door, and as I picked them up I marveled at how light they seemed. After seventeen years I didn't own much more than the clothes on my back, but somehow that suited me just fine. There wasn't much I wanted to remember about this house, and I hoisted the suitcases and grabbed my beaded new hat and stuck it under my arm before yanking the light string and closing the door behind me.

My footsteps were sure as I padded down the steps. The thud of a closing door echoed from the west wing, and the aunts' voices drifted toward me as they waited in the foyer. As I reached the bottom step and turned the corner to dart toward the double wood doors, Papa's pained voice froze me in my tracks.

"Beanie?"

I stopped but did not turn around.

"Why you up so early, Beanie Baby? Where you going with them there bags?"

It took every ounce of determination I had, but I refused to turn to face him. To do so would have been to forgive him for the years when he stood idle while I suffered racial abuse right under his nose. To forgive him for giving me this dark skin without providing the shelter and protection it required to remain toned and supple and loved.

"I'm leaving, Papa," I said simply.

His footsteps were heavy as he approached me.

"Leaving, going where?"

I shrugged my shoulders but they remained squared. "Anywhere. Away from here."

Papa came up behind me and put his arms around me. For the briefest moment I was tempted to lean back and find a small measure of comfort in his embrace.

"Oh, baby." He squeezed me tightly and let out a long sigh. "You just grieving, that's all. You can't just up and leave your home. What you gon' do out there in that big ole world?"

"I'ma live, Papa. I'ma find me some folks who love me for who I am, and I'ma live."

He tried to turn me around to face him, and when I resisted he chuckled and gently touched my hair. "You don't wanna look at your papa? Well, that's okay. I know you love me anyway. I know you loves your mama too."

I jerked away. "My *mama*? What mama? You talking 'bout Peaches? That evil, self-centered witch who ain't never gave me an ounce of mothering in my whole entire life? That same *mama* who hated my blackness so bad she refused to let me suck from her lily-white titties?" I did turn to face him then. "No, Papa," I said as I allowed the tears to run freely down my face. "I ain't got no love for Peaches or for nobody who looks anything like her either. As far as I'm concerned Peaches, Paline, Junior, and every other half-white nigger in Sweetwater can go straight to hell."

I softened my voice then because a large part of me did, in fact, love my daddy. "But watch out, Papa," I warned him. "Watch you ain't charged and found guilty by association. You a good man, but you color-struck and you weak. You one of them self-hating colored men who need a white woman—or the closest thing to a white woman—in his bed just so he can feel like he's almost as good as the white man."

I was fully prepared to bear his striking blow when I opened my mouth again.

"But you know what, Papa?" My eyes were full of loathing as I stared at him. "No matter how hard you sham and put on airs and rub up against Peaches or anybody else who looks white, when you roll over and get up you still gonna be a nigger!"

Why I was still standing and breathing I will never know.

I whirled away from him quickly before he could recover his senses and give me what I knew I deserved. I hoisted my suitcases once more and started toward the foyer. I could see the shock on the faces of the aunts as I walked toward them with my spine stiff, full of pride. My papa's eyes, hurt and pleading, caused pain to swell where they touched my retreating back. I was almost there. I reached the double doors, and just outside the foyer I paused for a moment. I set Ma'Dear's hat on my head and pushed it down snugly until it completely covered my ears. Heat immediately enveloped my head and my scalp broke out in a drenching sweat. The long row of colorful beads swung back and forth as I resumed my solitary strut toward the door, and at the first bolt of lightning I thought Papa had swung a sledgehammer and struck a blow high on the back of my skull, but suddenly the pain exploded outward in billions of violent splinters, and then I thought nothing at all.

Chapter EIGHT

I CAME AWAKE SLOWLY, and the first thing that struck me was a scratchy sensation on my arms, belly, and back. Somehow, my skin was ablaze from the coarse fabric sticking to my body and my limbs were limp and weak from exertion.

"Git up, gal," came a voice from the doorway. "You bin out chere long enuf. It don't take nobody half a mo'ning to lose they water. Po' baby. The massa let you stay outta his bed sometimes an' meybbe you won't be so weary you pass out on de hole."

She stood silhouetted against the sun, her face set in a tired grimace, her skin a soft beige, her thick body all but blocking the light from the doorway. The heat was suffocating. Dampness ran between my legs and seeped down my back. The putrid smell emanating from all around was enough to put me out again, and I gagged and coughed as I tried to sit up on the tightly packed lime-caked floor.

"Ain't gwine tell you no mo'. There is sheets an windahs yet to be washed an' rugs to be shook. An' next time you take Massa his supper late you'll git some skin ripped off'n yo' back. I'se goin' down yonder to de slave quarters an when I gits back you best have yo' hands in some hot water 'n' lye."

The door swung shut behind her leaving me in near darkness except for the small slice of sunlight streaming in from a circular hole cut in the rotting wood of the ceiling. I struggled to my feet, my hat lopsided and askew, wincing at the pain in my arms and aching in my legs. My skin was ablaze from the foreign material of my dress, and as my stomach heaved and retched, I pushed through the door and fell out into the bright sunshine.

What the hell?

As I lay upon a bed of sweet-smelling grass surrounded by gnats and gulping down lungfuls of moist morning air, an icy panic slid down my back as my eyes took in the unfamiliar scene. Scores of Negro shanties lined the dirt road to the east, where I saw several spotted hounds lying in shaded corners of porches and prowling around looking for scraps. One of the larger hounds trotted over to me with a lopsided gait and sniffed the air cautiously. He stood on three legs; his front left paw shriveled and mangled, his sad brown eyes almost human. Ignoring him, I turned my head. A large, white-columned mansion peeked over the crest of a hill to the west, and there was some sort of crude horse-drawn buggy sitting in the dusty road out front. Ahead of me I could barely make out rows and rows of black backs bent over what looked like cotton, their hands traveling rhythmically from the white crop to the sacks slung across their shoulders, then back to the crop.

Papa must have busted me up pretty good, I thought and rubbed my eyes with the back of my hands. Suddenly my heart stopped beating. My eyes bulged and my whole body began to tremble and I was overcome with terror and disbelief.

My hands had gone almost completely white.

For the first time since I could remember, I peed on myself.

Ignoring the warm pooling urine, I rubbed my hands together and then slid them rapidly up and down my arms, which were almost just as pale. I looked down at myself. I was dressed in some sort of sack. Made of rough burlap and tied around the waist with twine. I crawled to my knees and stood. Pee slid down my body and cut a clear track in the dust clinging to my legs. My legs. They were mottled with itchy red insect bites, and although my feet were bare, the bottoms hard and crusted, it was obvious what color they were. Yellow.

I grunted in horror and staggered forward. With my breath coming in gasps, I reached up to touch my face, my thin lips topped by a soft fuzzy mole, my straight nose, my soft stringy hair. Heaving in great gulps of air, I gurgled and choked as I staggered over to a nearby well. Clenching my fists and retching up scalding bile, I bent over and peered at my watery reflection, and when realization finally struck me I was bent nearly in half by the force of my own screams. Somehow I'd earned the second part of my name. The Oyi-Yansi Ma'Dear had predicted had finally come.

⁓

Feet came running, kicking up road dust and calling out my name.

"Gal, whatchoo m-m-makin all dat ruckus fer? Is somebody runnin' off? What the d-d-debil you hollrin' like a b-b-banshee fer?"

I would have recognized her anywhere.

She stood before me dressed in a layer of clean rags. Evil rolled off a face as black as tobacco juice, and two thick plaits fell from the back of her white bonnet and hung straight down her back. Her shoulders looked wide but strong, and a slight fullness settled near her belly. Her eyes were accusing and shrank me under her glare. I let my jaw drop.

"Fool! Shut yo' m-m-outh! You catchin' flies? Allus tryin' t-t-to git outta doin yo' w-w-work. Thank somebody g-g-gonna' do ever'thang fer you whilst you lay in de massa's b-b-bed!"

"Paline?"

"Pa-who? Gal I bin Queen-Esther all these y-y-years an' now I'se s'pposed to ansah to Paline?" She clucked her tongue and stomped off toward the big white house, then called out over her shoulder, "Them taters be w-w-waitin' to git peeled an' de yard birds n-n-need pluckin'. You know lak I do you best git in dat kitchin and g-g-git to werk!"

I watched as she walked toward the back of the house and disappeared. Then I took my yellow fingers and pinched my cheeks hard. I was real enough all right, but who was I? My face stung like the dickens as I closed my eyes and prayed. "Dear God up in heaven, please forgive me for hating Peaches and sassing Papa. Whatever evils I've done, please show me how I can make up for them so I can wake up from this nightmare before I lose my mind."

"Euleatha! Gal, you done finally crawled out de outhouse, huh? Whas wrong wit yo' face? Dem skeeters done bit you? Po' baby, you look right peaked." Her rough hand grabbed me by the arm, but somehow I sensed a bit of tenderness in the touch as well.

Mrs. Lemmon?

"C'mon in here," she fussed gently, "an' catch yo'self a teacake. I done baked a whole pan an' they is jes 'bout reddy to come out de stove. Dem pretty brown ones you like so much. I'se gonna take some down to my own chirren by an' by, but right now us needs to git back to de big house."

I was led to the rear of the stately white house as though in a dream. My whole body felt strange. Alien. It was neither the right color nor the right shape; I was filled out in places where I'd never had so much flesh before. My hips had widened and swung naturally, my breasts were full and ripe and strained against the sack of my dress. I now possessed the same dreaded skin color of Peaches and Paline, but it was my hands that scared me the most. Red and calloused, my fingernails were torn back and stumped, my knuckles raw and thick, each joint knobby and swollen from hard work and overuse. My palms were nearly as coarse and solid as the soles of my feet, and thick veins stood out prominently on the back of my hands.

I stumbled alongside Mrs. Lemmon woodenly, all the while refusing to believe the sights my eyes beheld. A teenage girl in a patched dress swept clouds of dust off the wide front porch. Her mouth was drawn down in a sullen line, and when our eyes met I felt her stabbing anger shoot right through me. Near the side of the house I saw an elderly black man wielding a garden hoe and pruning a colorful bed of wild azaleas and silver bells. Perspiration stained his faded brown shirt and darkened his back and his armpits. "Mo'ning, Aunt Mattie. Miss Euleatha." He tipped his straw hat in my direction and grinned crazily with a mouth full of pink gums. "You two ladies lookin' lovely as eber dis fine day."

I dug my fists into my eyes and almost tripped over a large rock.

Mr. Thomas! Sweetwater's sin on sobriety! He should have been at Chez LeMoyne scrubbing floors! My jaw hung uselessly as Mrs. Lemmon pulled me along, pausing to hold the screen door open as my alien body trailed along behind her.

She led me into a large kitchen where the girl who called herself Queen-Esther stood stoking a glowing stove. She cut her eye at me but continued with her task. I looked around and shuddered. An army of cast iron and copper-bottom pots hung from the ceiling by a metal rack, and two huge basins stood side by side filled with water. There was a long rectangular table in the center of the room bordered by low pine benches. A pile of potatoes stood off in a corner, and three scrawny chickens, minus their heads, were dangling upside down over a large kettle, bright blood draining from their carcasses and dripping lazily into a container.

"Take off Boxing Ben's old hat and git ta werk, gal." The woman they called Aunt Mattie gave me a gentle push in the small of my back.

I pulled the brown fedora from my head before speaking. "Uhm, Mrs. Lemm—I mean Aunt Mattie, ma'am," I stammered. My voice came out in a pitch and tone I'd never used before and a strange ringing sound echoed in my ears. My knees were ready to give out and send me crashing to the floor. "I want to go home now. Peaches and Top Jar are sure to be worried about me, so if you could please show me how to get back to Sweetwater I'll just be on my way."

She stared. "Gal, what you jes say?"

Queen-Esther snickered over at the stove. "You know how she be, Aunt Mattie! Jes 'cause she stay in de house an' beddin' wit the massa havin' his white babies she thank she white too. She allus had it easy. Didn't nevah have to werk hard like the rest of us. Now look at 'er. Gwin git herself kilt. Pretendin' like she white whilst she talkin'. Must be messin' wit some a Massa learnin's."

Aunt Mattie moved like lightning and slapped me across my bruised face. Hard. Once, twice, three times with her open palm. I stumbled under her heavy blows and recoiled with my back against the stove as she advanced on me.

"Go home? You is home! You thinkin' 'bout drawin' a pass and runnin'? Ain't you got enuf a that after Massa kilt yo' Ben? Lissen here, gal. You keep on sneakin' in the massa study foolin' with his learnin's! Ain't no nigger s'pposed to be foolin' wit no letterin'. Let alone talkin' like you jes did. You might be yella, but you best nevah forgit you is still a nigger. I don't care how much you thank Massa feel special fer you. You is still a nigger!"

Between the heat coming off the stove and Aunt Mattie, I was completely engulfed. Her face, stern and rigid, wavered like water before my eyes. I swallowed hard but managed to stay on my feet. I would need to be much smarter if I planned on making it back to Sweetwater in one piece. Mr. Brathwaite had always said I was a quick study, though, and I had no intentions of risking Aunt Mattie's wrath and being whacked again, so when I opened my mouth again I had everything just right.

"Yessum. I 'pologize. I musta fergot jes who I is, an' I cain't thank you enuf fer settin' me straight."

"Good." She stared at me for a long second and then seemed satisfied. "Now git yo'sef in dat back room an' git to werk."

I knew then that I was in some kind of coma. Either that, or Papa had killed me with that ax and I'd come back to life as somebody's slave. Who were these people who looked like folks from home but somehow didn't? I'd already figured out that Miss Lemmon was Aunt Mattie the cook minus the dark skin, and there was no doubt in my mind that that Queen-Esther girl was surely Paline. I'd recognize that look in her eyes anywhere. I'd often given Paline that same look whenever she used her charms to get over like a fat rat in a cheese factory—contempt rolled up in resentment. And although Queen-Esther was roughly my complexion—my old complexion—and wore her hair in the same thick plaits as I did, or used to, she was Paline through and through.

I walked stiffly into the backyard where water was boiling in two huge kettles. I looked down at the thick grooved callouses on my knuckles and palms and somehow I knew just what to do.

I'd never worked so hard in all my life. Not even the time Peaches fired her entire staff and made me and Ma'Dear pick up their slack. This new body of mine was strong, though. The muscles in my arms rippled and stretched as I dipped my hands in rough lye soap and scrubbed, dunked, and rinsed sheet after sheet after sheet. When I was through Aunt Mattie helped me wring them until my knuckles were white and my palms cracked and sore, then I struggled out to the back of the house with endless baskets and clothespins and hung them on the line to dry in the billowing breeze.

After the sheets came the silver. I polished crates of flatware, candlesticks, platters, and picture frames. Then I went through the house beating rugs with a scraggly excuse for a broom before moving from the top floor downward with a large, coarse brush, scrubbing floors and baseboards on my hands and knees. I was allowed to sit in the kitchen while the floors dried, where I plucked those gross, still-warm chickens, then peeled down that mound of potatoes until Aunt Mattie said it would soon be time to take Massa his supper.

"Gone down an' feed your lit'luns while I git the massa's tray ready," she said as she held the naked chickens over an open fire and singed the remaining feathers from their pale bodies.

Lit'luns? What lit'luns?

"Uhm, Aunt Mattie," I said carefully, not willing to risk another slap from her mitt of a hand. I wiped a few strands of my stringy brown hair from my eyes. "Where 'bout my lit'luns be?"

She looked at me like I was some kind of fool, then laughed out loud.

"Gal, I don't know what done got into you today, but you sho is actin' daft. Yo' lit'luns' is right where they s'pposed to be. In the slave quarters with the rest of the slaves! Ole Eliza should be fixin' to feed them tirectly, so git on down there an' help."

"Aunt Mattie?" I ventured timidly again. "Where 'bout the Massa be?"

Her face dropped and hard lines of exasperation creased her chin. "Euleatha Ray Sanders! Massa in the fields watchin' ober his proppity! Where you thank a white man what owns niggers s'pposed to be?"

The sun beat down fiercely and I was grateful for the protection of Boxing Ben's old hat as I walked down the heavily worn path toward the weather-beaten shacks. I saw things I had only heard about in Mr. Brathwaite's history lessons. I was on some sort of slave plantation where cotton and corn were the crops. My mind refused to delve too deeply into the mechanics of it all, but I was sure I was somebody else. Some other Euleatha who had surely come before me. Not Euleatha Oyi-Yansi, but Euleatha Ray. As I approached the lean-to cabins, I heard Aunt Charming's voice echoing in my mind. "You'll see Ma'Dear again. And Big Euleatha too." I took several deep breaths and an eerie sensation washed over me as I realized how close her prophecy was to coming true.

Chapter NINE

THE LOPSIDED HOUND was waiting in a clearing beside the shanties and limped ahead of me and led me to the proper door. I knocked softly on the dusty cross-wood planks, and when no one responded I pushed right in. The contrast between the brightness outside and the dimness in the interior of the log shanty hurt my eyes, and it took me a moment to make out the features inside.

It was a one-room shack with a small fire going in the hearth. A round black pot sat on some kind of platform in the center of the room, and roughly twenty-five to thirty children sat in a circle around it. For so many kids they were extremely quiet, and I got a sense that hunger had rendered them so. An old black woman with a red bandanna tied over her head was bent over the pot and ladling a thin liquid into bowls held in eager, outstretched hands. She was heavy and stooped in the back, and wore a clean white apron over a simple black frock. I caught a glimpse of her face when she turned to pass a full bowl to a small boy, and the shock made me let loose the door and cover my mouth in awe.

Fannie!

It was her all right. Older and much darker, but the jolly chin and prominent jaw were a dead ringer for Chez LeMoyne's head cook. As the door slammed behind me Fannie looked up and smiled.

"Hey thar, Euleatha. I wuz jes gwine send dis chile right'chere up de road to fetch ya! Hur'rup an' nuss yo babe so you kin hep out wit' dese hongry chilluns."

Nuss my babe?

My heart hammered wildly and I shifted from foot to foot as I mentally prepared my words. "Uhm. Miss Eliza, ma'am, Miss Mattie sunt me ta' hep you feed dese kids—I mean chilluns."

A sweet cackle of laughter escaped her lips. "Ole Euleatha. You de same as always. Standing dere lookin' like a whole pot a dirty rice." She walked over to the far side of the room and bent low over a corncob cradle. When she straightened up there was a wriggling bundle in her arms.

"Come git yo' baby, chile. Genessa done took Genera to de outhouse so you kin' nuss this'un till dey gits back."

Genessa? Genera? Ma'Dear and Aunt Charming? Lord have mercy! If these were my kids, then that would make me the first Euleatha! Euleatha the Brave!

My arms shook as I accepted the swaddled bundle and rocked a few moments before pushing aside the rough blanket to glimpse the beautiful face of the pale infant inside. Dressed in a soft cotton gown, she stared up at me with old eyes. Eyes that had been here before, and somehow I got the feeling it was the baby I stood rocking who was actually trying to comfort me.

Eliza laughed again. "Ain't she sumpthin' already, tho? That chile thar is gonna be a dish!"

I gazed into the blanket. Genevieve. Aunt Mary Mack. The baby of the family. The prettiest. The dish.

My mind reeled with the impossibility of it all, and I had no idea what to do next, but this new body of mine was familiar to the child and she nestled and pulled at the opening near my breasts until she had what she wanted and settled down to feed. I sat on an overturned wood crate and stared down at myself in amazement. The tops of my breasts were creamy and full, and the strangest feeling coursed through me as the milk rushed from my body. I was nursing a baby! Nursing my Aunt Mary Mack! I examined her clothing and played with her toes as she slurped and grinned happily, and for no reason at all I broke off a measure of twine securing the folded pieces of cloth that were meant to serve as baby socks and absentmindedly wound it around my index finger.

As I sat admiring and feeding the baby, the door opened again and a girl of about ten walked in holding the hand of another little girl who looked to be no more than three. The older girl wore clothes similar to the other children in the shack, but the younger child was dressed in finer garb. Faded and obviously handed down, but not nearly the simple homemade sacks that the others wore. I held my breath as they moved straight toward me, and when the older girl came close enough for me to see her eyes, I nearly dropped the baby and screamed out loud. *Ma'Dear!* One jellied eye sat uselessly in her brown face, and she peered at me with a mixture of sadness and love from the other. Her mouth was set in a serene line, and when I glanced down at her feet they were dusty but well formed and not at all displeasing to my eyes.

The smaller girl came over and rested her head upon my arm, and without thinking I reached up and ran my fingers through the wild tangles of her light brown hair. It was obvious that the two younger children were of mixed race, but Ma'Dear stood staring at me from a face that was much darker and had beautifully strong African features.

My heart wrenched as I stared into her eye, its hypnotic pull drawing me deeper and deeper into her soul. She did not speak but instead came forward and smoothed the hair back from my tired eyes, then took my free hand and rubbed the ache away with her fingers. I looked down and saw the contrast between our skin—hers a deep baked brown and mine raw, scarred, and pale. Her small brown hands moved down and massaged the ache that began in my inflamed ankles and flowed like the Nile straight out through the soles of my caked and calloused feet. I knew then how she had been able to love and understand Peaches, and why she'd never favored me over Paline. Why she had insisted we were all the same no matter what our outer wrappings. Why my great-great-grandmother had tried so hard to teach me how to love the skin I was in.

We sat like that for some time as Eliza spooned up bowl after bowl after bowl of hot mashed gruel and passed it out to the silent children, me nursing the little one, little Mary resting upon my shoulder, Ma'Dear rubbing my feet. I hated to move when Eliza finally told me it was time to get back to the big house to take the massa his supper.

"You be sure an' git it to him whilst it's still nice 'n' hot," she warned me. Massa John Sanders don't like nuthin' cold and he be right ornery now that we in pickin' season."

"Yessum." I placed the baby back in her rocker and stood before Ma'Dear. She took Aunt Mary's hand and gathered the small child to her. Her sole eye bore into me and fed me strength. I reached up and wove the piece of broken twine through the band of my hat, and then with tears in my eyes I kissed the tops of their heads and went back out into the bright sunlight.

⁓

Aunt Mattie had Massa's tray waiting when I returned to the kitchen. "Git down to de fields an' then git right back chere." She wrapped a clean white cloth over the tray of bread, what looked like a hunk of ham, and a thick wedge of cheese. "De afternoon werk still gots to be done, so don't you tarry."

As I walked down the dirt roads toward the mind-boggling fields of cotton, I stared all around me. There were wheelbarrows full of shucked corn, old women tending rows of collard and mustard greens and vines of red ripe tomatoes. Heads turned as I passed by, and in every eye I saw the same naked hostility and anger that had been in Paline's eyes so deeply set in Queen-Esther's face. I cast my eyes downward and passed on, tittering laughter hammering at my back as I made my way further down the trail.

The sun rode high in the sky as the black slaves streamed up from the cornfields on the left and the cotton fields on the right. I passed droves of full-bodied men dressed in tattered shirts and knee-high pants, and strong, muscular-looking women with picks and axes slung over their weary shoulders. As the dog-tired slaves filed past with long poles braced across their broad necks with empty water buckets hanging from each end, I studied their dark, sweat-drenched faces with great dismay. Some of these were faces I could swear I'd seen around Sweetwater and beyond, yet each of them was somehow very different. Deprivation and subjugation had been ground into the sun-baked lines of their faces, the resigned set of their chins, the slump of their shoulders.

They streamed around me, cutting a wide swath and walking onto the grass so as not to come too close. The stoniness of their glares singed my skin, and I felt alien and peculiar under the hostility in their eyes. Deep within this strange body of mine, under this pale, burnished skin I knew I held a different station. I knew they despised me. And I knew why too. There were men and women here of various shades of black and brown, but my skin was much lighter than theirs. They toiled in the fields and I worked in the big house. But at least they had each other. 'Cause as hard as I knew this life was for all slaves, surely it was harder still when you were ostracized by your own kind.

The massa sat beneath the leaves of a hardwood tree. Several slaves were just beyond him, some drawing water from a stonewashed well and others inspecting the cotton crop for signs of the dreaded boll weevil. "'Bout time you got down here, Euleatha. You sure is movin' slow today." Massa grinned a lecherous grin. "Musta been up too late pleasurin' ole Massa last night. Got mo' for ya where that come from too."

I stood there blinking in the bright sunlight. He was a scraggly-looking thing. Thin and sun hardened. Sweat stained his white undershirt and sparse gray hairs peeked out from his neckline. I had a vision of lying beneath him, his hands searching and pinching, his teeth gnashing and tearing, his pathetic white penis jabbing and probing me deep enough to deposit his seed firmly within the walls of my womb. I handed him the tray and stood there dumbly, waves of fear and revulsion coursing through me. He massaged his crotch with one filthy hand, then set the tray on the grass and grabbed my arm. Squeezing roughly, he pulled me close and clamped his mouth onto mine. The overpowering odor of an unwashed body and stale liquor assaulted me, and as I struggled against him my empty stomach rolled and lurched.

He shoved me away so hard I fell back into the grass. "After all this time you's fightin' me? He-he. I likes me a nigger wench who kin show some spunk! Keep some a that fer tonight, ya hear? Now git over there and fetch me some water!"

I ran shakily to the spigot and pumped until a stream of clear water burst from its mouth. I held a dusty tin cup beneath the flow until it was full, then scampered back over to give it to the massa. Our hands touched briefly as he accepted the cup from me, and in that moment I knew why my own kind despised me so. Because this Euleatha whose skin I wore also despised herself.

Back at the big house Aunt Mattie gave me instructions for my afternoon chores. Somehow I worked even harder than I had that morning, and by the time I was done washing windows, rubbing sweet lemon oil into highboys and chiffoniers and wardrobes, bringing in the sheets, folding linen, boiling spare blankets, and melting down lard and soapberry to use for cleaning, Aunt Mattie was calling to me from the kitchen.

"Euleatha! Git on in heah, Euleatha! De massa be wanting some corn pone wit his dinnah t'nite! Hur'rup and grind dis heah meal, then git yo' blackberry pies in de stove. I done kneaded de dough fer ya an' it's rising up real pretty right now."

Queen-Esther stood at one of the two large basins pulling fat and guts off the chicken, whose carcass had been expertly split and sliced into pieces that looked more acceptable and more familiar to my tired eyes. She looked up at me as I entered the kitchen and laughed bitterly. "Jes look at her, Aunt Mattie. Did the least bit a werk she could git 'way wit' all day and got th' nerve to look tuckered out."

I dragged myself over to the table to grind the corn for the pone. My arms and shoulders ached with an intensity I had never dreamed possible, and my eyes were blinded by tears of pain and frustration. But there was also fear within me. Fear that I would not be able to withstand the harshness of this life. Fear that I would somehow fail myself, and fail those who depended on me.

That evening after tying on a starched white apron and assisting Aunt Mattie serve dinner to the massa and his three grown sons who ate like slop hogs and completely devoured every scrap on the table, all I wanted to do was find a quiet corner and collapse.

I asked, "Where 'bout I sleep, Aunt Mattie?"

Queen-Esther laughed. A bitter, harsh sound that cut right through me.

"Hear that, Aunt Mattie? Dis wench is full a funnin' today! All day long she bin actin' like she daft an' don't know nuttin' 'bout the ways of de big house. She de only one Massa Sanders 'llow to feed her own chirren his food and walk 'round wearin' store-bought clothes. She gits all sorts a special privileges jes 'cause she a bright-skinned house nigger. An' now she cain't figger out where she sleeps?" Queen-Esther turned toward me with a look of pure disgust on her face. "Euleatha git yo' tail in Massa's chambers! You ain't nebber had to werk hard for nuttin' by day, it only be fittin' you gots to work hard to earn yo' keep by night!"

"Esther!" Aunt Mattie swung her around by the shoulder. "Look a here, gal! Jes 'cause you feelin' jittery 'bout stealin' off on tonight's journey, don't you go rilin' Eulea—"

Journey?

"Sssh!" Queen-Esther's face was a mask of pure terror. "You done tol' her! You ought to know better'n talkin' in front of Massa's wench! She be runnin' telling ever'thang she know jes to make hersef look better'n us!"

Aunt Mattie's eyes registered Queen-Esther's horror. "Oh, sweet Jeezus! Po' baby! Aunt Mattie sorry! Lord, what you an' Joshua gonna do now?"

Queen-Esther burst into tears of frustration and pointed at me. "You better act like you ain't heard nothin'! If'n you tell a livin' soul, I swear I'll kill you mahsef!"

I'd stood there dumbly up until now, but somehow I managed to find my voice. "I swear Paline—I mean Queen-Esther! I swear befo' God I'se nebber gonna tell a soul. You kin trust me. Honest Injun."

"You bettah be tellin' the troof or de massa gonna find his prime wench out in de hog feed!"

The three of us stood in the massa's kitchen trembling in fear. It seems Queen-Esther and her infant son were planning to steal away to a neighboring plantation whose owners were white abolitionists and who often helped escaping slaves on their journey north. These abolitionists were not only neighbors of the massa but had disagreed publicly about Massa's handling of his Negroes, while all the time they themselves were secretly known as a safe stop on the Underground Railroad.

I reassured Queen-Esther the best I could that I was trustworthy. Aunt Mattie apologized over and over again until Queen-Esther finally seemed to believe me. "We gots to leave tonight, Euleatha," she explained. "Josh gwine run off furst from the DuPont place an' be waitin' on me over to the Reynolds' plantation. I plans on gittin' there on time! You oughta know how bad it feels fer your man to git sold off from you. If'n Ben hadn't bin so fulla pride that he outboxed de massa's son, an' if'n de massa hadn't already wanted you fer hissef, den meybbe you'n Ben still be together. Prob'bly been done jumped de broom by now, but he gone alla dese years and that Genessa looking jes lak him an' missin' her eye." At the mention of Ma'Dear, I stiffened. "Fer sho'," Queen-Esther continued, "Massa woulda sold her off too if'n he could find somebody willin' to pay fer a one-eyed wench. If'n he kin kick out her eye an' blind yo' po' chile, don't thank jes 'cause you havin' his babies he won't sell dem 'way from you too."

By the time night fell and the three of us had cleaned the kitchen and scrubbed the floor, I had an ache in the center of my soul that could not be quelled. I'd learned from Aunt Mattie that Ma'Dear and the aunts slept down in the slave quarters with Miss Eliza, and that I was only permitted to see them once per day, right before taking Massa's supper out to the field. I felt this new Euleatha's pain. The pain of a mother who had no control over her children's lives. I felt Aunt Mattie's pain. The pain of a woman who cooked all day for whites yet never had enough to feed her own, 'cause whatever Massa and his sons didn't eat went to the hogs. But most of all I felt Queen-Esther's pain. The pain of a young woman who was willing to do whatever it took to keep her small family together. There was no way I'd even consider telling anyone what I knew, but a small part of me wished I could steal away too. Steal away back to Sweetwater where I'd find comfort in my papa and make peace with Peaches and Paline.

I lay in the darkness of the massa's room. A bed warmer is what Queen-Esther had called me, and I dreaded the moment the door would open and I'd find out firsthand just what that term meant. As tired as I was, I stayed awake for hours, tossing and turning upon the hard mat filled with sweet straw and hay. Sometime during the night I thought I heard Ma'Dear calling me. I thought I heard her raspy voice saying, *You don't know what all is in they hearts, Euleatha. What trials they done endured, 'cause you ain't learned yourself to wear they skin . . .* And I heard the grown-up voice of the baby that I had nestled earlier in my arms. *You gotta learn to understand folks so that you can love 'em better . . . you gots to learn folks before you can judge 'em. Gots to walk in their shoes, sleep in their beds, and live in their skin.* And then I heard Aunt Charming, *Hold on, Beanie . . . This ain't the end, baby. Brace yourself. 'Cause this ain't the end. You got a long road to travel, daughter. So save some of them tears for later, 'cause before it's all over you are sure to cry again.*

The tears came hard then as I realized how I'd arrived here. Why I was here. How my own intolerance and hatred had festered so deeply inside of me until it took a lesson of this magnitude to make me understand why I should love my people unconditionally. I didn't know what kind of woman this slave Euleatha was, but I knew how it felt to be treated wrongly just because of my skin tone. I'd always believed that those with lighter skin had lives of leisure, free from toil, but after the backbreaking work I'd done today I was beginning to see just how wrong I'd been. Here I lay looking for all the world like Peaches and Paline, yet my hands were cracked and bleeding, my feet so sore and swollen they felt ready to pop, and my soul lonely and in need of comfort.

As I sat there and sobbed and cried both for what I missed and for what was now my destiny, I was filled with understanding. The understanding of how we as a race of people had come to be so fractured and misaligned. My shoulders shook and I was filled to the top with the understanding of exactly what was stolen from us, from our psyches as well as from our souls.

How silly it was of black folks to polarize themselves along skin-tone lines. Didn't matter to the massa one damned whit. A nigger was a nigger was a nigger. He was the one who divided us up into groups of light and dark, house and field, and kept us biting and scratching at each other based on his divisions. He used us as weapons against one another to keep us fighting inward. That way we wouldn't have the time or the energy or the trust in one another to fight the external binds of slavery.

But as sad as it was, it seemed to me like almost every slave in America had bought Massa's lies lock, stock, and barrel, and it stood to reason that they'd passed these slave-owner beliefs onto their own children and their children after them. Fools! The dark slaves hated the light ones for supposedly living a life of luxury in the big house, and the lighter-skinned slaves secretly rejoiced in their lightness, fooled into believing they were somehow better than their kinfolks. Forgetting that no matter how light they were, they too were just slaves, and naïvely thanking the massa for making them look as far removed from African-black as they thought they could get.

Wasn't that the same way things were back in Sweetwater today?

Now I knew why Peaches had refused to nurse me. Why Paline had hated me so. I now knew why I hated her too. Why I felt somehow low before her light skin and hazel glare. Massa had told us that bold-faced lie and we'd both believed it. It was Massa's white blood that had poisoned us, weakened us, and neither of us had ever stopped to think that the very same blood ran through both of our veins, or that our outward expressions of race were just the by-product of a mixture of genes that dictated our hair texture and skin color but could never dictate our love. Euleatha Oyi-Yansi looked just like an African in America was supposed to look, and was lovely and beautiful when judged by the proper standards of African beauty. And after the horrors of American slavery, Euleatha Ray looked just like Africans in America were supposed to look too, and each was beautiful in her own right.

Chapter TEN

THE MOON WAS HIGH IN THE SKY when I awakened. I sat up with a start, pulling the scratchy blanket up to my neck as I peered through the darkness around me. I was alone in the massa's bedroom, my entire body screaming in agony from stiffened joints and bruised flesh. Muted voices had awakened me, and I pulled myself up to a shaky stand and tiptoed over to the window.

Outside under the glow of handheld lanterns, I saw several men on horseback. They were gathered in a circle around the massa, who seemed to be trying to settle a dispute of some sort. Cloaked in the shadows of the curtains, I counted the nightriders. There were fifteen all together. With deft fingers I slipped the latch off the window in order to hear more of the ruckus.

"I tell you, Sanders," one of the men was saying. He cradled a shotgun across his lap and I could hear the deadly tension in his voice. "My own driver told me! They is plannin' to run to Reynolds's farm at first light! I always knew he was a nigger lover, but come tomorrow we'll have every right to catch him an' skin him and his nigger-lovin' wife. Then you and DuPont can handle yo' property anyway y'all sees fit."

First light? I thought madly. Queen-Esther had said she was leaving when the moon started to slump in the sky! Maybe that would give her enough time to get to the Reynolds farm and then onward to safety, but I couldn't be sure. Even then this posse was sure to kill the white family they found living there.

I heard Massa Sanders say, "Ain't none of my nigras fool enough to run off, Sam. The last one tried it got his fingers cut off for boxing my boy, and then I put out his daughter's eye so she wouldn't have to watch her daddy burn up in that pyre. Smelled like dead nigger 'round here for two whole weeks." Massa laughed as he turned around to come back into the house. "Naw, ain't a one of my niggers plannin' no mess like that. They'd be too scared to run if'n I turned 'em loose and told 'em to go."

"Hold up, John." A burly man who held his rifle high on his shoulders guided his horse over to the massa. "Just in case you don't know yer niggers like you think you do, we'll be heading over to the Reynolds place in a while. You might wanna ride with us to make sure your property gits back to you in good condition."

I shrank back into the shadows as they continued to talk. My mind raced with the sure knowledge of Queen-Esther's and Josh's fate, even as I tried to give myself a million reasons why I should lie back down on my scratchy mat and wait for the massa to come in and have his way with me. As I pondered and planned, I told myself that helping Queen-Esther and betraying the massa would somehow fix him good for killing poor Ben and maiming Ma'Dear.

Shrug off your outer skin my child, and try on something new.
When the time is right to make your move,
you'll know just what to do.
The past always reveals the truth, so there's no need to fear it.
Be patient, loving, brave, and strong . . .
and if the hat fits you must wear it.

Ma'Dear had been right. I knew just what I had to do. Not only would I help Queen-Esther and Josh, I'd finally get to pay the massa back for all the terrible things he'd done to me. To Boxing Ben. To Ma'Dear. I reached beneath my mat and pulled on a tattered shawl, then took the hat from beneath the bed and pushed it down on my head. My bare feet were noiseless as I hurried down the steps to the kitchen and crept quietly out the back door.

The lame hound dog hobbled over to greet me as I made my way down the trail guided by the light of the moon. "Git, dawg!" I told him, but after gazing deeply into my eyes he licked at my feet and then followed on my heels. The slave shanties were completely dark as I hurriedly approached them. Crickets and light snoring were the only sounds in the night air as I crouched down low, trying to find a clue to which one was Queen-Esther's cabin.

The hound nipped at me playfully, then with his awkward gait ran over and sat down in front of a middle door on the right side of the row. He growled low in his throat.

"Dis one here?" I asked him, and he stuck out his tongue and panted in reply.

I knocked on the door once softly, and to my surprise it was snatched open and I was pulled inside. Queen-Esther clamped her hand over my mouth and I felt something sharp pressing at my throat. "Whatchoo d-d-doin' here, Euleatha?" Her eyes were wild in the darkness and I could smell the fear that washed over her in waves. Soft baby sounds came from a dark corner of the room, and despite the pressing knife I swallowed hard.

"They comin' fer ya', Esther." My words came out in a jumbled rush. "Massa DuPont's driver done told his massa bout you 'n' Josh meetin' up at the Reynolds place an' they gonna be there waitin' on you!"

She stared at me suspiciously. "How you know so much? You jes a nigger! Who bin talkin' to you?"

"I heard him! I stood right there in de windah and heard 'em talkin' 'bout killin' the Reynolds' and whuppin' you an' Josh!"

Queen-Esther eyed me for a long moment, and when she spoke again I could tell she believed me. "What I'se gonna do? Josh be waitin' on me. He won't leave wit'out me an' dis baby. He be right there when the pattyrollers come to kill Massa Reynolds, and he gonna get kilt too!"

I spoke without thinking. "I'll go warn him. I'll go to Massa Reynolds's house an' tell him to run an' hide until the white mens are gone!"

"You?" She snorted her disbelief. "Gal, you ain't wurf a damn! Ain't nebber picked a bale a cotton or toted a bale of hay in yo' life! How you gwine make it ober to the Reynolds place an' back by yo'sef?"

"I can do it, Queen-Esther!" You jes stay right here wit' de baby an' act like ever'thang is fine. I'll take care of de rest!" I pushed out of the cabin before she could protest any further and headed back up the dirt road, the lame hound dog trotting ahead of me leading the way.

At the crest of the hill I followed the hound and turned left, heading east toward the Reynolds farm. The grounds were well lit by the moon, still I was scared senseless as I picked my way through the thorny bushes and low, rambling underbrush. The hound stayed just ahead of me and despite his injured leg easily maneuvered his way around fallen trees and dangerous patches of brushwood and led me through the thickets by the safest means possible.

After an hour or so of sliding down spurs and climbing over dense ridges, sweat ran from my body in rivulets and my limp hair was plastered to the back of my neck. I stopped to rest a spell and took off my hat and used my shawl to wipe my face and chest. The air was moist and clammy and I could smell stagnant water nearby. Mosquitoes buzzed at my face, attracted by the stench of my perspiration as they searched for moisture in the corners of my eyes and in the recesses of my ears.

I removed my shawl and fanned at the insects a few times, and when the hound gave a low growl and resumed his irregular trot, I tossed the shawl to the ground and followed him. We ran through the black night as though the devil himself was chasing us. Every few hundred yards the hound would stop and turn to me, growl once, and then continue through the heavily wooded brush. I was completely exhausted when the hound stopped and perked up his ears. He whined softly, then walked back to me and grabbed the hem of my dress in his jaws. He yanked and pulled at me, and I had to duck low under a thistle bush to follow him. On the other side of the dense greenery, I stopped and stared. There was a high creek before us, and instinctively I knew we'd have to cross it if I meant to warn Josh in time.

The hound splashed in first, and I stepped in a little at a time. I'd never in life learned to swim, although Sweetwater had its fair share of creeks and man-made water holes. It just never seemed that important to me, seeing that I didn't have any friends, other than Cissy, to splash around with in the water.

I felt no fear of this water, though. Perhaps this Euleatha had swum before, because as I held the hound around his neck with one arm and pushed through the water with the other, my feet kicked right naturally and I had no problem holding my head up high and keeping my hat dry until we made it to the other side.

Standing on the far shore, the hound shook himself as I wrung water from the folds of my dress. I was still dripping when we took off running again, and although the gnats and mosquitoes came at me full force, the moisture actually felt good as it cooled my hot skin. We went another three miles or so, sometimes on the edge of the road, but mostly safely hidden in the tree line, before coming to a small house surrounded by several coops and barns. My bare feet were cut and torn, my arms and legs scratched and bleeding, but determination still pulsed in my heart.

According to Queen-Esther, Josh was hiding in the sty, and I followed the hound as both of our noses led us straight there. The animals were resting quietly, lying on their sides with their monumental bellies extended grotesquely. Patches of pink could be seen beneath the layers of brown mud, and the stench was so powerful even the hound abandoned me and trotted away.

"Josh," I whispered and stepped cautiousy through the stink, sucking mud of the pen. "Josh, it's me. Euleatha! There's gonna be trouble, Josh. Queen-Esther sunt me t'warn you that de massa an' his pattyrollers are on the way! Dey knows you plannin' t' meet here, an' dey's gonna kill Massa and Missus Reynolds if'n dey find ya!"

I almost didn't believe my eyes when one of the muddy pigs rolled over and sat upright. I squealed and tried to run from the pen as the dark form leaped up and grabbed me by the arm. Two bright eyes and a set of flashing white teeth emerged from the darkness of his mud-covered face as Josh squeezed my wrist and glared in fear. "Whatchoo talkin'? You sure, Euleatha? You sure? You bin t' see Esther an' my boy? You swear on yo' mama's grave you talkin' fer true?"

I nodded miserably as I held my breath against the odor rising from his body. "I swear, Josh. Dey be here soon. Us gotta go warn de Reynolds an' git back t' Massa Sanders's place befo' dey miss us!"

Josh climbed out of the pit of filth and pulled me out by the arm. He grabbed both of my shoulders and shook me hard. "Nebber mind 'bout dem Reynolds! I ain't getting' kilt ober no white folks, an' you betnot either!"

"But dem white folks was gonna hep you! Queen-Esther said dey been heppin' lots of slaves escape to de North!"

"Don't be no fool, Euleatha! If'n it come down 'tween us 'n' dem, then dey gots to go!"

Josh gave me one last pleading look, then took off running past the barns and into the dark woods. I had a mind to take off after him, but the hound limped over to me and tugged at the hem of my dress once more. He was pulling me toward the house, and I knew then what must be done. What I had to do.

The animals sensed our urgency as we ran toward the house. Chickens clucked and cows mooed, and horses stirred restlessly in their stalls. I started toward the back door, but then changed my mind and ran around to the front. I banged furiously on the door as I yelled out, "Massa Reynolds! Massa Reynolds! Please let me in!"

A light went on in an upstairs bedroom and a few seconds later an elderly white man came to the door. He was dressed in long underwear, and a nightcap, and held a candle in one shaking hand and a revolver, which was pointed straight at me, in the other.

"What do you want here? Why are you at my front door in the middle of the night?"

"Massa Reynolds," I panted. "I be Euleatha, from over to John Sanders's plantation—"

He snatched me inside and closed the door shut and locked it. "Gal, I knows who you is. I tried to help your Boxing Ben once."

"Well, Massa Sanders is on his way here to do to you what he did to Ben. He done found out Queen-Esther an' Josh was plannin' on runnin' an' you was plannin' to hep 'em. He wit 'bout fifteen other white men who is on horses and got rifles. They gwine come here at first light an' search yo' place lookin' fer runaways!"

His wrinkled face dropped. "Dear God! I've got to get out there and warn Josh!"

"Already did, Masssa. Josh done ran back to Massa DuPont's place an' Esther been warned t' stay put at Massa Sanders's."

He stared at me with a mixture of awe and respect. "You know, Euleatha. Not all white men are like John Sanders and Ken DuPont. More and more you will find there are decent, God-fearin' men who don't believe the Negro should have been taken out of Africa, let alone brought here to be tortured and worked as slaves." He put his gun down on the floor and pinched out the flame from his candle. We were engulfed in total darkness, except for what little moonlight filtered in from the windows.

"You have to get back to your plantation, Euleatha. You got to run. If they said first light, then that means they'll be here way before that." He led me through the dark house and around to the back door. "Slip out this way," he instructed me, "'cause when bad men come riding they always come to the front door." He gave my arm a small pat. "Thank you, Euleatha. The missus and I both thank you and we will be forever in your debt. Travel safe."

Massa Reynolds opened the door and I stepped out. The faithful hound was waiting by the back step, but as soon as I neared him he turned toward the house and began barking and howling and backing me toward the door. "What?" I whispered down at him. "What's wrong? Quit makin' all that noise fer you get us shot!"

But no sooner than the words were out of my mouth I saw something that made my blood run cold. Coming toward us mounted on horseback was Massa Sanders and the others. With his rifle pointed straight at me, Massa Sanders grinned, and for the first time I noticed how both of the aunts had his nose as well as his sloping forehead.

"Euleatha!" he sang out loudly. "Nigger wench! You s'pposed to be in my chambers warming my bed! Look at ya! All wet 'n' dirty an' smelling like a hog when you coulda been nice an' warm and pleasurin' me!"

He climbed down off his horse and slowly walked toward me. The lame little hound stepped between us and rushed at his feet. I cringed and cried out as Massa Sanders drew back his booted foot and swung it over and over full force into the dog's head. My heart splintered in pieces as my lame friend's lifeless body fell to the ground in a quiet heap.

Massa moved in closer, and every bit of me wanted to fall to my knees and cower before him, yet from somewhere deep within me I found the courage to stand before him and face him like a soldier. As he grabbed my dress and ripped it from my body, the men on horseback laughed and hooted and dismounted as they banged on the door and called Massa Reynolds out.

"Okay, boys," Massa Sanders told them as he led me, naked and trembling over to his horse. "Look like this nigger got here in time to warn them, so go easy on old Reynolds. If'n you don't find nothin' the law won't take too kindly to you killin' him. I'm gonna head back home and take care of a little bizness myself. I gots me a wench to whip an' I'm gonna enjoy every lick."

Massa pushed me toward the horse as I quaked in fear. He laughed wildly as he snatched my hat from my head and with an evil grin placed it atop his own mound of slick, oily hair. He found a long rope to tie around my neck and then climbed upon the mare and dug his heels into her sides. "You shoulda known better'n to try me. I'ma whip you jes like I whipped that big black buck of yourn! You ran all the way over here, huh, Euleatha? Well you's about to be a runnin' fool! Let's see jes how fast you kin run back!"

I cried out as he slapped the horse's flank and took off with me stumbling and tripping and running full speed to keep pace. My full breasts bounced against my body and my hair streamed out behind me as I galloped with that horse under the bright moonlit sky. I no longer felt the pain in my feet or the stiffness in my joints. My lungs heaved and strained and my heart hammered manically as it struggled to burst from my chest. The rope wrenched and bit into the soft skin of my neck, choking and bruising me as I ran and ran, and as the moon cried down and bathed me in her tears, I prayed to God that my suffering would not be in vain. I prayed that Queen-Esther and Josh would somehow make it to freedom. That Ma'Dear and the aunts would be taken care of. But most of all I prayed that the other Euleatha, the third one with the beautiful dark skin, would know the truth about her lighter-skinned ancestor. That she would understand that as I ran along beside that jet-black mare with the white man straddling her back and laughing out his glee, it didn't make a bit of difference to him whether my skin was light or dark.

I was still his nigger.

The sun was peeking over the horizon as he towed me onto the plantation. I was exhausted and felt near death. It had taken us less than an hour to return on a trip that had taken me almost three hours to make. There'd been several times during the journey when I'd tripped and fallen and was dragged along on my face and knees, ripping and tearing the skin away from my bloody flesh and cutting off my breath as Massa laughed above me and urged the horse on. I'd nearly drowned when crossing the creek, holding tightly to the rope as the dark water swirled around my head and seeped into my mouth and nose.

The field hands were just gathering their tools and preparing to begin another day of toiling in the fields when Massa shouted out to one of them to bring him a whip. "Boy! Fetch me a whip and go bring Big Bear in from the fields! But first make sure you get my stable boy out here to water my hoss and rub him down good wit some liniment!" His laughter was high pitched as he pushed my hat back on his head and called out to his sons who had rushed from the house upon hearing his voice.

"Bring every last nigger up here right now!" he ordered. "We gonna have us a good ole time today! I'm gonna give this ungrateful wench the same kinda lickin' I gave her buck. See how brave she be then!"

I lay in the dirt as Massa prepared to whip me. Wavering in and out of consciousness, I looked around as if in a dream, and I saw scores of slaves gathered around with fear in their eyes, the women with horrific pity and the men with gut-wrenching helplessness. I saw Queen-Esther crying softly and clutching her infant to her breast. I was grateful when Aunt Mattie braved the massa's wrath and pushed through the crowd to wrap my nakedness in a thin shawl, but my heart nearly stopped cold when I saw the gaze of my child upon me, her brown face an impassive unreadable mask as she held on tightly to her younger sisters and stared at me from the depths of her one seeing eye.

Massa ordered two young field hands to string me up on his whipping pole and hang me by the wrists. "Give her twenty-five!" he commanded Big Bear, and a shocked murmur rose from the crowd in alarm.

"But Massa," Big Bear protested, his muscles bulging from every crevice of his overalls. His face was kind and several of his front teeth were missing. Big Bear was simple, but he had a good soul. Everyone knew he hated this job, but since he was the biggest and the strongest on the plantation, Massa said the job belonged to him. "Nobody nebber got more'n twenty befo' an' I kilt that buck befo' you wuz through countin' to ten!"

Massa tried to clamp a hand on Big Bear's massive arm. "Do it, boy! And do it good, or I'll have yer black ass whupped alongside of her!"

Big Bear wrapped the horsewhip around his thick fists as tears welled up in his eyes. "I'se sorry, Miss Euleatha," he moaned. "Lawd knows I'se sorry."

"One!"

The first lash cut me so deeply and stung so badly that it restored me to full consciousness. It felt like someone had sent hot lightning shooting through my back, and every fiber of my being responded to the horrific pain.

"Two!"

The second stroke snaked around to the opposite side of my back and crisscrossed the first lashing, ripping deeply as it tore away my tender flesh. The scream that ripped from me was harsh and grating, the pain indescribable as my heart hammered in my ears and acrid bile rushed into my throat and spilled from the corners of my mouth.

"Three!"

The third blow cut me to the bone, and my body systems retreated into shock. A cry went up from the slaves as the air was knocked from my lungs and dark rivulets of blood poured down my buttocks and dripped like midnight tears into the dew-wet grass below. There were no more screams left in me. I could only pant shallowly through my cracked and bloodied lips as the pain reverberated and completely engulfed my senses.

"Four!"

The next lash was far worse than all the rest. I heard Big Bear cry out and moan, but not a sound escaped me as my bowels let go and my body twitched and convulsed upon the rope.

"Fi—"

I heard the air rush past as Big Bear drew back his arm and prepared to let his whip fly, but then suddenly I realized that Massa had hesitated in giving the command.

"Cut her down, Big Bear," Massa commanded instead. "Ain't worth much as it is! Sure to be worth even less if'n she dead."

Too late, Massa. I felt myself leaving this world and all I wanted was a cool drink of water. I hit the sweet grass with a hard thud, and my eyes flew open on impact. I made out the form of the massa as he stood towering above me, and through the haze of my pain I could have sworn my fedora glowed like a halo upon his head.

Some good soul had mercy on me and doused my face with a bucket of cool water, and Aunt Mattie rushed over and gathered my head in her arms. She rocked me like a baby as she whispered into my ear in perfect English. "You've earned your title, Euleatha the Brave, and because of that you've given Euleatha the Strong a new stance on life and another opportunity to live well."

"Fix her up, Aunt Mattie." Massa's voice stung my ears. "I want her back to work in three days' time."

I knew Aunt Mattie would fix me up real nice. No stranger would ever touch me and not a drop of blood would be drained from my body. I'd be laid out and put in the ground on the same day. Through the slits of my eyes, I peered past Aunt Mattie's shoulder and up at Massa Sanders. My descendants would carry this man's name as well as his blood, and I prayed it wouldn't sully them too badly or prevent them from loving and being loved by their own kind.

"Throw some more water over that gal," I heard Massa insist, and I winced as the blood poured from the pyre that blazed upon my back and seeped into the fertile North Carolina soil. I peered up at him, and for a final moment our eyes locked. As the last of my breath escaped me I felt a small glow of happiness as I watched a string of colorful beads dance from the band of the old brown hat, but then Massa reached up and cast the fedora down upon my face, cloaking my hot skin in cool, merciful shade and suddenly I felt nothing at all.

Epilogue

I AWOKE WITH A BURNING THIRST; my throat scraped raw, my head pounding furiously. I opened my eyes slowly, and somehow I was not surprised by what I saw. She sat on a wicker chair in the far corner of the room, a kiss of sunlight streaming in over her shoulder. She wore a loose-fitting dress in shades of soft pastel that were at once pleasing to my eyes and soothing to my spirit.

The old brown fedora that had once belonged to Boxing Ben sat atop the dresser, its brim turned upward, a thin ream of twine looped through its black band. The beads Cissy had given me dangled down the side, the last few resting peacefully on the polished surface of the dresser.

My eyes returned to hers and she looked at me expectantly, as though she'd been waiting for quite some time.

Ma'Dear can't leave here proper until your lesson done been learned.

I'd held up her progress long enough, and she watched patiently as I struggled to speak. I reached over and with shaking hands took a full water glass from my night table. I gulped greedily, the cool water rushing past my throat and filling my cheeks until it dribbled from both corners of my mouth and dripped from my chin.

A few seconds later I managed to speak. "How long?" I asked from a mouth that still felt worse than the Mojave.

"Three days."

I hated to ask but I had to know. "And you?"

She smiled and her love washed over me like an ancient river. "I got folks waitin' on me. Your job ain't yet done here Euleatha the Strong, but now your heart is free to get working on it."

She rose from her seat and drifted over to my side. Then she bent at the waist and placed her cool lips upon my forehead before gathering me into her lemon-scented arms one last time.

My love will keep you until we meet again.

I nodded and closed my eyes, reveling in her love. When I opened them the sun had dipped much lower on the horizon and shadows had gathered in the empty room. I sat up shakily, then swung my legs around and cautiously tested them on the floor. Blood rushed to my toes and set them to tingling, and I wiggled them gently back and forth as I gazed around the familiarity of my bedroom.

The chair where I'd seen Ma'Dear was now empty. Grasping the bed frame for support, I staggered over to the mirror and lowered my nightdress. The thin cloth stuck lightly to bits of healing skin, and pain still radiated outward from my mending wounds. As I turned around and dipped my shoulder just a few inches, the looking glass confirmed my suspicions. There on my back, crisscrossed in erratic patterns were the beginnings of the new skin I'd earned. Light patches of brown, subtle hints of yellow, and even lighter patches of beige were growing out of what used to be a horizon of almost jet-black. One day there'd be other colors there, I knew. Perhaps red and maybe even white.

I smiled at my dark face in the mirror and straightened my

clothing; thankful for the lessons I'd learned through the sacrifices of that other brave Euleatha. As sounds from Chez LeMoyne drifted up to the attic, I slipped a faded blue duster over my white nightgown and smoothed down my thick, coarse hair. I had some explaining to do, I knew.

And perhaps some apologizing too.

Things in our family weren't going to change overnight, and it wasn't only me who'd been wrong in my thinking, but I prayed they would be as willing to try as I was. Besides, real change always begins within. In your own heart. In your own skin. So I was heading downstairs. Heading downstairs to kiss my papa, hug my brother, and talk to my mother and sister. Because now that I'd learned how to live in their skin, it was time to teach them how it felt to live in mine.

DESIREE
New Birth
COOPER

Chapter ONE

LETTIE THREW THE SOPPING RAG into the dingy bath-water swirling white with disinfecting tub and tile cleanser. She sat back on her heels, wiped her wide, dark face with the back of her hands, and huffed as she pushed herself up. Beads of sweat glistened against the smooth ebony of her skin, sending the roots of her short, comb-straightened hair reverting back to their natural state.

Was this another hot flash, or just her temper rising? She stood looking down into the murky little pond for a moment, hands on her hips, disgusted.

"Have mercy," she breathed.

She was willing to clean up behind folks—to slosh her hands in the gray water that had been their bathtub rings, to lean over their yeasty toilet bowls, to scrape the hardened food from their dishes. But they ought to have the decency to make sure she didn't have to wallow in their filth, like a sow.

This was the third week she'd come to clean at Miz Catherine's only to find the vacuum cleaner still wasn't fixed (was she expected to sweep the entire upstairs and downstairs?), there was no Windex in the maid's closet (despite the fact that Lettie had put it on the shopping list each week), and the master bathtub still didn't drain. How hard could it be to call a plumber?

"I should have known better than to work for a redbone," she muttered. "Worked for Miz 'Lizabeth for fifteen years and that white lady never put me through nothing like this. These redbones 'round here pretending they have money when they're one paycheck away from the poorhouse just like the rest of us." Soon it would be time to find another job, she thought. Miz Catherine and her hinckty ways would surely wear her out.

Lettie, I want you to hand-wash my sweaters today. Lettie, use beeswax and orange oil on the paneling. That spray stuff just makes the wood look dull. Lettie, wash that box of summer nautical dishes in storage. We're using them for our boat race party on Saturday.

Not to mention the sly way she poked into Lettie's personal business. Like the day Lettie had come for an interview a few weeks earlier, Miz Catherine had all but given her an IQ test. Lettie was still bristling at the humiliating memory.

"Now, Lettie, I need you to write down a few things," Miz Catherine had said, flipping her long, bone-straight hair away from her face.

Lettie had taken the notepad quietly, noticing how Miz Catherine eyed her pencil grip before beginning to dictate slowly, her thin, glimmering garnet lips forming the words carefully, as if Lettie was mentally retarded or hard of hearing.

"Every other Monday, I need you to flip the mattress in the master bedroom," Miz Catherine pronounced. "Keep the dust cover clean—my husband has terrible allergies."

Miz Catherine's eyes yearned toward the paper as Lettie wrote down her tasks. She actually nodded when Lettie spelled "allergies" correctly.

She's trying to see if I can read and write! Lettie realized with amazement. As if a maid couldn't possibly have gone to college, couldn't possibly know the difference between a chifforobe and an armoire.

"Miz Catherine." Lettie put down the pencil abruptly. "If it's all the same to you, you can make out your list each week and leave it for me. I'll READ it and check off the things as I do them. I can also WRITE you a note listing the supplies I'll need as they run low."

Miz Catherine stared at her wide-eyed, almost fearfully. Her beige cheeks pinked and she took a tiny step backward. "Well, Lettie, you don't need to get hostile. I was just trying to . . . just trying . . . Well, I tell you what. I'll just leave you a list if that's okay with you," she said, spoon-feeding Lettie back her own suggestion.

"I'll pay you every two weeks," Miz Catherine continued, turning away as her cell phone rang. She reached into her suit pocket and retrieved it in the middle of the first bar of "Für Elise."

"Hello?" she asked, her voice syrupy sweet. She turned back and winked, then raised a manicured index finger at Lettie that said, "I'll be with you in a minute."

Lettie shifted her weight to her good leg and stood impatiently.

"Well, Sheila," she heard her employer snap, "I told you I'd be late today. I'm handling a domestic issue this morning. I'll be there in an hour, so just take care of it, would you please?"

Miz Catherine flipped the phone closed and smiled again. "Okay, where were we? Oh, yes, I'll leave the cash on the kitchen table. You do prefer cash don't you, so it won't interfere with your food stamps or anything?"

Lettie had stared at the woman in disbelief. She didn't get food stamps, nor had she ever been on welfare. She'd worked hard since her husband died, and she paid her own way. But when her employment agency, Baker Temporary Services, had closed, she'd found herself out of a job cleaning offices at night. Unfortunately, she needed this job with the Rollinses and she wasn't about to let her mouth rob her of it before she even got started.

"Cash would be fine," she'd told her, looking down at her feet to hide the fury in her eyes.

Miz Catherine smiled. "Good. Well, I think that's it. You can get started today if you like—unless you have to go home to make some arrangements with your grandchildren. How many do you have anyway?" Miz Catherine held her hands cupped in a one-person handshake in front of her tiny breasts, her elbows out, like a kindergarten teacher waiting for a child to recite her ABCs.

"My son is just twenty-two," Lettie said, wondering why Miz Catherine would presume she was already a grandmother at forty-five. "He doesn't have any kids. He's in Kansas."

"Oh? That's unusual . . ." Miz Catherine furrowed her brow. "No grandchildren? Well, lucky for you your son didn't leave you with loose children running all over Black Bottom. Good then. You can start today."

Bristling at the memory, Lettie gave the tub another twirl with the brush, grateful that she rarely had to face Miz Catherine when she started her day. Usually it was Mr. Rollins who was home reading the paper when Lettie arrived at eight, Miz Catherine already at work for an hour by then.

"Have a nice day, Lettie," Mr. Rollins would say each morning, a bright smile flashing over a face smooth and creamy as a café latte. "Catherine put your money on the table next to the list." He'd say "the list" as one would say "the Declaration of Independence," hinting that he didn't take things quite as seriously as his wife. "You'll particularly like item one: 'Wash the globes of the wall sconces today—and let them air-dry so that there won't be any water spots.'"

His cynicism made Lettie want to laugh, but she resisted. You could never play one employer against the other. And she knew that, in the end, it would be Miz Catherine who decided whether Lettie would stay or go.

"I'll do my best," she'd tell him seriously. "You have a good day, Mr. Rollins."

There were things you could tell about people after you worked for them for a while. Things they'd never want you to know. Like how often they had sex by the condition of the bedsheets. Like whether one of them had hemorrhoids—Tucks and Preparation H left on the bathroom counter. Like when they were in financial trouble by the number of automated phone calls left on the answering machine during the day.

As she stood in the bathroom looking over the drain that was still clogged after three months' worth of Mr. Plumber, Lettie knew there was trouble in the Rollins household. For one, Miz Catherine would come in from work these days and barely say "hello" before going straight to her bedroom and closing the door. She didn't even stop to inspect Lettie's work, to enjoy the pleasure of dismissing her like a boot camp drill sergeant.

Medications crowded the nightstand on Miz Catherine's side of the bed, some in little pink compacts with pills inside set in rows for the days of the week. Medicine for female trouble, for sure. The relationship seemed to be tense between Miz Catherine and Mr. Rollins. For several weeks, Lettie had arrived in the morning to find a comforter and his slippers by the sofa, his side of the master bed barely ruffled. And these days he was always gone before she arrived in the morning.

Miz Catherine, never very neat, had become a slob. Most women she'd worked for made an effort to "straighten up" before the maid came, and Miz Catherine had been no exception—at first. In the beginning the house would be generally picked up each time Lettie arrived, leaving Lettie to take care of the deep cleaning. But lately Miz Catherine's clothes were strewn through the house, her makeup lay open as if she'd jumped up and left in the middle of her morning regimen. Chocolate cookie crumbs lay in her sheets like pepper on grits.

And hair. Hair everywhere. At first when the light brown, curly strands began to fill the vacuum cleaner bag, Lettie thought the Rollinses had bought a dog. But no animals were allowed at River-house East—especially not in the penthouse apartments. Then she noticed hair in the lint trap in the dryer. Fluffy balls of the strands even lived beneath the dressing table and on the bathroom floor.

The wispy spiders of Miz Catherine's hair at once repulsed and angered Lettie. Is that what it was like to live with a hazel-eyed, blow-haired redbone? Like having a dog? Did all of them leave pieces of themselves everywhere like they owned the world?

"I'll bet that's what's been clogging the drain," Lettie mumbled to herself, marching out of the bathroom and into the walk-in closet. She yanked down one of the countless wire dry cleaner hangers and went back to the bathroom, her thick hands untwisting the neck of the wire as she walked.

She knelt down as if she was about to call Jesus but instead thrust the crook of the hanger down into the narrow throat of the drain. She plunged and fished, her eyes rolling skyward in concentration, her fingers judging the amount of resistance on the other end of the wire. Suddenly, she yanked the wire up, and with it came a bubble, then a slurp.

The water began swirling down the drain, still a bit slowly, but at least today it was flowing. Grunting, she stood holding a clot of long hair, slick and gently curling on the end of the hanger. It was the kind of hair she'd seen circling the crowns of mahogany babies at birth. The kind of hair many black women start with but not many get to keep.

"Don't matter what grade it is," Lettie lectured Miz Catherine in her absence. "If it gets wet, it's gonna go back. You need to learn how to wash your hair in the kitchen sink the way your mama should have taught you."

She walked over to the garbage can grimacing, holding the glob of hair in front of her as if it were alive.

Catherine examined the documents before her on the desk.

"Sheila?" she called from her office to her secretary sitting just outside. "I thought you were going to put these closing documents in a binder for me!"

"Oh, Mrs. Rollins, I'm sorry," said Sheila, rounding the corner. "Do you want me to do that now or after I finish typing the Mixco loan agreement?"

Catherine eyed her secretary critically. "I want you to do them both. You promised me you'd stay late and get it done yesterday."

"Well, I couldn't get a ride and the last bus left at seven . . ."

"Okay, okay, never mind." Catherine waved. "Just get that loan agreement done. You can bind these documents on your lunch hour."

Sheila nodded, on the verge of tears. Catherine followed her to the door and closed it.

Sheila wasn't working out. She'd been warned about hiring a black secretary, especially one who wore those matted, filthy dreadlocks. But what was she to do? Her old secretary, Mrs. Woolingham, had retired suddenly, leaving her in the lurch. She'd been infuriated when the office manager suggested she hire Sheila Hunt, a big-behind, stupid-looking, dark-skinned girl who hung her thick lips open when she was concentrating. And those beastly dreads!

It was a test, Catherine knew. Hawkins & Simons had never hired a black secretary in its 130-year history. Catherine had been only its second black lawyer. None of the other white attorneys would have put up with a black secretary and Catherine knew that they'd foisted Sheila on her for just that reason.

It pissed her off that she would be expected to take on a substandard secretary for the sake of political correctness. And couldn't they have found a more acceptable black woman somewhere in Detroit who at least *looked* professional?

She had to admit that Sheila had been a quick study and seemed willing enough to work. But she always had "personal" problems. Her sister was pregnant again and she had to help take care of her other three nieces. Her brother was arrested for drugs and she had to go to court. Her husband finally got a job and he needed the car to get to work because no buses ran out to the suburbs.

Well, Sheila and her kind weren't the only ones with personal problems.

Catherine walked to the window and looked out. Seemed like those welfare queens on the east side were kicking out babies every time they sneezed. And here she and Chas were—successful, married, longing for children—and she couldn't get pregnant.

It had been a year of doctors, of procedures, of drugs. She was losing her hair, getting acne, walking the hormonal tightrope between menstruation and a mustache, and still, no baby.

But you didn't see her bringing *her* problems to work, did you? Catherine shook her head. It wasn't easy keeping up appearances, maintaining professionalism when most times she felt like her life was crumbling, her womanhood fizzling.

If she could function under that kind of pressure, why couldn't Sheila get it together? Was she supposed to put up with Sheila's excuses just because they both were black women? And why didn't Sheila do something about her appearance? Her thrusting breasts, those tight skirts pulling across her full hips? Why didn't she do something with that embarrassing matted hair? Didn't she know she was reflecting poorly on the both of them?

The phone rang, jogging Catherine out of her thoughts.

"Hawkins & Simons, Catherine Rollins speaking," she said robotically.

"Ms. Rollins? You don't know me, but I heard you on the radio last week, on the *Don Franklin Show*?"

"Oh, yes!" said Catherine, flattered that a listener of one of the top-rated talk radio shows in the market had been impressed enough to call her. "How can I help you?"

"I'm Bob Freeman over at Hunter Realty. We're doing a project on the east side and we need an attorney with your experience."

Catherine sat down at her desk and crossed her legs primly. She had built a good reputation as a real estate lawyer, especially adept at assembling land for large new developments in the city. Don Franklin had talked to her on his show about the latest commercial developments springing up all over the city of Detroit.

"Well, I'm sure I can be of service," she said proudly. "What seems to be the issue?"

"The community isn't really in favor of the project. It's for a light-industrial park near Gabriel and St. Vick's. They're threatening to make this a political issue. We need a lawyer like you—you know, one who understands the community—to help smooth the way for the development."

Catherine was silent. A lawyer who knew "the community"? He meant a black lawyer, that's what he meant. Catherine was miffed. She was careful about her diction. How could he tell she was black from listening to her on the radio?

"Well, Mr. Freeman, is it?" she said with measured politeness. "I'm not sure I'm the woman for the job. If it's a good real estate lawyer you need, I know I can be of help. But if its help quelling a bunch of angry black people from the hood, well, maybe you'd be better off meeting with the NAACP. Why don't you think about it and let me know?"

She hung up, her heart racing. She hadn't gotten this far by being the liaison to the black community! She was the lawyer white people wanted on their side because she was good. She'd overcome too many obstacles and worked too hard to become somebody's nigger lawyer now.

Chapter TWO

WHEN THE FRONT DOOR OPENED, both Lettie and Catherine were startled.

"Oh! Miz Catherine, I didn't expect you home so early today!" Lettie exclaimed.

Catherine slumped against the door as she closed her eyes and held her breast. "My God, Lettie, you scared me to death. It's so dark in here and there you were standing there blending in with the shadows—I thought you were going to attack me!"

Lettie laughed too loudly, thinking Miz Catherine was joking. But when she flipped the switch of the crystal chandelier in the foyer, she could tell by the woman's stiff posture and heavy breathing that she wasn't.

"Well, I apologize," Lettie said, bristling. "I had just cut off all the lights in the house like I usually do, and was about to turn on the foyer light when you came in. I'm sorry I startled you."

"My God," said Catherine, calming down. "Living in the city is so dangerous, I get jumpy. You know, Chas is the one who wanted to live downtown. I was pushing for the suburbs—somewhere that's safer, more shops, nice restaurants . . ."

Lettie smiled tightly. "Yeah, somewhere far away from us," she said.

Catherine raised her chin. "You know as well as I do that when too many blacks move in things just start going all to hell. You can't possibly tell me you feel safe in your neighborhood."

"No, ma'am. I don't feel safe all the time," Lettie said. "But I'm not afraid of everyone just because they're black."

The two women stood glaring at each other.

"Lettie, I work too hard to put up with this type of crap from the maid," Catherine seethed. "You've got a big chip on your shoulder, miss. You're always so hostile, so damned militant. I'm just saying that I want what everyone sane wants: a decent, safe place to live. And the fact that I have to walk around this town feeling like some stink, big-lipped, charcoal-black monster is going to leap out of the shadows any minute and knock me down is a ridiculous way to have to live. Maybe *you're* used to living like that, but *I'm* not."

Lettie thought. She thought for a long time. She could give this high-yellow, Casper-looking witch a piece of her mind, or she could skip it and keep her job.

"I've got to go," said Lettie, pulling on her jacket. "If you'd prefer, I can start keeping all your lights on when I leave. That way, you won't even have your own black shadow to fear when you come home."

She brushed by Miz Catherine and left her standing in the door, mouth agape.

⌒

Lettie pulled her jacket tighter around her as she waited for the Jefferson bus. The air was still blustery even for April.

She thought about moving closer to the Plexiglas bus shelter, but it reeked of urine and malt liquor. Anyway, a man stood there smoking a cigarette, leaning heavily against the structure. His eyes, cloudy and red, met hers for a brief moment before she looked away. He's high, she thought, pulling her purse closer.

A younger man sat wide legged in the middle of the bench, his pants hanging loosely around his legs. He wore an expensive leather jacket bearing the black-and-silver insignia of the Oakland Raiders—a one-eyed pirate and crisscrossed sabers. The boy's head nodded rhythmically underneath a tight black skullcap as he listened to music from an iPod. For as long as the music played, he was in another world.

Lettie pulled her own hat over the tight curl of her spongy, thick hair and looked down the busy city street for the bus. If the bus didn't get here too late, she'd be home at least by seven. I guess that's the only good thing I can say about Miz Catherine coming home early today, Lettie thought. Green-eyed banshee, that's what she is. Lettie snorted and thrust her hands deeper into her pockets as she visualized her employer. A pure-D witch.

Lettie knew this job was costing her more than her pride. Her blood pressure was up and Miz Catherine had a lot to do with it. On the mornings when she had to go to the Rollinses', she could barely lift herself from bed she was so filled with dread. What new humiliations awaited her? Would she be expected to hand-wash that woman's nylons? Rinse dried saliva from the sink? Soak her bright lipstick from the cups and silverware?

Funny, she'd done all those things for white women a million times. But with Miz Catherine the chores took on a different meaning. Somehow she'd expected more from a black family. Maybe an apology that their fair skin and whitewashed accents had bought them the success that eluded other black people who were as dark as molasses on a wooden spoon. Not a formal apology, but a different level of kindness to acknowledge their common history.

But a few drops of white blood, white education, and white culture had bleached all memories of mutual suffering from the minds of black people like Miz Catherine. They were alien to their own nature, afraid of the dark rims circling the ears of their newborns, ashamed at the green-blue patches of pigment that stained the behinds of their sandy-haired children. Her mother had been right. Redbones couldn't be trusted. They would just as soon cut you down as lift you up. Miz Catherine had to be watched.

As the bus finally pulled up, the two waiting men pushed their way in front of Lettie. She stood back and allowed them to board, then lifted her leg carefully, placing her good foot first, then easing the arthritic one onto the high step.

"Afternoon," she said to the driver out of habit as she put her token in the slot.

The driver did not speak back.

⁓

Lettie got off the elevator of her east side apartment building and walked toward 5D. Two children, their bushy hair full of lint and their skinny legs and arms naked, ran by as they played with a plastic truck.

"Hey Mama Lettie!" they called, nearly tripping her in the tangle of their legs.

"Hey, LaShon, Lamont, where's your mama? Get inside and put some clothes on, it's cold out in the hallway . . ."

"She ain't home," said the oldest, a six-year-old who was used to watching his five-year-old brother whenever their mother stepped out. "She over at Niqua's."

Lettie paused. She was too tired today to take the boys in and feed them like she sometimes did. She put the key in her door, but feeling guilty, called back to them as she went inside.

"Well, you knock on my door if you need anything, hear?" she said. The boys nodded but kept playing.

Lettie dead-bolted the door behind her. Putting down her bag, she trudged to the sofa and plopped down heavily on the worn-out springs. Sighing, she thumbed through her mail.

"Gas bill, light bill, water bill," she mumbled. She read the outside of the brown envelope— "You may have already won $10 million!"—then eyed the stack of unread magazines over by the television stand.

"Humph," she said. "I wish they'd stop sending me this stuff."

The last envelope was a white one, with tall, looping handwriting scrawled on the front. "Nicholas Greene, 34904857, Leavenworth Correctional Facility, Leavenworth, Kansas."

She sucked in her breath and pressed the envelope against her heart.

"Nick," she whispered.

She placed the envelope on the coffee table and stood, suddenly euphoric. She opened the refrigerator door and bent down to peek in. A quart of whole milk, a block of Velveeta, a packet of fatback (even though the doctor told her to stay away from pork), eggs, a dish of macaroni and cheese, and some chicken left over from lunch at church last Sunday.

She frowned; not much for a meal. She pulled out the milk and got some flour from the cabinet. Outside, she could still hear the boys playing in the hallway, bumping against the walls with their truck. Maybe she'd fix them a little something after all. She hummed "Precious Lord" as her hands nimbly worked the flour into dough. She pinched off pieces and rounded them in her palm. Placing them on a greased cookie sheet, she popped them in the oven, while stirring grits into lightly salted, boiling water.

In minutes, the biscuits were golden, filling the apartment with their buttery aroma.

"Here, boys!" she said, opening her apartment door. "Want some hot biscuits? I don't have jelly for you today, want some cheese on them?"

The boys dashed to her door and lined up for a biscuit stuffed with a slice of melting Velveeta. They eagerly crammed them in their mouths, and without even a "thank you," they were back out in the hall, tumbling on the floor.

Lettie shook her head. Inside, the teakettle whistled. She gently shut the door, then made herself a cup of instant coffee. She placed the teacup and matching saucer on the special place mat, the yellow, flowered linen one she'd found at Goodwill along with a single bone china teacup and saucer. This would be a special dinner. Nick would be joining her tonight.

She piled her plate with grits and eggs and added two biscuits. She got a glass from the cupboard, not even minding that she thought she saw a bug scamper as she opened the cabinet door. She rinsed the glass, filled it with water, and placed it next to her coffee. Against it, she propped the letter from Nick.

She sat, eating slowly, mixing margarine into her grits, gazing at her son's writing on the envelope. Was he okay? Was he keeping up with his studies? Any news from his lawyer? When would he be home? She smiled, thinking how beautiful he'd become, tall and dark like his father, his eyes a magnetic deep sienna, his lips a full, perfect Cupid's bow. How he'd done so well in high school that local colleges wanted to give him a scholarship. How he'd taken his love of music after his father—at eighteen, his voice had become deep and full of rich tones. He had even auditioned for a place on the Brazeal Dennard Chorale so that he could continue learning classical music and Negro spirituals. The chorale had been holding him a spot in their summer program when . . .

Lettie looked away from the letter, her nose stinging with the salty burn of tears. She put a tiny forkful of food into her mouth, having suddenly lost her hankering for the creamy grits and flaky biscuits. Next door, a man's voice shouted in anger, something about "*my* money" and "*my* house." The ceiling above her throbbed with bass, as if she were living inside a giant heart, the continuous vibration of rap music the heartbeat.

She had expected more from life, to be sure, but not much more. Her place was clean, she had enough to eat, and had a good circle of friends at Greater Zion.

But for her children, her hopes had been higher. She and Horace had married young in rural Michigan. Lettie fell in love the moment she heard him singing as he delivered the mail. They'd come to the city in the seventies when Horace got a transfer from the post office. They'd scraped together a decent life—a house on the east side, a ragged car, and even an upright piano.

They'd waited to have kids. Lettie wanted to go to college to become a teacher. Horace agreed. She eventually enrolled in college full-time and worked nights cleaning office buildings. They rarely saw each other except on weekends when they'd go to the Enjoy to eat, or to Baker's Keyboard Lounge to listen to jazz.

But Lettie started her third year of college with a queasiness that wouldn't go away. She knew immediately she was pregnant. She waited a month—then two—to tell her husband, afraid of his reaction.

"Horace," she'd said one Friday night after she got home from work. "I don't feel much like going out tonight. I'm pregnant."

He'd looked at her, his brow wrinkled. Then his face broke into a wide smile and he'd said, "Well, it's about time. I thought I was shootin' blanks."

First Lois, then Nicholas two years later. At twenty-three, Lettie dropped out of school and exchanged her dreams of becoming an English teacher for cloth diapers and midnight feedings. Horace took a second job playing the piano at nightclubs. How could she have known that those years, however hard, would turn out to be the best of her life?

Lettie got up from the table and stood in front of the photos on the television. She picked up a picture of her daughter at six, her two front teeth missing, her braids sticking out from under a straw hat. Lois had been their smartest. She used to sleep on the couch waiting for her daddy to come home from his gigs. No matter how late it was, she'd wake up at the sound of his key in the lock and go running into his arms.

"Who loves you most?" he'd ask, planting kisses on her brown face.

She'd hug him tightly, inhaling the exciting aroma of booze and cigars. "My daddy!" she'd squeal as he blew kisses beneath her neck.

Horace died in '85, caught in the crossfire at a local bar. After that, Lois stopped waiting up at night for her dad and instead took to the streets searching for him. She was attracted to the fast life, and Lettie stayed up many nights by the window waiting for her daughter to come home. In the end, Lois died in 2001, a crack addict and a prostitute.

"Don't worry, Ma," Nicholas would say barely two years later as he, too, started hanging out late on weekends. "I'll be back. I'm just chillin' with Shay Shay."

Lettie didn't trust Shay Shay, a biracial boy so light his skin was nearly translucent. He had shoulder-length, straight wheat-colored hair, and Lettie was disturbed by his shifty eyes and the cruel curl to his thin lips. Her Nick was levelheaded and Lettie knew he had no stomach for trouble. Still, trouble was hard to avoid. Detroit had become a meaner place since the days she and Horace had bought their home in the area called Black Bottom. A depression in the eighties, along with a crack epidemic, plagued the neighborhoods with gangs and violence. Whole communities were abandoned, including Lettie's, and the houses left behind fell victim to scavengers and arsonists.

Lettie prayed that Nick's interest in music would keep him away from trash like his half-white friend and on the straight and narrow, but inevitably trouble came. The knock on the door from police, the hours at the precinct, the cries from her son that he was riding with Shay Shay when they'd been stopped at the Canadian border and searched. That gun and the crack cocaine in the car was not his, it was Shay Shay's. He hadn't even known what was in the glove compartment. But Shay Shay had fingered Nick, and the white cops believed the white-looking boy over Nick, who was as tall and dark as the vinyl on his dad's old albums. Lettie had mortgaged her home for a lawyer, and still her son received fifteen to thirty years in federal prison.

Lettie put down the photos and went back to the kitchen table. She pressed Nick's letter to her lips, then opened it.

Dear Mom—

You would be proud of me. I got another promotion. Now I manage the kitchen at dinnertime and on weekends. I have a new cell mate. Would you believe he's from Chicago? He's in for credit card fraud, so it's better than having to bunk with the guy who is in for murder one. I'm thankful.

Just finished Cry, the Beloved Country. *Seems like none of us will ever get over the white man's game. Divide and conquer. We can't get over cause we're too busy at each other's throats. But the weird thing is that no matter what, we are all alike in here. Faces light, dark, and hopeless. Even guys that look like Shay Shay.*

Well, enough of that. Thanks for the money—it comes in handy when I'm trying to get out of a jam here. I try not to worry you with the details, but everyone's on the take. It's worse than being on the outside.

I hope you are well. Are you taking care of your pressure? Don't work too hard. I will be there to help you retire in a few more years. (smile)

Mom, I just wanted to let you know that there are rumors they'll be moving me soon. I don't know where, but in the federal system, it could be anywhere. I'll tell you as soon as I know. I hope it won't be even further away. Maybe it won't matter—I'll be up for parole in a few more years. Please keep it in your prayers that they'll let me out.

I hope you get this letter in time for your birthday. Happy Birthday, Mom. I love you.

Nick

Birthday? Lettie looked up from the letter, her eyes blurred with tears. Yes, that's right, April 4. Yesterday had been her birthday and she'd totally forgotten.

She got up, holding the letter to her breast. She knelt on the floor and slid out an old, faded hatbox from beneath the sofa. Opening the worn, delicate lid, she placed Nick's letter among the bundles of letters inside. The envelopes on top were from Nick. The ones on the bottom were scrawled with her grandmother's handwriting, yellowed and tied with lavender ribbons.

She replaced the box gingerly, as if performing a ritual. She lay on the sofa, pulling her hand-crocheted afghan around her shoulders. Between her sobs and her prayers, she managed to find a quiet place in her soul to sleep.

Chapter THREE

CATHERINE PARKED her midnight-blue Jeep Cherokee by the waterfront and got out of the car. She walked along the rushing Detroit River, the air still stinging from the chill of late spring. She watched an old woman help three children feed the birds. The two girls, their hair in countless little beaded braids, like chocolate pickaninnies, lured the gulls with handfuls of crushed Saltines. As soon as the flock got close, the boy, a stocky preschooler with an infectious giggle, would run toward them, sending the screeching birds flapping skyward.

Watching the children, Catherine involuntarily placed her hand on her stomach, not knowing which hurt more: the gradually intensifying cramps, or the sorrow that grew within her.

To think, just yesterday she'd been happier than she'd been in years, walking around the law firm full of a quiet secret—she was eight weeks pregnant. She hadn't told a soul at work, especially not Sheila. But surely they had to notice that she had not been coming in at seven a.m. the way she had done for the last five years. That she'd moved all of her real estate closings to the afternoons, hoping that by then, her morning nausea would subside. That her smile came from a different place, a radiant new place that had quickened as soon as she'd read the plus sign on her home pregnancy test.

But this morning she had awakened oddly energized. She was on her way to work before she'd noticed her stomach was no longer a rollicking sea. She'd even stopped for a Big Breakfast on her way into the office.

It wasn't until she was in the middle of a conference call that she felt the warmness between her legs. Her eyes flew wide in terror. She somehow muddled through the end of the call without betraying what she already knew to be true—life was seeping from her.

In the bathroom, she sat on the toilet, trying to stem the blood. The fact that Hawkins & Simons only had a handful of female lawyers saved her from being discovered on the floor in the ladies' room, retching in grief. She stayed there twenty minutes, maybe more, afraid that by walking she might somehow disturb what was left of the new life clinging within her. But when the bleeding wouldn't stop, she knew all was lost.

She left the office without telling Sheila. She knew how women like her liked to blab, and couldn't trust the dumb girl to keep a secret, especially not something this personal. In the car, she called Chas on the cell phone as she made her way to the hospital.

"He's not in, Ms. Rollins," his secretary said, "Is there a message?"

Yes, tell him all of the drugs that had kept her up nights hot and sweating for a year had been for nothing. Tell him that he had weathered her mood swings, the doctor's visits, the desperate, task-oriented sex for nothing. That there would be no ornaments on the tree this year that said, "Baby's First Christmas." Tell him he'll have to take back the engraved, silver rattle he'd given her the day after they'd found out she was pregnant. "To the mother of my happiness," it read.

"No message," Catherine told his secretary. "I'll just call him later."

She couldn't bear the thought of another hospital waiting room, the stark white lights, and another pelvic examination while she lay on a paper-covered table. She needed to be alone, to go where she and her child could say good-bye, where the spirits could come and lift the fetus's soul on a gentle wind.

She had turned the car around and driven to Belle Isle, Detroit's island park just two miles from downtown. She had never been to the park unless there was a special event—the Grand Prix or the hydroplane races. Normally it was a place where she could never feel safe. Too many black people crowded the island on summer days like kindling in a tinderbox. Too many Mandingo-looking men on the prowl, looking at her and licking their chops as if she were a piece of meat. It always seemed that anything could happen on Belle Isle—a riot, a melee, a murder—at the drop of a hat. The gentle herds of deer and tall, broad-canopied trees in the park did little to soothe the urban beasts.

But on a cold spring day like today, the park was nearly deserted. She cruised by Scott Fountain, then by the old Prohibition-era Belle Isle casino. She had whispered Chas's name like a mantra, wishing he was there to hold her, to kiss her, to make her feel like his queen.

They'd met at the University of Michigan's law school during a moot court debate—Catherine arguing in support of a fraternity's right to ban gays, the tall, handsome Charles Rollins arguing against.

He had come up to her after she'd won the oral argument, smiling.

"I wouldn't want to be caught arguing against you in front of some federal judge." He'd laughed, extending his hand in congratulations

"Thanks," she'd said, giving his hand a firm squeeze. "If we ever meet again in court, I'll let you win next time."

"Do you really believe that under the Constitution, the national fraternities have a right to discriminate against gays?"

Catherine hadn't missed the way he'd taken her elbow to lead her down the hall as they talked, or the way he looked directly into her hazel eyes. He was as interested in her answers as she was interested in his attention.

"I'm all for people being selective about who they associate with," Catherine shot back. Chas looked at her, unable to hide his surprise. Her wit was as quick as her legal mind.

Charles Rollins, or "Chas," as everyone called him, was president of the school's Black Law Students' Association and as popular as he was handsome. His light tan complexion, his smooth, black, wavy hair, his twinkling dark eyes all made him as attractive to Catherine as he was to most of the women at Michigan—both white and black.

But up until then, Catherine had had little time for dating. Her mother had been killed when she was only seventeen, leaving Catherine and her ten-year-old brother, Marcus, the beneficiaries of a large insurance policy but with no close relatives to look after them. She'd never known her father.

Catherine had moved Marcus to an Ann Arbor public school while she attended college, then law school. Parenting her sibling had made Catherine more practical and serious than other freshmen. For her, college became a juggle of academics, soccer practice, and parent-teacher conferences.

Having worked hard her first two years of law school—and having talked Marcus into going to Notre Dame instead of his first choice, the historically black Hampton University—Catherine had felt that her third year of school would afford her more time for social activities. She was secretly pleased when Chas ended up opposite her during the moot court competition, and before their third year was over, the two were engaged and interviewing with top Detroit law firms.

Catherine's years as a single mother had also taught her a lot about juggling competing priorities. The partners at Hawkins & Simons noticed how eagerly she sought their assignments and how she always delivered on time. It wasn't long before she began to bring in her own clients. The partnership track was grueling, especially for a woman—and especially for a black woman. But Catherine moved easily through the white environment. Her tough golf swing, popular summer parties, and seemingly bottomless knowledge of English literature won them over. More than one partner had commented over the years that they were glad they had taken the risk with Catherine. She was so *different* from the other black students they'd interviewed. Catherine smiled at the compliment. If she continued to play her cards right, she'd be a shoe-in for partner.

Chas's outgoing personality and business savvy, however, was stifled by a silk-stocking legal firm. He left private practice three years later to start his own import-export business with a law school buddy from Sierra Leone. As with all new start-ups, the business had its ups and downs, theirs not helped by the country's raging civil war. But Americans were hungry for African imports (items Catherine thought too primitive and clumsy to qualify as art). For the last few years, business had been good. Chas kept busy shuttling between Detroit and Freetown while Catherine put in fifty, sometimes sixty hours a week at the firm.

Three years after they'd married, Chas had talked Catherine into buying the sky-top condo at Riverhouse East. She'd wanted to move to Birmingham, a neat little Detroit suburb with boutiques, five-star restaurants, and art galleries. But Chas insisted on living in Detroit. He thrived on city life, and a Detroit address was better for his business. Plus, he argued, the real estate market, depressed for decades, was beginning to skyrocket. If they got in on the ground floor, they could make a bundle off of the condo in a few short years.

The last argument had sway with Catherine as a budding real estate lawyer. She agreed that it wouldn't hurt to hold the property for now, especially since they had no kids to worry about raising in the city. Plus, the building had its own security gate, twenty-four hour doormen, and an elevator operator. She would probably be safe.

Chas and Catherine moved into the building, enthralled with its oak paneling, molded plaster ceilings, and Italian marble entranceway. Theirs was one of only two penthouse apartments, each a sprawling three thousand square feet.

While the condo made them feel connected to city life, it also made Catherine suddenly feel small and alone—especially when Chas was out of town. They had never really talked about children; both had been too busy with their careers. Plus, Catherine's experience raising her brother had made her leery of taking on the responsibility of motherhood again. But the half-million dollar condo with its echoing rooms made even their friends wonder out loud, "When are you guys going to start filling up this place?"

Chas would laugh, but the day came for Catherine when the question was no longer a joke. And now, after a year of fertility treatments, Catherine feared that motherhood would elude her for good.

Looking out over the flowing river, Catherine took a handful of pebbles and ceremoniously trickled them into the cold water, praying quietly as the children around her squealed at the gulls.

The moment reminded her of her last good-byes to her mother, when she and Marcus had driven to Lake Beulah with their mother's ashes in the backseat. Near sundown, they'd arrived at the tiny, rustic town, now full of prefab houses and ramshackle summer cottages. The town used to be a hot spot for black vacationers in the fifties and sixties when her grandfather had bought a cabin on the lake. But after the great move to integrate public places in the sixties, black resorts like Lake Beulah all but died.

By the time Catherine and Marcus were born, the splendor of

the little town had waned. Only long-rooted families still vaca-
tioned in the rustic town, now mostly peopled by the poor blacks
who'd lived there long before the black bourgeoisie had come and
remained long after they'd gone. Even without its fancy shops and
raucous nightclubs, Catherine's mother had loved the hot lazy days
of card playing, swimming, and barbecues.

Under the full moon, they'd buried their mother's ashes at the
foot of a live oak on the banks of the lake. They had sat underneath
the tree all night after that, telling stories and remembering the old
times. The next morning, they'd boarded up the two-room bunga-
low and driven back to Detroit. Neither had been back to Lake
Beulah since.

Her cramps worsening, Catherine got into her car and headed
home. She could barely say hello to the maid as she climbed the
stairs and threw herself on the bed. She wished she were alone so
that she could wail like the child she so much wanted. She wished
her mother were there to hold her, to tell her everything would be
all right.

"Miz Catherine, I'm all done now," came the maid's voice at her
door. "You need anything else?"

Catherine sat up abruptly. She wiped the tears from her face before rising and opening her bedroom door. "No, Lettie. Everything
looks fine," said Catherine, avoiding the woman's gaze.

They stood awkwardly. Catherine wondered what the woman
wanted, why she wouldn't just put on her jacket and go home.

"Is there something else?" she asked curtly.

Clearing her throat, Lettie said hesitantly, "Um, Miz Catherine,
about my pay . . ."

"What about your pay?" Catherine snapped. "Don't tell me you
want a raise already! You don't even vacuum under the beds! Don't
think I don't notice. You think just because we're both black you
can just ride all over me? You wouldn't do that if I was white, now
would you?"

Tears stung in Lettie's eyes, but she held her tongue. She needed this job. She needed it for Nick. She couldn't let him down.

"Miz Catherine," she said slowly, taking in deep breaths, "if you would like, I can vacuum beneath your bed before I leave today. I was just sayin' that you forgot to leave my pay on the table."

"No I didn't!" Catherine recoiled, the heavy grief of her lost child fueling her anger and resentment. "Are you trying to get me to pay double for your half-assed work? This is unreal!"

"No, no, ma'am! You didn't pay me, honest!" Lettie cried, wondering why Miz Catherine was so incredibly touchy. "You must have left out of here in a hurry this morning and forgot . . ."

"Forgot, my ass!" said Catherine. "Look, honey, I've had it. I told Chas this wasn't going to work. You people just want a handout—you want to make the rest of us look bad. I've worked to pull myself up from nothing—NOTHING, you hear?! I will not sit here and be extorted by a lazy nigger who won't even push a vacuum cleaner and expects to get paid for it!"

Her cramps worsening, Catherine clutched her stomach. "Just get out! And don't come back, dammit!"

She slammed her bedroom door and leaned against it, moaning in pain as the blood oozed down her leg. God, what had she done to deserve this? Why had the child escaped from her womb leaving her so lost and so empty? Why wasn't Chas there to hold her, to comfort her?

It was a few seconds before she realized that she'd heard no footsteps, no door slam. Lettie must be still standing on the other side of the door.

In horror, she turned and locked the door quickly. My God, she wondered. Did the woman have a gun? A knife? Was she going to stand there until Catherine came out only to slit her throat? Was she a crack addict who would steal her things—her mother's silver hand mirror, her diamond tennis bracelet, her Lladró porcelain figurines—and sell them for a fraction of their value for a short-lived high?

She was trapped. She needed medical attention. She needed her husband. She needed her mother. But there was no one to help her, no one to protect her from this murderous woman from Black Bottom. Riffraff who now threatened to take her life.

Doubled over, she walked to the nightstand and grabbed the phone. She sat on the edge of the bed, gathering the bedspread between her legs to stem the blood.

"I have a gun in here!" Catherine yelled at the door. "I'm taking it out and calling the police! You'd better be out of here before I open this door."

But she never called and never opened the door. She sat there on the bed in the dark, every muscle in her body tensed for attack, until, overcome, she fainted.

It might have been minutes, it might have been hours—she didn't know how long she was out. But suddenly there was a banging at the door.

"Go ahead, break it down!" came a man's voice, shrill and urgent.

There were gasps, voices. "Look at the blood!" someone said.

"Stand back!" Hands on her wrist. Someone touching her face. Oxygen, clear and pure. Blankets.

A whisper: "Kit, you're going to be okay, just hold on . . ."

Chas. Chas had come to save her. She waited for his arms around her, his kiss on the nape of her neck. But instead she felt herself being lifted, carried out of the condo toward the elevator.

The last thing she heard before blacking out was Chas's voice: "Lettie, thank God you called me. If you hadn't been here, Catherine would have died . . ."

Chapter FOUR

IVE MONTHS LATER Catherine sat on the hard, crinkling white paper of the examination table in the obstetrician's office. The air hung thick around her, heavy and warm. She moved her hands, clenched in a knot on her lap, only to find they had sweated a wet hole in the disposable dressing gown. Yet her feet were like blocks of ice. She scooted back on the table and pulled her legs up to sit cross-legged, so that her feet nestled like cool marble against the hot flesh of her thighs.

She looked at the clock: four-thirty. She'd been sitting in the examination room for forty minutes waiting for the doctor to come in. Why did she put up with these black doctors? She eyed the pamphlets on the wall. An Asian woman, maybe twenty, laughing from a cover that read, *Nutrition and PMS*. A graying, beautiful white woman, crow's feet snuggling the corners of her eyes: *The Menopausal Years*. A black woman, her skin silky as a chocolate bar, holding a round, smiling baby: *A Healthy Baby Begins with You*.

Here we go again, she thought fearfully. Pregnant again but still not out of the woods. She closed her eyes, trying to block everything out of her mind, breathing in slowly through her nose, out through her mouth like they'd taught her in meditation. But it made her feel light-headed, and her nausea seemed to be coming back.

Suddenly there was a knock on the door, and before she could move her legs and sit back on the end of the table, a nurse came in, smiling and holding her chart.

"The doctor will be right with you, Ms. Rollins," she said, her neat braids pulled back in a colorful elastic band. "We're still trying to track down the lab results from your last tests. They're faxing over another copy right now. Can I get you anything?"

You can't even find my paperwork! Catherine thought, near

tears. You can just get me out of here. But she simply shook her head. "No."

As the woman left, Catherine noticed how full the woman's body was—healthy breasts, round hips.

"I'll bet she has four children," she whispered. "Just got pregnant when she wanted to and popped them out, one after another . . ."

She covered her face, ashamed of the jealousy that had gripped her since her miscarriage. She couldn't look at a baby commercial, at a woman pushing a stroller at the mall, at a teenager with a baby on her hip without wondering why their wombs were more deserving than hers.

"Okay, I think we're set now," said Dr. Saunders, coming to the door. The doctor pulled a stool closer to Catherine and sat down. "Ms. Rollins, I have some good news and some bad news."

Catherine sat up, bracing herself. The doctor was an older brown-skinned woman, her hair shot with gray, her expression as sincere as it was compassionate.

"You've made it to twelve weeks," Dr. Saunders said. "You should be nearing the end of the morning sickness. Have you noticed it getting any better?"

Although she hadn't, Catherine nodded, "yes," bracing herself for the bad news. Dr. Saunders opened her charts and thumbed through the pages.

"You should begin to gain weight better now that you can start keeping down more food. I want you to take your prenatal vitamins at lunch, with a meal. Maybe that will help you tolerate them better."

Then the doctor put down the chart. "However, Ms. Rollins, there is some evidence that your cervix is beginning to open. It might be what caused your miscarriage last time." Sensing Catherine's mounting fear, the doctor stood and put her hand on Catherine's shoulder. "We can take care of that, don't worry. In a way you're lucky. The miscarriage gave us a lot of information. We learned that the fertility drugs are working; you can conceive. And we learned that we need to watch you more closely, which we have.

"I want you to hold on for another two weeks. That will be the beginning of your second trimester. If the fetus is still viable, I'm going to do a procedure called a cerclage. It's like fashioning a web that will hold your cervix closed. Then, when you're about thirty-seven weeks, we'll remove the stitches and you can deliver naturally. It's not a difficult procedure—we do it all the time. But there's one thing—you've got to stay off of your feet. I mean totally. Bed rest all day, no stairs, no jogging or aerobics."

Catherine could barely hear the doctor speaking. The baby is fine! My God, I'm going to be a mother! She looked into the doctor's eyes and burst into tears. "Thank you, Dr. Saunders," she said, grabbing the doctor and crushing her stethoscope between them. "I just can't believe it. I'm going to have a baby!"

The doctor, astonished, laughed and hugged Catherine back.

"Don't thank me, I didn't do anything," she said. "Thank your husband."

"Does that mean no sex?" asked Chas, as they sat at a corner table at the Whitney.

Catherine looked at her husband and winked. "Depends on what your definition of sex is."

He laughed and reached for her hand. "Kit, I'm so happy. I swear, I was tired of sleeping on the couch. Those drugs were turning you into a monster. Here's to parenthood, to the most beautiful mother-to-be in the world. I love you."

They clinked their glasses of sparkling water and sipped. Chas looked into his wife's beaming face.

"I can't wait to take my son—"

"Or daughter—"

"Or daughter with me to Sierra Leone as soon as they're old enough," he said. "I want them to see the coastline, the incredible beaches, the Loma Mountains, the villages in the hills, the museums—"

"And don't forget daddy's import shop in Freetown," Catherine interrupted. "Hey, before you get too gung-ho, what if Baby Rollins wants to be a lawyer like her mommy? Ever think of that?"

"She can be a lawyer," he said, without hesitation. "They need more lawyers in Sierra Leone!"

Catherine smiled. The pecan-coated whitefish had been exquisite; it was the first meal she'd been able to keep down in weeks. She'd spooned a little of Chas's warm spiced persimmon–walnut-raisin cake, afraid to push her stomach too far with a full, rich serving of her own. For the first time in almost a year, it felt like old times, like when they'd order pizza and cram for exams in law school, or like when they used to rent a movie and pop open a bottle of champagne on lazy weekends after they first got married.

In the dim candlelight, Catherine stared at Chas as he ate the last of his dessert. Would their son be like him—tall, muscular, his skin fair and smooth, his jaw square, his shoulders broad? If they had a girl, she prayed the baby would have her green eyes and straight hair. How would she manage if the child's hair was kinky? So nappy it was hard to tell when it was wet, so thick it took a whole day for it to dry?

"Coffee?" asked the waiter politely, interrupting Catherine's thoughts.

"No thank you," said Catherine, determined to avoid coffee while she was pregnant.

"Uh, no," said Chas in sympathy with his wife, although he eyed the silver pot longingly. "Just some milk to wash down the cake."

The waiter raised an eyebrow and nodded. "Very well."

"Now," said Chas, letting Catherine's hand go and pushing back slightly from the table, "about work."

"I'll tell Mr. Hawkins first thing Monday," said Catherine defensively.

"Tell him what?"

"Well, that I need to take some time off."

"No, Catherine, that's not what I understood the doctor to say. You need to tell them you won't be back—at least not until the baby is a few months old."

"Chas," said Catherine, miffed. "I know what that doctor said. I just think she was giving me the most conservative advice. I'll get a second opinion from another doctor, a specialist . . ."

"Catherine, Dr. Saunders *is* a specialist. Just because she's black doesn't mean she's not competent!" said Chas, an edge in his voice.

"No, Chas, I didn't mean that," said Catherine, backpedaling. Dr. Saunders had delivered Chas and most of his peers. When they'd moved to Detroit after they'd gotten married, Catherine inherited Dr. Saunders along with a bevy of black accountants, grocers, and dentists, all of whom were friends of Chas's family. "I meant that I have a high-risk pregnancy and I may need to go see a doctor who specializes in those. Maybe at a suburban hospital . . ."

"Catherine, I'm not going to argue with you about that—it's your call," said Chas. "But the bottom line is that you won't be going back to work no matter who your doctor is. After what happened last time, it's just too dangerous."

Catherine looked down in her lap and put both of her hands on her stomach. Maybe it was her imagination, or maybe it was the bulge of the night's meal, but it seemed she was already showing. This child was not something that would happen nine months from now. The tight, aching swell of her breasts, the death-like fatigue, the constant queasiness proved to her every second of every day that for her, the baby had already arrived. Suddenly it was clear to her that her life was going to be transformed forever.

"You're right," she said quietly. "I'll tell them on Monday that I'm not coming back for a while."

Chas breathed heavily with relief. "And one more thing," he said. "I'm going to talk to Lettie. I know she hasn't been back since the . . . since the incident, but I want her to quit her other jobs and come work for us full-time. I want her there to look after you."

"Chas!" Catherine almost burst into tears. "How could you go behind my back like that? I don't want Lettie in the house with me anymore. My God, the woman hates me."

"She does not hate you. She saved your life. If she hadn't gone downstairs and had the security desk call me and an ambulance, who knows what I would have found when I got home from work. You had lost so much blood, you were nearly comatose!"

Catherine sat, mortified. How could he be siding with that horrible woman who'd tried to hurt her? There was no doubt in her mind that Lettie was out to get her. Lettie only showed her true colors when they were alone, but with Chas, she was a sweet, innocent older woman—a mother figure. Why was she scheming to get back into their good graces after Catherine had fired her? Was there something in the condo she still wanted?

Chas was quiet a minute, as if he was struggling for the right words to say.

"Kit, think about it. Lettie comes to work on time. She's trustworthy . . ."

"Trustworthy?" Catherine asked, incredulous. "How do you know? Did you run a police check on her and her family? How do you know she doesn't have kids running around Detroit mixed up with gangs and drugs? How do you know who you're letting into our house?"

"Well, Catherine, what's your suggestion?" said Chas, sitting back in his chair. "You're about to have a baby. You cannot get out of bed for the next six or seven months. When the baby comes, we'll need a nanny. I say it's perfect. Lettie has come our way in the nick of time. If you have a better solution, I'd be glad to hear it."

Catherine opened her mouth, then closed it. For a moment, she tried to imagine the baby, dimpled with a head full of sandy, fine hair. She imagined her child gazing up into Lettie's face, and Lettie bringing the child to her large, black breasts to suckle, putting the dark knob of her nipple to the child's pink lips, letting her dangerous nectar slide down her child's throat . . .

She gasped and covered her face. My God, what was she thinking? That Lettie would take her own child from her, poison her with those ghetto ways, turn the Rollins baby into a child of the streets?

"Kit, are you okay?" Chas leaned forward, touching Catherine's arm.

"Yes," she said, unable to stop the tears. "I'll be fine."

She breathed deeply, trying to cork her deep-seated fears. "I'll agree to take Lettie back on one condition."

"What's that?" he asked.

"I want an alarm system in the house. One with sensors, cameras, and a panic button."

"What? Why? We live on the top floor of a building that's guarded like Alcatraz. If someone were to steal something they couldn't get out without being seen by fifty people!"

"Chas, those are my terms. You go out of town a lot. After the miscarriage, I just don't want to be left alone again. It will help me sleep at night . . ."

Chas looked at his wife sympathetically. "Okay," he said. "Consider it done."

"Here's your milk," said the waiter, placing the sweating glass in front of Chas. "Can I get you anything else?"

Chas looked Catherine in the eye. "No thank you," he said. "I think I have everything I need."

"We're finished, ma'am. Can you sign here?" Lettie took the clipboard from the workman and signed at the bottom of the work order as if she was the woman of the house.

The man tipped his hat, grabbed his metal toolbox, and left.

It had taken five months, but Lettie had gotten her job back. She'd left the house in a tizzy, unable to understand why Miz Catherine would refuse to pay her, then fire her for asking for the money she'd already earned. She was almost in the elevator when she'd heard Miz Catherine's screams.

The sound had been disconcerting and at first Lettie assumed the redbone had finally lost her mind. But by the time she got down to the first floor, she understood innately that Miz Catherine was in trouble. The strange behavior. The pallor of her face and the tremble of her hands. The shrill fear in her voice.

It was then that Lettie knew she had an opportunity to enlist Mr. Rollins to help her keep her job—the job she so desperately needed in order to be able to help her son get a new lawyer and a new trial. As soon as she reached the lobby, Lettie had alerted the security desk that she'd heard screams coming from the Rollins condo.

"They never gave me keys to their condo," she had explained to the security supervisor. "So I can't get back in, but I think you'd better call Mr. Rollins and EMS."

Even Lettie was shocked at the shape Miz Catherine was in when the EMS arrived. She'd figured they'd find Miz Catherine in a drunken stupor at worst, in the middle of a maniacal tirade at best. She had not even suspected that her employer was losing blood, evidently from a miscarriage.

Mr. Rollins had been eternally grateful that Lettie had been there for Miz Catherine, and in the end it was he who lobbied his wife to get Lettie's job back—and to keep her on as a nanny if Miz Catherine and her thin, white-girl bones could ever carry a baby to term.

Now she was back in the swing of things. If she ignored Miz

Catherine's pouting, things weren't so bad. And she had even managed to save more money for Nick's lawyer.

As the alarm installation men left, Lettie locked the door and returned to her work.

"Thank goodness, I thought they'd never leave!" she muttered. "Just look at this mess!"

She looked over the Rollinses' condo with her hands on her hips. The afternoon sun filtering through the leaded-glass windows lit upon the dust in the air, dust from the hours of drilling into the woodwork to install security cameras throughout the house, along with alarms around the front door and the service entrance behind the kitchen.

"All that trouble for a burglar alarm. And who in the name of Jesus can even get up here to steal anything? Got to go through the blessed secret service to get up here!"

She shook her head and went to the butler's pantry for the mop and a dust rag. She put a bottle of beeswax in the pocket of her apron and headed for the foyer where the marble was blanketed with fine dust. Rich folks sure have to spend a lot of money trying to keep what they have, she thought, laughing at the idea of a burglar alarm in her small apartment. Even if one went off, the police would never come to her street to investigate.

"The only one who will watch over us on the east side is the Lord Jesus," she murmured.

She pushed the mop over the floor once, then twice, before it dawned on her.

"I'll bet Miz Catherine made them put in those alarms to guard herself from *me!*" she said, eyes wide in revelation.

She sat down, suddenly feeling weak. That had to be it. During her employment one of the Rollinses' had met her at the door in the mornings. But in the months to come, Miz Catherine wouldn't be able to get up to let her in. They had to entrust Lettie with a key. Did Miz Catherine think she'd try to steal them blind?

Furious, Lettie stood up and thrust the mop over the white marble, sloshing water up on the wooden molding. She was glad Miz Catherine wasn't at home. Lettie just couldn't look at that woman right now, mad as she was. Who was that redbone to offer her a job, then accuse her of being a thief all in the same breath?

"I ought to walk out right now," she said. But she reminded herself that Mr. Rollins had offered her enough money so she could quit her other cleaning jobs. She was going to be paid full-time to sit and watch Miz Catherine's belly rise. What could be easier?

Catherine sat on the camel-backed, red paisley sofa outside of Winston Hawkins's office. She adjusted the skirt of her black suit, and pulled down the cuffs of her silk, goldenrod blouse. She smiled patiently at Mr. Hawkins's secretary.

"He'll be with you in just a moment, Ms. Rollins," said the secretary. "He's still on the phone."

Catherine practiced what she would say mentally. I've given you five good years, but now I need some time off. I know you'll understand. The doctor says that . . .

"Catherine? Come on in," said Winston Hawkins, filling the door with his six-foot-four-inch frame. The named partner of Hawkins & Simons, Winston Hawkins had been a kingmaker in city politics for the last thirty years. "Have a seat." He offered Catherine one of the Chippendale chairs in front of his desk. He sat behind the desk and picked up his pipe.

"What can I do for you?"

Catherine sat up on the edge of the chair. "Well, Mr. Hawkins, you know how much I enjoy my work . . ."

"Yes, Catherine, we're proud to have you here at our firm. You've been quite an asset over the years and we appreciate your hard work."

Catherine nodded, understanding the subtext of his compliment: It was good to have a black lawyer in a city like Detroit, where much of the political power structure was African-American. It didn't hurt that she was also smart and good-looking.

"Yes, well, I am hoping to have a long career here, Mr. Hawkins. I'm very happy. But I need to take some time off."

Mr. Hawkins considered Catherine carefully. He opened the ebony canister on his desk and spooned brandy-scented tobacco into the bowl of his pipe. The building had long ago banished smoking, but no one ever had the nerve to demand that Mr. Hawkins stop pulling on his pipe, as long as he smoked only in his office.

As he lit the tobacco and puffed, the blue-gray smoke wafted across the desk. The thickness of it clutched Catherine's throat unexpectedly. She'd been in his office a million times before, and had even loved the smell of the cured tobacco. It had reminded her of old leather, of richly bound books. But now, the smell turned her stomach. She struggled to keep from gagging.

"Time off, eh?" Mr. Hawkins said presently. "Are you and your husband finally going to do that traveling you talked about? Are you going to write that treatise on urban development like we discussed? That would be fine, Catherine, you know we would support you."

"Well, thank you, Mr. Hawkins, but this is another kind of project."

He crossed his hands in front of him and gazed at her. She didn't mean to, but she looked down into her lap, her bottom lip trembling. In that moment she knew she was about to sacrifice her career. She took a deep breath and looked up.

"I'm pregnant," she said, almost defiantly.

Years from now, she would laugh at the look that plastered the old man's face. It was a mixture of offense and shock, as if he'd just witnessed a three-hundred-pound woman tumble in front of him, exposing her dimpled thighs and huge expanse of underwear.

"Pregnant?" he said, barely masking his incredulity. "Well, that's, uh, that's . . . congratulations." There was an awkward silence, then he added perfunctorily, "When is the baby due?"

"Late August. But I need to take some time off now."

"Well, sure, that's no problem. How much do you need?"

Catherine frowned. He was not understanding. Her dilemma wasn't going to resolve itself in a few days. Maybe not even months. This was a child, not a client.

"The baby is at risk, Mr. Hawkins," she said, feeling more confident. "I have to be on bed rest until my due date. After that, we'll see when I can come back."

"Well, Catherine, I wish you all the best," said Mr. Hawkins. Then, his voice deepening, he spoke. "You know, I was beginning to worry about you, anyway. It's come back to me that you refused to take on a very big client a few months ago. Does Bob Freeman sound familiar to you?"

Freeman, who was . . . oh! The man who wanted her to be a buffer between his development and "the community"!

"I do remember Mr. Freeman." Catherine nodded. "It was my understanding that he was just looking for an African-American to smooth the project with the neighborhood residents. I'm not a—"

"What do you think we hired you for if it wasn't to take cases like that?" Mr. Hawkins fumed. "He took his business across the street! What good is it to have a black lawyer if the black lawyer doesn't want to do business with her own people?"

Catherine was stunned. Is that why they'd hired her? Is that why they'd kept her on for all these years? And all this time she thought it was because they needed her skills, that she fit in, that they liked her!

"Mr. Hawkins, I'm sorry, I just thought that—"

"Well, what's done is done," he said, standing. "I guess now you expect us to pay you to sit at home and have a baby. Or babies."

She squinted. Was he implying that she was just another black welfare queen, having babies right and left on somebody else's dime? Catherine stood, flipping her long hair.

"I have a doctor's opinion that I cannot work without endangering the life of my child." She tried to keep her voice from wavering. "I am going to take a medical leave of absence and you will pay me accordingly. When I return, we'll revisit this conversation, which borders dangerously on race discrimination."

"Interesting," he interrupted rudely. "Exactly when did you discover you were a black lawyer? A black woman? When you rejected Mr. Freeman's business, or just now when you threatened me with a discrimination suit? C'mon, Mrs. Rollins," he scoffed. "Which way are you going to have it?"

⌒

Even though she tried to ignore them, Lettie could feel the lenses of the security cameras on her back as she emptied the garbage or went from vase to vase watering the flowers. The demeaning little eyes were everywhere—above the kitchen sink, over the entertainment center in the den, outside the bathrooms, on the bookshelf in the library, in each corner of the four bedrooms—ready to convict her. Like they had her son. Like they had her grandmother.

She meticulously put everything back in its place, realizing that each article of clothing, each misplaced pair of earrings could be a trap. She lined up the slippers neatly in front of the loveseat. She moved the stack of books on each side of the master bed, dusted the floor beneath them, then replaced the books exactly as they had been left. She aired the cashmere throw on the chaise longue in the living room, then refolded it, draping it precisely across the brocade back.

The stress of trying to remember the order of things made her head hurt, her blood pressure rise. Deep down, she began to wonder if she had indeed been thinking about pocketing the change left in Mr. Rollins's suit pants or tucking a Waterford vase into her canvas bag to pawn it on the way home.

No, no that wasn't it. She'd never stolen a thing in her life. Most of the things these folks had she had no use for, anyway. Porcelain statues of silly, frail girls holding bouquets of flowers. Paintings that didn't make any more sense right side up than upside down. Silver forks and picture frames that only glimmered half the year, looking dull and tarnished the other half. Flimsy dresses cut from fabrics too expensive to launder yourself.

Who needed that kind of aggravation? "I don't want your useless, high-yellow stuff," Lettie announced to the cameras in the master bedroom. "Here, you think I'm gonna steal? See what you think of this . . ."

She picked up the box of chocolates Miz Catherine kept on her dressing table and stood in the middle of the room. She plucked a chocolate from its paper cradle and bit into it, its soft, mocha center spilling onto her full lips. She licked the sweetness and swept it into her mouth, rolling it arrogantly on her tongue, as she looked straight into the camera. She swallowed slowly, letting the bittersweet syrup trickle down her throat.

She grinned.

"How do you like that?" she said to the camera as she reached for another chocolate. She ate three in succession, only spitting out the fourth, because it turned out to be a cherry cordial. "Consider this payment for questioning what's in my heart," she said to no one there.

After that, the cameras lost their power. By the afternoon, they had instead become silent companions, like goldfish. They watched her go from room to room, scrubbing, sweeping, spraying, smoothing. They gazed as Lettie flapped fresh pima cotton sheets over the master bed, wondering out loud, "How much did these cost?"

They kept her company in the kitchen as she bent to clean the refrigerator.

"Who keeps leaving this mess uncovered?" she asked the cameras as she dumped out week-old, half-open containers of Yoplait.

They ogled her as she straightened the cosmetics on Miz Catherine's dressing table. "'Smoothing crème with UV protection,'" she read. "Wonder how much money she spends tryin' to keep her skin white?"

By the end of the day, she'd forgotten the cameras even existed. At five thirty, the front door opened and in walked Miz Catherine, back from her last day at work. All the blood had run from her cheeks, her eyes were sunken. Suddenly, Lettie remembered Mr. Rollins's instructions: "Watch her and let me know if you see her disobeying doctor's orders. I'm depending on you."

"Miz Catherine," she said, putting her arms around the woman's shoulders and trying to get her to go upstairs to bed. "If you don't mind me saying so, you don't look so good. Don't you think you should lay down now? Mr. Rollins didn't even want you to go in today. He told you to call and let them know you wouldn't be back."

Miz Catherine violently shrugged her shoulders, breaking Lettie's grasp.

"Leave me alone," she said, tears streaming. "I don't need Chas and I certainly don't need you telling me what to do for the next six months! You just stay out of my way and everything will be just fine. I know what you're up to, and believe me, as soon as I can find somebody else, you're out of here!"

Catherine went slowly up the stairs, wiping her nose with the back of her hand. She was out of a job and now she was reduced to being a prisoner in her own home. Her world had come crashing down.

Lettie watched Miz Catherine struggle up the stairs and smiled. Here was one redbone who was going to learn the hard way what it was like to live like the rest of us, she thought to herself as she went into the kitchen.

"Well, if there's anything I can do to help, Miz Catherine," she called sarcastically over her shoulder, "I'm at your service."

Chapter FIVE

SOMETHING WAS WRONG with Miz Catherine.

Lettie noticed how elated she'd been when she'd made it past fourteen weeks of pregnancy and the doctors did something to make sure the baby didn't fall from her womb. But in the days following the surgery, Miz Catherine had sunk deep into a depression.

It didn't help that the nausea was persisting long into the second trimester. Sometimes when she was downstairs, Lettie could hear Miz Catherine's footsteps trotting from the bed to the bathroom, then the sound of flushing and running water.

Lettie had seen it before. A woman whose spirit was so hard she was rejecting her own child. So venomous she was making her body a poisonous place for the child to grow.

Miz Catherine had slipped down to nothing, a fading, ivory waif against the white cotton sheets. She had no normal cravings, no kind words for her unborn child. The vomiting was continuing too long. Miz Catherine's stomach was an anger-whipped sea in which the child drifted, unanchored. At this rate, she's gonna lose another baby, Lettie thought. It's not for me to say, but something's got to loose the hardness in that woman.

"Mr. Rollins," Lettie said one Friday as she left for the weekend. "I think you need to take her to the doctor. Her color doesn't look right."

"You think so? At her checkup last week, the doctor said she was fine," said Chas, whispering in the kitchen.

"Yes, sir, but you can see she's not right."

Chas nodded. "I think she's depressed over her job—it's a lot of things. Neither of us realized how hard this would be. But I'll call the doctor and see if she wants to meet us at the hospital. Thanks, Lettie."

Lettie took the money he handed her and left. She knew that Mr. Rollins would call the doctor, but she suspected that what Miz Catherine needed was something no doctor would ever prescribe.

All the way home, she worried about what to do. She worried that if the baby was lost, she'd be too. It was the first time in twenty years she'd held only one job—and an easy one, at that. In just the last month, she'd even managed to pay five hundred dollars to Nick's lawyer. And Mr. Rollins had promised her a big raise after the baby came. If this kept up, she might be able to pay off Nick's whole bill—and even have some left to go visit him in Kansas.

At home, she put on some hot dogs and a can of pork and beans. She eased out of her clothes, slipped on a red floral house-dress, and tied a red bandanna around her thicket of hair. She knelt before the sofa and took out the large hatbox covered with faded lilacs. Inside she thumbed through the stacks of letters. This time, she ignored the ones from Nick and picked up the ones from her grandmother, the ones tied by the lilac ribbon.

"Hey, Mama Lettie, you there?" came a desperate knock at the door. It was LaShon.

"Coming!" she said, putting the box aside and trotting to the door.

"Hey, Mama Lettie, you seen Tina?" asked the little boy, his eyes so big, his skin so brown and smooth he looked like a baby seal.

Lettie frowned. She hated when the boys referred to their mother as "Tina." But Tina was a child herself—just eighteen—and she hardly acted like a mother worthy of anyone's respect, let alone her own children's. Tina was on the plump side, heavy breasts and rolling hips. Her skin was the color of freshly laid asphalt. So dark she glistened.

Not half-bad looking but no self-respect. Lettie remembered the night Tina had gone to her senior prom, all dressed up like the bride she never dreamed she'd be. Like that was the best day life was ever gonna bring her.

Tina didn't know it then, but she'd come home that night pregnant, believing the tan-faced, smiling boy with wet lips and a mouthful of sweet talk loved her. Was she the only one who didn't know that bright boys always wanted to sleep with black beauties but never wanted to marry them?

But by then, she was stung. Ever since, Tina would spread her legs eagerly for any yellow man, no matter who he was. Wouldn't be caught dead with a black man, no way nohow. So the light-skinned men used her, leaving her a broken heart and an arm full of babies, one right after the other. Eighteen and already the mother of two.

Lettie bent over and grabbed the six-year-old chin in her hand. "Where's Lamont?" she asked after giving him a kiss on the forehead.

"He lookin' for Tina, too."

"Well, baby, it's Friday night. I expect your mother will be busy for a while. Go get your brother and y'all can come in with me until she gets back."

"Yes!" the boy cheered, pumping his fist in joy. "I'll be right back."

Lettie smiled, knowing LaShon's search for his mother was a thinly veiled tactic to get an invitation to stay with her. She stood in the door waiting until the brothers stepped out of the elevator together and dashed for her apartment.

"Slow down!" she called. "You're going to bust your heads wide open!"

Twenty minutes later, the boys had blazed through two cans of beans, three hot dogs between them, and a half loaf of white bread. Lettie stood, watching them eat, admonishing them to chew their food carefully and keep their elbows off the table. The boys obliged with "Yes, ma'am," even while they ignored her.

"Can we watch TV?" asked LaShon, with a half slice of bread in his mouth.

"No," said Lettie. "You're going to help me clean up this kitchen. Then we'll put as much in your mind as you have in your bellies!"

The boys groaned in unison, although they didn't complain. She had taught them both their alphabets and how to read. She kept a stack of books for them in her apartment, but she never let them take the books home, or she'd never see them again.

Lamont, the younger of the two, stayed in the kitchen and helped dry the dishes while LaShon grabbed the watering can and began to fill it up.

"Hey, Mama Lettie," he called from the other room. "Who's this?"

Lettie came into the living room drying her hands on the dish-cloth.

"Oh, that's my oldest, Lois." Lettie smiled, taking the plastic picture frame from LaShon. "My Lord, she musta been just a bit older than you when we took this picture! Look at that child's head! That's when we lived over on Clairmont. In the summers, I used to put a plastic tablecloth on the ground in the backyard and wet it down with the hose. The kids would make a line and run and sliii-iiide!" she said, zipping her hands across each other like a plane tak-ing off. "Looks like Lois lost all her barrettes—and was almost about to lose her bathing suit!"

Lettie laughed, but the boys didn't. They sat with their mouths wide open, trying to imagine playing in a backyard. There wasn't even any grass around the apartment building.

"Where she now?" asked Lamont.

"Oh, Lois died years ago," said Lettie, putting the frame back among the others by the Bible on her bookshelf.

"Where your son?" LaShon asked. "Tina said he in the pen."

Lettie looked down, her smile suddenly gone.

"Nick isn't there because he did something bad," said Lettie quietly. "He's there because someone made a big mistake. I'm going to fix that mistake one day soon. He writes me all the time. I told him about you two and he said to tell you that prison isn't fun. You-all need to stay in school and stay out of trouble. He said he's going to teach you-all how to play the piano and sing when he comes home."

"Like Puff Daddy?" asked Lamont.

"He don't play the guitar, shithead!" scoffed LaShon. "Besides, I want to be a basketball player."

"Well, whatever you want to be, you won't get there cussin' like a sailor. No swearing in my house, young man, is that clear?"

Cowed, LaShon said, "Yes, ma'am."

"Besides, LaShon, when I look at how you pay attention to my medicine garden, I think you're gonna be a doctor."

LaShon beamed. "Can I water the plants now?"

He took the watering can and went to the window where Lettie kept her herb garden.

"Water the parsley well, it likes damp soil," Lettie instructed. "Okay, boys, smell this plant over here."

She rubbed a silvery-green leaf between her index finger and thumb and let the boys smell the scent it left behind.

"Smells like that stuff they put with the turkey at the soup kitchen on Thanksgiving," said Lamont.

"Smells like medicine," said LaShon.

"Well, you're both right," said Lettie. "You can cook with it or you can put it on your cuts. It's called sage."

"What's this stuff?" asked LaShon, whose short attention span led him to the pile of letters on the sofa.

"Oh!" said Lettie, moving quickly to put the letters back in the hatbox. "Those are letters. Some are from Nick, but the old ones are letters from my Grandma Sadie."

The boys looked at her quizzically. How could someone as old as Mama Lettie have a *grandmother*?

"Where does she live?" asked Lamont.

"She's gone now," said Lettie, sitting heavily down on the sofa and signaling for the boys to join her. They sat, one on each side, nestled into the soft cradle of her arms. "But she used to write me long letters.

"Long time ago, maybe seventy-five years now, Grandma Sadie and PaPa Black left Alabama for Detroit. PaPa Black got a good job at Ford's, but they just couldn't stand city life. 'A man's gotta be able to hunt a rabbit and turn the soil,' that's what PaPa used to say.

"So one day they just got in their buggy and headed north. They ended up in a tiny town called Lake Beulah. Most of the year it was practically deserted 'cept a handful of poor black folk. But in the summers, Negroes with a little bit of money would come in from Detroit, Chicago, Cleveland—you name it—to swim in the lake and have themselves a good time.

"PaPa took what little savings he had and bought a piece of land. He built a little house, not bigger than this room. Over the years, they'd just add on, bit by bit."

Lamont, full of hot dogs, began to yawn. But LaShon hung on Lettie's every word.

"PaPa spent most of his days as a lumberjack. In the summers, he'd sing and play guitar in the clubhouse for the rich folks. Grandma Sadie did what her ma did back in Alabama. She started helpin' the black women in the county deliver their babies. There was only one hospital anywhere near, and it was for whites. Sometimes the white doctor would come to the courthouse and the black folks would line up with their coughs and rashes and arthritis.

"But in between, there was Sadie with her herbs and potions. They said she could heal the mean off a snake. She was like magic. She must have delivered over sixty babies while she lived in Lake Beulah. Everybody loved her."

"Did any babies ever die?" asked LaShon, his voice growing high and whiny as he grew sleepy, too.

Lettie was quiet for a moment. "Yes, one baby died. It was the last one she ever delivered."

"Where is your grandma now?"

"She's in heaven, baby. She always told me, 'God gave women the blessings of heaven above, of the deep that lieth under, of the breast and of the womb.' Despite everything that happened to her, she always believed that."

"What does that mean?"

"It means she felt blessed to be able to bring babies like you into the world, and she loved each one equally no matter his skin color or lot in life," said Lettie. Then patting LaShon on the rump she said, "Lamont is already asleep. Why don't you two share the sofa? I'll wake you when your mother comes home."

Without argument, LaShon lay his head down on the sofa pillow while Lettie covered the brothers with her afghan.

"Good night," she said, giving each a kiss.

She went into her bedroom, wondering if Tina would even come home at all, and if she did, how long it would be before she noticed her boys were gone. She shook her head and got ready for bed herself. She fell asleep by midnight, reading her Bible.

Hours later, loud music blared through the paper-thin walls, waking her from a deep sleep. She got up and checked on the boys, who were tangled on the sofa like a litter of puppies. She went to the bathroom and got back in bed. As she turned off the light, she heard a loud crash come from next door, and the muffled sound of a man's voice, yelling. Minutes later, a door slammed. A woman's cries filled the night.

Tina was home, thought Lettie, but there was no need to wake the boys now.

"Here you go," said Lettie, backing into Miz Catherine's bedroom with a serving tray in her arms.

She tried to keep the smile plastered on her face when she turned to look at Miz Catherine, but the shock was too great. Miz Catherine had deteriorated over the weekend. Her face was swollen, her eyes puffy and weak. Her hair, once wavy and soft, stood on her head, dry and wiry. "Are . . . are you ready for breakfast?" she stuttered.

Catherine looked up, exhausted, even though it was ten a.m. She wouldn't speak.

Lettie sat the tray down on the nightstand. "You don't look well," she said. "Did Mr. Rollins call the doctor on Friday like I asked?"

"What's it to you?" Catherine bit back.

Lettie tried to remain pleasant. This redbone was milking it for all it was worth. How many black women had given birth in fields while mulatto women like her sat in the shade churning butter while they were pregnant? She was acting like she invented childbirth, like she was the first woman to ever suffer the discomfort of giving life.

Yet there was something in Miz Catherine's face that gave her pause. Something more than regular misery, something much darker.

Her eyes were deep set, her skinny mouth a grim line. Her hair was like straw, her fingernails thin and cracking. There was life in her stomach, but death on her face.

"Miz Catherine, if you don't mind me sayin' so, I think what you need is some woman advice—those doctors don't always know what's best. Where's your mother? Have you told her how bad off you are?"

Catherine shook her head but said nothing.

"Well, do you want me to call her for you? I think it would do you some good."

"My mother died of TB when I was seventeen," Catherine whispered in a harsh but measured tone. "She'd volunteered to help nurse tuberculosis patients in an all-black charity hospital ward and must have caught that nasty disease"—her next words were venomous— "from somebody who looked just like you!"

Lettie heard the words as if they were a slap. As if somehow her skin color made her responsible for the death of Catherine's mother. As if the darker the person, the more connected they were to an unspeakable evil, more connected to disease and to death.

"I-I'm sorry," Lettie stammered, looking for the first time into the heart of someone consumed by hatred. She wondered if someone looked deep into her, would he see the same thing? "I'm real sorry."

She backed out of the room as if running from a tiger and escaped to the kitchen. Her heart was pounding. In that moment she realized that Miz Catherine had been so deeply brainwashed by high Negro society that she was consumed with hatred of all that was black. That when Miz Catherine saw her, saw anybody with thick, kinky hair, nose wide as the Nile, lips full and ripe as melons, skin dark as a beautiful African night, she saw something inhuman. She saw a monster.

For the rest of the day, she stayed away from Miz Catherine's room, knocking on the door only twice more—once to deliver lunch, the other time to deliver dinner. She paced back and forth as the sun dipped below the windowsill of the eighteenth-floor condo, spreading its red like blood over the parchment-colored walls.

When Mr. Rollins finally put his key in the door, Lettie was there, facing him, nearly in tears.

"Mr. Rollins," she said, before he could put down his briefcase. "I've got to talk to you."

His eyes full of concern, Chas led Lettie to the kitchen.

"Stay here," he said, conspiratorially. He crept up the stairs and into the bedroom. Within minutes, he was back down again with the tray. Barely any of the food was touched.

"She's asleep," he said. Lettie could tell by the way his eyes evaded hers that he was lying.

"She wants me out of here and I can't stand being around her," Lettie said point-blank. "She's a cruel woman and it's not my job to take that kind of abuse."

"But . . ."

"Please, Mr. Rollins. Don't say a word. I just can't stay here anymore."

Chas looked at her, pleading with his eyes.

"Here's what you need to do," Lettie continued. "I thought about her over the weekend and I made her some tea. It's what my grandmother used to give all the women she took care of."

She pulled a plastic bag of loose tea out of her work bag by the kitchen door. "It's just chamomile and gingerroot. I got the herbs from Eastern Market and ground them myself," said Lettie. "Let it steep in the tea for about fifteen minutes. Serve her the tea lukewarm. The baby doesn't like anything too hot or too cold."

Chas eyed the amber and green crumbled leaves in the bag.

"And one more thing," said Lettie, getting up from the table. She went to the lazy Susan in the cupboard, spinning it around until she came to a bright yellow box.

"Now, I don't want you to ask any questions, hear?" she said to Mr. Rollins as she sat back down at the table. "We've been doing this in our family for generations, and I'd bet if Miz Catherine's mama was alive, she'd tell you the same."

Chas's eyes flew wide and met Lettie's. Yes, she knew about Catherine's mother. Now Chas understood why Lettie felt she had to go.

"Anyways, I can't get my hands on that rich, black Alabama soil, so this will have to do."

She gave the box to Mr. Rollins. "Give her a couple spoonfuls tonight. Let her keep the box by her bed, she'll start craving it as soon as she eats it."

"Starch?" he asked incredulously.

"I told you," she said, "no questions. Believe me, you'll see her improve in a matter of days."

Lettie stood and untied her apron, leaving it draped on the back of the chair.

"Mr. Rollins, I want to thank you for all you've done," she said. "You don't have to pay me for today. I'll see myself out."

She left Mr. Rollins sitting in the kitchen, his head in his hands. As she left the house, she could swear she heard the bedroom door upstairs click shut.

⌒

"Why didn't you eat your dinner?" Chas asked Catherine as he entered the bedroom.

"Chas, don't start in on me. I don't feel . . ."

"Catherine, I'm losing patience here. Right now I'm on the verge of saying I don't give a damn about how you feel, I'm worried about the baby. What are you trying to do?"

At his harsh words, Catherine's eyes grew watery. "Oh, Chas, you just don't know what it's like!" she wept as he came and sat on the bed, taking her into his arms. "I'm so afraid! I don't want to get too emotionally connected to this baby—what if I lose this one, too? I'm so sick all the time, I just feel like I'm afloat, like I don't recognize myself anymore.

"I want my mother back so much. I thought I had put all that behind me, but being pregnant, it's like I've lost her all over again. I have so many questions, so many fears, I need my mom to be here to help me through this.

"At night I dream. Sometimes she's there. She's holding me,

massaging my hands, my feet, my stomach. I feel safe, I feel peace. And then there's darkness, there are shadows . . ."

Her speech faltered. Her mouth was open, ready to form words that she could not find. Words that expressed what it was like to be the child of a murdered mother.

"Here, Kit," said Chas, "drink this tea. It's supposed to help with the nausea."

Catherine, emotionally spent, complied. She brought the cup to her lips and drank the ocher nectar. She waited for her stomach to convulse, to send the tepid water back up. But the tension inside her relaxed, soothed by the tang of ginger and the balm of chamomile.

"Thanks," she sighed gratefully. "Where'd you get this?"

"Here," said Chas, not answering her question. "I want you to try this, too."

He handed her a bowl of the corn starch.

"Chas! I'm pregnant! I can't eat a bowl of sugar!"

"It's not sugar." He laughed. "Go ahead."

Puzzled, she looked down at the bowl. The downy powder looked just fluffy enough to float to the bottom of her stomach, settling the roiling acids like morning fog over the sea.

She scooped some of the powder on the spoon and put it in her mouth. The starch stuck to her tongue, melting like a Communion host. It was salty and sweet at the same time, both tasteless and robust, crunchy beneath her teeth like fresh snow underfoot.

Then she swallowed.

It was as if that part of Catherine that still mourned for a mother had been pacified. A feeling of satisfaction overwhelmed her. The unborn child settled in her womb.

A single tear slid down her cheek.

Dear Mom:

In three months they're going to move me to a Colorado facility. I've been a model prisoner, especially considering the fact that I'm innocent. I have always done what I was told. Now this is what I get in return.

You've got to help me. Find Mr. Hastings. Tell him to file a brief or something. There's got to be a way to stop them until I can get paroled.

Please hurry.

Nick

LETTIE DROPPED THE LETTER in her lap. What was she going to do? She got up and went to her dresser. From beneath her underwear, she found the smooth vinyl savings account passbook. She opened it: two hundred and seventy-five dollars. She'd managed not to touch her savings for the two weeks since she'd quit her job. But unless she found something else quickly, she'd have to pull the money out by the first of the month when the rent was due.

But how could she pay her bills and Nick's lawyer at the same time? And unless she paid his legal bill in full, he'd never agree to represent Nick one more time.

Despair enveloped her. She knew what moving to a new prison would mean for Nick. More fights to establish himself, more money for bribes, more cell mates to overpower him. She wanted him to stay at Leavenworth. At least there he knew the ropes and how to function. At least there he had hope of keeping clean and getting out on parole.

She took a deep breath and pulled out her Bible.

"Didn't my Lord deliver Daniel?" she prayed. "God, what must I do?"

She thought ruefully of Miz Catherine, sitting at home like a roosting hen, having to concentrate on nothing but herself and the safety of her unborn child. Here her baby was all grown up—a kind young man with a gentle heart and a love of music—but where were the people looking out for him? Miz Catherine didn't know how lucky she . . .

Mr. Rollins! Lettie closed her eyes against the inevitability of what she knew she had to do. Mr. Rollins would be willing to find a lawyer to help. She hadn't talked to either of the Rollinses since the day she'd walked out. As much as she hated the thought of going anywhere near that vicious redbone, at this point she had no choice. Whatever it took to save Nick, she was willing to do.

⁓

Catherine rolled over in the bed. The room was still dim, and calming raindrops pattered on the roof. She lay there listening, eyes closed, a smile on her face.

For the last two weeks, her life had been heaven. With the teas Chas had brought her, she no longer woke to an urgent, violent feeling in her stomach. With the lessening of the nausea, she was keeping food down. She'd gained three pounds in the last ten days.

Her appetite for the starch became insatiable. Chas had wondered out loud if it was healthy.

"Tell the voodoo woman who recommended it that she's created a monster," Catherine had joked. Chas had told her that both the tea and the suggestion that she eat cornstarch had come from an old woman who worked in his store.

But healthy or not, the starch made her feel more grounded, more connected to the earth rather than the sea. The peach came back to her sallow cheeks, the tenderness into her smile.

She rolled over and stretched her arm across Chas's bare back, lifting her head to plant a kiss on his cheek while he slept. He stretched lazily, then lifted his head to kiss her back.

"Good morning," he said.

"Morning!" She smiled.

"What time is it?"

"Um, I think about eight . . ."

"Jesus! I've got to get out of here!"

Catherine frowned and hugged him tighter. "Noooo!" she whined. "Don't leave me!"

She'd been spoiled these last few weeks. Ever since Lettie walked off the job, Chas had been staying with her more, working most of the day from home. She felt guilty about the stress he was under, but it was nice to have him around, nursing her back to health.

"Catherine," he said seriously, "I told you last night that I had to start going back to the office. This is the heavy season for us—I can't handle it from home. I'm so glad you're feeling better now— you look great! The doctor yesterday was pleased with your weight gain and says you've turned the corner on the morning sickness.

"Look at me, Kit," he said, raising himself on his elbows to face her. "You may not be going back to work right away; we can't rely on your income for now. And if my business fails, I won't be able to support you and the baby. I'm doing the best I can, and it's time for you to do what you can to make this work. I can't stay with you all day every day, you know that. We've got to get some help . . ."

Catherine closed her eyes. Her throat tightened, she could barely swallow. She realized how hard this had all been on Chas. She knew that he was struggling to keep a million balls in the air and the strain showed. While she'd grown stronger, she'd watched him become more bedraggled, screaming into the phone at vendors, dressing down employees he couldn't effectively supervise from home. He'd often be short with her before coming back to apologize. Sometimes he forgot about her meals altogether. After he did it twice, he guiltily put a small refrigerator in the bedroom in case she needed something before he could get to her.

Even while she was feeling stronger, her moods less brittle, her manner more easy, he was growing colder. She prayed that the baby would be born healthy. She didn't think their marriage would be able to withstand any more stress.

"Chas," she said, "I know it's been hard. But it's only five more months and then . . ."

"Five more months if we're lucky, Catherine. Get real. This is touch-and-go. And once the baby's born, there will be a whole new level of demands. You'll be weak from the bed rest. But the baby, God willing, will be up demanding your attention around the clock. We've got to be more prepared. Having me home isn't the answer."

The two lay in bed silently, each absorbed in their own thoughts.

"Catherine," Chase said eventually, "I have something to tell you."

Catherine looked at him, afraid. What was it? Was he going to leave her? Was there someone else?

"Lettie called me a week ago."

At the sound of Lettie's name, Catherine bolted upright in the bed.

"She wanted my help. She has a nineteen-year-old son serving time in federal prison in Kansas. She says Nick is innocent, but her lawyer won't file any appeals until she pays off her legal bills. Now they're threatening to move her son to a Colorado facility."

Catherine bristled. "And?"

"Well, I've asked Walter Stevens to review the case. He says it looks like there are plenty of grounds for appeal. He wants to take it on."

Catherine thought carefully before she spoke. She didn't want to anger her husband any further. "Chas, do you think it's wise to get caught up in that woman's personal problems? Of course she says her son's innocent—what else would she say? The prisons are chock-full of 'innocent' murderers and thieves! Do you really want to have her son released back into society on a technicality? What did he do? Rape? Assault?"

"Drug possession," said Chas. "He got stopped at the Windsor Tunnel. He and his friend, Shannon Murphy. They call him 'Shay Shay.' His friend had a gun and cocaine in the car when the border patrol shook them down. But Shay Shay accused Nick of bringing the drugs across the border, and according to Nick, the cop actually gave Shay Shay some guidance. He said, 'Look man, here's some advice. Stop hanging out with niggers and you'll stay clean. You know they're moving drugs back and forth across this border like roaches.'"

Catherine looked at Chas in disbelief. How could he be a sucker for such a flimsy story?

Chas continued. "Shannon is half-white, and apparently with his freckles, green eyes, and long blond hair, he passes for white whenever its convenient. The cops actually thought he was a white boy and they let him go. And Nick got hit with fifteen to thirty years for illegal possession of a weapon and for attempting to smuggle crack cocaine across the border."

"Sounds like a bullshit story to me—his word against the cops'."

"Maybe so. Except that one of the arresting cops has since retired. He's willing to testify that Nick's version of the story is true."

"Chas, I know you're into this black-unity 'African' thing, but you can't just take on every Negro off of the streets with a sob story."

"You listen to me," said Chas, fuming. "And you listen good. This is a black woman who needs our help, and I'm glad I've arrived at the point in life where I can lend it. I'm going to make sure her son gets a fair trial. I don't want to hear anything else about it.

"And one more thing," he said, pointing his finger at her chest. "I told Lettie that I would help her on the condition that she come back to work. Whether you want her here or not, she starts back here tomorrow. You make it work this time, Kit, or I don't know what's going to happen."

He got up and went into the bathroom. When she heard the shower running, she turned over and buried her head in the pillow. How could he have gone behind her back and negotiated with that woman? How could he betray her like that?

She sat up and wiped her face. Chas had lost it. He was desperate and grasping at straws. Right now, she was in no position to argue with him. She'd put up with Lettie until the baby was born. As soon as she got her strength back, she'd take matters into her own hands and find a proper nanny. Maybe an au pair from London or Belgium who wanted to come study in the United States. Not some low-life ghetto woman with a drug-dealing son.

She nodded to herself and took a deep breath.

"I can do this," she resolved. "At least I was right: Lettie and her kind aren't anything but a bunch of raping, drug-dealing gangstas, just like I thought . . ."

By the time Chas came out of the bathroom, she was smiling.

Chapter SEVEN

WHEN CATHERINE HEARD the front door open at eight a.m., she called down immediately. "Lettie! Is that you? Guess what?"

Lettie put down her bag and lifted herself up the stairs. "Yes, ma'am?" she said tiredly when she reached the bedroom.

"My college roommate is coming over to see me today! I haven't seen Raj in ten years! I can't wait! She used to fix me the most fabulous meals: samosas, tandoori chicken, curried rice and peas. You never tasted anything so good!"

Lettie smiled politely. Somehow, she liked the other Miz Catherine better. The one who was moody and stayed to herself. Since she'd come back to work Miz Catherine had changed. Her health was much better, for one. But there was something exhausting about her fake friendliness, her patronizing attempts to be civil. Lettie felt like a calf being fattened for slaughter. "Do you want me to fix lunch for the two of you? I don't know anything about Indian food, but I could fix some chicken salad . . ."

"No, that's okay. Raj is bringing everything. What should I wear? I don't want her to see me sitting here like a pathetic hag . . ."

"Now don't overdo it, Miz Catherine," said Lettie, worried now that Miz Catherine was feeling better, she would push herself too hard. "Mr. Rollins told me you could use the lift to come downstairs today, but you still have to stay put in the living room while your company is here."

Catherine nodded, smiling. Nothing was going to ruin her day today. Not Chas's annoying hovering, not Lettie's spying eyes, not the restless tumbling of the infant in her womb.

Lettie nearly gasped when she'd opened the door for Raj. The young woman was dark. Much darker than Lettie, but her features were sharp and thin as a white person's. Somehow the strange juxtaposition of racial features made the woman as striking as an onyx statue. Her shiny black hair hung in a braid down her back. She wore a loose bright turquoise printed gown with matching pants and sandals. A yellow chiffon scarf was draped dramatically around her neck and over one shoulder. And she was pregnant.

Topping off the colorful ensemble was a dark brown man's fedora hat she wore on her head. It seemed so out of place that Lettie couldn't help but stare. Nothing about the elegant woman suggested a hankering for this unusual fashion punctuation. Maybe it was her personal trademark, something she was never without, Lettie mused.

Raj smiled with a row of sparkling white teeth and removed the hat with a slender hand. "Hello! I am Raj. I'm here to visit Catherine."

It was then that Lettie noticed a contrast even greater than that of her dark skin and keen features. While Raj's face was youthful and her smooth skin glowed with the radiance of pregnancy, her eyes were that of someone much older. They shone with a serenity and wisdom that somehow reminded Lettie of her grandmother, Sadie Mitchell. Lettie forced herself to stop staring, then nodded with a polite smile and reached out to take the shopping bag full of warm dishes from Raj's outstretched hands. "Thanks," Raj said. She smiled and looked expectantly at Lettie. "I am Raj," she repeated. "And you are . . . ?"

"She's the maid." Catherine's voice floated coldly from behind before Lettie could reply. "One of Chas's business associates referred her to us." Catherine's laugh was forced and bitter. "Lettie and Chas get along so well, in fact, that he's hired her to help us out. For now."

Raj nodded carefully and, seeing that Lettie was not going to accept her hand, lowered it gracefully to her side. "Look at you!" she patted Catherine's belly as the old friends enveloped each other in a warm embrace.

"Raj! Oh, Raj, it's so good to see you!" Catherine cried.

Lettie stepped aside to let them enjoy their reunion. She couldn't help but notice the contrast between Catherine's apricot skin and Raj's rich coffee hue. Hmph, Lettie thought, I wonder if Miz Catherine has any African-American friends who are that black. She chuckled mirthlessly to herself as she headed to the kitchen. Be a cold day down there before that happens, I'll bet.

Putting together a tray of brightly flowered plates and shining flatware, Lettie arranged the fragrant foods on crystal serving dishes, savoring the exotic blend of spices. Returning to the living room, Lettie heard Raj say, "You're due in August, right?"

"How'd you know?" Catherine asked peevishly. "Of course you always did have the answers before most of us had the questions."

Lettie stood, tray in hand, gazing at the hat Raj had hung on a hook on the coatrack in the foyer, the idle conversation washing over her.

"Well, I'm due around the same time and I just had a feeling that we were on the same schedule." Raj smiled. "I can't believe you and Chas finally decided to have kids," said Raj. "Shiv and I ended up buckling to family pressure. It was terrible what we went through."

"I can't imagine, Raj," said Catherine. "Your family has always been so traditional. I still don't know how you convinced them to let you go to law school."

"Shiv had a lot to do with that," Raj said softly. "When he made it clear how much money the two of us would be able to make and send back home to India, you'd be surprised how the objections calmed down. But not, however, the pressure to make some babies."

Lettie moved into the kitchen to serve the meal. The women's voices rose and fell outside the kitchen door. While Lettie couldn't make out their words, the warm comfort and affirmation of long-time friendship was unmistakable. Lettie felt a stab of loneliness, suddenly realizing how much she'd missed the simple pleasure of a woman friend with whom she could compare notes about life's ups and downs. Well, she reasoned, lifting the tray of luncheon delicacies, we all get what we need in life. Maybe I don't need a friend right now.

"Here," said Lettie, arranging the colorful food and plates before the laughing friends. There was something about Raj . . . those eyes, that hat . . . that made Lettie want to sit with her. Though she was younger in years, Lettie had a feeling that Raj had achieved a deeper understanding of life than many others her age. Especially Miz Catherine with her self-absorbed, childlike ways. "Can I get you anything else?" Lettie asked coldly.

"Um, may we please get some hot water for tea?" Raj asked, sending Lettie a look of apology.

"Certainly," Lettie said, articulating each syllable separately and heading back toward the kitchen.

"Now, how have you been feeling, my friend?" Raj leaned toward Catherine with a look of concern.

"Oh, Raj, I felt terrible for the longest time. Then Chas brought me some herbal tea and other things I guess I'd been craving without realizing it. I'm feeling much better now." Catherine smiled and rubbed her stomach. "Still, it is a high-risk pregnancy. If I survive this bed rest, I think I can survive anything."

Raj nodded while taking in each word. "Speaking of tea, I brought a special blend made by my aunts. They say it prepares your body to give birth and even to nurse your baby. One cup each day is all you need—and it's more than enough, because I tell you, it tastes terrible! But with a little honey, you can get it down."

Catherine startled her friend with her next question. "Raj, Shiv is so much lighter than you are and . . . well, have you thought about what complexion you baby might turn out to have?"

Lettie froze in her tracks and hovered near the doorway to the kitchen.

Raj leaned back from her plate and paused thoughtfully. The air in the room crackled with a new tension. "The aunts who gave me this tea used to make me drink a more bitter tea when I was a child," she said sadly. "While it tasted sweet, even without honey, it had a bitterness all its own. You see, my friend, this tea was supposed to lighten my shade, as they used to say. Make me have a 'fairer' complexion.

"Your people and mine, we put so much weight on the shade of our skin. In India, you know, the blackest of us are at the bottom of society—'untouchables,' they call us. My mother's family are of a lighter hue and higher caste, and they were devastated when she fell in love with my coal-black father. He was intelligent, hardworking, good-hearted, and he adored my mother. But all they saw was his skin, and they never fully accepted him. And when I was born, oh!

"My caramel-colored aunts huddled to discuss how I would ever find an Indian man to marry me. You can imagine their surprise—and relief—when I became engaged to Shiv. I'll try and answer your question gently, Catherine. Growing up as I have and knowing the truths of our world, and what is really important in life, I never agonize over what shade of skin my child will have. As long as he or she is healthy, it's the parent's responsibility to teach the children to love the skin they are in."

Catherine thought for a moment about how her nipples had darkened over the last few months. And a dark line had appeared from her navel and crept over her lower stomach and into her pubic area, cutting her abdomen in two like a peach. She'd worried that these were signs that she was darkening because of the pregnancy. Or worse, that the baby was dark and its pigment was somehow leaking out and affecting her coloring. "You know," she said to Raj, "I hear what you're saying, but I was raised with far different views on skin color. I can remember when as a child I used to steal sips of my grandma's coffee and one day she caught me and went berserk. She was livid, and not because coffee is bad for children, but because she was convinced that coffee would make my skin turn black! I never found out whether there was any truth to that, but I've never looked at a cup of coffee the same way, and just in case it *is* true, you can bet I haven't had a single sip since I've been pregnant!"

Raj ate silently for a few moments before responding. "Have you ever thought, dear friend, that you give far too much importance to skin color? Look at me. All my aunts' worries were for nothing. Even I—'the black one,' as they called me—found a wonderful man to love and marry. I was a top student at school, I'm self-confident, and I am successful in my career. And despite all of the things that were said to me and the way dark people were treated when I was growing up, I *like* what I see in the mirror, Catherine. And so do a lot of other women who look like me. We are not walking around hating ourselves and wanting to look like you or like those in your family. We are confident and assured about our own natural beauty, and I think that's all we can hope for. For our children, too, no matter what shade they turn out to be."

Catherine took a moment to absorb Raj's words. "Well, even though Chas and I are both light, I know there's always the possibility that our child won't be. I'm not sure what I would do if it wasn't . . ." Then she forced the brightness back into her voice and quickly changed the subject. "Hey, Raj! I remember when we were young my mom would take my brother and me up to Lake Beulah on vacation."

At the mention of Lake Beulah, Lettie took a sharp breath and inched closer to the sofa.

"It was so lovely back then." Catherine sighed. "Not run-down like it is now. Grandma would cook all day before we left and we'd eat all the way there—fried chicken, collard greens, candied yams, cornbread, even pigs' feet. Mother would make us pull over at a gas station about thirty miles outside of Lake Beulah and toss every shred of evidence of our country feast into the nearest trash can! My Lord, we don't eat those nigger delicacies anymore, but back then it sure was good!

"I remember how we'd go outside and play on our end of the lake—you know, where the vacationers all had cabins. We'd be outside all day just running around, swimming, making mud pies, just being free. Those were some of the best times of my life."

Catherine giggled, as both friends sipped their tea.

"Of course, it wasn't all milk and honey. I remember when Velda got caught in the woods alone and those black, bald-headed country girls held her down and cut all her beautiful hair off. You should have seen her hair—almost like yours—down to her waist and not a kink in it! Not even a wave! What a scene! I'm pretty sure her daddy pressed charges, he being a lawyer and everything.

"I tell you, those natives could be so mean to us! You'd think they'd want us there since we paid them to do our yards and clean our cabins during the summers. But no, they were completely rude. Didn't even appreciate us. So we stayed among ourselves on the lake. Frankly, we were afraid of them."

"Afraid?" Raj raised one eyebrow. "Why on earth would you be afraid of your own people?"

"My people? They looked different, spoke different, had lots of babies, no money, no real jobs . . . they weren't really our kind of people at all." Catherine grimaced. "I remember at night we used to stay up late and tell ghost stories about them. Our favorite was the one about Black Sadie." She spoke faster, as if the story still made her blood run cold. "She was a ghost—a big black woman with giant hands. She'd come into your room at night wearing an old man's hat that covered most of her face. You had to sleep with the sheets up to your forehead, because if Black Sadie saw your lips, she'd put her mouth over yours and suck your breath away."

Lettie felt her knees buckle. She reached for the back of the sofa. Black Sadie? Sadie Mitchell, her grandmother?

"All of us were terrified of Black Sadie," said Catherine, all tingles, "and not just because she was a ghost, but because she was so . . . so *black*. Not pretty and exotic black like you, Raj, with your beautiful hair and keen features. Just regular black. Ordinary African black. You know, that kind of black that takes the sun and doesn't let it out. Like the black in the back of your closet or beneath your bed. It was terrifying!" She paused to wrap an afghan around her shivering shoulders.

"The story was that she was jealous of one of the families vacationing on our side of the lake and killed their baby, then went to jail for the murder. Killed it fresh out of its mama's womb, just because the baby's parents were from a very successful family with beautiful features and lovely hair. That scandal was the biggest thing that ever happened in Lake Beulah, and the story was on everyone's lips year after year. So we grew up being terrified by the legend of Black Sadie and her big, murderous lips."

Raj's eyes bored into Catherine's as her friend continued to swim through her childhood memories. "And believe it or not, the natives of Lake Beulah had the *nerve* to look at us cabin folks like *we* were the trash, as though we'd done something unforgivable to *them* that made them hate the sight of us. It wasn't us decent folks who ran around killing their rusty-butt babies! I didn't understand it then and I'm not sure I understand it now," Catherine murmured, rubbing her belly lightly. She looked at her friend pointedly. "But color *does* matter and it doesn't do a bit of good to pretend that it doesn't."

Her eyes brimming with tears, Lettie unfroze and fled to the kitchen. To think that her grandmother, a woman who had loved everyone, no matter their skin color, who dedicated herself to bringing forth new life, was the town symbol of fear and hatred. Not remembered for her skills as a midwife, for her service to the poor people of Lake Beulah, but for the murder of an infant, a murder she didn't commit. A murder she *couldn't* have committed.

Lettie slumped against the cold marble of the countertop. How could she find the strength to kowtow to Miz Catherine, one of those high-yellow rich niggers who had demonized the memory of her grandmother, who had allowed the woman to spend her last years on earth confined to a six-by-eight-foot maximum-security cell?

"Lettie?" she heard Miz Catherine's voice calling a moment later. "Lettie? Raj has to leave now. I want you to walk her to the door."

Lettie murmured a prayer beneath her breath. "Yes, ma'am," she answered slowly.

"Lettie, it was so nice meeting you," said Raj as she hesitated near the doorway. "You're taking good care of Kit . . ." Raj's voice trailed off.

Lettie looked down, avoiding Raj's gaze. "I know Catherine is kind of . . ." Raj whispered apologetically. "Sometimes she can be . . . Well, you know. Just be there for her. She's clueless. Never been taught a thing about racial pride and identity. She needs you."

Lettie looked at Raj in disbelief. How could someone as dark as Raj befriend a redbone like Catherine?

Raj read the expression on Lettie's face and nodded. Without saying a word, she lifted the rich brown fedora hat from the coat-rack and extended it toward Lettie. "I know. It may not make sense now, but it will in time. Take this as a gift from me, please. And be sure to wear it, all right?"

Lettie hesitated, but Raj urged the hat toward her until she accepted it simply to be polite. What kind of foolishness was this? She was brain weary and bone tired, sick to death of crazy Miz Catherine and unsure what to make of her darkly exotic friend.

"Well, thanks again," said Raj, reaching out to give Lettie's shoulder a brief, warm squeeze. "You know more than you realize. And the truth never looks the same from opposite sides of the mirror."

Then calling past Lettie, "Take care, Kit! Let's promise to call whoever delivers first!"

Lettie closed the door firmly, wishing she could leave with Raj.

"Oh, Lettie, isn't Raj wonderful?" Miz Catherine called from the living room. "Not at all like most of the black women in my college dorm. I had such a lovely afternoon. It was like old times . . ."

Lettie only half heard the pregnant woman as she turned the fedora in her hands, amazed at its resemblance to the hat her grandmother had worn day and night, no matter what time of year. When folks saw that hat, they knew who was up under it, Lettie chuckled softly to herself. Well, who knows what will happen with this one.

"Lettie? Lettie? Don't you hear me calling you?" Catherine whined. "You'll need to clear these dishes up. And be sure to wrap the leftovers for Chas. I want to give him a special treat when he gets home."

Lettie sighed and returned the hat to its hook. "Coming, Miz Catherine," she answered. Then under her breath she added, "Lord, help me endure this woman for one more day."

Chapter Eight

FOR THE LAST WEEK, every day when Lettie got home from work, LaShon and Lamont had been playing by her door. Most days, they'd been playing there for up to three hours, since that was the time their school let out.

Lettie sat at her dinette table watching them eat the last of her macaroni and cheese. She'd forgotten how much boys, even little ones, could eat. Tomorrow if Tina didn't show up, she'd have to call protective services. Even as she gave the boys a reassuring smile and a second helping of macaroni, she grieved. She knew that once they were in the system they'd never get out. And they'd probably be separated in foster care. They were reaching the age that made them hard to adopt. Her heart grew heavy for the loss, even before it happened.

"Mama Lettie, can we turn on the TV?" asked LaShon, always trying her limits.

"Feed your belly and then feed your mind," she repeated for the hundredth time. "Tonight, we read!"

The boys groaned like they always did. Then LaShon asked, "Can you read us *Everett Anderson's Goodbye?*"

"Oh, that's so sad!" Lettie complained, wondering what on earth had possessed her to buy a book about a boy losing his father. But the boys loved it so much they'd almost memorized every page. "Well, okay," she gave in after seeing the crestfallen look on their cute little brown faces.

The boys cheered as they left their dirty dishes on the table, each scrambling to be the one to get the book. Lettie laughed and cleaned the plates up herself. She just didn't feel like lecturing tonight. It had been a good day. Miz Catherine had gone to the hospital to get her stitches removed, and Mr. Rollins had taken the rest of the week off to be with his wife. That had given Lettie an unexpected two days off.

She'd spent yesterday morning gloating, exuberant that she'd ushered Miz Catherine into her eighth month without incident. Just one more month to go. She'd treated herself to lunch at Big Boy's and then walked around Belle Isle before returning home to find the twins at her door.

But this morning she'd gotten up ready to attend to business. She got a letter off to Nick updating him on the case. The attorney, Mr. Walter Stevens, had said that they should know any day now whether or not the court would hear Nick's appeal.

> *I have a good feeling about this. Mr. Stevens is a good lawyer—the best. I know that a door will open for us soon. At least you won't be transferred to another prison until the appeals are complete. That buys us a little more time for now. God bless Mr. Rollins. Remember, son, God's eye is on the sparrow.*
>
> *Love, Mom*

She'd stopped by the bank to pay her utility bills and check on her savings balance: $1,150. Her heart skipped a beat. She'd even begun thinking about buying a used car. Then she went to the store to get more groceries in case she had to feed the boys again that evening. She was glad she did, because when she got back to the apartment at four o'clock (she'd meant to be there at three to beat them home), she found Lamont trotting in pain before her door.

"I have to go, Mama Lettie!" he said as she fumbled with the door key. "Hurry!" Lettie sighed after them as they ran toward the bathroom, removing the brown fedora hat and stroking its soft brim absentmindedly. She'd been wearing it every day, indoors and out, just as her grandmother had worn hers, and somehow the fedora brought her inner peace and tranquility during life's storms, especially as she remembered how Raj had looked in it, her old-soul eyes comforting and grandma familiar. Smiling wearily, Lettie set the hat on her hall table and hurried into the kitchen.

After she'd cooked for the boys and they'd eaten their fill, Lettie was happy but exhausted. She was about to settle down with a book when the doorbell rang.

"Who could that be?" she asked the boys, who shrugged in unison as if they were really expected to know.

Lettie pushed herself up from the sofa and walked to the door, peering out of the peephole. "Who is it?" she asked, not recognizing the man's face.

"I have a delivery for Lettie Greene," came the voice on the other side of the door.

A delivery? Nothing but bad news had ever been delivered in their neighborhood. She shrugged as the boys stood fascinated. The fact was, not even a newspaper or a pizza was ever delivered to anyone in the building. Lettie opened the door slowly with the security chain engaged. There was a man standing at the door with two packages. One was clearly a bundle of flowers in a ceramic vase. The other was a wrapped item the size of a cigar box.

Lettie closed the door to remove the chain then opened it wide.

"Here you go, ma'am," a short young man said, pushing the packages toward her. She took them and sat them on the dinette table. "Could you sign here?" he asked, pulling a clipboard from his armpit.

"What is it? What is it?" the boys chimed, ready for a new adventure.

Lettie let them rip open the paper on the flowers while she grabbed the card inside. *Congratulations,* it read. *The court has agreed to hear Nick's appeal! Charles Rollins.*

"Oh my God!" Lettie screamed, hugging the boys and jumping up and down. They screamed, too, laughing as they imitated Lettie. "Nick may be coming home soon!" The boys broke into a dance, hoping that one day soon Nick would be home to teach them how to play the piano.

"What's in the other box?" asked LaShon, taking it to the sofa to open it. He ripped the paper off with one tear, exposing a gleaming gold foil box underneath. "Oooo . . ." the boys cooed.

Lettie took the box, which looked oddly familiar. She opened it slowly to reveal a box of chocolates.

Enjoy, the card inside read. *Catherine told me how much you love Godivas. Charles.*

Lettie's face went hot. Leave it to Miz Catherine to ruin the happiest day of her life by taking the opportunity to throw five pieces of candy back in her face.

Lettie got the boys down at about nine o'clock, no small task since they were used to staying up until the wee hours. It didn't help that she'd let them gorge on the chocolates, too furious to eat them herself.

After tucking the boys in on the sofa, Lettie retrieved her fedora from the hall table. She reached under the sofa and got her hat box, then walked slowly into her small bedroom. Standing before her bed, she set the hat lightly on her head, then lowered herself gratefully onto the paisley bedspread. She sighed. Tonight, instead of reading her Bible, she opened the hatbox and thumbed through the letters inside.

Purposely, she skipped the ones from Nick and went directly to the ones tied with a lavender ribbon. The ones from her grandmother Sadie.

"Judge not, lest ye be judged," she read her grandmother's words.

> *That's what I'm trying to tell you, sugar. I'm fine here. Women's prison ain't like men's. I get my meals and my time to pray. I helps the other women with their troubles. I'm here for a reason. God is always with us.*
>
> *Sugar, when you write me, you seem so angry. But when I was sent here, you won't but nine or ten. What you got to be mad about?*
>
> *Yes, you right. It won't my fault that rich yella woman called me to her side the night she was giving birth. And it won't my fault that the baby was born blue, the cord wrapped around its poor little neck. I did what I could, Lord knows. Put my mouth to that child's and blew hard as I could.*
>
> *It was her husband that was the trouble. He was always too good for us county folk. You wonder why a Negro so scared the sun would darken his high-falutin skin felt a need to vacation in Lake Beulah anyway. Maybe it was the only place on earth he could feel better than someone else. He was boiling mad cause no white doctor would come into town to see about his wife. No matter how rich he was, them white folks at the hospital told him that anybody who stayed on Lake Beulah was a nigger, and their doctors didn't treat niggers for love or for money.*
>
> *So when that man saw me standing there, my black*

mouth nearly covering that baby's pale face and he near
bout had a fit. When I couldn't get the child to breathe, the
momma fainted away in grief. I think she just lost her
mind right there. But her husband was possessed of the
devil. He called the county sheriff while I was there trying
to get the momma to hold her dead baby. When the police
came and took me, that baby's soul was still sittin' there
waiting for her momma to send her to heaven.

Maybe what hurt me most was how that woman sat
there in that trial and ain't said nary a word in my defense. Not one. While her husband, mad that he couldn't
get back at those white doctors, made me pay for his blackness and his trouble.

When I heard about your Nick goin to prison, somethin in me just died all over again. I know exactly what it
feels like, sugar, to be betrayed by one a your own. Another
high-falutin Negro handing his brethren over to the white
man.

But you know, I can't carry that man's self-hatred on
my back. Every day I remember God's words. How when
Rebecca was pregnant with twins, God told her, "Two nations are in thy womb." That's what all black women carry
in their womb, two nations. They never know when the
white slave master seed will show itself in their children.
And then the babies got to be born fightin: fightin cause
they're either too black for their own people or fightin cause
they're too light for their own people.

You got to stop fightin, Lettie-girl. You gotta let it go.
Cause what we need here is a new birth. A new awakening. Take what I taught you and do something good for another person's sufferin. That's what God wants. You want to
see your Nicholas set free? You gotta love, child. Even when
it's hard.

Lettie put down the letter and wept. She thought about Miz Catherine and her fear of "Black Sadie." Miz Catherine, whose husband was paradoxically turning out to be the last hope for Lettie's only son. Lettie prayed for her grandmother's capacity to love and if possible, for a fraction of her courage.

Chapter Nine

LETTIE," SAID CATHERINE as Lettie dusted the bookshelves in the study. "I'm so tired of being cooped up in this apartment. The whole summer is passing me by! I think I'd like to get away for a week or so."

"Away?" asked Lettie, her hackles rising. "Where to? You know you can't fly in your condition."

"In my condition?" Catherine mimicked. "Do you know what my condition is? My condition is that if I don't get out from under you and Chas, I'm going to lose my damned mind. The doctor removed my stitches four days ago. She said that I could move around more. Besides, I don't want to fly anywhere. I want to drive."

"You can't drive! The doctor said—"

"No, no." Catherine shook her head in annoyance. "I want *you* to drive. I'll ride. To Lake Beulah. My mother's ashes are there and I just want to go and be there for a while before the baby comes. Just a week or so."

Lettie stood with her hands on her hips. "Now, Miz Catherine, you know if Mr. Rollins was here—"

"But he's not. Chas is in Sierra Leone and I'll call him as soon as we get to the lake. You don't work for him now, you work for *me*. And I say we're going. I'm not due for another month and I'm definitely in shape to ride for three or four hours in a car. We're leaving on Friday."

Lettie searched her mind for an excuse. She knew Mr. Rollins would have a fit if he found out. And what if something happened to Miz Catherine while Lettie was driving? The Rollinses were both lawyers. Would they press charges?

Plus, the mere thought of going back to Lake Beulah made her shudder. The courthouse, the run-down shacks where the towns-people lived—where she'd lived during the summers as a child with Grandma Sadie. The rows of spacious cabins around Lake Beulah, filled with out-of-town, uppity Negro vacationers, some whom could almost pass for white, and who had ample money and time to spare. And the lies about Sadie and that baby that had become legend among the townspeople. How could she return to such a place?

Lettie stared blankly, cornered. What could she say? If she didn't oblige, Miz Catherine might balk about her staying on to be the baby's nanny. If she did, Mr. Rollins might arrive at the same conclusion.

⟋

Lettie was deep in thought about how to get out of the trip to Lake Beulah when she stepped off of the Jefferson bus. She'd already plodded up DeGras and turned down Chalfonte when she noticed the flashing lights of police cars and EMS in front of her apartment building.

Her heart raced and her breath became short. She looked at her watch. Five-thirty. Thank God she was a little early today. If the boys were locked out of their apartment again, they'd be terrified by all the commotion.

As she came closer, she saw that the police were restraining a heavyset, dark-skinned woman dressed in a pair of blue Daisy Duke shorts and a halter top. The sound of her cries was un-mistakable.

It was Tina.

Lettie quickened into a trot, her eyes searching the crowd gathered outside for the boys.

"Mama Lettie!" She heard a small voice. She closed her eyes with relief. It was Lamont. "Mama Lettie!"

She ran toward the voice, finally spotting Lamont in the back of the police car.

"Oh my God, what's happened?" she screamed.

"No! No! Let me go, my boy, my baby!" wailed Tina, who was flailing so wildly that two policemen had to restrain her.

"Do you know this child?" came a voice over Lettie's shoulder. She turned to find a white woman in a blazer and slacks standing beside a police officer. White people never came into this neighborhood. She had to be a social worker.

"Y-yes," said Lettie, the fear rising. "What's happened? Where's LaShon?"

"Mama Lettie!" Lamont's voice became as shrill as the siren on the EMS truck as it sped away.

"How do you know the boys?" the white woman asked gently.

"I live next door," said Lettie, crying. "Where's LaShon?"

"Do you know the boys' mother?" The woman continued her line of questioning.

"No," Lettie wailed. "I mean, no one really knows her; she's never around. WHERE'S LASHON?"

"Ma'am, there's been an accident. It looks like the boy was hit by a stray bullet during a drive-by shooting."

"WHAT?" Lettie moaned, her knees buckling. "Is he okay? He's going to be okay, right?"

The social worker looked at her grimly without speaking.

"Mama Lettie!" Lamont cried. "They got my brother!"

The police handcuffed Tina and put her in another squad car and drove away. Lettie walked past the yellow police tape toward Lamont, her arms spread wide. A police officer reached to stop her, but the social worker grabbed his arm and nodded. "Let her see the boy," she said.

As Lettie neared the squad car, Lamont leaped out into her arms. They said nothing, just squeezed each other tight, believing if only for a moment they were both safe. Finally, the boy spoke.

"My brother." He wept, mucus and tears covering his terrified face. "We were going around the neighborhood lookin' for Tina. All of a sudden, there were shots and LaShon fell down. I couldn't get him to get back up. He wouldn't get up."

Lettie grabbed the tail of her skirt and wiped the boy's face. "Shh, now," she said. "Somehow, everything's gonna be all right. LaShon is going to heaven now where my grandma will take good care of him. Don't you worry, okay?"

The boy had been crying so long his sobs were coming in dry hiccups. His little body trembled against hers. If she could, she would have pushed him into her breast, absorbed him straight into her heart.

"Remember Everett Anderson?" she said, her voice rising with false hope. "No matter what happens when people die . . ." she began.

And the little boy added ever so softly, ". . . Love doesn't stop and neither will I."

Chapter TEN

B Y THE TIME THEY REACHED FLINT Catherine was sound asleep. With a little more than an hour's drive remaining, Lettie pushed the brown fedora further back on her head and looked over at her charge: Catherine's cheeks now full and plush against her high cheekbones. Even as she dozed, the pregnant woman twisted and turned in the seat belt trying to get comfortable. *She'll probably have to stop again to use the bathroom before we get to Frankenmuth*, Lettie predicted.

This whole scenario was wrong and they both knew it. Taking off for Lake Beulah a week after the doctor had removed Catherine's stitches, two days after Mr. Rollins had left for Africa.

"We've made it past the danger point now," he'd said to Lettie the evening before he left. "I want to thank you for all you've done. By the time I come back it will only be a matter of days before the baby is due. We're lucky to have found someone so wonderful and trustworthy to help get us through."

Lettie felt guilty that she was betraying the trust Mr. Rollins had placed in her. Miz Catherine could not have left home without Lettie's assistance. Lettie could have refused, but she hadn't.

Not after LaShon, not after the funeral.

Not after seeing that precious, innocent little boy in a powder-blue suit—the first suit he'd ever worn—laying in a white casket, smiling the way babies smile in their sleep. Not after having agreed to testify against Tina in order for Lamont to be taken away and placed in foster care.

Suddenly, Lettie's apartment became unbearable. At night she kept hearing thumping against the walls. She'd jump up from her bed, hobble to the door and open it, expecting to see the boys there, playing with their trucks.

But the halls were filled with nothing but ghosts now. Even Tina's apartment was strangely quiet. It was as if in a second, every-thing familiar to Lettie had suddenly disappeared. If it wasn't for Nick, she would have wanted to disappear herself.

So when Catherine demanded that Lettie get her suitcase from the storage room and call a maid service in Lake Beulah to have the cabin ready when they arrived, Lettie simply gave in. Why not get away from all this sorrow? The loss of her daughter. The imprison-ment of her son. The murder of little LaShon. How many more children could she bear to lose?

Her resentment of Catherine boiled higher each day. Mothers of black children were tucking their children into caskets while she sat there like a queen bee, nesting with a team of the best doctors waiting to bring her precious child into the world. The Rollins child stood little chance of being lost to life's darkest side. Its sun-yellow face and dimpled smile would radiate with privilege, love, and security. This one would be spared the threat of the real boogeymen of this world.

Unless the child was born on a road like this one. Or in the woods at Lake Beulah, where the rustic life leveled the playing field between the redbones and their dark-skinned shadows.

"Lord, Lord, Lord," Lettie breathed, looking over at the passenger side of the car where Catherine slept soundly. She couldn't help but wonder if she'd agreed to this trip on the slim chance that, while out in those woods, Miz Catherine finally would be forced take a sip of the nectar everyone else called real life.

Catherine's eyes flew wide open. Her hair curled tightly against the cold sweat on her scalp. Her breaths came hot and shallow. She was in her cabin at Lake Beulah. The crickets rubbed their legs together, kicking up an earthy ruckus outside of her window. Her mouth felt dry and parched. Had she screamed? Had she cried out her mother's name?

"You all right, Miz Catherine?" Lettie was knocking at her door, her voice slurred with drowsiness.

"I'm fine," said Catherine, wondering if Lettie had been snooping by her door in the middle of the night. "Go back to sleep."

Catherine sat up and eased her legs over the side of the bed. It seemed everything hurt now. Her back, her stomach, her legs. Her Braxton Hicks contractions were coming more frequently now. That sudden hardening of her stomach that the doctor had told her would start several weeks before the baby was due. But she hadn't thought they'd be strong enough to wake her from a deep sleep. And it didn't help that she'd had one of those frightening dreams.

All the way down in the car she'd been haunted by dream demons. A woman in a hat. A baby's cries growing louder and louder until they sounded like the wail of a police siren. Hysteria. Confusion. And each time, she awakened sweaty and panicked, reaching for Chas in the emptiness that surrounded her.

She stood slowly, pulled on a robe, and padded quietly down the cabin hall, past Lettie's room, to the bathroom. She stopped in the dark in front of the picture in the hall. A photo of Catherine, Marcus, and their mom sitting atop horses in front of Buster's Riding Stables.

In the darkness, the photo was only shadows, but Catherine didn't need light to remember how the sun had shone that day, bronze and glorious. How Marcus's horse, Kato, kept wandering off the trail scavenging for sweetgrass. How Mom had trotted ahead, her ponytail bobbing behind her, lovely and regal as a princess.

It's funny how sometimes you can't remember your first-grade teacher or your first valentine, but you can remember one single, ordinary day, Catherine thought. A day that was comforting in its routineness, spectacular only in that there were thousands more like it. What she wouldn't give to be out there again on those ponies, Marcus crying because his horse wouldn't move, Mom galloping ahead, free and laughing.

Catherine used the bathroom and went back to her room, pausing only to notice the light on in Lettie's room. That eternal eye, always watching her. That voodoo woman who was as stealthy and black as a bad-luck cat. She couldn't wait to get Lettie out of her life once and for all. It wouldn't be long now.

She lowered herself into the bed, noticing how the baby seemed suddenly heavier, like a rock slung low in a gunnysack. "I'll be glad to unload you!" She sighed, patting her stomach.

Catherine closed her eyes and breathed deeply, the scent of pine and honeysuckle wafting through the open window. She was glad to be at Lake Beulah. For the first time in months, she felt as if she was home.

⁓

"Good morning, Miz Catherine," Lettie said as she stood drinking a cup of coffee. "I'll get your eggs going. Your tea is already steeping."

"Just fix me some toast," Catherine said. "I'm not hungry this morning."

Lettie looked at Catherine, concerned. "You feelin' okay? You were up a lot last night."

"I feel great. I'm just not hungry," said Catherine, opening the patio door and walking out onto the deck.

Lettie poured Catherine's tea and gingerly followed her outside. Lettie hadn't been able to rest since they'd gotten to Lake Beulah. She was terrified about what would happen when Mr. Rollins found out they'd left Detroit. "Did you call Mr. Rollins and tell him where you are?" Lettie asked meekly.

"That's none of your business!" Catherine snapped. "That's between me and my husband. Where's my toast?"

Lettie nodded and scampered back into the kitchen to get the toast.

Catherine smiled to herself. Old woman was about to worry her hair straight! And she had reason to worry. Catherine was sure Chas would be furious, more so at Lettie, who had done the driving, than with her. Maybe he'd end up firing Lettie and saving Catherine all the trouble.

Lettie brought Catherine her toast. Beads of dew sparkled on the redwood deck. A gentle wind tossed the birch branches overhead.

"Gonna be hot today," said Lettie, pushing her hat back from her forehead to catch the breeze. "I think I'll walk to the food mart this morning before it gets unbearable. Did you make a list?"

"It's on the table," Catherine said. "Remember, I can only use Dove."

"Okay," said Lettie taking her coffee cup back into the cabin. "I'm going to change into my clothes and walk on down there."

"Take the car," said Catherine.

"No, thanks," said Lettie. "I've had enough of driving for one week. I'd rather walk."

Catherine shrugged. "Suit yourself."

When Lettie had left for the store, Catherine stood up, pacing. She had to call Chas before he called home and found out she was gone. Her heart throbbed as she picked up her cell phone. When she turned it on, she discovered that she had a voice mail.

Grateful for any diversion, she listened to it right away.

"Hey, Catherine, this is Walter Stevens. I've been trying to reach Chas, but I think he's out of the country right now. Can you deliver a message for me? Can you tell him that the court has agreed to hear Nick's appeal? He'll be released from Leavenworth pending the appeal and will be home within a week. I know Chas will be happy—he's really been concerned about this young man. Looks like he was right. The boy was set up, and our chances of getting a retrial are excellent. Anyway, hope you're doing well and good luck with the baby. . . ."

Catherine saved the message. Well, how about that? she marveled. Lettie had been telling the truth! Her son wasn't a drug dealer after all!

"But now that he's been to prison, rolling around with that nasty element, who knows what kind of animal he is!" she muttered. "I still don't trust her or her family around my baby."

Lettie strolled down the gravel path from the cabin to the tiny general store on the main road. It had been so long since she'd walked like this, down an isolated, heavily wooded path. Lake Beulah. She was surprised at all the good memories that came flooding back, the bad ones somehow dwarfed by the blue sky, the sweet air, the chirp of the nestlings. How she and her grandmother had walked these paths many times looking for wild blueberries or bringing a line of fish home for an afternoon fry. Past Beulah Island where the wealthy doctors, lawyers, and ministers used the logs her grandfather felled to build their cabins and retirement homes.

She had only been about ten when they left Lake Beulah, but it seemed like the placid lake and forests of pine and dogwoods had never left her blood. Maybe things are different now, she thought. Maybe one day Nick will be home and we can come back here to live. No gunshots. No police sirens, no streets full of dirty snow in the winter.

Nick. He'd never known what it was like to catch tadpoles in a jar, to chase fireflies at dusk, to weave halos out of dandelions, to chew the tangy rinds of watermelon pickles. Maybe if they'd stayed in Lake Beulah, Lois would still be alive and Nick wouldn't be trapped behind bars.

Lettie found herself praying in gratitude as she walked. Despite her dislike for Miz Catherine, the woman had been an unexpected blessing in her life. How could she have guessed that Miz Catherine would be the one to bring her home?

"Shows God can use anything for good," she said, tipping the fedora toward heaven in thanks.

Humming to herself, Lettie rounded the path and walked down the paved road toward the two buildings that comprised Lake Beulah's "downtown": a tiny general store and the Bantam Rooster Lounge. Outside the store, children rode rusted bikes, their dark legs ashy white from dried lake water. One boy flew by, a few playing cards clothespinned to the back spokes of his bicycle and making a grating noise like a revving engine. Lettie smiled and wished that LaShon and Lamont could have spent at least one summer here.

"Good mornin'," said Lettie as she stepped inside the store. She lifted the fedora momentarily to wipe the sweat from her forehead as she looked around.

"Mornin'," said an old woman sitting behind the counter. Her silver hair was a stunning contrast to her smooth, jet-black skin. She was one of those women who could have been any age between fifty and eighty, her ageless features never giving a clue. It was only her work-worn hands and crooked back that betrayed she was closer to the latter.

Lettie nodded, then looked around. She needed some cream for their coffee, some cheese, a packet of dry yeast, some hot sauce. And soap.

"Do you have any Dove?" asked Lettie.

The woman behind the counter turned and considered Lettie. Lettie sensed she had disturbed the woman, although it appeared that she wasn't doing anything but sitting on a stool behind the counter and soaking up the breeze from a noisy electric fan.

"Check back at the end of the week," said the woman. Then, squinting at Lettie she asked, "You from Beulah? Ain't I seen you somewhere before?"

Lettie smiled. "No, we're from Detroit. We're in the Johnson cabin on the lake."

"Oh," said the woman, still looking in Lettie's face. "But you ain't a Johnson. They're all bright skinned with wavy hair . . ."

"No," said Lettie, her smile now cold. "No, I'm a friend of the family."

"Yeah, a friend, all right," said the woman rudely. "Them Johnsons ain't got friends who look nowheres like you. Fact, you put me in the mind of them Mitchells used to live over near the tracks near Yardley Colored School. Matter of fact, with that hat on, you surely do favor—"

"How much?" Lettie interrupted, dropping her purchases firmly on the counter. The woman looked at her suspiciously before turning to add up her groceries with a pencil and paper. Lettie looked around anxiously. She had to get out of there before the woman put two and two together. That she was related to Sadie Mitchell, the midwife-turned-murderess. Folks had it in their minds that Sadie was guilty, but Lettie knew in her heart that her grandmother was innocent.

She drummed her fingers on the countertop impatiently and looked nervously around the store. Her eyes landed on a few sprigs of dried lavender tied in a matching bow. These would go nicely in my room, she thought. I can wrap the dried flowers in muslin and sleep with them under my pillow. Maybe it will help me sleep through all Miz Catherine's screamin' and tossin' and turnin'. Besides, she thought, lavender was her grandmother's favorite color. Maybe it will soothe my soul and bring me good luck.

"How much is the lavender?" asked Lettie.

"Four dollars a bunch," said the woman. "Want me to add it on?"

Lettie nodded and pulled out her wallet. She paid the lady, then took the bag of groceries. "Have a nice day," she said with forced politeness.

The woman just stared, her eyes widening as if viewing the specter of an old memory. Lettie's heart leaped as she closed the door. She stood on the steps for a moment to collect herself, praying there wouldn't be any more people still around who remembered her grandmother, who remembered the trial. Suddenly she was thankful that they'd only be in Lake Beulah a week. She was starting down the stairs to head home when the children's voices reached her ears.

Black Sadie, Black Sadie, why'd you kill that baby?

She turned to find one of the boys pointing at her accusingly. The other children gathered around, repeating the chant straight to her face. Their young brows were furrowed, their eyes narrowed, and their lips cruel as they chanted the taunt, daring her to stop them.

Black Sadie, Black Sadie, why'd you kill that baby?

Lettie worked to steady her nerves and her footsteps, muttering a prayer under her breath to shield her from the hateful words. Just as she was nearing a corner, she felt a thump, and her fedora flew to the dusty ground. Whirling, she faced the tallest boy, his arm cocked back and frozen in midair. Her eyes swept the group of suddenly silent children as she fought the urge to curse their ignorance while stooping to retrieve the hat. In her haste, her bag fell to the ground and her groceries spilled helter-skelter onto the dusty road.

"Black Sadie, Black Sadie," the children continued. "Why'd you kill that baby?"

Lettie pushed the groceries back into the bag, looped the handles securely over her wrist and stood slowly, brushing the dust from the brown fedora, her fingers teasing the wide black band. Her murmured prayer was now the hum of a favorite gospel hymn, one she'd known so long she forgot the title but had every note branded into the marrow of her bones.

The children encircled her, whispering the chant like a dirty secret, waiting to see what she would do. A jury, thought Lettie. A jury of children waiting to condemn her.

"Get out of my way!" she yelled, overcome with anger. One of the smaller boys noticed the bunch of lavender still on the roadway, some of its delicate dried flowers now crushed, and picked up the bouquet as if it were a peace offering.

"We didn't mean nothin'," he said, holding out the flowers.

When he looked into Lettie's eyes, he saw she was crying. He started crying, too.

"Shut up!" Lettie yelled and pushed the trembling boy. Towering over him as he staggered backward, she reached down and snatched the flowers from his hands. He flinched, fearing she was about to hit him. "If I ever hear that stupid rhyme again, you'll regret it!" She glowered.

"Ooh, she *is* Black Sadie," she heard one of them whisper as she pulled the fedora onto her head. She ducked beneath its brim in order to hide her own shame and began to march away from the store with the bag hanging from one hand and the flowers in the other. The children stood and watched her departure, their chant now a whisper propelling her from their reach.

Black Sadie, Black Sadie, why'd you kill that baby?

The silver-haired woman in the store let the curtain drop at the window where she'd stood watching Lettie in action. She shuffled away from the window and walked down the aisle past her fan.

"The baby killer's back," she mumbled, reaching for the telephone.

Chapter ELEVEN

NOTHING COULD HAVE PREPARED Catherine for the storm of Chas's anger.

"What the *hell* are you doing in Lake Beulah, Kit? Are you nuts?" he screamed through the cell phone.

"Chas, I've been cooped up in that condo for eight long, dull months, I just wanted to get out for a few days—"

"Well, I'm sorry, but that's not your call," he cut her off. "That's my child, too. If you want to endanger yourself, well, there's nothing I can do about that. But I can't believe you'd risk the life of our baby!"

"I'm not risking anything, Chas," said Catherine defensively. "The stitches are out and the doctor said I can move around more. Anyway, the baby's not due for another month."

"You don't know when the baby's coming and you're out there in the boonies. The nearest hospital is forty minutes away."

"Chas, calm down. I'm fine, honestly. Lettie's here with me. I'm not doing anything strenuous. I just wanted to relax by the lake."

"What did you do to Lettie? Did you threaten her? I know she wouldn't have willingly agreed to this!"

Wasn't it bad enough that he was angry at her without him taking up for Lettie too? "Chas, I—"

"I want you to leave this minute," said Chas, his voice so cold she barely recognized it.

"I can't do that," she said, holding her ground.

"Then I'm coming to get you," he said, hanging up the phone.

"Chas? Chas . . ." she begged into the dial tone.

She held the cell phone to her ear for a moment longer, hoping he would come back, say he loved her and wrap her in his warm embrace. The anger in his voice devastated her. Why couldn't he understand her need to be near the earth, near the sky, near her mother?

The baby inside of her curled against her sorrow. She wept as her stomach grew hard with grief, her muscles a tight drum skin, the child's heart its rhythm. She reached for a chair and sat heavily. It was only after her muscles relaxed that she realized she'd been holding her breath.

The air in the tiny cabin hung thick with electricity. A storm was coming on the heels of the heat, a storm just waiting for the sun to ignite it. Catherine wept noiselessly. She stood and went to Lettie's room, searching aimlessly for something of comfort.

Inside the neat little room, Catherine's eyes found Lettie's Bible. She hadn't read the Bible in years, not since her mother's funeral. She grabbed it desperately and burst out of the stifling house, gasping for air.

Outside, she stumbled the few yards to the lakefront, down to the tree where she and Marcus had buried their mother's ashes nearly two decades before. She fell heavily against the trunk, sliding down its hard spine, coming to rest on the lap of its roots.

Her eyes wet, she looked up into the limbs. The leaves rustled only slightly in the humid air. She dug her bare feet into the earth and, with the Bible in her lap, grabbed tufts of grass in her fists as the pain racked her body once more. This time she remembered to breathe. Her hot panting did little to move the air inside her clawing lungs.

The pain left like a wave washing over baking sand. She grabbed the Bible, opening it by heart—even after all these years—to her mother's favorite passage from the book of Ruth. The one she'd always recited to Catherine as a promise she'd never leave her:

"For whither thou goest, I will go," she panted, the sun raising sweat on her brow, "and where thou lodgest, I will lodge: thy people shall be my people, and thy God my God. Where thou diest, will I die, and there will I be buried."

Just then, a breeze tossed the limbs above her. She lifted her face skyward to catch its soothing coolness. Yes, her mother was there, watching over her.

Feeling calmer in spite of her pain, Catherine flipped through the pages of the Bible, hoping Lettie would be back soon. What was taking her so long? Her body was beginning to really ache and she was afraid to be alone.

Just then, a yellow page fell from the Bible to Catherine's feet. If the breeze hadn't been so short-lived, the paper would have blown into the lake. Catherine reached for it and was about to put it discreetly back into the Bible when she saw the headline. It was from the *Lake Beulah Herald,* August 10, 1959:

LOCAL WOMAN CONVICTED IN INFANT MURDER

Lake Beulah, Mich.—Sadie Mitchell, a 50-year-old native of Beulah Township, was convicted yesterday of first-degree murder. Mrs. Mitchell smothered the newborn infant of Dr. Roscoe and Mrs. Lillian DeWitt in July, after she had helped deliver the child.

Sadie Mitchell? Catherine read. Was this Black Sadie, the baby murderer? What was this doing in Lettie's Bible? Catherine read further:

"No one can bring my daughter back," said Dr. DeWitt, "but justice has been served."

Mrs. Mitchell has been a reputable midwife among the colored in Beulah for over 20 years.

"My mother did not kill the DeWitt baby," said Verna Simpson, speaking for the Mitchell family. "Everyone here knows that my mother's life has been spent healing those who could not afford to go to a doctor."

Mrs. Mitchell testified in her own defense at the trial. She claimed that Mrs. DeWitt had gone into labor prematurely while playing bridge at the Lake Beulah Clubhouse. Mrs. Mitchell, who worked in the clubhouse kitchen, was called to help in the delivery. She said the baby was not breathing when it was delivered.

No ambulance was available to take colored patients to the hospital in nearby Elk Springs.

Mrs. DeWitt offered no testimony during the trial.

The trial has split the Lake Beulah community.

Many natives of the area revered Mrs. Mitchell; the more affluent vacationers did not share that view.

"We have told her several times to keep her voodoo out of Lake Beulah," said Mrs. Delilah Matthews, vice president of the Lake Beulah Lot Owners Association. "This is a decent affluent community. Sadie Mitchell and her kind have long been jealous of Dr. DeWitt and other vacationers. We just never thought it would come to this."

Mrs. Mitchell will be sentenced on September 5. Given the seriousness of the crime, she could receive 25 years to life in prison.

"My God." Catherine breathed, amazed to see the legend verified in black and white. She reread the article, then gazed at the photo. It was barely discernible after so many years, but the woman in the photo wore a big man's hat. Her face was dark, her cheeks high, her nose strong, firmly set mouth. Catherine could feel the fear rise in her chest. Even through the stained ink and the age of the photograph, there was no mistaking one hard fact: The woman looked just like Lettie. And the fedora she wore in the picture was almost identical to the one Raj had worn and given to Lettie. The hat Lettie barely removed from her head these days, even when working indoors.

Pain rose up Catherine's spine. Her back tensed, feeling like it would buckle from the pressure. The ache radiated to her stomach, causing her to fall backward, where the sun beamed directly into her face, heat burning both inside and out.

Was Lettie related to the woman who killed a rich, light-skinned woman's baby out of jealousy? Did that explain Lettie's hostility toward her all these months? Had she been right? Was Lettie secretly envious of people like her and Chas? People with higher social status, better hair, lighter skin, more privilege? Who knew what the woman had been plotting all this time against Catherine and her baby!

Catherine was blacking out now, awakening minutes later in indescribable pain. The throbbing peaked, sending her clawing at the dirt, then passing out exhausted as it waned. Around her, the air stood still. Off through the shadowy trees in the woods, Catherine thought she saw a figure, a silhouette: a woman luminous and black. And wearing a man's fedora hat.

Old Black Sadie. Catherine moaned and bit her lip to quell the rising tide of pain. The legend was fact, and the nightmare had come back to life. Black Sadie was coming to steal the breath from her unborn baby's lungs.

"God," she prayed, "where are you? Please help me now." Where was Chas?

Another pain struck so intensely she couldn't even hear herself screaming.

Lettie was calmer now. She didn't know what had gotten into her. She hadn't meant to yell at those children. They were just youngsters; they didn't know the pain their words had caused her, the harm they were doing. They probably didn't even know that Sadie Mitchell had been a real person and that she'd safely delivered far more babies than she'd lost.

She made her way back along the path. In the distance, the dirt road baked and hardened under the sunlight. It had to be nearing ninety degrees. She looked down at the brown fedora in her hands. It was so much like the one Sadie had worn when they walked together through the woods searching for herbs and wild berries. Lettie gently dusted off the fine fabric and straightened the frayed black band. She flipped it over and ran her hand around the cool, dark chocolate silk lining inside. The hat seemed to vibrate in her work-worn palms, sending a comforting tingle from her hands, up to her shoulders and down her back. Something ancient and powerful surged through her, memories born of blood rather than of mental recollection.

She took the skinny bouquet of lavender and tied the flowers to the brim with the lilac ribbon. There, now it looked and felt more complete. Lettie plopped the fedora on her head and walked toward the cabin. She had a feeling she'd been gone too long. Miz Catherine would be wondering where she had been.

As she neared the cabin, she heard a sound resembling the call of a strange bird, the shriek of a wild animal. Immediately, she knew something was wrong. She darted inside.

"Miz Catherine?" she called, her throat tightening in fear. "Miz Catherine?"

The house was silent. She ran to the bedrooms. Miz Catherine's bed was still unmade. She looked in the bathroom, outside on the deck.

"Miz Catherine, where are you?" she yelled, the panic rising higher.

She went outside on the front porch where she heard a muffled groan, then a panicked scream. "Miz Catherine!"

She ran toward the noise in the direction of the lake. There on the bank, near an old oak tree, lay Catherine, writhing on the ground.

"Lord, Jesus!" Lettie whispered.

She thought about going back inside to call 911 but knew it would cost precious time. The baby was coming. Who knows how long Miz Catherine had been in labor. Lettie gathered her strength and ran back to the cabin and into the kitchen for a knife. She snatched the tablecloth off the table and propelled herself quickly back outdoors. Stifling her panic, she knelt by Catherine's side and cradled her in her arms. "Its okay, Miz Catherine," she said. "I'm right here."

Catherine looked up weakly. The sun blazed directly behind Lettie's back, blacking out the woman's face. All she could see was a silhouette, the outline of a dark figure wearing a fedora-type hat.

Catherine almost fainted with the realization. *Black Sadie had come back from the dead to suck the breath from her baby.*

"Nooo!" Catherine screamed. "Get away from me! Stay away from my baby!"

Faced with Catherine's sudden terror and the urgency of a new birth pushing itself into the world, Lettie finally understood the words in her grandmother's letters. All this time Lettie had wished ill on Miz Catherine, but she knew she could never stand back while a child was in need. This baby was innocent. Innocent of its mother's wrongs, beliefs, and misplaced fears. Miz Catherine was responsible for herself, but right now Lettie was responsible to the child.

Lettie ran down to the lake, removed her fedora, and filled it with cool water. She brought it back and poured the water over Catherine's body before placing the hat on the laboring woman's head to shelter her from the sun.

Catherine wept in relief, her parched face now blessedly shaded by the fedora's wide brim. The water soothed like a baptism, washing the scent of lavender over her, and for the first time Catherine could see that it was Lettie who was crouching over her. Not Black Sadie. It was Lettie who had come to save her.

Lettie grasped Catherine under her arms and propped her against the tree. She parted Catherine's legs and took stock of the situation unfolding between her thighs.

"You're gonna have to push soon," she told the laboring woman. "I know you're tired, but the baby's almost here. When you get the urge, bear down hard. Use the muscles down here," said Lettie, massaging the underside of Catherine's belly. "Like you have to use the bathroom. No screaming. Use all the pain to push. Okay?"

Catherine nodded. Suddenly her muscles tightened of their own accord.

"Here we go," said Lettie, feeling the woman's body tense. "PUSH!"

Lettie could see the baby crowning.

"My goodness, what a head of hair!" She laughed. Catherine ignored her and released a guttural groan.

"Lord, put your strength into it now. Push harder. Keep bearing down. It shouldn't be too much longer now . . ." Lettie alternated her words to Catherine with a nonstop prayer. "Lord, you know I ain't no midwife. I don't know how to do this, so I'll trust your wisdom to guide my hands and bring this baby safely to life. And please let everything be . . ."

Catherine let out a mighty holler and pushed until her face turned bright red.

She could feel her bones parting, her flesh ripping to make way for this new life. She struggled to maintain the pressure, to force the child from her. It seemed the sky itself was splitting, thunder rumbled, a siren wailed.

"Good, good, Yes!" cried Lettie. "Oh, Miz Catherine, it's a beautiful girl!"

But the child was blue. Her tiny eyes were closed, her perfect hands falling limp.

"Let me see her." Catherine panted. "Why isn't she crying?"

Lettie cut the umbilical cord with the knife and reached for the ribbon from the fedora. She tied the cord and wrapped the baby in the tablecloth. She carried it with her to the lake where the reeds grew high on the banks. In the distance, the sirens shrieked louder.

"Where are you going with my baby? Lettie, let me see her!" Catherine panicked, thrashing about on the grass and nearly dislodging the hat from her head. Had she trusted Lettie in her moment of weakness only to have the woman choke the air from her child?

A police car sped down the dirt path and screeched into the clearing. A uniformed officer jumped out of the car, along with the silver-haired old woman from the general store.

"There she is!" yelled the old woman. "Look at what Black Sadie's doing to that baby!"

"Don't move, lady! Lay the baby down and then freeze right where you're standing!" yelled the officer, moving closer.

Lettie looked up. The baby's color was a deepening violet. The light on the police car flashed red then blue. Catherine lay against the tree, bloody and wailing.

"Put the child on the ground!" the policeman commanded, reaching for his gun.

Love. Lettie could hear her grandmother's voice. *Love even when it's hard.*

Lettie lay the baby down gently in the grass and reached for the reeds. She broke one in half and quickly inserted a stem in each nostril. She sucked mucus through the straws while she gently tapped the child's chest.

"Move away from the child or I'll shoot!" warned the officer, aiming his gun as Lettie crouched over the infant at the lake.

Just then a terrible clap of thunder split the air. The startled baby opened her mouth; her cries rose up from the ground. Tiny droplets of rain began to fall.

Catherine pulled the fedora further down on her head and lifted herself to the sound of her child crying. A stream of tenderness flowed through her body, filling her breasts. At last she was a mother. Lettie had made it so. Her eyes darted between the posturing white officer and the dark face of her old maid.

"No!" yelled Catherine. "Don't shoot! Lettie! Is the baby all right?"

Lettie stood, cradling the crying baby in her arms. She carried her over to Catherine, stumbling once or twice, but never letting go of the precious life in her arms.

"Here you are, Miz Catherine," she said, her tears mixing with the falling rain. Then looking down at the pale child, Lettie planted a tender kiss on her rosy cheek and placed her in Catherine's arms. "Say hello to your mama."

Catherine rocked the wailing baby gently as she unbuttoned the top of her blouse to allow her to suckle. "I don't know how to thank you, Lettie," she said. "You saved her life."

"Ma'am, you're going to have to come down to the station," said the officer now standing behind Lettie.

Catherine looked up, startled. "Down to the station?" she asked wearily. "What for?"

"For endangering the life of your child, ma'am," the officer answered respectfully.

Lettie stood, soaking wet, too tired to fight. This was how justice had worked forty years before. It was how justice still worked today. Some things never changed. Her shoulders slumped as she turned away from Catherine and held her hands out for the officer's cuffs.

The rain began to stream from the sky.

Catherine spoke up sharply, thirty years' worth of authority and privilege boiling in her tone. "What do you mean, endangering a child?" She adjusted her infant and sat up straighter. "She saved my child's life! If you arrest her, I swear I'll have every attorney from here to the Detroit River crawling over this county! This woman is *not* a criminal." She reached up and took Lettie's hand. "She's my baby's godmother!"

The officer looked at the two women, confused. He looked questioningly at the accusing old woman from the store.

"Look at her!" the woman insisted, pointing a gnarled finger in Lettie's face. You can't tell me that ain't Black Sadie! I'd know her anywhere. Wish I had a picture on me, I'd show you for sure!"

The officer scratched his head and cleared his throat. "Well, if you're certain there's no danger," he said to Catherine.

She nodded. "Everything is fine, officer. Just fine."

The young officer gazed down at the nursing baby and grinned. "Then let's get you and your precious cargo to the hospital," he said, scooping Catherine and the baby into his arms and carrying them gingerly to his car.

In the back of the police cruiser, Catherine lay exhausted, propped against Lettie. The baby girl slept peacefully, lulled by the motion of the moving vehicle and the intermittent sound of raindrops.

"Lettie?" said Catherine, turning slightly in order to gaze directly into Lettie's dark brown face. "I have something to tell you. I'm not the only one whose child was saved today."

She sat up completely, facing Lettie head on. "I spoke to Chas today. Walter Stevens was successful. Lettie, Nick is finally coming home. Your son is free. The judge has released him and agreed to give him a new trial, and you can bet that this time he'll have the best possible legal team this county has ever seen."

Lettie gasped, her hands trembling. It was several moments before she could speak. "Oh, thank God!" she said finally, tears of gratitude streaming down her face. "Thank God and thank *you*, Miz Catherine."

Catherine smiled. "Lettie, please. Please drop the 'Miz' and just call me Catherine. After all, you've been better to me than I ever deserved, and you've also taught me a lot. Today, not only did you give me the gift of a daughter, you also gave me a lesson on selfless love. *And* about judging people harshly because of my own insecurities. I'm almost too embarrassed to admit this"—Catherine smiled sheepishly— "but I've been known to form opinions about people—even my own black sisters—based on what their skin and hair looks like and what social status they hold. But through your kindness and selflessness you've shown me that no matter what our backgrounds and what positions we hold, ultimately, we *are* sisters. And as sisters we have to be able to love each other and be there for each other during hard times—just like you were for me today."

Lettie did not answer right away. She stared at Catherine for a moment, then spoke. "We've both rushed to some judgments Miz—I mean Catherine. And we've both learned something good from it. But now that we know better, let's make a promise to each other to *live* better."

As the cruiser sped along over the rain-splattered road, lights flashing toward the hospital, the two women hugged the new birth nestled between them, then fell into each other's arms weeping thankful tears—one for the promise of the future, the other for the redemption of the past.

ELIZABETH

Take It Off!

ATKINS

Chapter ONE

"YOU GOT THE POWER, GIRL," Kyle whispered. His onyx eyes burned with affection as he stared up from his velvet playpen of red and gold and purple pillows.

"No, the power is yours, sweet soul mate of mine," Dahlia moaned. She slid her butter-hued thighs over the satiny black sheen of his hips and ran her fingertips down the luscious ridges of his collarbone, his pecs, and his tapered waist.

"You don't know," Kyle moaned over the sexy sounds of a Boney James CD. His skin glowed, from his high cheekbones now rouged with arousal, to his long, down-pointing nose, to his clean-shaven, angular jaw. His eyelashes, thick enough to give the illusion he was wearing mascara, came together as he said, "You don't know what you can do—"

"Ssshh." Dahlia tossed her head back, letting sandy braids tickle down her back and dance over his thighs. "Just love me, Kyle."

Hazy sunshine glowed through white sheers, which billowed in the open windows around them in the round turret. The light intensified the euphoric glaze in Kyle's eyes.

"One year of heaven," he whispered. "Give me a hundred more."

"I don't want to remember life before you," Dahlia whispered. "I send up a thank-you and a hallelujah and a praise the Lord every hour on the hour. Ooohh—"

She closed her eyes, savoring a sudden starburst between her legs that sent erotic ripples down to her toes and fingertips.

"Yeah, feel me, Baby Dolly-ya," he moaned deeply. "Feel the power of us."

"Yeah." Kyle's deep voice vibrated through her chest. "I'm tellin' you, Baby Dolly-ya—"

"Tell me," she moaned through parted lips. Dahlia's mind spun in a psychedelic swirl as they literally became one: eyes blending into two black sapphires . . . skin blurring into hot pools of butterscotch . . . amber braids coiling around little black twists like flowers . . . two pounding, pink hearts afloat in a sea of red blood.

"This power," he whispered. "The power of us. Of me. And you. Together, we could move mountains—"

Eyes open, staring at him, she traced his lips with a fingertip.

"Kyle, you know I love your brain." She pressed her palms to the sides of his head; a few of his little black hair twists poked between her fingers. "But right now," she whispered, "while we're alone without Angie *for once,* I just want your body."

"So it's like that," he said playfully.

"Mmm, no, it's like this," she purred, leaning down. Her honey-colored braids formed a curtain around them as Dahlia sucked his bottom lip. The tip of her tongue slid up his cheek.

He groaned, and in a flash, he clenched her waist and flipped her onto her back. Kyle stroked her braids into a fan over the hills and valleys of velvet pillows.

"You need to let the world see how fine you are," he whispered. "Stop hiding under your glasses, your hat—" Her brown felt fedora rested on the arm. "Those baggy clothes covering up this brick house—"

"No, Kyle, not now. We've had this—"

"For me," he said. "I see something in you that you need to share with—"

The tenderness radiating from his eyes melted her inside. But cold arrows of anger chilled her just as quickly.

"Let me up." Dahlia pushed against his chest.

"Babydoll, I'm tellin' you—"

Dahlia rolled out from under him. The muscles in her legs quivered with lust and rage as she rose to her feet. She pulled her braids to the front, their coarseness prickling the firm, beige points of her breasts.

Kyle propped on his elbows. "You can see," he said, glancing downward, "coitus interruptus is not part of the program this morning. Come here, Baby Dahlia."

Standing at his feet, Dahlia stared at him, wishing he would understand that she did not want to expose herself to the world again, or put herself in the headlines once more. Never again did she want to be the hot topic burning up the black grapevine that coiled into every dorm room and Alpha party on campus.

"Kyle," Dahlia whispered, straddling him and taking small, teasing steps alongside his legs.

"Yeah, Babydoll." He cast smiling eyes upward.

"I'm going to tell you something," she said with a seductive tone.

"I'm listening."

"Kyle," she whispered. "You like leading rallies and marching down State Street, having all the TV stations know you as"—she lowered her voice like a broadcaster— "'fiery student activist, Kyle Robard.'

"But me, Kyle," she whispered, "me, for the millionth time, I prefer the power of the pen. The anonymity of—"

"You're trying to hide the black blood pulsing through this red-hot sistah-shape. People think you're ashamed—"

"People think!" Dahlia shouted. "Those are the two most toxic words in the English language! I'm sick of what people think!"

Kyle took her hands, pulled her downward, so their eyes were just inches apart. He kissed her gently. "Baby Dahlia," he said with a piercing stare, "you need to understand the responsibility that comes with looking like you do—"

"Kyle, you know better than anyone," she said over a burning throat, "I took care of my responsibility before I got here. Nursing my parents, watching them die! Now the responsibility I feel in the world is using my work as a journalist to make change."

He finger-combed a handful of braids over her shoulder, holding the uncurling, coconut-oiled ends to his nose. "You're doing it at the expense of your reputation with the black students. But I know how you can change that—"

Her lips tightened. "Kyle, I don't know how many times I've explained this over the past year, but here's one last time. That's a game I can't win. People think I'm too white to be all the way black. Or too black to be all the way white. So I'm not playing anymore. I'm watching and analyzing from behind a shield of newsprint."

Dahlia's mind filled with a collage of images: dozens of people scowling and shouting at her during the Black Student Union strike last year when she'd refused to honor their picket line and crossed it in order to attend a literature class. The black students had been furious with her, calling her a sellout and a honky-lover, and the white students had simply stared past her. With her fedora pushed down snugly over her jumble of coarse braids, had they suspected she was black?

Although she tried to be invisible and quell their suspicions, she remembered the curious stares from white students and professors, their eyes roving her brown hat, her yellow skin, and that question making their lips twitch: What exactly are you, Dahlia Jenkins?

"Dahlia," Kyle said, "it's different here now. I think you have more freedom to do and write what you want. So I have a proposal, a way for you to put your money where your mouth is and earn back the respect of the BSU."

Dahlia sat up, stood up, stepped back, her mouth open with shock. "Please, please don't tell me you're about to put me through some black litmus test. If you don't know what's in my heart and soul after all this time—"

"No, Baby Dahlia," Kyle said, standing up. "All that drama last year, it was more about my relationship with Josette than—"

Dahlia spun away, stepping onto the cold pine floor, into the apricot-walled living room. On the far wall, above the fireplace, she admired the large wooden African mask with a spray of straw hair that she and Kyle had picked out at the art fair last summer. Just after their picnic in the park when he fed her giant chocolate-covered strawberries and said, "I love you, Baby Dahlia," for the first time.

Now, the huge mirror near the stained wood door showed Kyle striding toward her. Without her glasses, their reflection was a blur, like a stick of butter next to a big bar of dark chocolate.

"Dahlia," he said, wrapping his long arms around her chest, pulling her backside into him. He kissed the top of her head. "You're a symbol of what America can, and should, be. United. But you put up so many defenses, you're not living up to your full potential."

"Your sister," Dahlia said, glimpsing one of Angie's tennis rackets lying on the low wooden coffee table, "and your ex-girlfriend took the hammers and the nails and the boards, and they built these defenses in me."

"Forget all that drama," Kyle said, towering over her with six foot three inches of broad shoulders, a round, firm behind, and long, muscular legs.

"They're not forgetting it for one minute," Dahlia said.

His hot palms cupped her trembling shoulders. "I need my Baby Dahlia. When my tax law class is kickin' my ass, or I'm goin' head-to-head with the administration, the thought of you . . . of you smiling at me, that's like my opium. Can't live without—"

"Then promise me, no more pressure—"

"Someday, you'll see," he said.

"Someday won't come if you keep it up." Dahlia pulled away.

"Dahlia, you don't need to cover up that fine, round ass, either." Kyle sliced the air with a flat hand, first in a straight downward line, then a pronounced half circle, then straight again. "It's like, 'Pow!' Curv-a-licious. You should be proud of your black woman shape—"

Dahlia's cheeks burned; she glimpsed her slim body in the mirror as she pulled her jeans up and over her full behind. "People always tease me about my bubble butt. No one needs to see it but you." She pulled on black hiking boots.

"You need to learn how to celebrate yourself, Dahlia," he said softly. "Let down your guard—"

"I want to celebrate you and us, Kyle, but you're making it hard," Dahlia said. "And I don't know how much more I can take—"

The door clinked. A key.

Dahlia quickly pulled her black turtleneck sweater over her head.

"Shit," Kyle said, diving for his baggy jeans. He slid them on. "She's supposed to be at practice—"

The door opened.

Angie stepped in, looking fashion-model fabulous in her pink tennis sweater, the same cotton candy shade as her tennis skirt.

"It's the Invisible Sister," Angie said. Her eyes, a similar feline shape as Kyle's, glowed with disapproval as she scanned Dahlia and Kyle through big pink-tinted sunglasses. "Denial and hypocrisy, live and in color. Good thing Josette didn't come up."

"Don't start, Angie," Kyle said. "It's time to call a truce."

A jolt of longing shot through Dahlia. She stepped toward Angie, whose deep bronze complexion had a postworkout glow.

"Angie, I agree with Kyle. I want to be friends again," Dahlia said, remembering giving Angie a brown leather folder engraved with her initials for her birthday. Taking her to Cottage Inn for wine and pizza to celebrate her getting the summer internship at the advertising firm in Chicago. And bringing her chicken soup when she caught that nasty flu bug that was going around campus. But then the boycott controversy and her budding romance with Kyle, was like a butcher knife cleaving right down the middle of their friendship. "I still don't understand what happened."

"I used to think you was cool people," Angie said, her white sneakers silent as she strode past Dahlia, a tennis racket in one hand and a shiny white tote bag in the other. "Until I saw your true colors. Or lack thereof."

Angie's long, black, curled ponytail flipped over a shoulder as she sat on the couch. The toned muscles of her deep bronze legs rippled as she lifted her right leg onto the coffee table. "Kyle, I twisted my ankle at practice."

Kyle knelt, pulling off her sock. "Want ice?"

"Coach says it's fine," Angie said, grimacing. The soft scent of Ralph Lauren perfume lingered in the air around her. "But, ow!"

Kyle stepped around the stools and breakfast bar, into the open kitchen, filling a Ziploc bag with ice cubes.

Dahlia sat next to Angie. "Kyle's got Aspercreme and Tylenol in the bathroom," Dahlia said, "for when he lifts too many weights. Want me to get you some—"

Angie scowled at her ankle. "I know what my brother has in our bathroom! I don't need you—"

"Angie, I'm extending the olive branch," Dahlia said despite her trembling fingers. She bunched her braids into a thick rope, twisted them, then grabbed Grandpop's hat. In one well-practiced motion the hat came down, its brown satin folds enveloping the braided coil. A cool gust of relief hit the back of her neck. "I do not want there to be this friction between us anymore."

"I can't respect some of the decisions you make," Angie said with a bored tone, leaning back on the couch and turning toward Dahlia. "You betrayed us for your career. You think hiding behind the white folks' newspaper—which could blot some Wite-Out over your picture just as fast as they gave you that column—is more important that the quality of life for thousands of black students!"

Dahlia shook her head. "No, Angie. I put the issues out there by writing about them. That has much more impact than me, one person, can have by revealing my race or by boycotting classes one day a year."

"It's the principle of it," Angie said. "You got the column but you don't take a stand for us. They should call it 'Perpetrating Sister' instead of 'Perspectives.'" Angie pinched her fingers in the air. "Then in tiny print it should say, 'Dahlia Jenkins—A sellout, fence-straddlin', wanna-be white girl who's scared to show the world she's black.'"

"Angie!" Kyle stepped between them, holding the bag of ice. "I'm not havin' this anymore!" His deep voice echoed through the apartment.

"You got all that from Josette," Dahlia said. "You never used to say things like that, Angie, until Kyle broke up with your best friend!"

Angie glanced up at Kyle. "Kyle, you're such a hypocrite." She took the bag, held it to her ankle. "My blacker-than-thou brother takes over the administration building, then can't stop fucking the whitest black chick on campus."

"You are so crass," Kyle said. He glanced at Dahlia. "Baby Dahlia, I'm sorry."

Dahlia's cheeks burned. The shame and rage heating her face, prickling with a hot sheen of sweat over her body, was so intense she imagined disintegrating into one of those sparkly columns of space dust on *Star Trek*.

Like so many times in her life—over her parents' deathbed,

under the cruel taunts of classmates, in the disapproving glares of blacks and whites, standing over Grandpop's grave—she wanted to disappear.

She hated that people always had something to say about the way she looked. No matter what she said or did, relatives, friends, and strangers alike filtered their perceptions of her through how they thought she should think, act, and feel based on her white skin and coarse sandy hair and the hourglass body she was born with.

Now it seemed all the more intense when charged by the emotion and longing and political allegiances tied up in her relationships with Kyle and Angie.

"I'm not listening to this again," Dahlia said. She grabbed her black leather backpack from the chaise facing the TV and stereo. She put on her black plastic framed glasses, then glanced at Kyle through the rectangular lenses. "Gotta go, Kyle. Can't be late for my presentation."

She centered her backpack on her shoulders, then pulled her hat down further. She stepped toward the stained-wood doorway leading to the upstairs hall of this old Victorian house divided into student apartments.

Kyle pulled on his maize-colored sweater embroidered with "University of Michigan" in navy blue block letters. He glanced down at Angie. "How are you gonna get to Finch's class today for your presentation?"

"I'll get there," she said.

"I'll drive you," Kyle said. "I will not let you flunk his class again."

"Ask your girl here what grade she got on the midterm. A little more pigment, she'd be in the same boat as me. Maybe I should drop a dime to old man Finch: His darling Dahlia ain't as pristine as she looks."

"It's not a secret, Angie," Dahlia said.

"Pfftt. All the white folks on campus think you're white!" Angie said. "And you don't offer any evidence to the contrary, either."

Kyle closed his eyes, shaking his head. "Angie, she doesn't deserve this from you!"

"She does when she's up here in our apartment, leavin' blond hair all over my furniture! I never shoulda listened to Mama saying we should live together—"

"Then move out," Kyle said. "Because Dahlia's not goin' anywhere."

"Kyle, your allegiances are just as whack as hers," Angie said. "I think she crossed the picket line so nobody would know she's one of us! Can't you see she's trying to pass?"

Dahlia stiffened in an effort to stop a shudder of rage from racking her body. She turned back toward Angie.

"Angie, if I were trying to pass, do you think I would be in love with your brother?"

Angie pulled off her sunglasses. "Plenty of white girls have jungle fever. Lots of them are secretly fiending for that majestic Mandingo. But still, you'd be with us in some capacity if your heart and pride was in the right place."

"They are," Dahlia said. "And that's becoming the first person in my family to go to—and finish—college. My grades mean everything. You have your rich family to pay for school and help you in a bind. Me, I'm on my own. By myself. Had to bust my butt to get here, and every dime I pay for tuition you better believe will come back to me in the form of a four-point."

"You don't see the bigger picture," Angie said.

"Yes, I do," Dahlia said. "I'll make my mark on the world as a journalist. Not as a fifth-year senior."

"It's more important to take a stand," Angie said. "And I can't respect you for hiding in that gray area, wrapped up in the white privilege you got from your momma—"

"Angie!" Kyle shouted. He stepped between them, putting an arm around Dahlia. "One more word—" He glanced down at Dahlia, pain radiating from his eyes. "Come on." He led her toward the door.

In the hallway, Kyle's face blurred through the tears burning in Dahlia's eyes.

"It's not her decision how I live my life," Dahlia said, the steps creaking under their feet as they passed the tall window on the landing. She pulled her hat down so it covered her ears and her hairline at the back of her neck.

"Kyle, I could understand if I were some video diva always flipping my hair around, acting like I'm a goddess or something. But—"

"It doesn't matter if you're as sweet as honey," he said, "as you are. When she thinks you're trying to pass for white it pushes all these buttons inside her. Our grandmother looked like you and she passed for a long time. And Gran always had something to say about us being so dark."

"But Angie and you are gorgeous!"

Kyle shrugged. "I know. I just understood Gran was from a different generation. A generation where it was a crime to be black. But even though she is very beautiful, as a female, it really messed with my sister."

"Well I'm not your grandmother, and I'm not apologizing for it," she said as they stepped into the paneled foyer. Hazy sunshine streamed through the stained-glass windows on each side of the heavy wood door. "If I get treated like that when I'm downplaying my looks, imagine—"

Kyle shook his head. "No, baby. That's where you're wrong. I love you, but beauty comes in all shades so it's not even about your looks. If you let your inner self shine and use what you've got, you could make people like my sister see that you're not trying to run. That you want to help uplift the race."

He pulled off her hat. Her braids tumbled over her shoulders, down her back.

"Kyle, stop." She grabbed the hat, fluffing the black silk flower held in place at the front by a black ribbon. "Seriously, I like hiding behind my byline, behind the boldface type of newsprint, to get my point across."

Kyle ran a large hand over his hair twists. "But Dahlia, you—"

"No, Kyle. I don't want to stand in the middle of campus shouting into a microphone. You make me proud when you do it, but—"

He opened the door. The hazy brightness illuminated a glint in his eyes that made her stomach cramp. His tone was a little too sharp when he said, "You want all those folks out there who think you're white to keep thinkin' that, don't you?"

Dahlia drew her brows together, studying his eyes. "Kyle!"

"You like it that people don't know you're black, don't you?"

She exhaled angrily. "Just because I don't wear a sign saying 'My father was black' doesn't mean I want to keep it a secret. I just don't owe the world an explanation."

"Maybe you do," he said deeply, crossing his arms as a cool gust shot through the doorway. "Maybe it's your responsibility to teach that we come in all shades. Yes, your father was black, but what are you?"

"I don't need this from you, too." Dahlia stepped into the crisp fall air. Orange and brown leaves blew across the wood planks of the covered porch. She turned back toward Kyle, seeing a flash of Angie's attitude in his eyes. "I fell in love with you, Kyle, because I thought you appreciated me just the way I am. But if you keep trying to change me—"

"It's because I love you, too, that I think you should do the right thing."

Dahlia crossed her arms. "Which is what, exactly?"

"Make folks stop and think," he said. "Check this out. Every black student who's ever been through Finch's English class has either gotten a D or flat-out flunked. But you, he gives you As. Because he doesn't know—"

"I study my butt off, Kyle. I read every book and write papers like my life depends on it. That's why I get As. It has nothing to do with—"

Kyle shook his head. "It's no coincidence, Dahlia. I heard about that racist bastard way back when some student recruiters came to my high school. Somebody asked if the grading system here at U of M was fair, and the young lady said, 'Not if you take an English class with Dale "Willie Lynch" Finch.'"

Dahlia sat on the top step. "I still don't get it. What's he got to do with me?"

"I've been thinking," Kyle said, sitting next to her, glancing out at the tree-lined street of stately older homes. "Some students who flunked his class last semester, we got their blue books. They brought their midterms and finals to the Black Student Union meeting. They want us to get someone to investigate this guy."

"He can be a jerk," Dahlia said, watching a few students pass by on the sidewalk. "But I hear white students complain about Ds and Fs, too. If you don't know James from Joyce or Lord Tennyson from *Lord of the Flies,* you're in trouble. Plain and simple."

The damp wind cut into her burning cheeks.

"Let me tell you, baby. Some white students came to the meeting with their blue books, too. We compared the answers. And I'm tellin' you, nearly identical responses got marked A for our Caucasian brothers and sisters but D or F for black kids. No joke."

She turned to Kyle. "You know, Kyle, Angie and her friends are in my class. If they didn't spend so much time criticizing me for getting assigned to work in a white project group—"

He pounded his palm on his knee. "We have not found one black student—ever!—to get an A from that motherfucker."

A car rumbled past on the narrow street whose curbs were

crammed with students' cars, including Kyle's black Jeep at the foot of the front walk.

"Then why," Dahlia asked, "hasn't someone done something about it already?"

"We need a linchpin, if you will. One dramatic and undeniable example."

Dahlia met his intense stare. "That's me, I take it?"

"You got it," he said. "You can be our spy. Gathering secret intelligence—"

"Uh-huh," Dahlia said. "And I'm doing this to help who? Josette?"

"Of course my ex-girlfriend can't stand you, Dahlia. And you were already on her list because you wouldn't pledge Gamma."

"Which gets to the core issue here. If I based all my decisions on what other people think—"

"Some say you care about what white folks think by siding with them over the newspaper issue." The hard glint in Kyle's eyes made Dahlia wonder if he were speaking for himself.

"You know, Kyle, sometimes I think you supported my decision to take the column and cross the picket line so you could control what I write." She crossed her arms, staring into his eyes.

"That's crazy," he said.

"Then why are you always trying to tell me what to write?"

"I simply make suggestions. That you don't take."

"Well, this is my senior year," Dahlia said, raising her brows. "I'm not going to betray myself and my hard work. You don't understand the discomfort I go through. The way people have reacted to my mix. I'd just rather not deal with it."

"But it's power, girl," he said. "Don't you get it?"

"You don't get it, Mister Middle-Class Comfort." She nodded toward his Jeep. "Your dad's a doctor. You went to college right out of your private high school. Me, I had to wait."

Dahlia swallowed over a hot lump in her throat. "I went

through three years of hell to get here, Kyle. You don't know—
working in that office to save money, and nursing my parents when
they couldn't walk, then they couldn't talk, then they didn't know
who I was . . ."

Dahlia covered her face with her hands to block out the image
of drool spilling over her father's brown lips, her emaciated mother
moaning in pain, and her just standing there, trembling, wishing
the nurse would get there with the new morphine drip.

Now, she stiffened and then stood up. "You know, even though
my parents are dead, I'm doing this for them. Every time I write my
column for the *Daily*," Dahlia said, remembering she had to file her
story later today, "and every time I hear people talking about it in
the hallway or in class, I know I'm contributing."

"You could do so much more."

"I will," Dahlia said. "My stories are gonna jump out of the
newspaper and change the world. First my internship next summer
at the *Detroit News*, then the *New York Times*. You watch."

Kyle stood, taking her hands. "This would let you make your
mark. Write a big column about it. I can see it on CNN: 'Student
Journalist's Bold Exposé Ousts Racist Professor.'"

"You're not hearing me, Kyle. The answer to whatever it is you
want me to do is no. N-O." She glanced at her watch. "I don't want
to be late for my presentation. I stayed up 'til three getting ready."

"For Finch's class," he said with an accusing tone. "Think about
it. Don't sell me out like this, Baby Dahlia." His eyes pleaded.

"I will not jeopardize my education." Dahlia stuck her thumbs
in the front straps of her backpack. "Kyle, I am so disappointed that
you can't respect how I feel on this."

His eyes raked her up and down. "Yeah, respect. I don't know
how much longer I can respect somebody who hides under that hat.
Keeps all her power to herself, when it can make a difference." He
dashed up the steps, glaring down from the porch. "You need to take
it off and show your true colors. 'Cause what I'm seein' now—"

Dahlia's boots thumped on the wooden steps as she hurried up onto the porch. She probed his eyes, then pressed her mouth into his. His lips parted, and he sucked hungrily for long moments.

She pulled back. "Kyle, don't let this, or anything, come between us."

"It already has," he said, staring down with glassy eyes.

The unfeeling mask stiffening his face stabbed at Dahlia's senses. She closed her eyes, taking a deep breath. But suddenly she remembered Angie upstairs in the apartment. The image of a crowbar came to mind, as if suddenly the politics of race were prying Kyle out of Dahlia's life. No. They were made for each other; she could not, would not imagine life without hearing him call her Baby Dahlia or listening to him read Maya Angelou poems over ice cream at three in the morning or crying with pride over his commitment to helping others.

"Kyle," she said softly, opening her eyes.

But he was gone.

Chapter TWO

D AHLIA HURRIED UP THE STONE STAIRS of Angell Hall, through the double doors, and into the cavernous, white-columned lobby. Her heart was pounding, her hot palms were slick. After a ten-minute run-walk from Kyle's apartment, sweat plastered the coils of braids to her forehead under her fedora.

But no way would she take it off.

Her writer's eye envisioned giant letters sitting atop her head like the Hollywood sign, reading, WHERE DO I BELONG?

Not just that, but who knew? After last year's media hailstorm, it seemed everyone knew. But now she was back to those same wrenching questions that had gnawed her for a quarter century: Who knows I'm black? Who cares? And why does it matter to me, and them, so much?

"Relax," she whispered as she pressed through the crowded hallway echoing with chatting students. Her every muscle was trembling with the fear of losing Kyle or letting his proposal erode the composure and confidence she would need to get an A on this report.

If she could bring herself to form an intelligent sentence. The practiced words and ideas clashed in her mind with Kyle's deep, smooth voice and the understanding and tenderness in his eyes. She had to make both situations right—acing the presentation to maintain her 4.0 average in Finch's class and quieting Kyle's demands that she do something brazen to prove her blackness.

"Hey, girl, let me help you lift the weight of the world off your shoulders." A friendly female voice made Dahlia look up.

Sharmane put an arm around her, engulfing her in a warm waft of patchouli oil. Her best friend's brown eyes twinkled; a peaceful glow emanated from her heart-shaped face, the same smooth, rich hue as maple syrup. "Dahlia, girl, I'm makin' you a rum relaxer when we get home."

Dahlia laughed, pecking Sharmane's soft cheek. "No, no, I remember the aftermath of the last time. Wasted a whole day's worth of studying. But if I could have a bottle of your sunshine for just one hour—"

"Life's too short," Sharmane said, hoisting her fake-fur trimmed bag over the shoulder of her brown suede fringed jacket. "Too short to lug all these books around, that's for sure."

Dahlia smiled. Until she heard another female voice shoot through the crowded hallway: "Always rushin' around, trying to look so important."

Dahlia glanced toward the benches lining the hall. Josette McGee and three other black female students were glaring at her.

"She thinks she's all that, having Kyle. But I had him first. And Angie's gonna help me get him back, in a big red bow, just in time for Christmas. You watch."

Josette locked her hazel eyes on Dahlia, then winked, making her curled-up bob bounce over the shoulders of her denim jacket. Then she raised a green apple to her cinnamon-glossed lips and took a loud bite, glaring at Dahlia as she chewed.

Dahlia's blood bubbled with rage.

"This way!" Sharmane said playfully, yanking Dahlia into the women's restroom on their left.

The anger pounding through her filled her ears with static. Her trembling hands prickled as sweat dampened her palms. A quick glimpse in the fluorescent-lit mirror—her full, rose-colored lips curled into a tight slash.

"Dahlia, girl, whatever Kyle's got goin' on must be pure magic," Sharmane said, facing Dahlia in the mirror. "To keep a hex on Josette a whole year later. Is he that good?"

A small smile lifted Dahlia's burning cheeks. "Kyle is everything. He'll quote Langston Hughes while he whips up the best omelettes and French toast you've ever tasted. And he gets this intense look in his eyes when he reads—sometimes I think the book will catch fire, he's staring so hard."

"I don't think it's memories of his brain makin' Josette's claws come out when she sees you," Sharmane said, tucking an errant braid under Dahlia's hat behind her ear. "You cool now?"

Dahlia snatched off her hat. "Do you see it?" Dahlia focused her dark blue eyes on the face she'd been looking into since second grade.

Sharmane nodded, forming dimples without moving her lips. "I thought we had turned the lights out on that big ol' sign up there," Sharmane said. She stood on the tiptoes of her brown platform boots, making her flowy beige dress sway as she peered into the aura of sandy frizz shrouding the bases of Dahlia's braids like opalescent morning mist in a forest. "But I see it's back on bright today," Sharmane said.

"Kyle flipped the switch," Dahlia said, drawing warmth and comfort from the soft folds of brown and cream silk wrapped high around Sharmane's head. Three skinny black braids, weighted with cowrie shells, dangled from the center of the silky hive.

"Yep, girl, no doubt," Sharmane said. "It says, WHERE DO I BE-LONG?"

Dahlia stared at the imaginary sign atop her head. She and Sharmane had made up the joke back in fourth grade, when Sara Horowitz and Tamika Johnson both invited them to a birthday party on the same day. Dahlia had felt that picking one would somehow define her allegiance to one race over the other. So with the help of parental taxis, she and Sharmane had bowled and eaten pizza at Sara's party, then headed over to Tamika's just in time for water balloon games fueled by the sugar rush of cake and ice cream.

Dahlia cast a mock-serious look at Sharmane. "What about the meter?"

Sharmane's beaded earrings dangled as she raised up again, studying Dahlia's head. "Right now, girl, the needle is on 'Leave me alone,' but it's threatening to shoot back into the 'Militant mulatto' zone at any moment."

Dahlia exhaled loudly. The frustration casting a gray pallor over her face in the mirror made her stomach cramp. She glanced at her mother's Timex.

"I can't be late," she said, not wanting to leave the comfort of her kindred spirit. She and Sharmane both grooved on anything by Anita Baker and the Gap Band, couldn't get enough fire-hot rasta wings with bleu cheese dip at the campus jazz joint, and loved all things hazelnut, whether coffee, candles, or hand lotion. "Finch will call you out if you dare walk in while he's talking."

Sharmane twisted Dahlia's braids into a rope, coiled them on her head, and secured them under Grandpop's fedora. "I'm not lettin' you outta here until I see peace and serenity on your face," Sharmane said.

Dahlia shook her head. "Sharmane, on one hand, I just don't care what everyone thinks, even Kyle. I'm just tired of wondering and worrying about it."

"Then don't."

"But he keeps talking about 'the power,'" Dahlia said. "And Grandpop used to always say God made me like this for a reason— to blur the color line and make a difference. I just haven't figured out exactly how."

Sharmane's smooth lips parted over straight white teeth; her dimples became deep and adorable. "Girl, it's not supposed to be spelled out in black and white. Pardon the pun. You have to figure it out for yourself."

"Right now the only thing I'm sure of is I'll be late if I don't get in gear."

"Come on." Sharmane led her back into the noisy hallway. A few yards away, Josette and her friends were pushing through double doors into the lecture hall.

"As for them," Sharmane said, "some folks need a soap opera. And they put the most interesting characters in the cast. Starring Dahlia Jenkins."

Dahlia kissed her friend's cheek. "Sharmane, thank you." Dahlia pressed the metal bar to open the double doors into the giant lecture hall.

Sharmane's warm palm and fingers gave Dahlia's hand a gentle squeeze. "Always, girl. I got my women's studies lit class right now. But we'll turn off that sign later."

Dahlia's heart pounded as she stepped inside. She was sure she was late, but down at the front of the blue-carpeted hall, Finch sat hunched over a desk, writing on a stack of papers.

She was about to exhale with relief and dash down to her usual seat, when she glimpsed Josette standing to her right with another woman in a blue Gamma sweatshirt.

"Good luck with your presentation," Dahlia said in a neutral tone.

But the expression in Josette's hazel eyes made Dahlia's insides churn. She stiffened her face into the apathetic mask she'd learned to wear in second grade, when Veronica Mears pushed her off the swings on the playground, calling her a "honkey." Then, while Veronica stood over her with hands on her hips, hate in her eyes, Dahlia had risen to her feet with a poker face, ignoring the sting of scraped knees. She dusted off her blue dress and black patent leather Mary Janes. Then she looked Veronica straight in the eyes . . . and whacked her in the jaw. No tears, no teachers, no telling. Just self-defense. And no more harassment from Veronica.

But plenty of other girls. In middle school: Michelle What-was-her-name in gym class, leaving those "white nigger" notes on her locker. Then there were the Willard twins on the school bus, who made it their daily sport to see who could pull Dahlia's long braids or ponytails the hardest. Those rapper chicks in high school, cornering her in the bathroom, saying things like, "Pass my ass. I'll call you out, black girl." Another, the one with the blue fingernails and platinum-blond natural, would hiss. "We'll see how stuck-up she stays when my boot goes up her booty."

Though her insides quaked with terror, Dahlia never reacted. She just looked at them with boredom in her eyes, waiting for the torment to end. Then she wrote a passionate essay about her experiences as a biracial girl, whipped by the turbulence between black and white. And that essay, along with a 4.0, won her admission to the University of Michigan.

"Good luck on your presentation," Josette mocked in a prim and proper voice. "Golly gee, girls, invisible sisters like me have lots of time to study because we don't want to be bothered with all those Negro problems!"

Dahlia wished she could disappear as she hurried down the staircase dividing three huge sections of stadium-style seats. At the front, she took her usual blue tweed fold-down chair. Her brain was like an out-of-control radio, spinning past Kyle's deep voice, Josette's catty comments, Sharmane's comforting words, Angie's unfriendliness.

With trembling fingers, she unzipped her backpack, pulled out the red folder holding her presentation, and reviewed the words spawned during a late-night writing frenzy. Sitting at the desk in the one-bedroom apartment she shared with Sharmane (who'd been asleep), she'd gulped down coffee spiked with a shot of espresso, while typing away at the desktop computer Kyle had given her when he bought his laptop. ·

"Ladies and gentlemen," Professor Dale Finch said into the microphone at the front of the auditorium. Bright yellow lights illuminated his gossamer shock of white hair and those silver brows always drawn toward that deep crease between his blue eyes. His saggy cheeks shook slightly as he spoke, and his lips were so pale there was no distinction between them and his milky skin. "Today we will continue our reports, starting with Tony Jacobs."

A guy a few seats down from Dahlia stood, his red Kappa sweatshirt highlighting his rye bread complexion as he stepped to the podium. Professor Finch, in brown slacks and a scotch plaid sweater, sat at a desk facing the podium.

"Richard Wright made his mark on the world with some of the most graphic and provocative writing . . ." Tony began. He looked at Finch, whose head was down. With pale hands marbled with blue veins, he scribbled on papers with a red pen. Tony cleared his throat.

". . . that made him one of the most controversial and celebrated writers." Tony's jaw muscle flexed, but he continued with a strong tone for the next five minutes. Finch glanced up once, nodding when Tony said *Native Son* was "a must-read for all Americans."

Dahlia's heart pounded as Finch took the podium. "Thank you, Mr."—he looked down at his notebook—"Jacobs. Next, Dahlia Jenkins."

Dahlia grasped her papers. With her spine straight, shoulders squared, she stepped under the hot lights to the podium. She could smell Kyle's musk, his Donna Karan cologne, the faint scent of those ginger-peach candles mixed with sex . . .

An unintelligible snicker shot toward her from the right, where Josette McGee always sat.

Staring down at the papers, Dahlia pushed her glasses up her tiny bump of a nose, taking some comfort from the fact that the brim of her hat shielded her from the hundreds of stares before her.

"My presentation is comparing the lives of women in *Portrait of a Lady* by Henry James and *The Color Purple* by Alice Walker."

"Interesting contrast there," Finch said from his desk. Intrigue burned in his blue eyes as he watched her.

"Both novels delve into the sensibilities of American women," Dahlia said with a strong, smooth voice, "all torn by the conventions of their day versus the desire for freedom burning in their hearts." A sort of autopilot switched on, fueled by the confidence that she had thoroughly prepared for this and that the bottom half of her face—and her voice—were all she had to expose.

Dahlia glanced up, then continued reading. "I want to explore just how James and Walker—"

"Ms. Jenkins," Professor Finch interrupted, "please remove your hat."

Her brows drew together as she gazed up at his sharp stare. She wanted to shout, no! What does my hat have to do with anything? Muffled laughter shot toward her from the Josette McGee zone.

"You may begin again, without your hat," he said.

She froze. Sweat prickled under her turtleneck. She glanced out at the still, expectant faces. The Asian-American woman in the second row with the silver hoop earrings. The blond frat guy with the

Lacrosse sweatshirt a few seats back. And higher up, the trio of sorority girls she was assigned to for the team project due later in the semester. All watching, waiting . . .

"I'd prefer to keep it on," Dahlia said firmly.

"It's a distraction," the professor said. "Remove it."

Dahlia's face burned with embarrassment. Hushed chatter spread throughout the auditorium.

Finch turned toward the audience. "Silence." Then that crease between his eyes deepened as he looked at Dahlia. "Time is of the essence, Ms. Jenkins."

She set her pages on the dark wood podium. She raised her hands, grasping the velvety brim between her thumbs and forefingers. She raised it slightly, causing a cool rush of air on her hot, damp forehead.

"Ms. Jenkins, this is not theater. This is high-level English. Unless you want to forfeit your slot for an instant F—"

Dahlia pulled the hat off.

Long braids tumbled over her shoulders like a dumped basket of yellow-brown snakes. One hit the podium. Another grazed the back of her hand as she set Grandpop's fedora down next to her report. The big, double-spaced words blurred as excited whispers spread like fire through the auditorium.

"She is so bizarre," a white woman whispered with a gasp.

"That's kinda hot," the Lacrosse guy said with a deep chuckle. "Imagine all those braids flyin' around while you're—" One of his friends laughed.

A raspy white female voice snickered, "Like, what *look* is she going for?"

"I told you!" a female voice struck like a gong. "Ain't no denyin' what she is now."

"Extra! Extra! Read all about it!" a brother called. "Invisible Sister called out for all to see!"

Dahlia's face burned as if she were standing too close to a fire.

All those curious eyes and whispers boring into her made her want to turn, to run away. The recessed lights made her hands glow white-bright; she was sure her sweat-dampened face was glowing with a moon-silver sheen as well.

And she could almost hear the question blaring through the hundreds of minds before her: What is she?

For those who knew, especially the Josette crew, she was sure their minds were streaming with a steady flow of negative adjectives that she'd heard before: high-yella studious snob . . . can't nobody that white be black . . . thinks she's smarter than us all . . . professor's favorite . . . not an ebonic bone in her body.

And for the black guys: Damn, what does Kyle do with all that hair . . . wouldn't touch her, somebody might think I'm with a white chick . . . she got it rough . . . way too much cream in that coffee.

"Ms. Jenkins!"

Gasps and laughter rippled through the audience.

Dahlia bristled. She thought of the anguish in her parents' eyes, right after the diagnosis. The terror on their ashen faces as their bodies shut down. Their pleas for her not to nurse them, lest she get infected . . .

No! I have to excel for them, to show that their love was not for naught. That people like me can handle the pressure, the scrutiny, the tug-of-war . . .

She took a deep breath, staring at Grandpop's hat. If he could don that stylish fedora and wear it with his head high in segregated Atlanta, then surely she could withstand the scrutiny of her classmates for the next few minutes. With that thought, a cool gust, his spirit, seemed to waft around her, calming her, giving her a shot of adrenaline and confidence.

"Yes, Professor Finch. Let me start over. As I said, my presentation compares the lives of women in *Portrait of a Lady* by Henry James and *The Color Purple* by Alice Walker."

She glanced up at the audience.

Right into Kyle's eyes. He was sitting two rows back, on the end, just a few yards away. Staring. Hard. Radiating that intensity that made him so gorgeous and mesmerizing.

She swallowed, trying to suck in air to quiet her pounding heart. "Both novels delve," she said with a quavering voice, "into the sensibilities of American women"—the words of her prepared text seemed to dance on the page— "all torn by the conventions of their day—" She could feel Kyle's stare. Or was it a glare?

Again, so many questions. Dahlia did not know if Finch had paid attention to all the news articles last year when the furor exploded in *Michigan Daily* headlines; "Black Student Crosses BSU Picket Line!" Had Finch, or any of the white students, paid it any mind? Did they know she was black? Did they care? Did all the black students even know?

Regardless, right now without her hat in front of hundreds of curious stares, Dahlia felt exposed, just like Kyle had requested.

Was he here to further "out" her racial identity? Was he going to shout out, "Hey Willie Lynch Finch! Bet you didn't know Dahlia Jenkins is black like me!" But did she owe her professor an explanation? Had he heard any of the students' comments? Was she supposed to have gone to his office and said, "By the way, my father was black"? Why couldn't Kyle understand that she just wanted to be accepted as a hardworking student? Not an intelligent black student or a gifted white student or even a diligent biracial student.

Just a senior at the University of Michigan in Ann Arbor.

Stop! Just do it, Dahlia.

"—versus the desire for freedom burning in their hearts." Finally, a strong, confident tone. And when her five-minute report was over, applause from the audience.

"Very well done, Ms. Jenkins," the professor said. "Thank you. Now, John Kincaid."

With trembling fingers, Dahlia gathered up her speech,

grabbed her fedora, and dashed out of the spotlight. To her seat, no, up the steps, to the back of the lecture hall. She pushed the metal bar on the double doors, hearing Kyle's footsteps behind her.

She shot into the hallway. She would dash to the ladies' room, put her hat on, catch her breath, compose herself, then get back into the lecture hall.

"Dahlia," Kyle said behind her.

She kept walking.

"Dahlia, I'm sorry."

She spun to face him. "Why are you with me?"

His eyes widened.

"Did you ever stop to think about it? Your sister is right. You and me, it's like Malcolm X hooking up with Sarah Jane in *Imitation of Life*. The Odd Couple at best."

"Dahlia," he said, grasping her upper arms. "I'll make a truce between you and my sister if it kills me. This conflict over your racial allegiance, it's got to stop."

Dahlia crossed her arms, pulling back. "Then go tell that to Josette McGee and Company. She says she wants you back."

Kyle chuckled. "She's my ex-girlfriend, Dahlia. She can't stand the idea that I, the head of the BSU, dumped her, the president of the Gammas, for a someone who is nonpolitical and looks like you."

"Exactly. So don't ask me to put my neck on the line to help her."

"No, Baby Dahlia, I—"

"Kyle!" A high-pitched voice screeched down the hall. Dahlia and Kyle turned, just as a half dozen women in blue Gamma sweatshirts surrounded Kyle.

"What time is the BSU meeting?" asked Marla Harris, a Gamma whom Dahlia had interviewed at a recent women's health fair sponsored by the Gammas. "Why don't you have your nose in one of those fat books over in the law library?"

"Yeah," another woman, who looked all of sixteen, asked, "What are you doin'"—she looked Dahlia up and down—"over here with us young folk?"

"Angie hurt her ankle at practice," Kyle said. "Just doing the big brother thing. Listen, we were talking—"

The young woman peered at Dahlia from under a blue baseball cap. Her light brown hair curled under at her ears, then her thin, oatmeal-colored face lit up. She smiled and held out a hand. "We've never met," the woman said, "but I'm Wendy Hutchinson. I read your column."

"Thank you," Dahlia said.

One of the women whispered to another, "Isn't she the one who wouldn't pledge?"

Dahlia met her eye. "No, I did not pledge, because of my long hours at the paper."

"Well, you sure found your place in the world, girlfriend," Wendy said. "Because you can write."

Dahlia smiled. "That means a lot. Thank you." She heard one of them whisper "Invisible Sister" and something about her braids.

Dahlia turned to Kyle. "I really don't need this," she said, grasping the metal bar on the double doors leading back into the lecture hall. "Kyle, I'll see you later."

"Hold up," he said. "Marla, listen to yourself. Didn't the Gammas just hold that forum on women's issues?"

"Yeah. Dahlia did a nice job with that huge write-up in the *Daily.* But that doesn't mean I can forgive her for choosing that over us. Or the BSU."

"Tell me, Marla, even though you're enjoying the fruits of my decision—because believe me, the *Daily* wouldn't have given you half that space, if any, if I hadn't pushed for it. I reminded them every day, then insisted on covering it myself, on a Saturday—"

Marla smiled up at Kyle. "Kyle, we did have a bomb panel on women entrepreneurs, blood-pressure screenings . . ."

He glanced at Dahlia, then back at Marla. "So did you talk about catfights between women of color? How do you think you can move forward in business or education, or just life, when you're always at each other's throats?"

Marla crossed her arms. "Women of color? Everybody knows, since the first day she came to this campus, the Invisible Sister does not count as black. By choice. She disses us, we dismiss her."

"How does giving your event all that ink equate to dissing you?" Dahlia asked. "You are unbelievable. You don't want to admit—"

"How can you, as a black student leader on campus," Kyle asked, "engage in racism against one of our own?"

"She's not one of *us,*" Marla said. "I mean, she can be white and get all the privileges of being white, as long as she covers up that nappy hair—"

"Until you walk a mile in my shoes," Dahlia said through tight lips, "you can't dictate who or what I should be. And my father's black blood in my veins does not give you permission to decide how I live my life."

"Yes, it does," Marla said with that same glare and sense of power that she'd had freshman year in the dorm cafeteria, when she'd urged Dahlia to pledge the Gammas.

At the time, Dahlia's dorm friend Rhonda—a soprano on scholarship to the music school from a family of auto workers back in Detroit—wanted desperately to become a Gamma. But Marla never even looked Rhonda in the eye when she approached. Dahlia got the feeling Rhonda's working-class roots just didn't measure up to the Gamma image.

Now, Dahlia smiled. Rhonda had somehow gotten an audition on Broadway, then left school to star in a hit musical called *Triumph*.

"You just don't want to be one of us," Marla said.

Dahlia shook her head, drawing on her grandfather's spirit for strength. "And just what does 'one of us' mean? A woman? A black woman? Someone with x amount of pigment?" Dahlia turned toward the freckled, fair-skinned woman in the bunch.

"It means," Marla snapped, "women who have our issues."

"Such as?" Kyle asked.

"Well, being judged by our skin color, for one," Marla said. "Go in that classroom and see how the professor looks at her, then see how he looks at me."

Dahlia's cheeks burned. She spun, pushing the metal bar on the door, back into the lecture hall. Kyle's grip on her arm made her turn back. "And you wanted me to do what?" Dahlia glanced at the six pairs of question-filled eyes.

"It's bigger than this," he said. "You'll see."

"Excuse me," a blond woman said, slipping through the Gammas. "Oh, Dahlia, Lori changed the meeting for our group project to four o'clock, at Café Royale. See you there?"

"Okay," Dahlia said.

"See what I mean?" Marla said, crossing her arms.

"Excuse me, ladies," Dahlia said flatly. She returned to the silent tension of the auditorium, where a bulky football player was reading his report.

Standing in the dimness, she stuffed her braids back into her hat, then walked down to her seat, hating the feeling of so many eyes on her. And hating even more that she cared so much.

Chapter THREE

THE FACE STARING BACK from the bathroom mirror was pale and angry. And it made Dahlia's heart ache. Her parents never would have wanted her to go through this self-consciousness that bordered on self-loathing when she viewed herself through the prism of what she thought others saw.

"This has got to stop," Dahlia whispered into the steam. Her skin still burned, and was pink, after that nearly scalding shower. But at least the beating water had melted some of the tension from her shoulders and helped her forget those five minutes in front of her class. Something about it had made her feel dirty, like she needed emotional cleansing. "I can't go the rest of my life like this . . ."

Suddenly, her image blurred; she wiped steam from the mirror with her palm. And looking back were her mother's dark blue eyes, her father's full lips, the distinctly V-shaped jaw identical to her mother's and her maternal grandfather's—Nathan Rochester, an army soldier who died while liberating Europe from the Nazis during World War II. Dahlia had only seen pictures of the man even her mother had never met; Mom had worn his image in a locket around her neck until her dying breath.

The thought of him raised still more questions: He died fighting bigotry, but what would he have thought about his daughter's choice of a spouse?

Also in the mirror, Dahlia saw Grandpop's light pecan complexion. His spirit was with her so strong that she could hear his deep voice, with that Southern twang, singing his self-styled lullaby:

When I wish upon a twinkling little star tonight,
I say tickle my sweet baby girl with delight.
My little Dahlia, happy child with eyes so bright,
The world done me wrong, but it'll treat you right.

"Not yet, Grandpop," Dahlia said, smiling. Sometimes Grandpop was off-key as they swung in the big swing by the river, behind the house where he grew up, raised his kids, and was now buried. But the love and tenderness in his voice always made up for it.

Love. Grandpop had loved her. Her parents had loved her. Kyle loved her.

"But do I love myself?" And if the answer were no, how could she expect anyone else to love her?

She was glad that Grandpop had told her never to cut her hair, because he said when she was born he had a dream that she would need it. That it would be a source of pain and pleasure, that it would be celebrated and scorned.

She twisted a few braids between her fingers. How cool that the hair could stay together in triple strands woven together without any fasteners at the bottoms. How liberating that she did not have to deal with blow dryers or curling irons. Grandpop would be proud now, to see that her braids dangled nearly to her butt.

The round curves of her butt. Dahlia studied her ample backside in the mirror. So many voices of strangers over the years popped up and out of her memory: "Booty" and "Baby got back" and "Dang, she got a big ass for a white chick." And that white guy at a rock concert once calling her "lard ass."

She hated that the world felt it was their place, their business, to comment on the shape and size of her body. That was one thing she loved about being with Daddy's family. Big, prominent behinds were cherished and admired. So she felt comfortable showing it in jeans or slacks to all the dozens of relatives packed into Aunt Lola's house for Thanksgiving and Christmas.

But out in the world—especially in situations where if she did not make an announcement about her black blood and when she was wearing her hat, people assumed she was white—she hated the size two, buttless, bony standard of beauty perpetuated by Hollywood. For a while, when she first came to college she tried to diet her butt away. But it always came back.

And the braids, she'd worn those since middle school, when she took a cue from Sharmane and discovered braids were the perfect way to control the massive cloud of sandy frizz that reminded her of a tumbleweed stuck on top of her head. No more tangles, no more comments from classmates about sticking her finger in a light socket, no more dreading the wash and comb routine.

Just cool, easy braids, courtesy of Daddy's sister, Aunt Lola. The less she had to think about it, the better. The same, she thought, about her skin.

Yes, she did understand that with her white-looking skin came privilege. But what was she supposed to do about that? Whatever it was, it was something big. She just had to figure it out.

Right now, she wrapped a big towel around her damp skin, just as Sharmane knocked and entered the steamy room.

"Okay, what'd Romeo say?" Sharmane asked.

Dahlia explained her conversation with Kyle and his proposal that she do an exposé on Finch.

"I hear you, girl," Sharmane said. "But that's how the world is. In this women's studies class, sometimes I feel like my professor saves the As for lesbians only. But I just do my own thing and hope for the best."

"Well," Dahlia said, "I don't want to be singled out for being half this or half that. In my father's family people range from my color with straight hair to blue-black and it's no big deal."

"We come in all colors," Sharmane said. "But it's still a big deal, girl, you know it."

"I hate that it is. I hate that when I meet people I have to stop and think about how they're reacting to how I look, on top of whatever I say and do. And what I really can't stand is I'll be walking around wishing I could hide or disappear, that I didn't have to show a face or an eye color or a hair texture, that I could just be accepted on my spirit alone without all the distractions, for black folks about where my hair falls on the scale from bad to good, or whether I look more like the brown paper bag or the white one, or if I'm wearing contacts—"

"Girl, somebody last week, in the library, she asked me if you do," Sharmane said as they walked into the bedroom. "She said she's in your Harlem Renaissance class, and she thinks you're aloof—"

Dahlia closed her eyes. "Sharmane, the thing is, I can be really down on myself and so uncomfortable about where I fit in, and people still want to accuse me of being too proud. No matter what I say or do."

Sharmane stepped to the oak dresser, where she pumped some lotion from a green bottle and caressed it into her hands. "Folks are always trying to say it doesn't matter. But we know it does."

"I want to do something to change that," Dahlia said. "Help me think of what, though."

"Writing," Sharmane said, making her dimples. "You're doing it. Just step a little farther into the militant mulatto zone, and bam, girl, you can change the world."

Dahlia shook her head. "But half the time I haven't figure out who I am yet. Or why Kyle is with me. I mean, family dinner parties at our house meant the Yamamotos from down the street, and the Jacksons from Daddy's old neighborhood, and the Weingartens from Mom's office. They taught me not to segment myself off from any group. Just be with everybody—"

"But girl you know the world isn't like that."

"Well, I hate how everything is so divided here," Dahlia said, pulling on black panties and a bra. "I am not going to put on labels or be a certain way to please everybody else."

"I heard that," Sharmane said. "But just 'cause my mother wants me to take over her accounting firm when she retires doesn't stop me from being a history major. It's my decision."

"Decisions," Dahlia said.

"One thing I do know, Dahlia, is that nursing your parents like you did, that was a testament to your character. And working to save money for college, that showed your determination and discipline. You are stronger than half the folks out here."

Tears of fatigue burned Dahlia's eyes, blurring the pale blue wallpaper, the cherub-covered shower curtain, the digital clock on the wicker shelves next to the sink. It blinked: 3:45.

"Ugh," Dahlia groaned. "The last thing I feel like doing is meeting the sorority trio for Finch's group project. But it's due next week. And today we're supposed to review each other's reports to make sure they're accurate, not redundant."

"Dahlia, just remember," Sharmane said, "stay true to yourself. That's what counts."

Sharmane's words echoed in Dahlia's mind as she examined her braids. They still looked smooth, but soon it would be time to have them redone. Dahlia glanced at the clock, then dialed Aunt Lola in Detroit, about forty-five minutes away.

"It's the Little Professor," Lola announced over the chatter and soap opera noise filling the basement boutique. Her cousins had given her that nickname as a child when Dahlia preferred to read and swing in Grandpop's hammock by the river as opposed to climbing trees and catching frogs with the other kids.

"Tell her," Dahlia heard an older woman say, "her daddy would be proud."

Dahlia's eyes burned. "When are you coming? My braids are—"

"Little Professor, why don't you let me cut—"

"Lola, you know I promised Grandpop I would never cut it." Dahlia remembered her grandfather stroking Grandma's cloud of black hair as she died, then turning to Dahlia and saying a woman's hair holds mystical powers, that he was always upset that Grandma wore hers short. And then he said Dahlia looked just like his baby sister who died as an infant of chicken pox, back in the day in Georgia.

"I know," Lola said. "I'll be there in two weeks."

"Bring your newsletter stuff," Dahlia said. In exchange for the hours and hours it took to wash and braid her hair, Dahlia would pay her cousin by composing the newsletter Lola did every month for her church.

Dahlia slipped into black jeans, a beige turtleneck, boots, and a blazer. Then she twisted her damp braids up, grabbed her bag, and headed out.

About fifteen minutes later, Dahlia approached her project group at an outdoor table at Café Royale on State Street.

"I was like so stunned, Dahlia, today," Lori said as traffic roared past on one side of the umbrella table. A steady stream of students and professor types passed on the crowded sidewalk.

"It's so windy," Dahlia said, grasping her hat. "Weren't there any seats inside?"

"It's packed," Lori said, shrugging. "Plus, pretty soon it'll be too cold to sit outside, so we wanna make the best of it now." She smiled at Mikki. "Except for those of us going to Aruba for Thanksgiving!"

Mikki flipped her silky brown ponytail over the shoulder of her puffy red down vest. "Sorry. We go every year. This is a sin?"

"I'm jealous," said Nora, in a white nylon jogging suit and baseball cap with their sorority's logo across the front. Her red curls sprayed from the back of the cap. "I'll take Aruba over our place in Florida anytime. The same thing every year gets so boring. And Scott can't come. He's gotta go to Aspen with—"

"C'mon, you guys, we got work to do," Lori said. "Dahlia, need a java jolt?"

Dahlia thought about the last time they met here: She'd ordered something new that ended up costing four bucks. And that was her lunch money for the day. "No thanks," she said, sitting down in the black iron café chair. She spread her report in front of her. "I'm fine."

"Old man Finch was a super asshole today," Lori said, widening her eyes behind gold-rimmed glasses. "I was like, floored—"

"I survived," Dahlia said, feeling mature among the twenty-one-year-olds. "If that's the worst thing that happens to me during college—"

"And what was up with those black chicks in the corner?" Mikki said, a grimace twisting her round face. "Like, everything you said, they were whispering and ridiculing you."

"Hello!" Nora raised a palm and twisted her neck a bit.

Dahlia bit the inside of her lip as Nora said, "I wanted to stand up and yell, 'Ladies, listen to the girl, you might learn something from her brilliant presentation. Because she's getting an A, and you're not!'"

"Let's play nice now," Lori said.

Dahlia studied each woman for a few seconds. They had no idea she was half black. Why would they? Her skin was as white as theirs—whiter, if you compared her to their sun-bronzed glows after their winter getaways. And what would they think if they found out? Would they treat her any differently? Would they still describe her presentation as "brilliant"? Or, what if Kyle walked up on them, planted his full, dark lips on her mouth and said in his best Barry White, "Hey, baby"?

Dahlia started to smile, but a sudden wind gust made her press her hat down. "It's so windy," she said again, trying to peek into the glass front of the packed coffee bar.

"I don't know how you can be so cool," Lori said, gripping her fluttering papers. An aquamarine ringed with diamonds sparkled on her right hand. A graduation gift from her parents, she had said at their last meeting. "After today, I mean, so what if you want to wear your hat. It's not like we were in church or something! That old guy is a lunatic, I'm sorry!"

"But my God, Dahlia, your braids are so bold!" Mikki said. "I wish I could make a statement like that."

"Well, why do you wear it up all the time?" Nora asked. "If I had your hair, I would be a royal bitch. Because," she said, flipping her head with a sort of Miss America smile, "I'd toss it around all day like I was a perfect ten. Bo Derek. Everybody would adore me."

Mikki tossed a balled-up white napkin at her. "You're conceited enough. No wonder you got voted queen of the homecoming ball." Mikki turned to Lori. "How does Rick stand her?"

"Ladies," Lori said, "let's get to work." She gulped a tall coffee, her metallic pink fingernails glistening in the haze. "Now, after reading everybody's report, I have to say, Dahlia's makes us all look like idiots." She laughed.

"Great," Mikki said.

Dahlia wanted to say thank you and cringe all at once.

"The good news is," Lori said, "I made copies. So all of you can study Dahlia's format and use it to improve your own. As in tight sentences, organized paragraphs, and interesting—did you hear that word? Interesting! If your paper makes me drowsy, then it sure won't impress Old Man Finch."

Nora rolled her eyes. "Dahlia writes for the *Daily*. Of course hers is the best."

"Learn from it," Lori said with a glare. "After that C on the midterm, I need an A on this. 'Cause if I don't get at least a B in this class, my GPA goes down. As in good-bye summer on the Vineyard. Hello summer school. No thanks! So get to work, ladies."

Dahlia raised a finger. "Lori, what about the presentation itself? Will all four of us do it like we talked about before? I think that's how most of the groups are doing it."

"Yes, but since you did such a fabulous job today," Lori said, "we'd like you to do the most talking. If that's okay with you?"

Dahlia's stomach cramped at the idea of standing up there again, all those eyes on her . . .

The wind gusted; her hat flew off. Mikki shot out of her seat, grabbed it as it hit the base of a nearby cement planter holding a tree.

"Here," Mikki said.

Another breeze whipped up Dahlia's braids. She pulled them back in a twist. But her papers started to blow, so she let go, slapping a palm down on the table. "Anybody got a rubber band?"

The other women shrugged, but questions glowed in their eyes as they all stared at her hair. With her fedora in her lap, Dahlia glanced down the street at the drugstore. She thought about running in to buy a package of hair bands to hold back her hair.

And then she saw them.

Angie Robard. Josette McGee. Marla the Gamma. And the fair-skinned woman from earlier. They all walked toward her, in slow motion it seemed.

Dahlia glanced at the coffee bar. In the glass window, her braids blowing all over reflected bright yellow in the sunshine. Her face looked as white as the three women around her.

Her heart pounded. No telling what Angie and Company might do or say.

Their laughter and whispers seemed amplified as they approached. Dahlia glanced down at her papers and tried to listen to what Lori was saying about their reports. But she couldn't stop her eyes from focusing back on Angie.

Her leave-my-brother-alone glare. Her pink lips and glamorous aura as she turned toward the other women, who all stared at Dahlia.

They stopped about a dozen feet away.

Angie's eyes blazed, as if she'd never seen anything so disgusting.

Dahlia felt hot and cold; her stomach cramped. As her mind spun, she tried to pinpoint exactly what she was afraid of. That Angie would confront her in front of her project mates? That she would divulge her race and make an issue of it? Or just that she would create an ugly scene, leaving a bitter impression on these rich white girls to reinforce their already negative perception of black students?

"Dahlia, is that cool with you?" Lori asked.

Dahlia's eyes widened. "I'm sorry, that car going by, I didn't hear you."

"If we have our final drafts in by Monday," Lori said. "Spell-checked, proofed, ready to put together."

"Oh, of course," Dahlia said. "We can meet—"

Those boots pounding the cement became deafening.

"Sarah Jane!" Josette said, sparking deep laughing from Angie and the two other women.

"Sarah Jane got her ass kicked," the light-skinned woman said. "Her mama died. She was all fucked up."

Dahlia remembered the tragic mulatto character Sarah Jane who tried to pass for white in the 1959 movie *Imitation of Life*. Her boyfriend beat her up when he found out she was half black, and the film ends with Sarah Jane coming home, screaming over her mother's casket.

"Sarah Jane!" Angie laughed. "Let my brother 'lone, Sarah Jane!"

The four of them bumped into each other, laughing.

"That Invisible Sister wishes she could be one a them," Marla said.

Embarrassment burned Dahlia's cheeks. Not for herself. But for Angie and her friends, for representing the black race like that. Sure, white girls acted silly, too. But right now, on the sidewalk crowded with white students and professors and teaching assistants, it seemed they were doing a disservice to the race with their cattiness. Dahlia had a scary thought. Perhaps she was also doing a disservice to the race by denying and rejecting her blackness.

"White bitch," Angie snarled. "Thinks she smarter than all of us put together. Ssshhh. Don't interrupt the dream team. They got work to do—"

Marla let out a loud laugh as they walked slowly past, glaring at Dahlia. "She looks just like 'em. And that's just where she wants to be."

Lori turned around, wrinkling her brow. "Can I help you ladies?"

Dahlia's stomach cramped. She wished she could disappear.

"No thank you," Angie said in a mimicking tone. They walked away, tossing their heads back in laughter.

Mikki sucked her teeth. She tossed her pen down. "Why are they so hostile?"

Nora widened her eyes. "I swear, if the blacks hate it here so much, why don't they just go back to where they came from."

"Yeah, like the ghetto or prison or—" She turned to Dahlia. "It's like they single you out, Dahlia."

"Well, look at her," Mikki said, looking at Dahlia. "They wish they had your cool braids. And they wish they were smart enough to get an A like us."

"Ladies, let's not stoop that low."

Dahlia glanced from face to face. A tirade at them, at Angie, at the world, threatened to explode on the tip of her tongue. She could stand up and shout, "I'm black, too!"

Or she could come to Angie's defense and say, "If you could spend ten minutes inside black skin, you'd have a whole new attitude and understanding." Or she could keep quiet, not get into it. And not jeopardize the A she would probably get on this project. Because squabbling with these women and having to get reassigned to a new group this close to the deadline just wasn't worth it.

Still, Dahlia's stomach burned. She had to do something. She felt like she had one foot on each side of an earthquake. And every day the crack was growing wider, splitting her in half, making her ache and hurt.

Suddenly, she craved the comfort of Kyle's embrace. She needed to hear him say something intelligent about them disliking her because he broke up with Josette. That their feelings were motivated by nothing more than ex-girlfriend emotions.

But what would he say about her silence at this moment? He would call it collusion. Agreement. Endorsement.

And just plain wrong.

Dahlia pressed a hand to her stomach. The wind whipped her hair over her face, which she was sure was ashen.

"You guys," she said. "I got a deadline at the *Daily* tonight. I better run. Lori, I'll have my report on Monday in class."

"Cool," Lori said. "Dahlia, you were fabulous today. I hope you don't let that old geezer get you down."

Dahlia tucked her hair into her hat. "Not for a second," she said.

"And those black chicks . . ." Mikki said with a shudder. She raised her hand, making a slapping motion back and forth. "God, can we get a little more hostile?"

Dahlia's face started to twist into a snarl. Her lips and tongue started to form the words, "Shut up you stupid bitch, you have no idea—"

But something was building inside her. And she would not let it explode until just the right moment.

Chapter FOUR

ALL OF THE MEAN LOOKS and harsh words of the day were clamoring inside Dahlia's head at a deafening pitch as she bounded into the Tudor-style building that housed the *Daily*. She pounded out her frustration and anger as her boots clunked up the open, Pewabic tiled staircase. She grasped the iron railing, inhaling air thick with the scent of ink and dust.

At least here she could lose herself in the rush of deadline pressure, in case her editor wanted any changes to her column, which was due in about ten minutes. And she could do some online research for next week's column that would coincide with a campus forum on AIDS.

She dashed past the red glow of the Coca-Cola machine on the upper landing, past a group of artsy writers talking about some new rock band.

"Hey, Dahlia."

She turned back. Smiling at her was a bald, chalky-hued woman wearing a long flowy dress and Birkenstocks. She was holding hands with a Latina woman in black and lots of turquoise beads around her neck. "Great story on that women's forum the other day," the bald woman said.

Dahlia smiled, remembering the inner triumph of hearing Miss Gamma Marla's compliment on the story before she knew Dahlia had written it.

"Thank you," Dahlia said. Deep in her mind a seed was germinating for a future column about the head-spinning and heartbreaking dynamics of identity she'd had to face today. And her whole life. But today had provided more than enough material, and the sun had yet to set. Still, she'd have to wait until the time and the emotions were just right for that report. She smiled back at the women. "I appreciate—"

A deep male voice caught her attention inside the double glass doors leading to the sleek gray newsroom. A familiar voice. Kyle's voice.

She stopped, scanning the row of computers, where student editors and reporters were hunched over, chomping pizza, arguing, typing furiously, chugging coffee and soda.

And Kyle, sitting at the head of the table in the glass-walled conference room, talking heatedly with the editor in chief, Barbara Mendelson. He stopped for a moment, meeting Dahlia's stare. Then he pressed a forefinger into a black folder on the table, locking his intense gaze back on Barbara. Dahlia could not see her face, as Barbara's pouf of dark hair and the green paisley print of her back were to the newsroom.

For an instant, she relived the tension of a year ago—the former and now graduated editor in chief calling her into the conference room to say she had to choose between being a reporter and an officer of the BSU, which organized rallies and protests and sit-ins to force the university to recruit more minority students and faculty, and create curriculum requirements that included African-American authors and more in-depth history.

She relived, for one heart-pumping moment, the dizzying anxiety about how the BSU would react to her decision, then the heart-pounding heat of that meeting, of being called a sellout and a traitor, even though she'd argued that the power of the pen could do far more than one extra body in the BSU.

Now, much of the *Daily* staff had moved on to other endeavors or graduated, so few people who witnessed the debates last year remained.

But seeing Kyle in the conference room, the same place where he'd tried to negotiate for Dahlia to do both, raked up all those nerve-racking emotions once again.

"What is he doing now?" she whispered.

Her own reflection came into focus in the glass: A long yellow braid hung from her hat. She quickly shoved it inside, then straightened her black glasses. Suddenly, her head seemed small against the broad shoulders of her black blazer; her face seemed little behind her glasses, as Grandpop's fedora was pulled down to her arched brown brows. Her book-filled backpack tugged down her shoulders—

"Eh, Dahlia, you think fifteen inches is enough for your piece on admissions standards?"

She spun to face Carl, her editor. He ran a hand through shoulder-length brown hair, then pushed red-framed glasses up his thick nose. He squinted, as if to draw out an answer.

"Here's fifteen," Dahlia said, pulling a green disk from the zipper pouch of her backpack. A white student was suing the law school, accusing the university of discriminating against white students by admitting minorities with lower grades and test scores.

Dahlia had written that she agreed with the federal judge who said all students got a better education among classmates of diverse races and cultures. "It's ready to run."

"Excellent," he said. "Can you stick around? Barbara might want you to interview Kyle Robard." Carl nodded toward the conference room. "His latest crusade: He wants Old Man Finch's head on a stick. Says the BSU isn't stopping until they get it."

Dahlia glanced around the newsroom, looking for the Asian-American graduate student who covered minority affairs. "Where's Eugene?"

"Death in the family. He's back in Philly for the week. Everyone else is swamped. So you're it."

Dahlia peered in at Kyle, gorgeous in his cream turtleneck sweater contrasting with his deep dark chocolate chiseled features. The intense aura of power that glowed around him when he spoke sent a molten ripple through her middle, stopping in a hot swell between her legs. She smiled slightly; she was not sure if anybody in the newsroom knew they were a couple. In fact, few people on campus were aware of just how serious they were, as their time together was typically in their respective apartments.

"Sweet soul mate of mine," she whispered, trying to read his lips. Would she spend the rest of her life with him, after he graduated from law school and she landed her dream job as a reporter at some big-city newspaper?

But now, her stomach cramped. Did Kyle want to keep her a secret? Was he a hypocrite, as his sister said?

On the surface, it seemed Dahlia and Kyle didn't go out of their way to keep their relationship behind closed doors. But she'd taken a hint soon after they'd met in the cavernous reading room of the law library, with sunshine pouring through the high stained-glass windows, slicing through the silent, dusty air over long rows of dark wood tables packed with students. He'd said something about how it would not bode well for his image as a fiery student activist to be seen with a white-looking blond—even with those coarse braids—on his arm.

Besides, during the days and evenings, Kyle was consumed with classes at the law school, BSU affairs, and a diligent weight-lifting routine at the campus recreation building. At the same time, Dahlia's long hours at the *Daily*, on top of sixteen credits and end-less hours of studying, left little time for leisure. After working so hard to get here, the last thing Dahlia wanted to do was loll around at the bars or coffee joints, wasting time, energy, and money.

Neither she nor Kyle liked to take time out for lunch or coffee dates, although they did occasionally indulge in a late-night scoop of strawberry cheesecake swirl at the campus ice cream parlor. And he did enjoy spooning the gooiest chunks into her mouth, even while they sat in the window.

"Dahlia?"

"Yeah, Carl. Sure, I'll interview him. Just let me know—"

"Dahlia!" Barbara's New York accent shot across the newsroom. "I hope you've filed already. I've got—"

Dahlia turned around. Kyle smiled down at her, holding out his hand. "Ms. Jenkins. I admire your work."

"The feeling is mutual," she said with smiling eyes.

"Dahlia, think about a story, maybe a column, based on what he just told me." Barbara turned toward Kyle. "Now tell her every-thing you told me. Can't say I liked Old Man Finch when I had him, but we need proof. Serious allegations you got there." Barbara nodded toward his black folder.

"Whatever you need," he said.

Dahlia glared at him. Was this a trick? Did he think he could come in and railroad his way onto the news pages? Sure, he'd been here plenty of times before. But he always spoke with Eugene or the editorial page editor. Now Kyle's eyes smiled down at her, but his face was stiff, his jaw muscle flexed.

"Come in here," Dahlia said, leading him into the conference room. With the doors closed, she pulled her tiny black tape recorder from her backpack, then set it to record on the table between them. "How'd your little meeting with those Gamma chicks go? You know, Kyle, that's the kind of crap—"

"Ssshhh. I got a plan. The more I see of that, and my sister"— he shook his head— "and all that pain in your eyes, and their eyes, I've got to do something to stop it."

"We had a second encounter of the nasty kind today," Dahlia said, "when I met with my project group. It was embarrassing, Kyle. Doesn't do any good for the image of black women on campus when they act like that."

His eyes sharpened. "And what do you care about the image of black women? As a black woman yourself, what did you do about it today?"

"I'm not the attitude police," Dahlia said. "I told you where I stand when it comes to jeopardizing my grades for that nonsense. I won't do it."

He crossed his arms, sat back in the chair, staring hard.

"So Kyle, if you launch a media campaign against Finch, it could backfire. He and all his cronies will hide every shred of perceived evidence, and you, along with the BSU, will look like a bunch of hotheads."

Kyle's dark brows drew together. He sat up straight. "You know I'm more calculating than that," he said. "I just came here to test the waters. See if there's any interest for when I do drop the bomb."

"And?"

"And I want to know how many of your *Daily* colleagues know you're black."

Dahlia raised her brows. "I want to know how many of your BSU brothers and sisters know that I'm your girlfriend."

He stared hard, then said, "They know."

"Good. I'll go to your meeting tonight and you can introduce me," Dahlia said. "Now, why don't you go out and ask. Just yell it out, 'Excuse me, I'm taking a poll here. How many of you know that Dahlia Jenkins is—' Wait, better yet, call Angie." Dahlia pointed to the phone. "That would make her *month* to watch something like that!"

Kyle grasped her hand on the table. "Stop it, baby. It's all about the power. To heal. To enlighten. And you have it. But you won't use it."

"I don't see it, Kyle. I feel like I have to work my ass off just as hard as the next student. Or harder, since it took so long for me to get here."

"You don't see how those folks out there respond to you? How the lecture hall applauded you? Did you hear clapping for any other student?"

Dahlia drew her brows together. "No."

"If you could unleash your power—let your hair down, show your face, shine—"

"Yeah, make myself a target for the likes of your sister. No thank you."

"She would respect you more if you showed that kind of courage—"

Dahlia shot to her feet. "Courage? What the hell do you know about courage? Courage is walking into your dying parents' bedroom every morning and smiling. Fighting back the tears, keeping an upbeat face and voice when your father who used to play football looks like a brown sheet draped over some long sticks. And your mother who won't make eye contact with her own child because she's ashamed of the lesions all over her face!"

The pain of those moments shot up through her in a hot gush, bursting from her mouth. With her back to the newsroom, she stared down at Kyle.

"Both of them in diapers," she said softly. "And me, alone, twenty years old. Changing my parents' diapers, Kyle! Do you know what AIDS does to your body? I should be crazy for that alone, for watching my wonderful parents waste away, all because . . ."

She described that night, in the park, that wild-eyed white woman coming at them with a needle. Yelling that any white girl who crossed the color line and had a baby deserved to die.

Dahlia could still hear her mother screaming, raising her hands, trying to run. Her father shielding them both, getting stabbed in the arm and the cheek.

"Nigger lover!" the woman shouted, jabbing the bloody metal point into her mother's neck, her hand. Blood dripping down, making a red splotch on Dahlia's pink pants.

Then her father, knocking the woman to the grass before she could get Dahlia—

Now, Dahlia's every cell burned with the terror of those moments and the anguish of the years that followed. At the time, when she was a little girl, she had never heard of AIDS. Neither had her parents. But they both got sick at the same time and died at the same rate, as if their souls were linked and fed off each other.

Now Dahlia closed her eyes, shaking her head.

"Kyle, don't ever say the word 'courage' around me again." She shoved her trembling hands into the front pockets of her jeans. She strode to the window, staring out at the colonial-style women's dorm across the street.

He stood, putting his hands on her shoulders, looking out the window with her. "I'm sorry, baby. You never told me that's how they died."

"It doesn't matter. They're dead. And I'm here. Alone. With nobody, Kyle. I am fending for myself the best I can. So don't ask me—"

"Sshh. You're not alone, baby. You got me."

She turned, staring up through burning tears that dripped onto her cheeks. Kyle's thumb wiped them away.

She took his hand. "This is hardly the time or place for all that, but I don't know. I feel like today is a turning point. I'm seeing things in a new light. I think we should spend some time apart."

His fingers gripped hers. "No, baby. I can't be without you."

"I need to take some time to reflect on who I am, where I fit in—"

"Let me hold your hand while you do that," Kyle said, desperation and tenderness deepening his voice. "Because Dahlia, baby, when you realize some things, I wanna be right there beside you. Watchin' you work your magic."

She probed his eyes. She still had no idea what he was talking about. But she was going to find out.

Chapter FIVE

ABOUT FIFTY FACES TURNED toward the door as Dahlia entered with Kyle. Chatter about homework and weekend plans and romantic gossip stopped. A tense silence chilled the dark-paneled room on the third floor of the Michigan Union.

"Kyle, wazzup?" one of the guys at the U-shaped table said with a nod.

Marla, the Gamma she'd met earlier, whispered to Angie in much the same way Dahlia used to chat with Angie about homework and their latest dates. Now the rawness of losing a friend made Dahlia glance downward as she sat with Kyle at the head of the table.

"Hey, girl," Sharmane said, hurrying in. She squeezed into a seat next to Dahlia, setting a steaming cup of hazelnut coffee on the table.

"Mmm, that smells delicious," Dahlia said.

"Everybody, some of you know Dahlia Jenkins," Kyle said, resting a hand on her shoulder. "You might recognize her from her picture in the *Daily*. She writes that weekly column, 'Perspectives.'"

A hot wave of déjà vu prickled Dahlia's skin. It was as if all the probing stares were ripping away chunks of her flesh, just like this afternoon in Finch's lecture hall. But this was even worse, because these were black students, scrutinizing her in a new way. At least she was still wearing her hat, with all her braids tucked inside. If she held her head at a certain angle, the lights caught in her glasses, making her unable to focus on all the faces. And despite the emotion searing her senses, her face was a steely mask of calm.

"Dahlia also covers some news stories for the paper," Kyle said, "like the women's forum sponsored by the Gammas last week. But for those of you who don't know, Dahlia is a sister. She's my girlfriend. And she can help us."

"Oh no she isn't," a woman in red said from the door. "None of the above."

Another woman sighed. "If he wants to go that way, I don't *need* to know about it."

A guy in an orange sweatshirt and ornate gold glasses pushed back from the table. "This ain't the dating game, man. We got serious business to discuss tonight. I don't give a damn about your love life. Especially with—" The guy looked Dahlia up and down. "Some white chick."

Dahlia held his gaze. Her stomach cramped. Her mind spun. Her heart pounded. This fear of rejection and ridicule was exactly what had kept her away from the BSU. But now, something was pulling her back.

Kyle glared at him. "This is business, man."

"Monkey business," Marla said. She pressed toward the door. "I can't believe you'd bring that yellow Uncle Tom back in here. She already showed us where she stands—"

"Marla!" Kyle bellowed.

She stopped in her tracks. "Have you looked in the mirror

lately? Or taken a good look at some of the faces in your sorority?" He glanced at the light-skinned, freckled woman from earlier. "In case you've forgotten, we come in all shades."

Someone whispered, "We do. But she's off the chart. And she doesn't want to be on the chart at all. That's her choice."

Kyle stood. "A house divided cannot stand. Now how do you expect us to make change on this campus if we can't even accept one of our own?"

The guy in the orange sweatshirt pulled off his glasses, rubbed his eyes, exhaled loudly. "She already showed us her true colors back during the boycott," he said. "Loud and clear, she was sayin' she didn't want any part of what we stand for. So why the sudden change of heart?"

"Listen," Kyle said, "in order to execute our plans regarding Willie Lynch Finch, we need a strategic campaign. And Dahlia here, being a journalist, can share valuable insight into how—"

Marla crossed her arms over her blue sweatshirt. "She can't just show up one night and say, 'Oh, I'm black again. Let me join the cause.' I don't trust the Invisible Sister for a second. We don't call her that for nothing. She might be working for the other side, try-ing to infiltrate us—"

"I think," Kyle said, "you've seen too many bad spy movies, Marla. If you can just see past the hate—"

Marla tilted her head. "What do you mean, hate?"

"Hate," he said loudly. "Today I have seen so much hate directed from us, at us, it makes me sick. Sick in my heart, black people!"

He pounded the table.

Dahlia bristled. She could almost hear her heart railing against her ribs in the still silence.

"Our women are supposed to nurture and protect," he said. "But today"—he shook his head—"today, I saw venom. From the eyes and the mouths of my sisters. Poisoning their own blood." He cast sad eyes on Angie, who stared at her dangling feet. "Including my own sister."

His voice quavered. "As ashamed as I am to admit it, today, Angie, what I saw come out of you—it's wrong. All wrong. And Marla—" He shook his head. "We have to heal this. And I think accepting Dahlia—and Dahlia accepting herself, is the first step toward healing."

Dahlia's cheeks burned; she could feel people glaring at her, but she stared down at the horizontal grain of the wood table, as if Kyle were a preacher leading a prayer.

"Are you with me?" he asked loudly.

Silence.

"I said, are you with me?"

"If she's not for us, then what can she do for us?" the guy in orange asked. He put his glasses back on, looking around the room. "And what's up under the hat?"

Dahlia stared back at him. She shouldn't have to prove anything to that guy. But somehow, the power she was absorbing from Kyle gave her an idea. She pulled off her hat. Her braids rolled downward, over her shoulders, a few hitting the table in front of her.

"Aw, hell no," someone whispered from the other side of the room. "She look like fuckin' Jan Brady after a vacation in Jamaica."

"With blue eyes to boot," someone else said, then snickered.

"Kyle, you crazy, man," the guy in orange said. "She might have black hair, but her heart is pure white."

"If she's ready to accept her color and love it, I'm game." It was a female voice.

Silence.

That was Angie. She was sitting on a table, her hands shoved under her legs, feet dangling. Warmth and curiosity glowed from her face as she focused on Kyle.

"My baby sister," he said, smiling. "All right, yawl. The diva has spoken. That should be all the endorsement you need."

"Probation," Marla said. "If she can stay down with the program long enough, we'll trust her. But I still say she can turn the other way in the blink of an eye and leave us all coughin' in the dust."

Marla cast a still-disgusted look at Dahlia.

And that snapped her to her senses. She suddenly had the feeling she was at the center of some Salem witch trial hundreds of years ago. Being judged and ruled over by people who had no right, no power to decide her fate.

Just a day before she never would have entered this room, knowing she might face just this type of visual and verbal dissection. Yet, right now, something was making her stay. She had the sense that she could leave at any moment, and that even if folks decided tonight that she was welcome, she would probably always be viewed through a lens of suspicion.

But she drew strength from Kyle and had faith that this night, somehow, would help her harness that mysterious power he kept talking about.

"I wanna hear just what she can do and how she can do it, to help us," the guy in orange said.

"Deal," Kyle said. "Here's what I got in mind—"

Chapter SIX

PROFESSOR FINCH'S OFFICE smelled like Ben-Gay, coffee, and mint as Dahlia stepped in. Hot beams of sunshine shot through the slatted wooden blinds on the high windows, illuminating dust particles floating through the air.

"Have a seat, Ms. Jenkins," he said as he turned his wingback oxblood chair away from his ancient-looking roll-top desk. He gestured toward a big wooden chair with a needlepoint cushion arranged in front of floor-to-ceiling shelves of books that covered three walls.

"Thank you," she said, sitting down. She rested her backpack on her lap, as the Persian rug looked kind of dusty.

"Coffee?" he asked, raising a steaming mug to his lips.

"No thank you," she said.

It felt odd to be this close to the man whose larger-than-life image haunted the minds of thousands of students across campus. For whites, he was just an ornery old geezer who was too tough with grades. For blacks, a racist jerk who flunked them for sport.

He swallowed loudly, then plunked the cup on the desk. "That wind die down any?" he asked while pulling his infamous grade book, bound in oxblood leather, from a scattering of papers on the desk.

"Almost knocked me down," Dahlia said with a slight laugh, remembering how she'd held her hat down, pushing into the wind as she walked the ten minutes from her apartment to Angell Hall.

She glanced around, feeling a mini-chill snake up her back, despite the hot sunshine heating her hat and her black blazer. How many students had sat in this chair and been told they were flunking his class? Paying all that money for four credit hours only to fail and have to do it all over again? If only she could, somehow, get a breakdown of how many white versus how many black students had heard that news . . .

Her journalistic instinct made her want to jump inside his head and find out just how he felt about her darker brothers and sisters. However things unfolded down the line with Old Man Finch, it could earn her the respect and trust of Angie and Marla and the other women in the BSU. For some reason, that mattered now.

Meanwhile, she bit down a smile at the idea of saying something like, "Did you know my dad grew up on a peanut farm in Georgia . . . that he was black . . . and he married a white woman?" She wanted to ask if he had any idea that when he talked about some of the letters that Thomas Jefferson wrote to his slave mistress Sally Hemings, that she—Dahlia Jenkins from suburban Detroit— was also a white-looking black woman? She wanted to say something to the effect that she was in love with the tall, muscular black man who was always leading rallies in the middle of campus, and that Kyle Robard had made her squeal into this morning with a lovemaking that was tender and torrid beyond words.

Dahlia smiled. All that would have to wait. For now, she just had to talk about her work this semester, before the Thanksgiving break.

"Ms. Jenkins, the three major markings," he said, opening his oxblood leather grade book over his crossed legs. A maroon Rockport, in need of polishing or at least a good wipe down, dangled from a thin leg in hunter green slacks, the same shade as his sweater. "Ah," he said. The phone on his desk rang; he ignored it. "Here. An A on your midterm. Another A on your oral report. And an A on your group project. You're well on your way."

"I study hard," Dahlia said, meeting his probing gaze. "And I'm a little older than most of the students in class."

He shrugged. "So was I, when I came here. After World War II. I saw combat. Normandy. Nothing like it. Makes me proud, to this day, to say it. See there," he said, pointing toward one of the book-shelves above and behind Dahlia.

She glanced that way, without looking.

"That was my best buddy," he said. "Nathan Rochester."

Dahlia's breath caught in her throat. Her pulse quickened. She turned, slowly, glancing up and back. A black-and-white photo, probably a five by seven, sat in a frame in front of leather-bound books.

"What was his name again?" she asked coolly, standing up. She set her backpack on the chair. Then she tiptoed to focus on the man in uniform.

"Nathan Rochester. From a good family, in Detroit. Died within arm's reach of me." He ran a hand down his face, letting out an anguished sigh. "Not a day goes by that I don't think about him. Left behind a wife. A little boy. Never even saw his baby girl."

Dahlia felt dizzy. Was he talking about her mother? Could there be two Nathan Rochesters who left behind a wife, a little boy, and a baby girl? She stretched for a closer look. Dahlia's every cell ached to find out if Finch was talking about the flesh and blood that created her.

He stood. "Here," he said, reaching up, handing her the cold, dusty frame. "That's history there."

Dahlia's mind spun. There was no doubt. The man in the black-and-white picture had Mommy's nose, a sort of upturned A shape with narrow nostrils. And the broad forehead, the dash-shaped brows.

"What color were his eyes?" Dahlia asked. "I'm always intrigued by people's eyes."

"I'll never forget," he said. "We'd be standing on board the ship. I'd look at him, then look at the ice-cold Atlantic. Same color. The deepest blue you can imagine."

Dahlia glanced downward. Her mind spun. Kyle's voice. The BSU. The *Daily*. This connection she felt with him, it wasn't supposed to happen.

But if Finch were her one link to the family neither she nor her own mother ever knew, yet whose genetic code was helping to make her heart beat and her brain work at this very moment, Dahlia could not knowingly bring him down. She glanced at the closed door, imagining Angie and Marla bursting in, glaring at her, shouting, "I told you this white bitch couldn't be trusted to represent us!" Kyle staring over their shoulders, shaking his head, eyes burning with disgust.

But Dahlia could not think about them right now. At least until she found out more about Finch's real character. And her own grandfather. Longing and regret stabbed through her. If only her mother were here to see this, to believe this.

How many times had Mommy, her own blue eyes aglow with reverence, talked about how her father died on the D-Day beaches in France, saving the world from the Nazis? Fighting oppression and bigotry, giving his life so that millions could live in freedom? Now Dahlia's eyes burned as she remembered her mother's tears of pride and heartache.

"Did you ever meet his family?" Dahlia asked without taking her gaze from her grandfather's picture. "I mean, once you got back from the war?"

He turned down the corners of his mouth. "No. Would have been too hard to take. I was in Wisconsin at the time, anyway, with my own young wife and kids. Then I got caught up in teaching. Came here, got on tenure track, never looked back. But I think about Nate all the time. Wondering what he'd be like now, what happened to his family, his little girl—"

Dahlia was afraid to look him in the eye. He might see some similarity between her and her grandfather. And she couldn't stop thinking about Kyle. What in the world would he think about this? A sort of kinship—unbelievably—with Willie Lynch Finch . . .

Exactly the kind of suspicion Marla raised about the BSU meeting. And for that, Dahlia would be the first to admit that perhaps she could not be completely trusted to bring down Finch. Because he was now a link to a man she wanted to learn more, much more about.

"Professor Finch," she said, staring at the picture, "this is fascinating. Why don't you ever talk about that in class?"

He shrugged. "Ah, your generation. Half the kids don't have a clue when World War II was, or *where* it was, for that matter. And they care even less."

"But I think to hear it from a real person—"

"Ah! If it's not moving a mile a minute, or ringing or paging or flashing video, I don't think my students care." He looked back down at the grade book. "Besides, all this political correctness. Last time I talked about the war a German exchange student accused me of bias. I had hearings and the whole hullaballoo. Not worth it."

"I think we could all learn from your war experiences," Dahlia said. "That was such a fascinating period. So much hatred and intolerance. Even here in the U.S. The Japanese internment camps—I can't believe that actually happened."

He shrugged. "Ah, I don't want some Jap kid in my class jumping up and down, calling me a bigot. So I keep my mouth shut on that, too. A shame," he said, gazing up at the bookshelf behind her. "I teach literature. That which immortalizes the words of man. Words that some men risked life and limb to commit to paper. Yet I'm censoring myself out of fear—"

"Fear of what?" Dahlia held the gaze of his sad blue eyes. Her nonchalant expression masked the shock snaking through her. And she hoped, with her glasses and hat, he would not notice any similarity between herself and her grandfather.

"I'm a dinosaur, heading for extinction," he said. "Us old white males are being rooted out of the ivory towers like the plague. Our time has passed. If you're not black or homosexual or a woman, forget it. We're as passé as hoopskirts."

He gulped coffee. "Ah, anyway, why am I telling you this?" His eyes trailed up the tall plant by the closed door. He shrugged, then looked at her with a distracted gaze. "I don't know. I just feel something special about you. Can't put my finger on it right now. Anyway—"

Dahlia raised her brows.

"Any questions, concerns?" he asked. The phone on his desk rang again, flashing red, but he ignored it. "Do you have a grasp as to what's expected of you the rest of the semester?"

Dahlia smiled. "Yeah, more late nights. Papers. And lots of books to read. Then cramming for the final and praying for the best."

He closed the grade book loudly, then plunked it on the desk. "Not a worry for you, Ms. Jenkins. You're well on your way to the rare straight-A in Old Man Finch's class."

Dahlia couldn't stop the question from escaping her lips. "Do you know what else they call you?"

"Ah, how much time do you have?" He tossed his head back, letting out a long, deep laugh. The loose skin on his pale neck jiggled. "I suppose the second most common one is Willie Lynch Finch?"

Dahlia did not join his laughter. "You know I write for the *Daily*. That's the only other one I've heard around the newsroom. But—"

"Oh, years back," he said, lacing his fingers over his knee, "his name was Bill Price. Had a chip on his shoulder the size of Texas. Everything to him was about black or white. And of course, me being the old white male that I am, even back then, I was easy prey for his militant assault."

Dahlia wondered if he would be sharing this story with her if she looked different. Darker, like Marla or Angie.

"And?" she asked.

"Well Bill, I remember, he had a huge"—Finch held out his hands about a foot from his head— "afro. So big, it reminded me of Jupiter. He was always reciting the latest black power slogan. Well, you wouldn't know, but they said things like 'power to the people' or 'let my people go' or my favorite was simply, 'black power.'"

"Your favorite?" Dahlia asked.

"Yes. It's ridiculous. Was then, is now. What could that possibly mean? Have we ever had a black president? A black chairman of the Big Three automakers? A black Steven Spielberg? A black pope?"

Dahlia drew her brows together. "I think—"

"They say black power, I say, what power? Blacks had no power then. And they have only a token of power now." He shrugged.

"Quite sad, actually. A friend of mine, fought in the war with me, in a segregated camp, of course. Took him forty years to get the recognition he deserved for saving dozens of lives. But he never saw it. His widow went to Washington to collect the medal just a couple weeks after he died of cancer."

Finch stared up at the bookcase. "Yep, the power is all ours," he said softly. "Wrong as it is, that's just how things are set up."

"Ours?" Dahlia asked.

He held up open palms. "You and me. Caucasian Americans."

Dahlia swallowed hard.

"I want to ask," he said. "With all that beautiful hair, why do you keep it hidden under that hat?"

Dahlia fingered the silk flower. A bolt of annoyance shot through her as she remembered her extreme discomfort when he'd made her remove the hat in front of the lecture hall. But its snugness around her head now, the warmth and shade, gave her a sense of comfort and strength.

"I don't," she started. "My hair, it just gets in the way. A distraction. And the hat, I inherited it from my grandfather."

My other grandfather, she wanted to say. The black one. But she didn't dare.

"Professor Finch, you still haven't told me how you got that nickname," she said.

"Ah. Bill and his afro. I got sidetracked. Well, Bill of course challenged my every move. He could speak with the eloquence of any great orator, of any race. But ask him to write a paper—" Finch threw up his hands. "The word they use now is dyslexic. But back then we just called it illiterate. Anyway—"

"Did you flunk him?"

"Not exactly. I gave him an F on his first paper, and he withdrew from the class. But then he went on a campus crusade to smear my name, likening me to that infamous slave dealer named Willie Lynch."

"That's it?" Dahlia asked. After the way he'd just spoken about blacks, surely there had to be something more sinister or malicious or—

"I'm afraid so. A weighty condemnation, I'd say."

"Are you sure there's not more to it?"

"Not that I'm aware of. Just one student with a grudge, and now we understand a recognized and treatable learning disorder—"

Dahlia drew her brows together.

A knock on the door made her jump. She remembered her vision of Angie, Marla, Kyle . . . witnessing this cozy visit with the man they viewed as the pariah of campus race relations.

"Oh, who is that?" he asked, casting an annoyed look at the door. "I have a quarter hour before the next appointment—"

The door opened.

Dahlia's heart raced.

A brown-skinned woman, with a cloud of silver-streaked black hair around a bright smile, stood in the doorway, holding a brown bag. She wore a beige wool coat with a mink collar and a rhinestone brooch at her neck.

"Ah," he said, grinning, standing up. "My day is made."

Dahlia looked back and forth between the two. Was she his housekeeper, delivering lunch? Finch stepped toward her, taking the bag and kissing the woman's cheek.

"Helen, my ray of light, I would be lost without you," he said tenderly. "Meet one of my star students, Dahlia Jenkins." He waved a hand toward Dahlia. "Ms. Jenkins, let me introduce my beautiful wife."

Chapter SEVEN

KYLE BOLTED UPRIGHT from the cozy cushion of pillows covering the floor of the round turret room in his apartment. The white sheers around him glowed from the small reading lamp illuminating a stack of law books balanced on a red pillow. And near the pillows, the scent of ginger-peach wafted from thick pillar candles burning on a long, flat metal stand.

"So you think he can't be racist because his wife is black?" Kyle asked. Candlelight magnified the suspicion in his eyes, which scraped Dahlia's heart. It was worse, more intense, than she'd feared. But she had to convince him that he could still trust her to find out more, to help him and the BSU expose Finch's discriminatory grading practices.

"I think it should raise questions about how he really feels," Dahlia said, tossing her hat and blazer onto the black corduroy couch in the living room.

"I'm not buyin' it," Kyle said, devouring her with his eyes. "Maybe he knows about you, and he's playin' you. Maybe she was his housekeeper and—"

"Kyle, you're bordering on a conspiracy theory here," she said, straddling him, her lips inches from his. "He's really not the monster that people think he is. He's just been burned in the past and puts up a sort of protective shell. And his explanation of the Willie Lynch nickname—"

"He told you that?"

"I asked."

"Are you crazy?"

"It was no big deal. I think people have built him up—"

"Excuse me," Kyle said angrily, "Finch's discriminatory grading practices have built up his own reputation."

Dahlia shook her head. "I don't know, Kyle. I just get the feeling that his whole situation is different than it seems."

"You are defending that man." His hard stare sliced over her senses.

"Kyle, you wanted a fact-finding mission." Dahlia didn't dare tell him about the connection between Finch and her grandfather. Her white grandfather.

"This is whack, Dahlia. I wanted you to find out things that prove the BSU platform correct."

"Is that what you're going to say when you start practicing law? Only see or cite the facts that prove your point?"

"You got it. That's Lawyering 101, baby."

"It's wrong," Dahlia said. "You can't make fair decisions unless you analyze all the facts. In journalism, we call it objectivity."

"A myth," Kyle said. "We color everything through our own biases. That's why your column is called 'Perspectives.' It's your point of view."

"That's why it's a column, not a news story, which would be less opinionated." Dahlia huffed. "This is impossible."

Kyle's eyes glowed with tenderness. "Dahlia," he whispered, "kiss me."

She pressed her lips into his burning mouth. "Mmm," she said, as he gently gripped the sides of her head. "You taste so good."

"Kyle," she whispered, "don't you ever question yourself? Don't you ever wonder if the things you believed in so strongly are suddenly wrong? Or misinformed?"

He pulled back, probing her eyes. "Sometimes," he said. "For a while, before I met you, I wondered if going to law school was what I really wanted, or if I was just doing what I thought my parents expected. But now I know."

"How?" she whispered.

"It's just a feeling. Intuition. You have to be still and silent, let it guide you." Kyle kissed her eyelids. "Like with you. At first, when that love bug bit me I was like man, I can't get with her. What would that look like?"

Dahlia stiffened. "You thought that?"

Kyle closed his eyes, pressing his cheek into her chest. "Yeah, for a minute. But I sat right here, meditated on it, on you. And my heart told me you're all I need on the inside."

Dahlia smiled. "I never sit still long enough to do that."

"Try it," he whispered. "It works. Otherwise you wouldn't be here right now."

"Where's Angie?" Dahlia asked.

"Meeting with a tutor for Finch's class," he said. "Don't tell her I told you. I told her you'd help her write her paper, but she—"

"Would never go for that," Dahlia said.

"Too much pride. And I think the idea of getting academic help from someone as light as you would trip her out."

"Kyle, it all makes me sick," she said. "Every day, I'm still torn between wanting to do something to help, but then wondering . . ."

She craved oblivion, to turn off her mind, make her stop thinking about everything: who she was, where she fit in, why her actions should define her in the eyes of blacks and whites. And whether the BSU's targeting of Finch was justified.

"Give your love to me," she whispered.

He smiled. "Your wish is my command. If—"

She balanced upward, on her elbows. "If what?"

"If you agree to take it off, for good," he said.

"Take what off?"

"Your hat," he said. "I want you to shine, Dahlia. Look at you. You're gorgeous. And the power . . . nobody I know has ever had a full-fledged visit with Finch. Then you go meeting his wife, hearing about his life."

Dahlia twisted her face. "Kyle, I—"

"But listen," he said. "It's all part of your power."

Dahlia sat upright. "This is twisted, Kyle. I'm trying to forget about all that, just for a little while."

He grasped her arms. "Dahlia—"

"No, there's enough pressure on me. As if how I handle the Finch thing will either buy or forfeit my credibility with every brown face on campus. I never should've cared enough to—"

"Yes, Dahlia, you should. Come here," he said.

She stared at the dark sheen of his muscular chest as that idea, for a column on all these emotions and insights about her racial identity, about how she related to the world, to other women, began streaming through her mind. Sentence by sentence. Revelations and thoughts that would surely rock the campus. And make her feel that she was taking a stand—a public stand—once and for all.

"Kyle," she said, "this is getting too intense for me. If all this political stuff is going to interfere with us—"

"It's political," he said, holding her pale hand up to his, lacing their fingers in the candlelight, "when my skin presses against your skin. The contrast—"

"What about my heart beating next to your heart?" she asked, her voice cracking with emotion. "If you still can't see past my exterior to the point that it's making your—"

"My what? I'm ready, Dahlia. It's you."

She shook her head. "Why can't we just stop talking about race for once?"

"Because when I look into those blue eyes, and bury my face in your hair, and press my black body next to yours, I can't *not* think about it. It's a constant reminder."

Dahlia thought about storming out right then. And never coming back. Because if he were that preoccupied with her appearance, he would never get over it.

"So for the past year that we've been together, you've been thinking this?" she asked.

"More or less."

"And in the past, when you've been with someone with brown skin, does her complexion consume you like this? Do you think and talk about it constantly?"

"I don't think about it," he said. "Don't need to—"

"Then don't with me," Dahlia said forcefully. "I don't want you to look at me or treat me any differently than you would any other woman of color—"

He kissed her back hard; she pulled away.

"—standing here, or laying here, waiting to love you," she said. "You say you listened to your heart when you decided to stay with me or pursue a relationship. Then if that's true, act like it."

In one graceful and strong swoop, he scooped her into his arms.

Dahlia's mind became a molten swirl. She imagined a swirl of flesh, a color somewhere between hers and Kyle's.

One body. One heart. One mind. One color.

Chapter EIGHT

DAHLIA COULD FEEL Angie's probing stare as she balanced on a stool at the breakfast bar, pouring amaretto creamer into the red coffee cup. She took a sip, letting the heat seep down her throat, warming her empty stomach.

"I'm ready now," Angie said, blowing on her own steaming mug. She wrapped her fingers around the red cup, holding it close to her lips as she sat on the stool next to Dahlia. "My paper," Angie said, "for Finch's class, it sings as smooth as Sade."

"I would've helped you," Dahlia said. "I didn't know you were going to pay someone."

"A grad student," Angie said. "He's kinda fine, and smart as hell, so it was far from a painful experience."

Dahlia smiled. Her body felt languid and loose after hours of lovemaking with Kyle. Wordless passion spoken only with their eyes, their hands, their bodies. Even as she tucked him into bed in his room. And just as she'd started to leave, Angie came home, offering a coffee nightcap.

"But the important thing is," Angie said, "I'll know I did everything I could to get the best grade in Finch's class. So if he flunks me, I'll know something is foul."

Dahlia clunked her cup on the counter. "I've been meaning to ask you, how did your office conference go with him?"

Angie sipped her coffee, grimacing. "Just like I expected. He didn't look up from the grade book. Not once. I think Michael Jordan coulda been sitting in that old dusty chair, makin' a girl voice, and Finch wouldn't even notice."

"What about Marla and Josette?" Dahlia asked. "The same treatment?"

"That's what they told me," Angie said. "Why?"

"I'm trying to figure out if he treats everyone that way," Dahlia said. "Because the white women in my group project, they said he just kind a grunted during their conferences, too. So . . ."

"How'd he treat you?" Angie asked with a piercing stare.

"That wasn't what tripped me out," Dahlia said. "I met his wife."

Angie rolled her eyes. "I can just imagine what she's like."

"You won't believe it."

"What?"

Dahlia widened her eyes. "Mrs. Finch is black."

"He was jackin' you," Angie said with a wave.

Dahlia shook her head. "No, it seemed like a surprise, that she came by while I was there."

"They have kids?"

"I didn't see any pictures, but we mostly talked about the class . . ."

"Mostly?" Angie drew her head back. Her gaze rolled down Dahlia, back up to her eyes. "What else is there?"

"Nothing," Dahlia said. She never should have raised the issue of Finch or the office conference with Angie. But she had to know if he treated anyone else the way he'd spoken with her. "Just, when his wife came in, he introduced us. That's all."

Angie shook her head. "Doesn't change my opinion. Because the proof is in the grade discrepancies. His wife might be the biggest Aunt Jemima, yes-Massah-Finch kinda sell-out Oreo—"

"No, she didn't strike me that way," Dahlia said.

"I don't think you got the same kinda radar as us," Angie said. "We can tell—"

Dahlia's cheeks stung. "Radar?"

"Yeah," Angie said, stirring more creamer into her coffee. "You know, to feel a person out. So you can tell where their allegiances lie."

"So I don't have that same intuition about people—"

"About white people," Angie said.

"Because what? Is it directly proportional to how dark a person's skin is?" Dahlia asked.

"You could say that," Angie said. An air of superiority glowed around her, as if she were talking about some magic power she possessed over everyone else.

Dahlia asked, "So, if I get a gut feeling about a person of any race, I'm not supposed to trust it because—"

"No, I didn't say that. It's just, I guess this was a self-defense technique that we developed during slavery. You had to know who you could trust, who was the Uncle Tom."

"And if my sense of who to trust is different from yours—"

"It would be," Angie said, "because your radar wouldn't be as honed or as sharp as mine."

"So it's honed by melanin?"

"No, by experience. I've had to go through certain things because of my color," Angie said, running her fingertips over the back of her hand, "that you have never been subjected to."

Dahlia thought of the crazy homeless woman stabbing her parents with an HIV-infected syringe, killing them because they loved, married, and created a new life across the color line. Angie's words, "go through certain things," echoed in her mind.

"I see," Dahlia said. She was not, at one-thirty in the morning, going to engage in a who's-suffered-the-most contest. Or try say anything to diminish Angie's apparent sense of superiority over insight gained through her oppression. "Is there any way I can develop this radar? Or will I always have an intuition deficit about people of color?"

"Don't mock me," Angie said, pulling a box of Cheez-Its from the end of the counter. "I'm just tellin' you straight. I can sense certain things that you can't." She popped a couple crackers into her mouth. "Want some?"

Dahlia took a handful, savoring the cheesy crunch. "Here's something—where does your privileged background come into play in all of this? I mean, my mom and dad always struggled with money. Even—" Dahlia glanced down at the beige countertop.

"You've never told me about them," Angie said.

"Even," Dahlia said, "when they were sick, we had to fight with the insurance company."

Angie's eyes radiated sympathy. "That's tight. But I could have all the money in the world. I'm still black. And still treated accordingly. Unlike you, I don't have a choice."

"A choice?"

"Yeah, you could go the other way if you wanted," Angie said. "If you didn't want anybody to know you're black."

"The choice is whether I want to announce it everywhere I go. Think of it this way. Kyle said your grandmother was Cherokee."

Angie smiled, pointing to her high cheekbones. "Yeah, that's where I got these."

"Well, how would you feel if there was a Cherokee Student Union, and they wanted you to announce to the whole campus that you're part Cherokee—"

"That's cool," Angie said.

"No, think about how much energy it would take. Think about every time you saw a Cherokee student in the library or at the ice cream joint—complete strangers—think about going up to them and saying, 'Hi, my name is Angie. I'm Cherokee, too.'"

Angie's brows drew together.

"Then imagine them looking at you, and their eyes are saying, 'But you don't look Cherokee. Why should we trust you?'"

"That's deep, girlfriend. That's how you—"

Dahlia nodded. "Take it a step further now. You feel strongly that this Cherokee is an important part of who Angie Robard is. But in the past, other Cherokees have beaten you up, yelled mean things at you, accused you of not being one of them."

Angie lowered her lashes.

"So you've developed a sort of defensive shell, because you never know how people will respond," Dahlia said. "And you reach a point where you're like, why should I bother to tell those Cherokee students that I'm one of them, too, when they won't trust me, they won't include me, and I don't even look like them?"

"You're makin' my brain hurt," Angie said. "I never thought about you like that. It must be—"

"Tough." Dahlia slid off the stool. "I'd better get home. My column is due tomorrow, and I haven't even started. Thanks for the caffeine jolt. I needed it."

"No, wait, Dahlia." Angie touched her arm. "So where do you stand now?"

"To tell you the truth," Dahlia said, slipping on her jacket, "I don't know. Some days I want to tell the world. But other times, I'd just as soon keep hiding under this hat, behind this skin."

Angie dumped her coffee in the sink. "I can't respect that. I think you owe it to the world to decide."

"It's not your decision, Angie. Or Kyle's, or Marla's, or all of the BSU put together. It's my decision."

"You act like you're gay, trying to decide if you're gonna come out of the closet," Angie said with an accusatory tone. "It ain't that deep, Dahlia. You're *black,* so get with the program."

Dahlia snatched up her backpack and left.

Chapter NINE

THE LECTURE HALL was silent as Dahlia centered on her desk the blue book and the white sheet covered with columns of bubbles marked A-B-C-D-E for the multiple-choice section of the final exam for Finch's class. He sat writing at the desk at the head of the class, as graduate student assistants wrote the time on the chalkboard and handed out the exam forms.

"He could at least," the guy down the row in the Lacrosse sweatshirt whispered, "look into the eyes of the persecuted before we face the firing squad." Another guy laughed.

"Good luck, Dahlia," a female voice came from behind.

Dahlia peeked back. Lori, the blond sorority girl from her group project waved.

"You won't need it, though," Lori said, her face tight with tension. Someone behind her was whispering about how he'd stayed up until three in the morning reviewing notes on Finch's lectures since September.

Across the aisle, Josette McGee and Angie hunched over their desks, writing frantically. Angie peeked over, her slight smile forming a dimple in her right cheek.

Dahlia felt like a giant clock was ticking in her head. It

would either explode like a bomb, or finally turn off and let her be.

With a deep breath, and a brain gush of all the material she'd reviewed the previous night, she started the test. She would have her grade before Christmas break, because Finch scheduled his final two weeks earlier than other professors. That way, he and his teaching assistants could complete all grading before the holiday vacation, and students would leave knowing whether or not they passed his class.

"I was ready," Angie said with a slight smile, two hours later in the hallway. "I got tripped up on a couple questions, but I jammed on the essay part."

Dahlia smiled. Until Lori burst through the doors, tears streaming down her face. "My dad's gonna kill me," she said with a trembling lip and bloodshot blue eyes. "If my grade is as bad as I think it will be, I am in such deep shit right now."

Angie's eyes raked her up and down. "Didn't you study?"

"Of course," Lori said, twisting her face into a scowl at Angie.

Dahlia wondered if they remembered each other from that day at the sidewalk café. Or was that incident in Angie's mind just about a blurry-faced blond, while Lori thought of it, if either thought of it at all, as just another angry black chick?

"But," Lori said, pulling her hair from the collar of her camel-colored wool trench coat, "the way he asks those questions, you could write your answer for five years straight and still not cover everything."

"You just have to be concise," Dahlia said. "Go straight down the middle, not get caught up in irrelevant tangents."

Angie and Lori both stared at her.

"Relax, you guys. I'm sure you both aced it. We'll know soon enough."

A week later, Dahlia pressed through a cluster of students outside Finch's office, where their grades were posted.

Lori slumped on the floor nearby, crying into her hands. At the same time, a sleek black leather coat emerged from the crowd. Angie. And the rage in her eyes made arrows of panic shoot through Dahlia's gut.

"That old motherfucker is gonna pay for this," Angie said, not stopping to talk. But she slowed long enough to glare at Dahlia, a deep, sharp, hurtful glare that made Dahlia's palms prickle with sweat. Her heart pounded.

"You got an A," Angie said. As she walked away, flipping her braids, she whispered, "Sell-out bitch."

Dahlia's insides spiraled with rage and betrayal. How could her relationship with Angie be so tenuous that it hinged on one grade? Was the distrust so deep that the action of their professor determined whether Angie would be sweet or sinister from day to day?

"We gotta do it, Dahlia," Kyle shouted an hour later in their apartment. "It's on you to expose that racist wretch for what he is. And I don't care who's at home in his bed. Black or white. Willie Lynch Finch goes down!"

Angie stormed out of the room, her boots stomping the hardwood floor as she headed into the hallway leading to the bedrooms. A door slammed; a deep bass beat vibrated the walls.

"She had a 3.5 until today," Kyle said. "Dahlia, are you with me?"

"White students bombed, too," she said.

"But the percentages speak for themselves," he said. "We analyzed all the scores. Out of three hundred students in the lecture, fifty-one are black. In total, seventy-five kids got a D or worse. And you, Dahlia—"

"What?"

"You are the only African-American student in the class to get an A on Finch's final." Kyle slammed his hand on the breakfast bar counter. "Based on everything I've seen, you are in fact the only

African American *ever* to get an A as a final grade from that man."

"I don't want to believe that," Dahlia said.

"What will it take to convince you, Dahlia?" Kyle's eyes blazed with rage. "Marla and that Kappa brother, they got Cs. This is no coincidence. I'm going to the administration this afternoon, demanding an investigation. And I want you to come with me."

"Why?"

"As proof."

"Oh yeah, I look so black."

"Then bring your application. Get it from your guidance counselor. You checked black and white, right?"

"Yeah, but—"

"Then that's all the proof they need. I'm also going to the Justice Department and the media. Someone I know at ABC said they'd send a crew for the rally tomorrow. Noon, on the steps of the graduate library. I want you to speak out, Dahlia. You got the power, girl, people will listen to you. See things in a new light."

"Kyle, that public speaking thing it's not my bag at all. You go for it. I don't care what you say about me. But—"

"You talk about being a bridge and a symbol and all that," Kyle said. "Well, here's your chance to put your money where your mouth is."

"Yeah, tuition money that I worked my ass off to save."

"Dahlia, the power! Haven't you been hearin' me? You!" he stroked his knuckles on her cheek. He pulled off her hat, letting her braids fall. He stroked the side of her head with his palm. "You, baby, are proof that a black student has the intellect to pull A-pluses from him—as long as he doesn't know it. The motherfucker."

The potent energy coursing through him, and into her, aroused something angry, something rebellious, inside Dahlia. She was trembling as she peered back into Kyle's dark eyes, alternately blazing with affection and desperation and raw anger.

"Kyle, if this is true, if he's grading based on race and not merit, then I will do all I can to help expose it and stop him, make things right."

"What do you mean 'if'?"he demanded. "What more proof do you need?"

"The journalist in me, the objective side. I need to do some investigating on my own."

"That's stupid, Dahlia—"

"I'll be at the BSU meeting tonight, with whatever I find out." She pressed her mouth to his, feeling the tension melt from his stiff lips under her heat. He kissed her deeply, then pulled away.

"This could make or break us," Kyle said.

"For the record, I resent that. I won't be bullied by you, or the BSU, or the fear of losing my boyfriend. Like I said, Kyle, I'll see you tonight."

She picked up her hat but did not put it on.

"Dahlia, baby—"

She dashed out the door, walking briskly to Finch's office. Her heart pounded as she knocked.

But a graduate student opened the door.

"Come on in, but he's gone," the guy said. "He never sticks around on grade day. You can imagine why."

She had to find something with his home address. She scanned his desk, but all the scattered papers were gone.

"Is he coming back today?" she asked, stepping toward the bookcase. There was a stack of magazines. A mail label would be all she needed.

"He's actually gone for the semester. Maybe a couple hours tomorrow," the guy said, returning to the oxblood wingback chair. He picked up a turkey sandwich bursting with sprouts from an open green wrapper on the desk. He leaned down to take a bite—

Dahlia picked up *Life* magazine from the shelf. Yes! 4210 Oaktree Drive, Ann Arbor. A fifteen-minute walk from here.

"Well, I guess I'll try to catch him tomorrow," Dahlia said. "Enjoy your sandwich."

She dashed out, through the center of campus, down the snowy, tree-lined streets to Oaktree Drive. There, the Cape Cod–style beige house with green shutters. The mailbox at the curb was shaped like a red farmhouse.

She dusted away a clump of snow. Big black letters said "Finch."

"Bingo," Dahlia said, bounding up the front walk, and for a second, she froze, wondering what exactly she would say. Her reflection in the glass of the front door made her pause. She was wearing the hat. With her braids flowing down the shoulders of her black wool coat.

She stared at herself for long moments, awed by how different she looked.

"The power," she whispered, thinking of Kyle's face and voice. And for the first time, she saw it. Felt it. In her mind flashed all the people looking at her, listening to her, clapping after her presentation in class. "I see it."

And she was going to use it. Now.

She raised her hand to knock or ring the doorbell.

But the door opened.

"Mrs. Finch," Dahlia said.

"Hey, sweetheart," Mrs. Finch said, smiling. "I was just coming out for the mail." She opened the door. "Nippy out here today. What can I do for you?"

Dahlia smiled. "You remember me, from Professor Finch's office a while back?"

"Sure I do, the day the rascal forgot his lunch," she said. "You and your pretty braids. But I remember those eyes of yours, remind me of Dale's army buddy. Maybe you saw Nate's picture. The spitting image."

Dahlia smiled, still stunned that Mrs. Finch was talking about her grandfather.

"Well, pardon my manners," Mrs. Finch said. "Come on in, girl. Hot chocolate? Tea? I just put some water on. You know they say green tea works wonders for the soul."

"No, thank you," Dahlia said, stepping inside. The house smelled sweet, like cinnamon.

"I'm baking." Mrs. Finch tapped her svelte waistline, clad in navy blue wool trousers and a silky blouse. "This time of year, I crave sweets something fierce. Always put on a couple pounds between Christmas and Easter. But it comes right off."

"Mrs. Finch, is Professor Finch home?"

"Sure is," she said, leading Dahlia through a bright, cozy kitchen. "He's in the back room, with the newspaper. You know, you remind me of my great-aunt Lucille, down in N'awlins. I saw all those reports about you last year. I told Dale, but he said—"

"You told him what?"

"Well he didn't believe you could be the same person as the woman in that big to-do with the BSU and the newspaper," Mrs. Finch said. "He wasn't hearing it." Mrs. Finch pointed toward the archway into a paneled family room with high windows and a roaring fireplace. Professor Finch sat in an oversized tweed chair, his leather-slippered feet on a matching ottoman. His head was back, eyes closed, newspaper blanketing his lap.

"Here, let me take your coat and hat."

Dahlia peeled out of her coat, handed over the fedora.

"Well, sister, I come from Creoles, so I know black blood when I see it," she said, turning back to wink. Her silver and black hair was pulled back in an ornate, antique silver barrette. "X-ray vision, you could say, when it comes to recognizing those part of our beautiful heritage."

Tension melted from Dahlia's shoulders, the same way it did when she stepped into Aunt Lola's house. "If I wanted to keep my black blood a secret, my hair certainly wouldn't let me. Although some of my majority peers have made comments like they think I'm just some kind of freestyle hippie who likes braids."

"So why do you hide it under that hat? The yellow hue of your skin is another sure sign, and you should be proud of that too," Mrs. Finch said with a smile. "Most folks wouldn't pay it no mind. Think you're suntanned. Or jaundiced. Here." She placed two mugs on the counter as the teakettle screamed. She picked it up. "But like you said, your hair is straight from the motherland. Now I have met some Jewish folk with hair so kinky I thought they were one of us, but—"

"It sometimes puts me in an odd position," Dahlia said.

Mrs. Finch prepared two cups of tea, saying, "And why is that? You should be proud of what you are. Eleanor Roosevelt said nobody can make you feel inferior unless you let them. Well, I say, nobody can make you feel odd or out of place unless you allow it, sweetheart. You can never be fully accepted by others until you accept your true self."

A nervous laugh escaped Dahlia's lips. "A lot of times I feel people try to play on my am-I-black-enough insecurities to mold me into what suits them best." The words came out before she could stop them.

Mrs. Finch froze, turned toward her with sharp brown eyes. "Well, do you consider yourself to be black at all? And why does being black seem to make you so uncomfortable? It seems to me that you want to be accepted and respected by black people while denying the fact that you *are* black."

"I don't mean to deny it—"

"But you do. You listen to me, sweetheart. God made you like this." She stroked Dahlia's hair and took her hand, tapping her knuckles. "He doesn't want you to fit a mold or be in denial. He wants you to love yourself, and let folks love you, just the way you are."

Dahlia's eyes stung with tears. "But why is it so hard?"

"I think when you try to hide, you make it harder on yourself. The minute I saw that old man's hat you wear, I could tell you're struggling with your blackness."

"I'm not—"

Mrs. Finch's sharp gaze made her stop.

"I don't like it when people look at me, and analyze me," Dahlia said. "I guess because I'm not done doing that myself. I haven't figured it all out yet—"

"Neither have I, and I'm sixty-three." Mrs. Finch laughed as she pulled open the oven, letting out a hot, sweet-scented gust.

"I've had my own struggles being a proud black woman married to a cantankerous white man. But I do know one thing," she said, turning away from the glistening brown-sugar mounds. "I had to figure out who I, Geraldine Finch, was before I let him"—she pointed to the family room— "or my sisters or the ladies at church decide who and what I *should* be. Long as I'm breathing, that's my cardinal rule."

Dahlia sighed. On one hand, she did not want to let down her defenses to the wife of the professor she was about to confront— tactfully, but what she planned to ask Finch could have a negative outcome. Yet who else could she speak to about this issue that gnawed at her every waking minute and even haunted her dreams? Did Sharmane take her side just because they were friends and she felt the need to comfort Dahlia?

Her parents used to talk to her about it, but over the past three years on campus, she felt that her mind and personality had matured and evolved dramatically.

Mrs. Finch grasped her hand. "I can feel what you're going through. I can see it in those pretty eyes. And it's all right, girl." Her tender gaze moved back and forth from Dahlia's left eye to her right and back. "Just remember what I said. You need to be true to what you are."

A small smile lifted Dahlia's hot cheeks. "Thank you," she said softly.

"Now," Mrs. Finch said, pulling the cinnamon rolls out of the oven. She spread white icing on their steaming tops. "Mmm, a tray full of heaven. I will be downright insulted if you don't sample at least two."

"I won't disappoint you," Dahlia said, lifting one of the white china plates next to the stove. She imagined herself coming here often, visiting with Mrs. Finch. Because this was the closest thing to motherly advice, motherly love, she could remember for far too long. Her heart ached for her mother. And when Dahlia remembered why she was here, her stomach cramped.

But maybe, "the power" meant being able to tiptoe through a serious conversation with Professor Finch without rousing anger or vengeance.

"Wow," Dahlia said, as Mrs. Finch used a spatula to put two cinnamon rolls on her plate.

"Have a seat," she said, pointing to the sunny nook.

Dahlia sat down. She used a fork to take the first bite, savoring the gooey treat. "Mrs. Finch, this is heavenly. Thank you."

"Happy to share," she said, placing a glass of milk in front of Dahlia.

"Geraldine?" Finch sounded groggy. "You talking to me?"

"We got a visitor, sweetheart," she called. "A student."

"Did you pat him down at the door?"

Mrs. Finch swallowed, then laughed. With eyes smiling at Dahlia, she said, "He can be orn'ry if I let him."

"I don't think she's armed," Mrs. Finch said playfully. "Come join us, Dale."

A minute or two later, Finch came into the kitchen, his slippers scraping the linoleum. He helped himself to the cinnamon rolls, then plunked his plate on the table.

"Ms. Jenkins," he said sternly. "I know my wife's baked goods are extraordinary, but that's not why you came. Here to contest your A?"

Dahlia smiled nervously. "No, actually I'm thrilled about that. I worked hard."

"Mmm-hmmm," he said, not looking up from his plate. He chewed silently.

"But I guess you could say," Dahlia said, "I'm here as a sort of delegate for the members of the Black Student Union. Students who feel—" She glanced at Mrs. Finch, whose brows drew together.

Dahlia willed the right words to come out of her mouth, despite her racing pulse, her sweaty palms.

"They feel," she said as he met her gaze, "that your grading is biased."

The sweet scent of the cinnamon rolls suddenly made her feel nauseous.

"Biased," he said, balancing a bite before his mouth. "Wouldn't you argue that grading is supposed to be biased? And in a field such as English, evaluations are rather arbitrary by nature?"

"People feel your grading is *racially* biased," Dahlia said, stunned that the words came out of her mouth so forcefully, so confidently. "I'm black, Professor Finch. And as long as you thought I was white you gave me the As I studied for and deserved. And I should hope our discussion today does not have a negative impact on my final grade."

She could feel Mrs. Finch's gaze, but Dahlia did not look away from her professor's sharp eyes. She wondered how Kyle would react if he saw her, heard her at this moment. But that thought faded. Because she was suddenly fueled by a new energy. An energy coming from her own heart and soul, now that she saw with perfect clarity that she was doing the right thing. The journalistically and racially correct thing: identifying herself as a black woman while getting a response and an explanation from the person in question.

"You've got guts," Professor Finch said.

"Give her credit for that," Mrs. Finch said flatly. She took another bite.

Were they going to tell her off and kick her out of their home? Would she suddenly get marked down from an A to an F? Or would she suffer some other consequence? Would she be blacklisted throughout the English department for her final semester come January?

"Ms. Jenkins," Finch said, "I've heard all about the Black Student Union wanting to run me off campus. But do you think I would be such an imbecile as to give them the rope with which to hang me?"

Dahlia sat frozen under his gaze.

"If I were to flunk all the African-American students and give As to the Caucasians or those I *assumed* were Caucasians, I would be digging my own grave."

"But the grades are posted!"

"Did you go through all three hundred markings?"

"No, but—"

His voice became loud and angry. "Then what, Ms. Jenkins, is the basis for this interrogation?"

"I'm a journalist, Professor Finch. Since my first day on campus, I've been hearing about your reputation. After our talk in your office, the talk where you *assumed* I was white, I started to question it. And now I had to find out for myself, from you."

"I appreciate that," he said. "Should I ever come under some sort of official investigation, I am prepared to provide proof that I grade solely on merit. In fact, there are no names on exams or papers, as you know. So it would be impossible to—"

"People think you use the number codes to identify us by name."

"If I had the time and energy—or malice—in me to do that—"

"Oh, Dale," Mrs. Finch said, clattering her fork on her empty plate. "I say walk up on that rally tomorrow and say all this to set the record straight yourself."

"No, Geraldine. I would no sooner swim into a school of piranhas than do that." He turned to Dahlia. "But as a journalist, Ms. Jenkins can speak for me."

Dahlia felt her eyes grow larger.

"Dale, sweetheart, that's an awfully tall order—"

"Isn't that why you came here?" he asked with a hard stare.

"Actually, yes," she said. "However—"

"You've taken it to this bold level," he said, "so I say go for it, Ms. Jenkins. Rest easy, your A is not in jeopardy for coming here and revealing your race. But your integrity as a journalist would be if you bowed to the pressures of those who may not have your best interest at heart. Student activists by nature have their own interests first and foremost."

Dahlia thought of Angie and Kyle and Lori, and the idea of conveying the tenor of this visit to Kyle, and to the BSU tonight, made a wicked claw of worry cramp her stomach.

Chapter TEN

THE COOL AIR inside the small paneled room in the student union was so charged that Dahlia sensed it could ignite with one spark. As she stood in the doorway, all sixty-some pairs of eyes, including Marla's, were on her. But Kyle was sitting at the table, surrounded by people, as he wrote in a notebook.

"There she is," Angie said, sipping a bottle of water.

Dahlia struggled to catch her breath. She'd run here from home, after spending hours writing her column, then turning it in at the *Daily* just minutes ago.

Kyle shot up from his seat, wedged through the standing-room-only crowd, and came toward her, a pillar of brown corduroy and cashmere.

"Give me a minute," he told the group. Then he guided her gently into the hallway, closed the door.

"Dahlia, I've been trying to reach you—"

"I said I'd be here. Why do you look so mad?" His face was taut with disapproval as he stared down at her.

"I want to know what you're up to," he said. "All afternoon, it just burned me up. Not knowing where you stand."

"Maybe I didn't know where I stand," she said. "Maybe I'm tired of you trying to tell me where to stand. And making veiled threats that if I don't take the right side, our relationship is over."

"What are you saying?"

"I'm saying I had to do some checking on my own," she said. "Then I wrote about it, and that helped me clarify some things."

"And?"

"And I think the whole Finch thing is not as cut-and-dry as you"—she nodded toward the door— "and everyone else thinks."

"What does this mean, Baby Dahlia? Are you on board for tomorrow or not?" The angry rasp in his voice scraped her nerves.

"Kyle, I analyzed the grades myself. In fact I got my hands on a sample for the past couple years—"

"What?"

"Wait, Kyle. This semester, the grades form a perfect bell curve. And there are several other black students who got As and Bs. Why did you happen to omit that information?"

"Two of them are African," he said with an annoyed tone. "Raised in London. Another, the biggest Oreo on campus. And one of them, a stuck-up snob I used to date—"

"Kyle!" she said angrily. "So if people don't pass your personal litmus test of blackness, they just don't count? In your so-called scientific analysis of information that you want to use to destroy a man who's devoted his life to education?"

"Whoa!" Kyle held up his hand, his eyes wide with surprise. "You're jumpin' ship all the way on me now."

"Kyle," she said, "I'm just trying to be fair to all parties involved."

"The *white* parties involved," he said. "How'd he get to you, Dahlia? Promise you an A-plus? As long as you don't join the niggers in their witch hunt?" Rage blazed in his eyes.

"Look Kyle, I've already admitted to Finch that I'm black, and he said it wouldn't affect my grade. I'm not going to let it affect my position as a journalist either." Dahlia closed her eyes tightly, shaking her head. "I don't believe you, Kyle. I don't believe you can turn on me in a split second if my racial allegiance isn't as skewed as you think it should be. Right now, I feel you've been using me like a puppet."

He slammed his hand on the door. "They're all waiting for you. We're depending on you to speak out tomorrow."

"Kyle! What you want me to speak out on is wrong! I am not the only African-American student to get an A from Finch. So what is your point?"

"My sister bombed his final," Kyle said angrily. "He is marring her college career."

"That is not my responsibility, Kyle. Lori Hudson—the white sorority girl—she tanked, too. And Lori puts the lily in white."

"We're through," Kyle said.

The tears Dahlia thought she would shed at this moment had already been soaked into the soft cotton of Sharmane's shoulder. She'd blotted a river of loss into those clumps of tissues back in her apartment, piled high inside the small wastepaper basket by her desk, as she wrote the column that was going to press as they spoke.

"I think you should call off the protest tomorrow," Dahlia said. "I think you should analyze the grades across campus, the law school, the chemistry department, engineering. Everywhere. Then see if you have hard evidence."

"Dahlia, you're letting me down."

"You're letting *me* down, Kyle. I'm sure there are racist professors out there. On this campus. But I just don't think you should go after Finch without solid evidence."

"This is whack, Dahlia."

"That's what I've been thinking all day. You wanted to use me, Kyle. Like a prop. Or some kind of mouthpiece, like I don't have a brain of my own."

"No, Baby Dahlia—"

"I'm not a baby, Kyle. I'm a grown woman. And I've had to grapple with some issues. But I've figured it out now. I've figured out the power you've been talking about. I'm not, however, going to misuse it."

The door flew open. Angie was a peripheral blur of light blue denim and a fuzzy angora sweater. "This is not the time for a romantic interlude," she said, glaring at Dahlia. "You're holding up our meeting. And we have a lot to go over for tomorrow. Kyle?"

"Yeah," he said flatly, not taking his gaze from Dahlia.

Angie glared at her. "I told you that sellout wouldn't stick with us. I told you. She got her A, and she's 'bout to run with it. With or without you, Kyle. To hell with us—"

"Angie." The rage in Kyle's voice echoed through the hallway. "I'll be in—"

"You break my brother's heart on top of everything else, Dahlia Jenkins, and you'd better stay more invisible than ever," Angie said.

Dahlia closed her eyes, hating to see and hear her ex-friend talk to her like that. The pain in Kyle's eyes scraped her heart.

Dahlia froze as his large hands came toward her shoulders. He gently grasped her, tangling his hands in her braids.

"Baby Dahlia, I did love you," he said softly. "You made a mark on my heart, girl. It will always be there. But I can't stay with . . . a *bitch* who's not down with what I represent."

Dahlia lifted his hands from her shoulders. "What you repre-

sent, Kyle, that's the problem. I just wanna say, thank you for helping me feel the power. Because nothing is more powerful than
doing what feels right in your heart, in your gut."

She stared into his eyes for one final time. "Problem is, you and
I just can't agree on what that is."

She kissed his cheek. "Bye, Kyle."

Then with her hat in her hand, she spun and walked away.

Chapter ELEVEN

THE WINDOW LEDGE in the empty third-floor classroom was
cold under the weight of Dahlia's behind as she looked down at
Kyle through the ceiling-high glass. He stood on the steps in
front of the massive brick and glass graduate library. Before him,
hundreds of students, mostly black, were cheering and raising their
fists in support.

Her reflection in the glass came into focus, as if her face were
superimposed on the crowd below. Errant hairs had escaped the
confines of her braids and glowed like an aura around her head; it
was definitely time to have them redone. The braids themselves
coiled down past her shoulders, over her chest, down her back. She
thought of Grandpop's fedora back in her apartment, tucked neatly
into green tissue paper inside a floral-print hatbox.

"Here goes," she said softly. Dahlia grasped a few curly ends
that were threatening to untwist altogether. At the same time, the
heat blowing up from the register under the ledge made the newspaper flutter in her lap. There, staring up in shades of gray was her
own smiling face, under the "Perspectives" banner over her column.

Kyle's deep voice, and the cheering students below, grew louder
as she read the words she had cried and sweat over yesterday:

For those of you who read my column every week, you already know my name is Dahlia Jenkins.

But there's something you may not know about me: I'm black.

At least half.

And my parents' marriage across the color line showed me, told me, reminded me, that love is color-blind. And I believed them, for the most part.

Why? For one, there was something about the way my mother's blue eyes lit up and her cheeks turned red and lifted into a grin when Daddy strode into the room in his FedEx uniform after a long day of delivering packages all over Detroit.

Another clue that affection and adoration do not see black or white was the way Daddy would sing Marvin Gaye songs to Mommy, and his eyes would sparkle like black diamonds, and he'd smile so much that the tiny lines around his mouth would stay there for hours, like parentheses marking off the happiness etched onto his face.

Then, when my parents would press their cheeks into mine, so we formed a collage of smiles in the mirror, I knew I was the bridge between them, the loving link that could bring all people together, somehow.

But for most of my twenty-five years, I have not known how to express that, how to let down my guard, take off this mask of ambiguity, and make a difference. Sure, plenty of people wanted to tell me and show me what they thought I should do to take a stand.

However, my heart had not yet heard the call to action. But now, after traversing this past semester that felt like a minefield of emotion, I'm ready.

Ready to take off the hat.

You see, for those of you who know me, I've always worn this hat, since my first day at orientation here. Because my grandfather gave it to me just before he died, a week after I was accepted to U of M. When I arrived on campus I was grieving for him and for my parents who'd also died. I didn't want to reveal my racial identity, I didn't want to take a stand. All I wanted to do was study and succeed.

I did not want—as people have done my whole life—to be put under that racial microscope so folks could ask, What is she? and treat me according to whatever hypothesis they came up with.

I wanted to be treated as Dahlia Jenkins.

But I'm learning the world is not that black and white.

I have to take a stand.

And the stand is this:

The next time you see me walking across campus or standing in front of a lecture hall or sitting at a café, I will be holding my chin high. I will be showing off the coarse texture of my hair with pride—after all, I got it from my beloved father. I will let you look into my eyes so you can see the confidence of a black woman who now knows her place in the world. And I will be writing about issues—racial issues—through a new prism of consciousness.

Because I, Dahlia Jenkins, have nothing to hide. I am baring myself, my soul, to the world, to share the power.

What power is that?

The power to report the truth, no matter what your race or mine. And as for our struggles within the black community, what is too light? What is too dark? And why is skin tone so important to us? Why do we allow it to so insidiously divide us within the race? These are questions I've had to honestly ask of myself.

Now fueled by my personal struggles and my newly emerging sense of pride, every jolt of anger, every ounce of denial, every tear of longing to stop fighting this battle within myself, every ounce of energy I once used to hide my true identity—all of that will go into my quest as a senior in my final semester, and as a journalist, as a black woman, as a human being.

I am going to shed light on these issues and feelings, the evils that divide us—both black and white, light and dark—through the written word.

Starting now.

Dahlia set the newspaper on her lap, then gazed out the window and down at Kyle.

"Thank you, sweet soul mate of mine," she whispered, "for helping me find the power."

Acknowledgments

I give thanks to God for the abundance of blessings that have been showered upon me. To my literary manager, Ken Atchity, for championing this project and for pursuing its publication with zest and passion. Huge thanks to my editor, Emily Bestler, for her role in the empowerment and edification of black women through the written word. You gave our project the nurturing and nourishment it needed to evolve from a simple dream into a blessed reality, and we love you for it. To TaRessa, Elizabeth, and Desiree, thank you for the gift of your literary sistah friendships as we strive to continue our efforts in the acknowledgment, examination, and healing of this skin/hair thang among black women everywhere.

—Tracy Price-Thompson

All praises and gratitude to Father Mother God, Olodumare, One Great Spirit, from whom all life and blessings flow. Thanks to everyone involved in the growth and birth of this wonderful project, especially my wonderful literary agent, Neeti Madan. It has been a true honor to join forces with such brilliant, talented sistah writers as Tracy Price-Thompson, Elizabeth Atkins, and Desiree Cooper. It is a privilege to be able to explore a topic that touches all of our people in so many profound ways, and to imagine different paths to healing the wounds caused by the skin/hair thang.

I would like to give special thanks to my wonderful family, from my ancestors to my mother, son and daughter, sister and brother, and to the incomparable circle of friends who provide non-stop inspiration, support, and honest feedback.

And deepest appreciation to our readers, who provide the impetus for us to dream on paper and allow our words into your lives.

—TaRessa Stovall

Thank you, God, for the blessings of family, friends, and fresh ways to tell stories that uplift and inspire all people. Tracy, TaRessa, and Desiree . . . I appreciate the sister spirit that sparkles on these pages!

—Elizabeth Atkins

Thanks to Elizabeth Atkins for bringing me into this wonderful sisterhood of writers, to TaRessa Stovall for her brilliant feedback, and to Tracy Price-Thompson for her devotion to healing the wounds of black women everywhere.

—Desiree Cooper

About the Authors

TaRessa Stovall is a Seattle native and playwright. She is the coauthor of *A Love Supreme: Real-Life Stories of Black Love* and *Catching Good Health: An Introduction to Homeopathic Medicine* and the author of *The Buffalo Soldiers*. She coedited *Proverbs for the People* with Tracy Price-Thompson. Her first novel, *The Hot Spot*, was published by BET Books in 2005. She lives in New Jersey with her two children.

Tracy Price-Thompson is the 2005 Hurston/Wright Award winner and national bestselling author of the novels *Black Coffee, Chocolate Sangria, A Woman's Worth, Knockin' Boots,* and *Gather Together in My Name.* She coedited *Proverbs for the People* with TaRessa Stovall. Tracy is a highly decorated Desert Storm veteran who graduated from the Army's Infantry Officer Candidate School after more than ten years as an enlisted soldier. A Brooklyn, New York, native who has traveled extensively and lived in amazing places around the world, Tracy is a retired Army engineer officer and Ralph Bunche Graduate Fellow who holds a bachelor's degree in business administration and a master's degree in social work. Tracy lives in Hawaii with her wonderfully supportive husband and several of their six bright, beautiful, incredible children. Her contribution to this collection, "Other People's Skin," won a Hurston/Wright Award for short fiction in 2002.

Desiree Cooper is a regular commentator on National Public Radio's *All Things Considered.* A 2002 Pulitzer Prize nominee for her regular column in the *Detroit Free Press,* Cooper graduated Phi Beta Kappa from the University of Maryland with degrees in journalism and economics and earned a law degree from the University of Virginia. Cooper was born in Japan to a military family and now makes her home in Detroit, where she is married to her law school sweetheart and has two children.

Elizabeth Atkins, a former race relations reporter for the *Detroit News,* is the author of the bestselling novels *White Chocolate, Dark Secret,* and *Twilight,* which was coauthored with actor/painter Billy Dee Williams. A motivational speaker with the American Program Bureau, Elizabeth has written for the *New York Times, Essence, Ms.,* BET.com, *Black Issues Book Review, HOUR Detroit,* and the *San Diego Tribune* and contributed to a national tribute program for Rosa Parks. She lives in Detroit with her son.